Also By Ashley Hawthorne

Deliver Me

Death Sentence

Beneath Calm Waters is the first in the Window's Point Duology
The second book, Against the Tide, is coming June 2026

Beneath Calm Waters

Beneath Calm Waters

ASHLEY HAWTHORNE

Published in the United States by Creative James Media.

www.creativejamesmedia.com

978-1-7353926-7-7 (trade paperback)

First U.S. Edition 2023

To anyone who's ever had to make tough choices to survive and then had to live with the consequences. May you all find peace and healing.

Author's Note

This book contains potentially upsetting themes including death, violence, pregnancy/childbirth, discussions of past abuse, and sexually explicit content. A full list is available at ashleyhawthorne.net

Prologue

George

A late summer breeze blew steadily across the bay beneath the wide windows of Barlow House. The setting sun threw pinks and oranges into the sky, a radiant explosion of color above the shimmering sea below. The peaceful scene might have seemed welcoming to someone else, but George Barlow knew better. He had been born in this house, raised in it, lived almost every day of a long life within its walls.

No one knew the truth about this place better than George.

Though the nearing autumn had not quite brought a chill to the air, the water off the northern Oregon coast was never warm. It was never friendly. Much like George himself, it was cold and hard. Greedy and grasping. Picturesque on the surface, it sent a chill straight to the bone. Riptides and unpredictable currents pulled at those brave and foolish enough to tempt fate.

Once, the small town founded by George's great-grandfather was intended to be named after their family.

Instead it was known as Widow's Point, an acknowledgment of those who had drowned or been lost. The early townspeople, trapped between the sea with its vicious nature and a man with a will like stone, had bent in favor of the sea. There had always been very little in this small slice of the world that was powerful enough to challenge a Barlow, but the ocean was one of them.

George had always enjoyed a challenge.

There had never been a woman he couldn't tame, a man he couldn't control, or a goal he hadn't reached. He'd asserted his dominance over everything within reach, master of his domain, and there was no task too difficult, no obstacle too tough.

Only the fickle sea, with its glorious violence and mercurial unpredictability had ever been a match for him, and more than forty years had passed since he'd first taken an evening swim off the small private beach that made up his backyard. All he'd really needed was a wet suit and a stubbornness that, even back then, had had everyone else subtly rolling their eyes. Now, at more than sixty and with more white than brown in his hair, he still had both.

There had never been peace between him and the sea and there never would be.

It beckoned to him now, as it did every day, but he ran a hand over his face as he hesitated. He had been uncharacteristically tired since dinner. Age creeping up on him, undoubtedly, a point that rankled sorely. Caution warred against his pride as he calculated the distance between the house and the gathering clouds barely visible against the darkening sky.

Rain would arrive within the hour and when it did, the ocean would become a restless beast, hungry and wild. Already it had begun to roll as though it yearned for the storm. A more timid man would have tucked himself away in his library, cozy with a good book in one hand and a glass of brandy in the other as he listened to the wind rage outside.

George had never admired such men. They were nothing but cowards, every last one.

He stepped away from the window, rolling his shoulders in a brief stretch. One quick swim wouldn't hurt. It would take him only a few minutes to change and not much more to swim a satisfactory distance from the shore and back again. It was a good bet he'd be inside before the worst of the storm even arrived.

Behind him, barely illuminated by the last rays of the sun, the white capped waves waited just beyond the pebbled shore.

Chapter One

Grayson

George Barlow was dead.

Grayson cradled his phone in his hands, the screen still lit though the call was over, and wondered how such a thing could be true. His grandfather had seemed inhuman. Invincible. Practically fucking immortal. He had always been a man stronger, in many ways, than Grayson had ever aspired to be. If someone had told him humanity had somehow pulled God down from the sky, he would have been only slightly more surprised.

Drowned.

That's what that man, that lawyer—whatever his name was—who'd notified him had said. That George Barlow, who had been swimming in those waters nearly every day for decades, had drowned in them. They had found his body less than a stone's throw from his own back door.

Christ.

It was impossible and yet ...

Grayson set the phone aside and eyed the nearly empty

one-bedroom apartment around him. He had a bottle of whiskey, gifted by a friend and never opened, tucked away somewhere. He wasn't much on drinking, but if there had ever been a time, surely this was it.

Countless thoughts tumbled around inside a head emptied by shock as he rummaged through the kitchen cabinets, searched the back corners of the pantry shelves, and finally found it shoved in a rarely opened drawer in the bedroom dresser.

He carried the bottle, amber liquid swirling, back to the kitchen to find a glass, wondering as he went what else he might have stashed in that dresser and promptly forgotten about. It wasn't like it got much use. If the place hadn't come fully furnished, he wouldn't even have the thing. Most of his personal items were still packed in the bags he dragged from city to city, apartment to apartment.

Settling in would have meant making a home, and, quite frankly, Grayson didn't think he was capable. He'd spent every waking hour of his adult life trying to escape his home. Running from Barlow House, its people, and its legacy.

For all the good it had done him, he thought, an edge of bitterness sneaking in to sour his stomach.

His grandfather was dead, and the lawyers were already calling. Looking for the heir, the next in line to step up and take over. Being a Barlow meant having responsibility, after all.

To the house.

To the town.

To his *grandmother.*

He took a long swallow straight from the bottle at that thought, sour stomach be damned. Edith Barlow was still alive, apparently. He'd wondered for years but had never had the courage to find out. He should have been relieved, but all he felt was another rolling twist of nausea and guilt that was strong enough to knock him on his ass.

And that little weaselly fucking lawyer ... Grayson abandoned his search for a glass and threw himself down in the nearest chair. The little eat-in kitchen had a dining set that was probably a holdover from the 70s and the orange and green plastic on the seat creaked beneath his weight.

That lawyer with his quiet judgment and his expectations. It was all *"Yes, Mr. Barlow"* and *"No, Mr. Barlow"* and *"I'm sure your grandmother is looking forward to seeing you again, Mr. Barlow."*

No, the lawyer didn't just have expectations. He had *assumptions.* He assumed Grayson was going to drop everything and go running home like a good little boy because ... Because his grandmother needed him.

Damn it.

Could he really ignore that?

Okay, sure, it bothered him that they assumed. Bothered him more how quickly they'd found him, as though he'd never really been lost to them at all. Had they always known? Tracked him from place to place as he ran away like a frightened child all these years?

Surely if they had, though, that would have been his grandfather's doing. Edith had never been anything but kind to anyone, and he had no reason to believe his leaving would have changed that.

Grayson took another swig from the bottle and let the burn chase away the churning spin of his emotions. Mixed feelings about his grandfather aside, he couldn't pin his anger on Edith. She'd been through enough. She deserved better than his resentment now and, if he was being honest with himself, better than he'd treated her when he'd left all those years ago.

He'd had his reasons, but those things were in the past. Dead and fucking buried, he realized with a little drunken snort. Besides, it wasn't like anyone else would have understood those reasons anyway. Barlow House held its secrets well, as old houses tended to do. People saw what they wanted to see and judged you accordingly.

Damn it.

Widow's Point was the same when Grayson returned to it as it had been the day he left. Well, not *exactly* the same. There were some small differences here and there. A house painted a different color. A business with a new sign. A fresh layer of asphalt down the main street. Despite that, the heart of the place was untouched and the few details that were different didn't change the feeling that he had come home.

He hadn't expected that after twelve years. Surely, he'd grown and changed, even if the town had not. It should have been like trying to put on a shirt that had grown too small since the last time he'd worn it. Instead, peace settled over him the moment the town came into view on the thin and winding highway. The feeling was butter soft and warm, like a pair of worn-in slippers.

Maybe it shouldn't have surprised him as much as it did. Generations of Barlows had walked these quiet streets. Built their quiet little houses and this quiet little town. Too stubborn to move on to bigger and better places, they'd made a life on this rocky shoreline. Typical, Grayson thought. They'd always had too much pride.

Still, he winced a little as he drove past the sign welcoming him to Widow's Point. The town might have grown faster if that far-back grandfather had been successful in naming the place Barlow. Widow's Point, however accurate, didn't sound like the kind of place most people would like to set down roots.

Of those that called the town home, most were families

that had been here since the beginning. Since before they realized how dangerous the waters were for boats and people. Grayson could see the bay just beyond the town, below the cliffs. Shimmering in the near autumn afternoon sunlight.

If there was one thing around here more powerful than the Barlows, it was the sea itself. Some said it was an unpredictable riptide and strong currents that made it so difficult to navigate, but it often felt more sinister than that. Temperamental and selfish, it seemed as though the bay had a mind of its own. Either way, it showed no mercy to the people of the town or anyone else.

Not that his family had ever seen sense.

They'd sniffed and rolled their eyes and then built their houses closer to the shore. Pride or stubbornness or simple foolish vanity hadn't stopped them. Eventually they had built Barlow House. Tall against the cliffside, it loomed over the small semi-circular beach below. A tower triumph built of aged wooden siding and spotless glass that shone bright against the often-cloudy gray sky.

George had embraced that inheritance as a testament to his superiority. Grayson, on the other hand, had fled from it at the first opportunity and refused to look back.

He sincerely hoped that wasn't the only difference between them, though the chance at comparison would have been better before the old man had died. Maybe if Grayson had come back sooner, made an effort to reach out once in a while ... People changed sometimes. It was possible George had mellowed in his twilight years. Become more reasonable and less ... less ... well, less like George.

Grayson shook his head, unable to picture his grandfather as anything other than what he'd always been, as he passed the grocery store and a familiar park. It amused him to see the local teenagers were still fond of placing brightly colored ladies' hats on an old statue of the original Barlow, standing stern and unsmiling in bronze as he looked out over the playground and browning grass.

Today's choice was a wide brimmed monstrosity of a beach hat in a stunning pink with what looked to be red and purple flowers on one side. Truly inspired fashion choices, and he wondered which terribly embarrassed mother would have to climb up and reclaim her borrowed property.

Alone in the car, he didn't bother to try and hide his laugh.

He'd done the same thing in his high school days, the fact that the man was a direct ancestor of his somehow making it even funnier. George would have come down on him like a hammer if he'd known, but it was one of the few things Grayson had ever truly gotten away with.

Hell, knowing how much George looked like that statue, the same cruel face, the same pinched disapproval in the mouth, might have been why he was so determined to do it, even knowing the risk. He'd never been liked well enough by the other kids to worry about peer pressure, though that was the excuse he'd given himself at the time for one of his few rebellions.

There had been plenty to rebel against, but he'd been too afraid to do more. It was fear that had kept him in line then, it was fear that had kept him from contacting anyone here since he'd left home at eighteen, and it was fear that had him pulling his car into the parking lot of a downtown diner to grab a late lunch instead of driving straight to Barlow House.

The diner, cleverly named On the Rocks, was still in the same tiny white building at one end of Main Street, noticeable only because of the hand-painted sign out front. Touched up every year, it bore the diner's name above an uncannily accurate depiction of the town's rocky cliff side above a restless sea. Operational in Widow's Point since 1935, the place might as well have had its own historical marker. Diner by day and the town's only bar by night, Grayson had thought the name was pretty funny once he was old enough to understand the pun.

Some of his first memories were made in that building, and he sat in the parking lot for several minutes trying to get up the courage to go inside. What would he do if no one recognized him? What would he do if they did?

He couldn't decide which one would be worse, and imagined both scenarios in painful detail, unable to convince himself to reach for the door handle. As long as he stayed in the car, he still had the choice to simply turn around and leave. He could make himself lost again and pretend he'd never been found. Once he went inside, he ran the risk of being recognized and if he was recognized, someone would tell Edith. She'd be heartbroken that he'd been so close and hadn't come home.

The inside of his mouth tasted like sawdust.

The door of the diner swung open, a laughing woman with arms full of take-out bags suddenly taking up all the space in Grayson's panicked tunnel vision. His first impression was of a pair of legs in a pair of thin cotton shorts—not much time left for those before autumn rain and colder temperatures set in—with a gray T-shirt that must have been two sizes too big and hot pink flip flops.

Not exactly the most fashionable woman Grayson had ever seen, but there was something about her that drew his gaze and held it there as she stepped out onto the sidewalk. Sunlight glinted off the gold necklace she wore as he took her in, shamelessly staring and cataloging one rich feature after another. Wild, wavy brown hair that barely touched her shoulders lifted with the breeze, fluttering around a face that was as captivating as it was surprising. Dark brows cut thick lines over wide eyes, high cheekbones, and a thin nose. She was beautiful, any fool could see that, but even in laughter, there was a closed wariness about her. Her expression was almost devoid of the softness one might expect to find there, a contrast that made him feel uneasy.

There was red lipstick on her wide mouth, and that mouth quirked up on one side when she met his gaze and found him staring. She gave him a look, part confusion and part warning, and he flushed, ducking down behind the steering wheel, and pretending to look for something he had dropped. Exactly what he needed, the first person he'd seen since he arrived in town now had perfectly good reason to think he was a creep. He didn't think he recognized her, so he'd just gotten caught making odd faces at a stranger.

Whether that was preferable to getting caught making faces at someone he'd once known and probably grown up with remained up for debate.

It took several minutes for him to finally lift his head above the dashboard, but when he did, he was relieved to see the mystery woman had left. A quick look around the parking lot confirmed she was nowhere in sight, and he popped open the driver's side door and made his way to the entrance of the diner as fast as he could without drawing any more attention to himself. It was best to get inside before anything else happened.

He greeted the waitress when he walked in, looking around the seating area as he followed her to a booth at the back. Same wood paneled walls. Same forest green upholstery. It seemed the only thing new was the waitress herself. She looked about the same age as Grayson, and this woman he definitely did recognize, though he couldn't immediately recall her name.

She gave him a subtle second glance as he sat down but didn't say anything as she took his drink order. Her brow was furrowed in thought as she walked away, and he would have been willing to bet she'd have his identity worked out by nightfall if she kept at it.

Unfortunately for him, it didn't take everyone quite so long. His peace lasted only long enough for her to return with his coffee and take his order for a heaping plate of fries and fried fish.

"Grayson!" A man in jeans and a red T-shirt sat down in the booth across the table without waiting for a response or an invitation. "I wondered if we'd be seeing you around here again."

Widow's Point's sheriff had aged since Grayson had left town, but he was still recognizable enough even without the uniform he'd worn nearly every day for most of his life. At more than six and a half feet tall, with hair whiter than the driven snow, he was a hard figure to miss. He had also been close friends with George for more than five decades.

Grayson tried to keep the irritation he felt out of his expression. Of all the people he could have run into, it would be someone that had been in and out of Barlow House so often they'd practically helped raise him.

"Sheriff Levine." Grayson rubbed a hand over the short stubble of his beard, rough from days on the road when shaving was the last thing on his mind. "How'd you know it was me?"

Sheriff Levine laughed loudly enough to have the waitress lifting an eyebrow as she passed by on her way back to the kitchen. "After all these years, you still can't call me Patrick? And what do you mean, how did I know it was you? You look just like your grandpa and your dad, too."

Grayson nodded, but he was more than half lost in thought. He'd always resented those Barlow genes, but the older he got the harder it was to deny that they'd made their mark on him. The sheriff had known at least three generations of Barlow men, and they all had the same easily tanned complexion, the same square jaw and long nose, the same deep brown hair and eyes the blue-gray color of a storm-tossed sky.

Sheriff Levine's smile faltered for a moment when Grayson didn't immediately respond. He drummed his fingers on the tabletop, a short and nervous beat. "Ah, sorry about that. Getting careless in my old age. Losing your parents when you're just a kid and now this? Like losing a dad all over again, isn't it?"

Not exactly.

That's what Grayson thought, but he had the self-control to keep it to himself. If it showed in his face, Sheriff Levine didn't notice. No one ever did.

"I can't believe he's gone." There was a tug in the sheriff's voice, a little glimmer in his eyes, that made Grayson shift in his seat and glance over his shoulder for a distraction. Any distraction. He was in no condition to shoulder someone else's grief over George's unexpected death. Not when his own feelings were still so conflicted.

Luck was on his side, and the waitress chose that exact moment to emerge from the kitchen with his lunch. He turned back to Sheriff Levine with an apologetic smile. "Well, looks like that's my order ..." The implication couldn't have been any clearer if he'd handed the sheriff a business card with the words *Please Leave* emblazoned across the front, yet he remained at the table after Grayson had received his plate and the waitress had left again.

"It sure is strange, though, isn't it?"

Grayson paused with his first fry halfway to his mouth. "I'm sorry?"

"That whole thing with George." Sheriff Levine had turned to look out the window, taking in the water of the bay with a far-off expression. "He'd been swimming out there for most of his life."

Grayson ate his fry, mouth full to keep from having to

answer the unspoken question. He didn't have an opinion on this, because he hadn't seen George in twelve years. He had no idea what kind of condition George's health had been in when he died.

"Not just that," Sheriff Levine continued. "He'd been at the doctor a week or two before. Full checkup, that's what he told me. Healthy as a horse."

He eyed Grayson in the silence that followed, waiting for a reaction Grayson wasn't comfortable giving him.

"Wanted to do an autopsy, but Edith said no."

Grayson lifted an eyebrow. "Edith did?" His grandmother never said no to anybody, especially someone like the sheriff. "If Edith said no, she must have had a good reason."

Sheriff Levine shrugged and took a fry from the side of Grayson's plate without asking. "If she did, I wish I knew what it was."

"I wouldn't know." The guilt of Grayson's absence once again rose to choke him and he swallowed it down with the next bite of his lunch. "I haven't made it out to the house yet. Figured I'd get some lunch, maybe stop off at the hotel and get a room first."

"You'd better not try to stay anywhere but Barlow House." Sheriff Levine shifted in the booth, draped his arm over the back as he considered Grayson the way he might have a kid he'd caught with a beer on a Friday night. Disappointment and disapproval on nearly parental levels. "You know you'd break Edith's heart if you did. She's been sad since you left."

"Has she?" It was not much more than a murmur, and Grayson didn't wait for an answer. "You're right. It's just ... Well, just a habit, I guess. I tend to move around a lot for my job, and I usually grab a room when I come into town until I can find something a little more stable."

"Oh? What kind of work do you do?"

Grayson resisted the urge to squirm under his stare like the guilty teenager he'd once been. "Been doing website design for a while now. Freelance stuff mostly. Nothing flashy but it keeps the bills paid."

"Yeah? You have to go to school for that?"

Grayson shrugged and popped a piece of fish in his mouth. Maybe it was rude to eat and talk, but he'd driven straight through more than one meal and, besides, he'd been living in Indiana last. They didn't have fresh seafood in Indiana.

"I'm sure they offer classes for it, degrees or whatever, but that's not how I got started."

Patrick looked interested, but Grayson kept the rest to himself. The memory of it was too intimate. That kid, fresh out of high school with no degree and no future, fucking around on the laptop he'd taken with him when he'd snuck out of his bedroom window and skipped town with some truck driver headed anywhere else.

He'd been a waiter for a while, a shitty one, and happened to mention he'd been good with computers when the owner was looking for a website upgrade. They'd offered him an extra fifty bucks, cash, under the table. Too good for him to pass up back in those days.

It had taken him a week of digging through tutorials and watching YouTube videos to figure it out, but he'd gotten it done. His boss had been impressed enough to recommend him to a friend, and that friend had done the same for some more friends, and before Grayson had quite figured out what was happening, he hadn't needed the job waiting tables.

He'd built a solid portfolio in the years since, and his services cost a lot more than a lousy fifty dollars these days. It had kept him going, kept him fed, and was flexible enough to let him move from place to place whenever he got too settled and started to feel jumpy.

"Well," Patrick said, apparently giving up on waiting for

Grayson to elaborate, "I guess you won't have to worry about paying the bills now. Sorry you missed the funeral though."

He hadn't even known his grandfather was dead until he was already buried, and the thought of the funeral hadn't occurred to him. Had someone been there for Edith? Someone to hold her hand and make sure she was alright?

"Me too." Grayson dropped the last piece of fish back onto his plate, appetite suddenly gone. "I should have been here."

"I won't argue with that." Patrick got to his feet and patted Grayson on the back. "Make sure you tell your grandma hello from me when you see her, alright?"

"Will do."

"Enjoy your visit, not that it'll be hard to do." Patrick laughed and shot Grayson a confusing, conspiratorial wink. "Barlow House has never been short on spectacular views, but there is something special about having such a nice-looking woman around."

It was difficult for Grayson to imagine a remark about his own grandmother that could have made him desire a long shower in scalding, cleansing water more than that one did. Sheriff Levine was gone before he could manage to close his mouth and think of a proper response.

Fucking weird.

Everyone and everything in this town was just fucking weird. He'd forgotten what it was like, and maybe he had been better off forgetting. He certainly hadn't needed *that* as a reminder.

He tried to put it out of his mind as he left the diner, making a quick stop by the register to pay what's-her-name for his meal, and by the time he'd made it to the edge of town, he'd forgotten about everything but his own nerves. It was a short drive from Widow's Point to the small private section of the bay that his family owned. To the house perched on the cliff side, with its faded shingles and shining glass and long winding stairway that led from the back porch to the beach below.

It was all familiar except the glaring yellow of an old VW bus parked in the driveway. It certainly didn't belong to his grandparents. George would never have bought something like that. Grayson could almost hear the disdain in the old man's voice whenever he'd seen something that he considered *hippie trash*.

No, it definitely didn't belong to George.

A visitor, maybe? A delivery driver?

He'd hoped he'd be able to have this little reunion without an audience, especially since he wasn't sure how his grandmother would react to his sudden arrival. Maybe he should have called first, but it was too late for that. Calling from the woman's own driveway seemed like a cowardly move. He considered waiting for the owner of the bus to leave, but he had no way of knowing how long that might take.

Whoever it was, they were going to have to deal with an awkward family moment.

He stood on the front porch for five full minutes before he worked up the courage to ring the bell, and even then it was only the potential humiliation of getting caught that kept him from trying to run back to his car. There was an explosion of sound from the other side of the door, a rough clattering of nails on hardwood, something landing and shattering with a crash, a stream of inventive curses using words he didn't think his grandmother had ever spoken in her life. Over it all, raising the volume to truly surprising levels, was a layer of rapid-fire barking. His grandparents had a *dog*?

The front door flew open and someone—not his grandmother, judging by the brown hair that was nearly all he could see of her at first—filled the doorway. He took a step back to see more than the top of her head and was met with an angry gaze over a newly familiar red mouth. She was still wearing the same outfit, and it was as unflattering as it had been when he'd seen her in town, but now there was a snarling ball of gray and brown fur tucked under her arm.

Probably a Schnauzer, he thought wildly, one of the little ones.

The woman holding it leveled him with a look, all five-foot-nothing of her bristling as she recognized him from their awkward moment outside the diner. Any doubt about her inexplicable hostility was erased the moment she opened her mouth, a single brutal question leaving no doubt that he was now a stranger here.

"Who the hell are you?"

Chapter Two

Grayson

Grayson could feel the muscle working in his jaw as the tiny guardian blocking the door impatiently shifted the still barking dog from one arm to the other. Who the hell was he? He was pretty sure that's what she'd asked him over the continuing noise, and it was hard for him to wrap his mind around the audacity.

Who the hell was he?

Who the hell was *she*?

"Well?" She was staring up at him expectantly, brown eyes so dark he could barely see the boundary between iris and pupil. She lifted her right eyebrow, her attitude and the dog's converging in a place that was all bristling challenge, and he had to resist the urge to smooth it back into place with his thumb. If the dog didn't bite him for his efforts, he had a strong suspicion the woman holding it might.

"I'm Grayson." He had to raise his voice to be heard, another level of awkward humiliation. "Grayson Barlow?"

"Yeah?"

"I've come to see Edith." He tried to stand a little straighter, make his voice a little more authoritative. "She's my grandmother."

The woman looked him over, a slow head-to-toe as she seemed to evaluate the truth of his statement. It had him grateful for those pesky Barlow genes for once, because whatever she saw apparently satisfied her. "Wondered if you were going to show up."

The fuck? He didn't have a clue who this woman was, but he was already sure he didn't like her or her infuriating attitude. He'd be catching enough hell from his grandmother, and he didn't need additional servings from some stranger.

"Well, I have." Grayson didn't say anything else for a long moment, engaged in a silent battle of wills with his small and apparently stubborn adversary. The dog finally settled from full barking to a consistent rumbling growl, a welcome reprieve to his eardrums. It didn't escape his notice that the woman holding it was cradling it in careful arms, gently petting away as it snarled at him. Apparently, her bad attitude was reserved for him alone, which pissed him off as he waited for her to move aside and let him into his own damn house. "Is she at home?"

"Oh, she's home." The mystery woman tightened her grip on the dog and cast a quick glance over her shoulder. "And she'll be thrilled to see that you've arrived just in time to cash in on whatever your portion of the inheritance is, but you better hear me now, Mr. Barlow Junior or whatever the hell your name is ... If you hurt her, I'll cut you up into little pieces and feed you to Ruffles."

"What?" He was still trying to puzzle out why she thought he'd shown up just for money he didn't need when the last part of her threat finally hit him. "Who the hell is Ruffles?"

She lifted the dog with both hands and held it out in front

of her like a weapon while Grayson stood there with his mouth open and his head empty. "Ruffles."

"Okay..." He drew the syllable out, let it linger and cast his doubts for him, but inside he was resigned. Being fed to a small Schnauzer couldn't be any weirder than anything else that had happened to him today.

She tucked the still growling dog back under her arm and walked away, leaving him standing in the open doorway as she called back, "Come on in, then, if you're serious about seeing Edith, but remember what I said to you."

How was he supposed to forget it? Some strange woman standing on the front porch of the house he'd grown up in and threatening him over the well-being of his own grandmother? Unforgettable. And who the hell named a dog Ruffles?

He should have stayed in Indiana.

He should turn around and go back to Indiana right now.

Memories of Edith flooded his mind as the familiar smell of home hit him, and he did neither of those things. Instead, he followed the faint sound of growling into the entryway and beyond, closing the door behind him as he went. It echoed inside like the closing of a tomb.

A fitting thought since nothing in this house had ever really felt alive.

The house, like the town, remained much as it had been when he'd left. George had been particular about the look and feel of the place, and it had been kept fairly sparse in terms of decorations. No private or intimate things on the walls or surfaces. No personal treasures. No photos. More of a display case for furniture and ugly art than a home.

Grayson pictured the apartment he'd lived in most recently, the bare walls and empty countertops. Unused drawers and windows with no curtains over the blinds. It was easy to see, now that he was looking at the place he'd come from, how closely the apple had landed when it had fallen from the tree. It made him a little sick to think of it, and he ran a finger along the cool glass of the ceiling high windows as they passed through the living area. A little smudge wasn't much to leave behind, but it was something at least. Something to tell the house he'd come back, even if he wasn't planning to stay.

His change was temporary, and would be wiped away during the next cleaning, but he realized as he walked the familiar path from the front door to the kitchen, that George's absence had suddenly opened up a wealth of possibilities for more permanent alterations. Maybe now that she was the only one living here, Edith could finally make her own mark on the house she'd lived in most of her life. Hang a photo or buy a chair that was actually comfortable to sit in. Take the mounted fish off the wall in George's library and throw them in the trash.

Actually, maybe he wouldn't wait for Edith to do that. If she let him stay a night or two, he might take care of it himself before he left. Those damn fish and their dull, sightless eyes had given him nightmares as a child and George had banished him from the library because of it. Grayson had been a real bookworm back then, finding solace in fantastical fictional worlds after the deaths of his parents, and it had made him cry for weeks afterward.

He pushed away the memory and tried to focus on the task ahead of him. There would be time to deal with the fish later—and with all the memories that came with them—once he'd tackled the more immediate problem. A problem that, as far as he could tell, was about to be made worse by the apparent grudge the tiny diner woman held toward him.

"So ..." He took a few longer steps to get closer to her so he didn't have to raise his voice to be heard. "You never told me your name."

"No, I didn't."

He waited long enough to make sure she wasn't going to say more, his jaw tightening as the seconds passed. "And? What is it?"

She ignored him, stepping out of his way as they entered the kitchen. Edith was seated at the island, an empty barstool pulled out beside her and two glasses of wine waiting on the granite countertop. Whoever the mystery woman was, she was obviously close with his grandmother. Grayson couldn't remember the last time someone actually sat at that island instead of at the long formal dining table down the hall. There was a pretty decent chance it had *never* happened before since George hadn't approved of actually using the eat-in kitchen space.

"Oh, good, Becka, you're back. I was getting a little worried Ruffles had managed to get out, and you were having to chase her down the beach again. We really should hire someone to come in and help teach her some manners, don't you ..."

Her voice faded away, the color draining from her face until all that was left was the artificial pink on her cheeks and her lips. Once, her hair had been blonde, but all that remained now was a soft white, pulled back away from her face in a tidy bun that sat just above the nape of her neck. He still remembered the dress she was wearing, a pale blue to match the color of her eyes and always paired with her favorite cream-colored silk scarf.

She had always dressed the part of the lady of the house. A bit prim. A bit proper. Elegant and soft-spoken. Everything she'd been raised to be and more. He absolutely adored her, something he'd tried hard to block out. It hit him then, as she looked at him like a ghost had walked into her kitchen, a punch to the gut of affection and regret.

"Grandma Edith." He was rooted to the spot, unable to do more than shrug helplessly and hope she somehow understood all the years of emotions contained in that single, unremarkable gesture.

"You came back." She was off her barstool and across the kitchen before he'd had time to do more than open his arms to receive her. She was a tall woman, slender and fragile as he enveloped her in a soft hug. More than a dozen years and she still smelled of lilac perfume and old woman. He hadn't even had to ask for forgiveness, and she'd already given it.

She couldn't have been more different from the wild looking woman now peering at him over a half empty wine glass, eyes narrowed like she was waiting for him to make a wrong move so she could toss him out on his ass. Nothing elegant or forgiving about that one, and she seemed to have all the ladylike grace of her poorly behaved dog. The Schnauzer wasn't the only one that needed training. The woman could do with some manners of her own.

"Oh, have you met Becka Simmons?" Edith pulled away, dabbing at her eyes with a discreet knuckle. "And Ruffles, of course."

"We've met," Becka said, her wide mouth stretching into a fake smile at the same time Grayson said, "We haven't been properly introduced."

"Where are my manners?" Edith was practically beaming. "Becka, this is my grandson, Grayson. I've already told you so much about him that you must feel like you know him already. Grayson, darling, I know it's been a while since we spoke," she glossed over the reason for that entirely, much to his relief, "but this is my caretaker, Becka."

"Caretaker?"

"Oh." The flush on Edith's cheeks was no longer fully synthetic. "Well, your grandfather was such a busy man, and I was starting to have a hard time getting up and down the stairs and such, you know? Becka helps with the chores and the cooking and things like that."

Grayson couldn't imagine how bad his grandmother had to have been struggling before George would have agreed to hire someone to help with chores. That was simply Edith's job, and she had best get on with doing it herself. At least, that's what his grandfather would have said. Grayson could almost still hear it.

He wasn't quite sure what to say to Becka, and her expression hadn't warmed a single degree, so he turned his attention to the dog she was still holding. "And, uh, Ruffles?" He thought about reaching out a hand for her to sniff but she still didn't seem much friendlier than the woman holding her, and he was afraid he might lose a finger.

"Becka's idea!" Edith beamed as she took the dog, who seemed to have no problem being nice to everyone but him. "She thought it would be good for me to have someone to spend time with, other than her, of course. I've always wanted a dog, and you know how much your grandfather hated them, so I never could have one, but then Becka suggested I get one now. That was after George's funeral, so he wasn't here to object, and we went to the animal shelter—what a terrible place that is and we are making monthly donations now to help fix it up—but we went to the shelter, and Becka told them we were looking for a little dog, and they had this one ..."

He waited for a moment, as he always had when she got too excited and started to ramble, timing it perfectly for when she had to stop and take a breath. "But why did you name the dog Ruffles?"

"She likes potato chips." The answer came from Becka, her voice and expression deadpan. "That brand particularly."

"So you have a potato chip dog, and you're drinking wine in the kitchen?" None of that seemed like the kind of thing Edith would have done on her own. After all, she'd been living under George's rules for more than forty years. It would have taken more than a few weeks to get her to start acting like that.

What exactly had been going on at Barlow House before his grandfather died?

Edith's smile faltered.

That was all it took to unleash the tiny terror of a woman behind her. "That potato chip dog makes her happy and so does having an occasional glass of wine in her own kitchen. Do you have a problem with that, Barlow?"

"What?" Not even in this town, where his family had been everything anyone needed to know about him, had anyone ever called him Barlow instead of his first name. "I wasn't complaining, I was just—"

"Just upsetting her." Becka glared at him across the kitchen, the tension in her bunched shoulders, a clear indication of how much anger she was holding back, all of it somehow seemingly directed at him. She reached for the gold necklace she wore—a small gold heart at the end of a short chain—and began to fidget with it as she turned away from him to smile at Edith instead.

"Becka, dear, that's not true at all." Edith took a breath, sliding on a mask of composure Grayson was well acquainted with. This was her hostess face, and nothing could crack it. "Grayson would never intentionally upset me. I'm just a little surprised to see him."

"I would be, too, after twelve years of not bothering to call." Becka downed the rest of her wine and poured another glass. She did not offer him one.

Grayson expected his grandmother to chastise her a bit, put her in her place as an employee speaking out of turn to a family member, but after a swift look was exchanged between them, Becka looked away with a sour expression on her face, and Edith turned back to him as though the comment had never happened.

They were definitely close, and he tried to ignore a swift rush of unreasonable jealousy. He had no right to be upset. He hadn't been here for Edith, a decision he'd made of his own free will, and instead it had been this woman, this prickly and ill-mannered stranger, who had filled his shoes. He couldn't blame Edith for forming a bond with someone else, even if that someone had the basic personality of a badger with one foot caught in a bear trap.

"Would you like something to eat?" Edith sat back on her barstool and looked around the kitchen. "Becka didn't pick up enough from the diner because we didn't know you were coming, but I'm sure I can think of something that can be put together quickly."

"No, it's okay." He thanked his lucky stars he'd already eaten. If Becka did the cooking, he was likely to end up poisoned or with spit in his food. "I stopped for a bite coming into town. Ran into the sheriff."

He'd also run into Becka, but he kept that awkward tidbit to himself and was relieved when she just rolled her eyes and didn't mention it, either.

"Patrick does seem to be everywhere, doesn't he?" There was something in Edith's voice that he couldn't quite catch before it faded. "I'm sure he was pleased to see you."

"He seemed to be." A little too much in Grayson's honest opinion, but he didn't mention that to Edith. "Told me to tell you hello."

He'd asked a bunch of questions, too, Grayson remembered. Most of them had been about his grandfather. Did Edith know that Patrick wasn't entirely sold on drowning being George's cause of death? Or at least that maybe it hadn't been an accident? And why had she denied his request for an autopsy?

He weighed the questions in his mind for a moment, debating the wisdom of asking her about it directly before clearing his throat and trying to sound as casual as possible.

"He mentioned some other stuff, too. Stuff about George. Have you talked to him about any of that?"

Edith reached for her wine, her gaze truly leaving Grayson for the first time since he'd walked in, moving instead to take in the view out over the water. "Did you know your father loved to swim? I wouldn't let him swim in the bay, of course. That was too dangerous for a kid his age, but he loved the pool and probably would have swum in the bathtub if I would have let him. Funny how he had that in common with George, don't you think?

"Grandma Edith, did you hear what I said? About the sheriff?" Her hearing had seemed perfectly adequate a moment before, and he wasn't sure why she was suddenly acting like she hadn't understood a word he'd said.

"Of course she heard you." Becka rolled her eyes again and Grayson had to resist the urge to roll his back at her. "You're standing right there. She just doesn't want to talk about that. Why would you bring him up to her and make her sad again?"

"I wasn't *trying* to make her sad. I was just—"

"It doesn't matter if you were trying to." She leaned in for emphasis, brown eyes sparkling with protective menace. "You *did*."

It was fascinating—and God help him somehow arousing —to watch her puff up with annoyance until she seemed much more intimidating than anyone her size had the right to be. He half expected her to start spitting chewed nails at any moment. Still, he was the one on the receiving end of her barb, and he wasn't able to pretend it hadn't hurt.

"I noticed."

His tone seemed to shut her down—he hadn't done a good job of concealing the naked grief in it—and she stepped back, deflating in on herself as her anger drained away in the face of his ready acceptance of his fault. She seemed determined to be mad at him for reasons he didn't quite understand, but at least she was able to see when it wasn't called for. He'd bet she was going to find something else to get fired up about pretty quickly, but for now she was back in her more docile role as semi-hostile observer.

Edith had remained quiet through their altercation, the dog in her arms relaxed as she petted it rhythmically. She hated having raised voices around her, it always made her so uneasy no matter who was talking, but she seemed calmer about it than he'd ever seen her before. Either time had changed her or having the dog had been a good idea. He hated to think that Becka might have made a good suggestion—if she wanted to hate him for no good reason two could play at that game—but he was in full support of whatever made Edith happy.

Even if it was a snarling hellhound that hadn't taken its eyes off him for even a moment since he'd arrived.

Everyone settled into a tense silence and after a few seconds, Edith seemed to realize they were done with their little verbal sparring session. The two women exchanged another silent look—Edith's expression tired and Becka's apologetic—before Edith stepped in again to take control of the situation.

"Perhaps you should take your things upstairs, dear." Edith stopped petting the dog long enough to pat his arm instead. Her hands looked so fragile, the bones so long and thin and protected by nothing more than crepe-paper skin. Her wedding ring still sat on her finger, a brilliant diamond, white and cold against a classic gold band. "You must be tired after such a long trip, and I think we'll all feel better after some rest."

He recognized it for what it was, a polite dismissal. He left them alone and in less than five minutes he was climbing the stairs to the second floor carrying the bag he'd gone out to grab from the trunk of his car. Nothing had changed there either, and he passed by his grandparents'—Edith's—room on his way to his own childhood bedroom. Knowing she was now the only occupant of what had been their room didn't keep him from walking a little more softly, a little more quickly, as he passed.

Some things were too ingrained to change, though the realization of what he'd done shamed him. He was an adult now, a fully grown man jumping at ghosts and shadows.

His bedroom had been the last door on the right, and he turned the knob slowly, wondering if Edith had kept it as it had been when he'd left. He half expected to find the same posters on the walls, the same blue bedspread on the mattress.

What he had not expected to find—and yet very much did as soon as he opened the door—was a whirlwind of chaos and clutter. Shoes tossed on the floor. Red lace bra hanging from the back of the desk chair. A pink blanket wadded up and tossed haphazardly on the bed.

"What the fuck?"

"That room is already occupied, champ."

He turned to find Becka leaning on the hallway wall, a little smirk playing at the corners of her mouth. Her lipstick was nearly the exact color of what was apparently *her* bra, and he found his eyes darting back and forth from lips to lace.

"This is my bedroom." He couldn't let go of the doorknob, once again frozen in indecision as she stared at him.

"It *was* your bedroom, but it's the biggest of the guest rooms in the house, and George and Edith didn't think you were coming back." She shrugged, clearly waiting for him to let go of her door and move out of her way. "You snooze, you lose, or whatever the saying is."

"I didn't *snooze*." He pushed his objection out through clenched teeth. "I was here *first*."

"You wanna take it up with Edith or can we settle this like men?" She had the most irritating face he'd ever seen, and he was convinced it was mostly because of that red mouth of hers. It drew your gaze right to it so you didn't miss a single amused twitch of her lips. "You'd have your pick of the other two guest rooms."

He let go of the doorknob like it burned him. "Fine, keep it, but remember who had it first."

"Yes, sir!" She gave him a mocking salute—he deserved no less after the childish pettiness of that last remark—and he ignored her as he grabbed his bag off the floor and tried not to stomp his way over to the slightly smaller bedroom directly across from the one she now apparently occupied.

At least the new one was clean.

It grated on his nerves and offended his pride to be ousted from his own room but, at least his grandmother was alive, and she'd let him stay. He was willing to put up with a few obstacles to make sure she was okay, including the aggressive dog and the bitchy neighbor across the hall.

He would worry about them later. For now, all he wanted was to close his eyes and get some sleep. It had been a long drive from Indiana, and nothing had gone quite the way he'd planned once he'd arrived. Surely he'd feel better once he had a few hours of rest.

That thought was interrupted by the sound of incessant barking coming from the first floor and he pulled the pillow over his head to drown out the sound. It didn't work. He could hear each aggravating woof and yip as it drove straight through his skull and into the soft tissue of his brain. For a small dog, she was really quite loud.

Happy fucking homecoming.

<h1 style="text-align:center">Chapter Three</h1>

Becka stared at the closed door across the hall from what she had come to think of as her bedroom, a shaky hand pressed to a nervous stomach. Nothing could have prepared her for the sudden reappearance of the notorious Grayson Barlow, and she was still reeling from the series of confrontations that had begun in the On the Rocks' parking lot and ended in the house she'd long ago come to view as her home.

She'd been here, taking care of Edith and keeping a watchful eye on Barlow House, for well over a year now. It was more to her than just a place of employment, just as Edith was more than some old woman who wrote her a weekly paycheck. That he'd shown up here, after all this time, pretending like he hadn't done a thing wrong and clearly looking down his nose at her for being nothing more than an employee, pissed her off. It pissed her off even more that he'd had the balls to act like she was the one in the wrong for being protective of someone she cared deeply about.

How many times in the past year had she heard stories about the prodigal grandson? Edith spoke of him often and with a pained fondness, even more so now that George wasn't around to chastise her for bringing it up the way he'd done in the past. The hole Grayson had left in Edith's life had been a gaping wound, one that never stopped aching, and if Becka had come to resent him for it, well, that seemed perfectly natural to her.

She was, after all, the one that had been around to see it. He might have been able to brush it off, put it in the back of his mind, or pretend it wasn't happening, but Edith hadn't had that luxury and neither had Becka. Actions had consequences, whether Grayson wanted them to or not.

Still buzzing with adrenaline and excess energy, Becka tossed her shoes in the closet and took a good look around the chaotic mess that was her bedroom. Truthfully, she probably should be embarrassed that he'd seen it in this state—she *did* wince a little as she picked the bra up off the back of her chair —but she had pretty thick skin when it came to things like that.

It wasn't normally quite *this* bad, but she'd spent most of the afternoon getting ready for her first date in over a year. Well, trying on all the clothes in her closet for it, anyway, and obsessing over her hair and makeup choices for hours. A humiliating waste of time and effort, since the woman had canceled on her at the last minute, leaving her throwing a pity party in the kitchen with Edith instead, drinking wine and pouting over dinner, instead of cleaning up her room or washing her face.

Which was why the bedroom had still been destroyed when Grayson had poked his head in and—as she'd realized when she'd finally caught a glimpse of herself in the bus's rear-view mirror after her stop at the diner—she was still wearing her best *fuck me* red lipstick with her slouchiest lounge wear.

She'd initially thought the strange man staring at her in the diner parking lot was taking her in from head to toe because he thought she was attractive, then she'd decided it must have been because she looked decidedly weird with her mismatched clothing and makeup choices. Either way, she hadn't expected to run into him again, much less to do so on her own front porch. When she'd found him standing there, her mind had immediately started blaring alarm bells and thinking about stalkers and serial killers.

How could she have known the truth was somehow almost worse?

After hearing every word there was to hear about him from the moment he drew his first breath to the night he'd climbed out the window of the very room she slept in, Becka had been sure that if Grayson Barlow ever did show up she'd recognize him on the spot. The pictures of him that Edith had hidden away all showed a tall and spindly kid, ears a little too big for his head, nose a little too long for his face. Brown hair, gray eyes. Edith had sworn he would grow up to look exactly like George, or, if not his grandfather, then his father, Thomas.

Like Grayson, Becka only knew Thomas through pictures, but the resemblance between father and son was clear enough. It wouldn't have been surprising for the grandson to follow suit. It seemed to her that the way the townspeople spoke of them was basically true.

If you'd seen one Barlow man, you'd seen them all.

At least that's what she'd believed until she'd come face to face with one on her front porch step. The coloring was right but if she was being honest, she'd been too distracted to notice. He'd grown into his nose, and his hair—brown, yes, but shot through with a golden glow in the warm afternoon sun—was kept long enough to help hide the ears. The facial hair, more stubble than actual beard, had emphasized a hard jawline that hadn't existed in those childhood photos.

Her first thought had not been that the long-lost lamb had returned to the flock, but rather that the weight of his gaze was as heavy upon the second encounter as it had been outside the diner. There was something about the way he looked at her, like he could see through her to the secrets she was trying to hide, that made her uncomfortable.

The quickening of her pulse had been entirely due to his unsettlingly direct assessment and had had nothing at all to do with what was a nearly perfect face and body. She had more sense than that and that was *before* she'd figured out who he was.

Now that it was *after* that discovery, well... All the more reason to keep her distance. She'd hold her tongue—for the most part—purely for Edith's sake but she had no plans to be any friendlier than she had to. If he'd wanted to be here, he'd had plenty of time and opportunity. She was willing to tolerate him because his grandmother wanted him around, but a last-minute, guilt-driven arrival wasn't winning him any points in Becka's book.

Thinking about it made her mad all over again as she stalked around the room, hanging clothes back on their hangers and returning her makeup and hair products to their proper places, her stuff taking up space in what used to be Grayson's bedroom.

She'd originally wanted to take the room across the hall, since all his stuff had still been in here when George had hired her, but Edith had insisted that wasn't fair to her. The largest bedroom should belong to someone who was here to use it.

They'd climbed the stairs together, filled row after row of empty boxes with remnants of his childhood as Edith tried to hold back tears and told stories about her grandson. It wasn't until later, when Becka tried to tell her how sorry she was for her loss, that she found out he hadn't died.

What kind of man would do that to an old woman?

It wasn't that she wasn't empathetic. No one recognized the look of a kid who'd had it rough better than someone else that had been through it. She could see the evidence of it in the brackets at his mouth and the haunted look in his eyes. Even if she hadn't already pieced most of it together from Edith, she would have recognized it in him anyway.

No, the problem wasn't that she didn't feel bad for him and everything he'd gone through. It was that he'd run off and left Edith behind.

And in all the years since, not one letter, not one phone call, not one attempt to say, *'Hey, I've got my own money now and a rundown one-bedroom apartment, wanna run away with me to someplace safe?'* Running away wasn't really Becka's style, but for God's sake, if you were going to do it, don't do it alone. Take your loved ones with you or come back for them when you had the chance.

Some people—him included apparently—didn't seem to understand the obligation they had to others. Of course, George was the one at fault, mostly, but didn't Grayson understand that the rest of the family should have stuck together? That leaving his fragile grandmother behind to deal with it all alone didn't exactly make him a decent person?

He'd been just a kid, she knew that, but that was no excuse as far as she was concerned. Hadn't she also been a kid the first time she'd stood up against one of the monsters in the weird pseudo-hippie cult her parents had raised her in? They'd tossed her out on her ass for being defiant when she'd still been a teenager, for not keeping silent when some nut job that called himself a prophet had picked out yet another underage bride.

The joke had been on them, since she'd burned down their

shitty 'church' and stolen her parents' car on the way out, but wasn't that exactly her point? If she could do it, overcome years of abuse and conditioning and be forced out into the world all alone because of it, then Grayson could have done it.

Payton could have done it, too, if she'd wanted to badly enough. Becka's stomach dropped at the unbidden thought of her older sister, the one that definitely hadn't needed to run off with the first boy that asked as soon as she turned sixteen, leaving Becka alone to deal with their fucked-up church and the wrath of their parents...

Becka's hand wandered, habitually, to the necklace she wore, the gold warm against her skin even as the edges of the heart shaped locket dug into her palm. It was the last thing she'd gotten from Payton. The necklace that had been her sister's, with a picture of the two of them together already tucked safely inside it, had been in the envelope with her goodbye letter. As angry as Becka had been, as hurt, she hadn't taken it off since.

She flopped down on the unmade bed, pulling a pillow with a pink silk pillowcase tight against her chest, right over the old, familiar ache that she'd never been able to escape or outrun. Thinking about Payton was always painful, and Becka had a feeling seeing Grayson was going to be dragging up a lot of feelings that were better off buried.

Her heart hurt, and she stayed on the bed for a long time, counting her breaths and listening to the rhythmic rush of blood in her ears. When she started to calm down, she sat up and reached for her bedside table.

She had one other picture of her childhood, besides the one in her locket, and she kept it tucked out of sight on the nightstand in a plain black frame. Careful not to drop it, she picked it up, cradled it in her hand as she tried to untangle the resentment she felt toward her sister and the anger she felt at the unwelcome—to her at least—guest in the next room.

No matter how hard she tried, it seemed like an impossible task.

In the photo, she was young enough to be missing her two front teeth, and beside her, only a few years older, was Payton. They leaned into one another, heads together until the onlooker couldn't tell when the brown hair of one girl ended and that of the one beside her began. With the same wide mouths and freckled noses, they were nearly identical except in age and eye color. Two peas in the same fucked up pod, they'd practically been inseparable in those days, held together by a bond that united them against their world and its horrors.

Becka flipped the frame so the picture faced down on the table and pressed her palms hard to her eyelids to keep the tears from falling.

It had been years and she still hadn't gotten over it. The way she'd felt when she'd realized she was all alone, that the one person that understood what she was going through had simply packed up in the middle of the night and left her there alone.

Her heart, no matter what the wisdom of her mind said, was still stuck in the moment she'd realized Payton, the one good thing she'd had in a life of suffering, had left her. She'd sealed off that hurt, the breathless loss of a frightened fourteen-year-old, behind a wall of anger so high and so thick she didn't think she could pull it down if she wanted to.

Maybe that was why she'd felt such an instant bond with Edith. They both knew what it felt like to find yourself the only one left in a bad situation. Edith blamed herself for being the adult and not having the courage to leave and take Grayson with her, but if Becka knew one thing in her heart, it was that all survivors had a responsibility to help the rest, and there was no excuse for the strong ones to leave the rest behind.

She'd never forgiven Payton and she damn sure wasn't about to forgive Grayson for it, either.

Edith wanted him to stay, and Becka wanted Edith to be happy, but as long as he was in Barlow House, as long as he was around Edith, he'd mind his manners if he knew what was good for him.

And if he didn't ... Well, she knew how to handle a Barlow man.

Chapter Four

Grayson

Pulled from a dreamless sleep by the smell of bacon cooking, it took Grayson several confused seconds to realize where—and when—he was. Not only was he back in Barlow House, but he was also pretty sure he'd somehow managed to sleep through the evening and into the next morning. A quick look out the window at the sun shining over the evergreens from the east proved it.

He hated to think what Becka and Edith were going to think of his manners, but he'd apparently needed the extra shut eye. His muscles were sore and his throat dry, but his head was much clearer after a good night's rest. It had been years since he'd slept through the night without waking to shake off a nightmare, but then it was to be at least somewhat expected after too many hours awake.

That could have been avoided if he'd stopped more often on the way from Indiana, maybe gotten a motel room and some actual sleep, instead of pulling off to the side of the road to have a farce of a catnap behind the wheel. If he had, he might have been able to avoid the awkwardness of showing his face again downstairs after such a long disappearance. His first day back and he had already made an ass of himself.

Edith wouldn't say a word, but if she was upset he'd be able to see the thin lines of hurt or disappointment at the sides of her mouth. Most people wouldn't even have noticed a change so small, but Grayson had always been attuned to her every move and emotion. Not just her, George, too.

The little worry brackets beside her mouth. The telltale twitch of his fingers. The charged silence when every second that ticked by felt as though it might last forever. He'd prayed then that it would end, that the quiet would not last forever, even though he knew what came after. Sometimes the waiting had been the hardest part.

"Grayson?" Edith's voice was thin and far away, and he realized after a short pause that she was calling him from downstairs. She had never been one to raise her voice before and even now it was tentative.

He didn't know if she'd ever heal enough to not be afraid, but he did know that leaving her here alone had been the most cowardly thing he had ever done. And even knowing it, he didn't want to face it. Every instinct he had was telling him to pack his shit and run, that he didn't have the right stuff to linger here and try to make amends.

Unfamiliar floorboards creaked beneath his weight as he crossed the room and opened the bedroom door, casting a quick glance across the hall to make sure *that woman* wasn't around before poking his head out. "Yeah?"

"Becka asked me to tell you breakfast is nearly ready."

He opened the door wider, confident now that he wasn't going to be accosted by an ill-tempered pixie woman in the hallway. She was already downstairs and was likely the source of the delicious smells wafting up the stairs and making his stomach rumble. His body warred with his survival instincts, but he was hungry, damn it. "I'll be down in just a second."

"Take your time, dear."

Grayson snorted as he shut the door. That was easy for her to say. He had a feeling Becka wouldn't be particularly forgiving if he was late for something, even if he hadn't been aware he was supposed to be there in the first place. If he didn't hurry, she'd probably throw the whole damn plate in his face. He really needed to figure out what her problem was before he ended up the topic of some true crime podcast as a missing person.

He changed into fresh clothes as quickly as he could—some of what he had stuffed in his bag was almost tolerably unwrinkled—and followed the smell of food and the sound of laughter until he found both women in the kitchen again. They stopped talking when he entered the room, and an uncomfortable silence descended in the place of their easy chatter. The only sounds that remained were the sizzling skillet and the low growls of a still grumpy dog.

Becka clearly wasn't the only one still holding onto a dislike for him, and he walked a wide path around the dog on his way to sit . She watched him from her place on the floor, comfortably settled at his grandmother's feet, and the look in her eyes was nearly identical to the one Becka wore as she watched him from her place beside the stove.

Two against one.

"Hush now." Edith seemed more than a little flustered as Ruffles huffed and quieted down but continued to stare at him with suspicion. "I don't know what has gotten into her since you got here. Try not to take it personally."

"She doesn't like men." Becka waved her spatula at him, a wide gesture that encompassed Grayson from the top of his head to the bottoms of his feet. "Who can blame her, though?"

"Well, I don't think that's—"

Edith cut him off with a shake of her head and a diplomatic smile. "Now, no arguing before breakfast. Isn't that right Becka?"

There was a long stretch of silence, a full beat or longer than was natural, and then Becka's shoulders drooped, her combative stance melting away. She turned back to the meal she was making with a barely perceptible shrug. "If that's what you want. I can be nice for at least one meal."

"Of course you can." Edith seemed oblivious to the reluctant tone of Becka's agreement, and she forged ahead in the conversation as though the tension in the room didn't exist. "I'm sure the two of you will learn to get along splendidly, don't you think so?"

"Actually—" Grayson started.

Edith forged ahead, smile bright and firm as she plowed over his objection. "Oh, please, Becka, would you mind refilling this coffee cup for me? I'm afraid I've finished the first one already this morning."

Becka stood still for a moment, the rest of what she had been about to say left unsaid as she set the spatula down and reached for Edith's coffee cup. Grayson had plenty of things he could say about her already, but she clearly cared for his grandmother. Not just in providing for her physical needs as she was paid to do, but in the emotional sense. No amount of money could buy the silent look that passed between the two women as the empty cup was handed over and returned replenished.

Like the previous evening, there was a warning there, sent and received, but beneath it was fondness, patience, and understanding. He felt like exactly what he was, an outsider in his own childhood home, an uncomfortable observer of a bond that did not include him. He could have had that here—*should* have had it. A place to be in his adulthood. A comfortable companionship with the only family member he had left. Instead, he watched from the sidelines as the urge to run burned like an unscratchable itch between his shoulder blades.

Edith was happy, and he could finally let go of some of the guilt he'd carried where she was concerned, but it was obvious now that she didn't need him. He'd done what he needed to do. The trip back home had given him confirmation that she was doing well and was being cared for. Now that it was done, he could let it go and move on.

He didn't belong here any more than he had when he was a child.

"You seem to be doing well." He tried to ease into the conversation, tapping his finger absently on the countertop as he wondered how best to explain to her that he wouldn't be staying another night. "Better than I expected, actually, so—"

"So?" Becka leaned across the counter to drop a plate in front of him. It landed hard enough to make the silverware rattle and he was surprised it didn't shatter. The food looked good but her face was bitter. He couldn't put his finger on it, but for some reason it seemed too intimate, too personal an anger to have for a stranger.

No matter how much love she had for his grandmother, it seemed like something more was bubbling beneath her surface. Not that it was any of his business. He'd be out of here before he had time to unpack any of that. Still, she might want to try doing what he'd always managed not to do himself and talk to a professional about that.

"I'm sure you're just glad she's doing okay, right?" Becka tipped her head as she spoke, evaluating him with cold eyes as he struggled not to squirm under her scrutiny. "You're planning to stay and have a nice long visit? It's been such a long time, after all. A nice extended visit from her only grandson is bound to help her do even better, don't you think?"

He didn't think he'd ever been threatened in such a sickly-sweet tone in his life, and he wiped a bead of sweat off his forehead with the back of his hand. His mind was working as fast as it had ever worked, but he was coming up empty as she waited in silence for him to say something. He could feel Edith looking at him, and he didn't have to turn his head and look to know that she was also waiting to see what he was going to say.

Becka's smile was sharply expectant—no red lipstick today—and it was clear she knew exactly what she was doing. The option to announce his intention to leave without coming across as a total ass had just been almost entirely demolished, and he could feel the two of them closing the exit door behind him.

The itch between his shoulder blades intensified.

"It's just that I have to work..." He shrugged and tried to look sad as he took a bite of the bacon Becka had put on his plate. "I'm in the middle of a big project."

"Oh, that's right." Edith took a sip of her coffee and patted his hand. "I remember now, there was some mention of you doing computer work."

Grayson thought about that lawyer and how quickly they'd tracked him down. He didn't know how Edith had known about his job or who had told her, but his suspicions that George had always been far closer to him than he'd ever wanted to believe deepened with her unwitting admission.

"Yeah, that's right." Grayson tried to hide the relief in his voice—a job was a great excuse to skip town—but Becka's glare told him he hadn't been as successful as he'd hoped. "Website design."

"Where's your office then?"

"What?"

He could almost feel the good feelings drain out of him as Becka leaned back against the edge of the stove, ankles crossed and coffee cup in her hands. She took a slow drink, her eyes locked on his for several seconds before she repeated herself.

Slowly.

For emphasis.

"Where is your office?"

"Uh, well, I was working in Indiana—"

"The office is in Indiana?"

"No, that's not—"

"Well? Where is it then? Because when we talked to the lawyer he made it pretty clear that keeping up with you wasn't exactly an easy task for them. You'd only been in Indiana for a few months. And it was Kentucky before that. Utah before that. I can't remember where he said you were before that, but it might have been one of those 'new' states. New Jersey? New York?"

"I've never been to New Jersey—"

"No, you're right!" She snapped her fingers and pointed at him, sarcasm dripping from every word. "I think it was North Dakota."

"Okay." He held up a hand, somewhere between a command for silence and a plea for mercy. "I don't have to go into an office. I just need somewhere that I can work in peace and quiet."

"You can do that here." Edith had been looking back and forth between them as they argued, her concern growing as their voices rose, but now she was positively beaming again. "You can work in the library if you want or we can set up a space in your room. I'm not sure what you need for work, but we probably have most of it. Anything we don't have, we can buy."

"You don't need to buy anything, Grandma Edith." He shot Becka a look, his own hostility on full display, but she only grinned back at him and saluted him with her coffee cup. "I'll take care of it."

And just like that, his chances of getting out of Barlow House unscathed vanished right before his eyes. Two hours later he still wasn't sure how they'd managed it. Had it been a spontaneous hijacking of his life or a planned one? Either way, his grandmother had been thrilled all morning and Becka had been giving him knowing, taunting, frustratingly beautiful smiles whenever Edith wasn't looking.

As it turned out, that was pretty often, since Edith had been bustling about the house since they'd finished breakfast, tucking things here and there and moving them from place to place. She said she was just tidying up so he could get settled in —to live and apparently to work—but he knew what she was really doing.

Fussing.

That's what she'd always called it when he was a child. Not really doing much but still needing the constant movement to soothe her frazzled nerves. He'd caught her ironing all their socks once and the two of them had laughed about that absurdity for days. Still, she'd always insisted it was worth it. That it kept her hands and her mind busy. It had made George angry, but Grayson had always found it funny and endearing in an odd sort of way.

Watching her shuffle the same stack of paper in the library for the third time, he realized she must be almost as nervous about him coming home as he was. She wanted him to stay, that much he knew, but he hadn't anticipated that she, too, might be a little uneasy at the idea of reconnecting.

Somehow that made it easier for him. He wasn't the only one worried. Not the only one feeling awkward. Not the only one that was curious or concerned. They were in it together and it was... kind of nice. Kind of like old times. He'd been dreading all of this—and he still wasn't entirely sure it was a good idea—but it surprised him how much he'd missed her and her little quirks.

He thought they were getting along pretty well until she kicked him out of the library.

"Go." Edith flapped her arms, hands waving as she tried to shoo him out like a pesky bird that had flown in an open window. "I want to get this room all set up for you, but I want it to be a surprise so you can't be in here. You have to go, and I'll have Becka help me finish up."

"Okay, okay." He backed out of the room, arms up to ward off her aggressive forced evacuation tactics. "I'll go sit in the kitchen."

"No." Edith shook her head, but she wasn't really paying attention to him anymore. She was already up on her toes, looking over his shoulder down the hallway for Becka. "Go outside. Walk on the beach or something. Before you do, though, can you ask Becka to come up?"

"I'll find her."

And find her, he did. After a quick and ultimately fruitless search of most of the downstairs, he found her waiting in the kitchen, her back to the doorway as she leaned against the countertop and stared out over the water.

Now that Edith was down the hall and not staring at him over the rim of her coffee cup, he had the chance to notice that Becka's shorts were even more revealing than the day before, and that she'd chosen a form fitting blue tank top to go with it. Without the oversized T-shirt, it was even clearer how small she actually was.

He'd known she was short, that much was glaringly obvious even to someone with his average height of 5'9", but though she was undoubtedly petite, she was hardly delicate. From the way she carried herself, he'd expected a dancer's body, with a lean, willowy grace. Instead, her arms were firm, with defined muscle that spoke to time spent in some sort of intense workout. She was far from bulky, but there was a strength there that surprised him.

He dragged his eyes away from taking in the details of her form—he didn't know what the hell he was doing staring at her like that—and tried to focus on the view. The water was calm, calmer than almost any other time he'd seen it.

"Nice out today," he said, ignoring the dog as she growled at him from her spot on the floor. She always seemed to be right beside one woman or the other, taking turns protecting them from imaginary boogeymen. "The water looks good."

"Tricky." She backed away from the window and turned her astute gaze on him instead of the waves. "Sometimes it looks good on the surface, but the riptide can still get you. You can lose people on days like today, when the weather is clear and the water is inviting. That's when your guard is down, you know?"

"I was raised here." He chewed on a thumbnail, frustration driving him back into bad habits he'd thought he'd left behind in this house years ago. It was unnerving to find they'd been here the whole time, waiting for him. "I know how the riptides work."

Charged, irritable silence dragged them both under as she turned back to face the water.

"My grandmother needs you." He should have led with that and not tried to make small talk. "She's in the library."

Becka set her cup in the sink and walked away without saying anything else to him. Fine. That was fine with him. She was half the reason he was trapped here in the first place and it's not like he wanted to talk to her anyway.

He brooded about it as he left the house through the back door but put it out of his mind as soon as he took his first gulp of fresh sea air. Let her hate him, he had a grandmother he barely understood anymore and a past he couldn't face. It was enough to deal with without adding on a temperamental slip of a woman and her perpetual attitude problem.

It had been more than a decade since he'd walked the path

to the beach but he still knew the way. Not much had changed, the water and the rocks and the salty tang in the air were the same as they had always been. The old stairs had seen quite a few boards replaced, but not the one he had carved his initials into.

"Guess I made a mark on this place, after all." Time had worn away the sharp edges of the lines, weathered the railing until the letters were nearly the same color as the wood around them, but he could still see the grooves he'd made with his own hands and a beat-up old pocket knife he'd stolen from George's garage.

Back then he'd doubted whether it had been worth getting knocked around—half the blows a punishment for the theft and the other half for the property damage—but now...

He ran his thumb over his name, knocking the loose dirt from the indents so he could see it more clearly. That beating would have come one way or another. He knew that now. If time and distance had taught Grayson anything, it had been that his transgressions were nothing more than an excuse for George to let his frustrations out on a smaller, weaker body.

He no longer blamed himself for what had been done to him, and the vandalism—all thirteen letters of it—had outlasted the man who'd tormented him. There was a petty satisfaction in that, one that Grayson carried with him to the water's edge.

Someday, probably soon, Edith would drag him to the cemetery. She'd insist that he pay his respects at whatever plot of land they'd buried his grandfather in. It was important, not so much because she thought Grayson would mourn, but because it was the proper thing to do. If he didn't go, people would talk. There would be gossip, whispers and speculation that maybe everything wasn't as picturesque at Barlow House as they'd all been led to believe.

So, she'd nag, and, because he loved her, he'd go and stand cold sentry over a headstone.

But this...

This little slice of rocky beach with its crashing waves and towering evergreen trees that marched straight up to the shore...

This was George's grave.

If there was a place where his grandfather's spirit would linger, where the people that had known him in life could visit and feel his presence, it certainly wouldn't be at the cemetery. George would have no interest in haunting the well-trimmed grass with its neat and tidy little rows of the dearly departed. He would be here, part of the wind and the waves and the high-pitched scream of the gulls as they scoured the beach for their dinners.

For a moment Grayson was tempted to speak George's name—to let his voice carry across the bay and see what might answer—but his courage failed him. Instead, he stood on the shore, feet inches from the water, and wondered what it was like to drown.

Chapter Five

Grayson

The next several days, he was busy trying to get settled in and set up to work from Barlow House. He was used to moving from place to place, so his system was fairly efficient, but it was difficult to stay on task when every move he made risked him running into his grandmother, her prickly caretaker, or her even pricklier dog.

Years of living an unsettled lifestyle meant he was used to moving, what he was *not* used to having was other people in his space.

Making sure he had regular mealtimes.

Talking to him.

Asking questions.

Insisting he go outside and breathe fresh air periodically.

Becka was indifferent beyond shoving a plateful of food under his nose three times a day, but his grandmother was a different story. She seemed determined to make up for lost time by coddling him, and he couldn't go longer than an hour without her turning up at his door with some invented errand.

More than a decade of worry seemed to lie dormant just behind her teeth, words that she couldn't say getting stuck on her tongue as she smiled at him and hovered over his shoulder every chance she had. Maybe, if he had been a better, braver man, he would have been the one to speak first. If he asked her how she'd been—*really* been—since he'd left, would she tell him? Would that loosen her voice, pry open her heart, and let her spill out everything she was clearly holding back?

Part of him thought it might and that was why he kept his own silence. He wanted her to know she was safe, that she was loved, that he appreciated what she'd done for him after he'd lost his parents, but he wasn't ready to talk about George. Barlow House had never been the kind of place that welcomed those types of discussions, and Grayson somehow didn't think that had changed with George's death. Some things were simply not meant to be talked about and there was a half-formed fear in Grayson's mind that any attempt to rehash the past would invoke some kind of wrathful spirit.

His grandfather had been a stubborn man, if anyone was capable of popping back in from the afterlife like some kind of corpse-ified Gothic ghost, it was George. It was not a pleasant image and Grayson let it keep him quiet. He patted Edith's hand, took the food she gave him, smiled at her in return... but he did not talk to her. Not about that anyway. The worst of it was behind them all, and there was no reason now to speak ill of the dead.

Edith didn't seem to mind it, happy to chatter away about his job and his travels and the lives of the various townspeople he still remembered from so long ago. Soon he knew all about the families that had stuck around. The deaths, births, and marriages that had taken place since he'd left were all stored inside Edith's perfect memory.

She was basically as reliable as the town hall.

"Aren't you too busy with everything else you do around this town to spend so much time remembering all that?" He was already up and working as the dawn turned the brilliant sky pink outside the windows. George had always insisted everyone in the house be early risers, a habit Grayson thought he'd broken over the years but had fallen back into almost immediately once he'd moved back in.

She frowned at him over the rim of her coffee cup—carried hesitantly over the threshold and into the library like she, too, half expected George to jump out and scold her for breaking a rule—and shook her head.

"These things are important, Grayson." She clucked her tongue at him, her disapproval written in the faint line between her brows. "I've known the people in this town all of my life. Every baby born here feels like it might as well be my own grandchild."

Ah.

Grayson knew she had always treated the townspeople well. As a Barlow, even by marriage, it was widely considered her duty to be part of every committee, to be seated on every board. Her donations to the church food banks and PTA fundraisers had never been late.

Still, there was more to this dedication than the duty of being a rich man's wife in a small town. She had lost her son and her daughter-in-law to a drunk driver in one stunning tragedy and then, not so many years later, had lost the only other connection to the future she had when Grayson had cut and run. There were no other children in her family—no other grandchildren for her to dote on—and she had latched onto the town as a replacement source of happiness.

What other choice had she had? God knew George wouldn't have cared that she was suffering.

Grayson's leaving had affected her more deeply than he

had been willing to consider and it seemed that each day he spent with her, he unearthed some new way that he'd wounded her with his choice to run. It had made sense to him at the time—hell, who was he kidding, it had been the only option in his mind back then—and he had justified it at every turn since, but he had been so focused on his own survival that he hadn't ever allowed himself to really think about what it had meant to those left behind.

"Grandma Edith." He wasn't sure what he wanted to say, how to comfort her without bringing up a past he was determined not to talk about, not to even think about if he could avoid it. "They're all lucky to have you."

It didn't seem like enough, a weak and paltry approximation of the depth of his feelings for her, but the crease between her brows disappeared and a full smile, untainted by her usual anxious hesitation, replaced the worry on her face. It warmed him and did more than a little to chase away the edges of nervousness that seemed to haunt all of their conversations.

Soon, she was perched lightly on the arm of a sofa—another small rebellion against the old rules—hands still wrapped around her coffee cup, a pleasant conversation bringing more smiles and even laughter to her lined face. He didn't remember ever seeing her so vibrant, so free. It had been worth coming back here to see her like this, to have these memories of her to keep and cherish.

It would never replace all the others, the ones that always made anxious knots twist in his stomach when he thought about them too closely, but it was good to have them. When he woke in the night with those other memories tangled in his nightmares, he would have these to call upon instead. Life moved on, and when it did, sometimes there was light on the other side of the darkness.

Not that he deserved it after what he'd done, running

away and leaving her here, but it meant more to him than he could say that she seemed to have been able to pass through it and find something good for herself. Some peace. Some quiet. He hadn't been there to help her, but she'd made it on her own.

He was still thinking about that, her strength in the face of so much adversity, as he wandered down the stairs to the beach after breakfast, his feet bare and his hair blowing in the wind coming in off the water. It felt good being here. Better than he'd thought possible. He'd miss all of this—the sea salt air, his grandmother, the feeling of being in a place he recognized even if the house had never felt quite like a home—when he was ready to move on again.

Grandma Edith would be upset—even he wasn't so deep in denial that he could pretend otherwise—but he promised himself it would be different this time. No hiding the way he had done before. He couldn't stay but he would keep in touch. There was no reason for him not to, not anymore. Without the possibility of dealing with George there was nothing stopping him from calling her to check in once or twice a week. She would know where he was and how he was doing and that was much better than the way it had been before. Everyone would understand, surely, that this way was the best for both of them.

The bark of a dog, high pitched and unfortunately familiar, broke into his thoughts before he could dwell too long on all the reasons that maybe they *wouldn't* understand. He knew that bark and a few seconds of scanning the small beach confirmed it. Ruffles had scented him on the wind and was barreling across the gravel at breakneck speed, paws flying and teeth bared.

She really hated him.

He was still frozen on the last step of the staircase, debating rapidly about whether to run or fight, when he realized Becka was standing near the water, doubled over with laughter and holding her sides.

"Call your dog!" If she waited much longer, he was going to end up needing stitches in his ankles or be forced to football punt a snarling Schnauzer and he didn't think either of those options would win him any points with the other residents of Barlow House.

"Ruffles!" The first attempt was swallowed up in the wind and the crash of the waves, her voice breathy and still more than half laugh. He glared at her, seconds flying by as the dog got closer and she tried to get control of herself enough to put some authority in the call. "Ruffles!"

Twelve pounds of fur skidded to a stop less than a foot away from him as Ruffles looked over her shoulder with a whine. It was clear that Becka had been working with her since she did have *some* manners, but it was still a struggle to let go of the opportunity to make her displeasure known. She trotted back to Becka's side and stayed there as Grayson crossed the beach to get close enough to be heard over the noise of the water.

Once he was sure Becka could hear him clearly, he got no closer, watching the dog as he evaluated the safety of his distance. "Thanks." He winced at the stiffness of his tone. Sure, they didn't exactly get along, but he had to give credit where it was due. She had saved his ass, so some genuine gratitude was in order.

"She wouldn't actually bite you." Becka's tone was certain, and a hint of a smile played at the edges of her mouth. "Ruffles is an excellent watchdog, but running in circles around your legs is about the most you can expect from her."

"Hmm." She probably couldn't hear the low, skeptical hum, but he was at a loss for what else to say. He wasn't as sure as Becka was that her feisty companion wouldn't resort to violence at the first opportunity. "She doesn't seem to like me."

"She doesn't like men." Grayson remembered her saying something like that before, but he still raised a brow, and she held her hands up, palms open to show she had no hidden tricks. "Not my fault! Edith got her from the shelter and they think her previous owner must have been an asshole."

Grayson thought that over for a minute, watching the dog as she watched him with cautious eyes. He couldn't blame her for that. Who wouldn't be a little edgy and defensive under those circumstances? He certainly was, and he couldn't expect any different from a defenseless dog. "Maybe it would be better if I gave her some treats sometimes? Tried to show her I'm not so bad?"

Becka ran a hand through her hair at that, gaze cutting out across the water. He hadn't really had time to look at her properly since he'd come down, and he realized now that her hair, usually pulled back in a ponytail or short braid, was loose and wavy around her shoulders like it had been on that first day. Dark brown and cut in choppy layers, it danced in the breeze, wild tendrils framing her face and sticking to the tinted color on her lips.

That wasn't the only thing different about her. In place of her usual shorts, she was wearing a flowing black skirt made from some kind of light, natural material. Her tank top, still casual, had been fancied up a little with a cute sweater. She had on gold earrings, little hearts that matched the locket she always wore.

He wondered if she kept a photo in it, but it didn't feel like they knew each other well enough for him to ask.

She turned her head to speak to him, none of the words actually making it to his brain, as it hit him then that she was wearing eyeliner, a fact that seemed both trivial enough that he wasn't sure why he had even noticed, and also dangerous enough that it made him want to take a step back and put some additional distance between them.

She looked pretty, softer and more approachable than he'd seen her look since he'd arrived, but he didn't think she'd appreciate that observation. He'd made the mistake of walking out on the deck when she'd been doing evening yoga a few nights after he'd moved in and he'd thought she might toss him directly into the ocean for seeing her in just yoga pants and a sports bra, even if it had been an accident.

It wasn't like he'd even been trying to look or anything, tempting as it had been. The smallness of her stature did nothing to keep her body from being ripe with curves that he had definitely *not* been staring at when she wasn't looking.

Like he was definitely not noticing now how the hem of her skirt blowing around her calves made it impossible not to look at her legs, or how the glint of an anklet against summer tanned skin made him absolutely sure it was the most erotic piece of jewelry he'd ever seen on a woman.

Stress.

It had to be the stress of George's death and his subsequent unwilling relocation to Barlow House. Life had gotten a little turned around, and he was just suffering the natural consequences of that. He couldn't run this time, so he was looking for some kind of distraction. It was the same kind of self-destructive urge that had had him drinking in his kitchen the day he'd gotten the news about George.

That had to be it, because there was no other explanation for this misplaced sexual interest in a pocket-sized hellion that just so happened to be the only person his Grandma Edith loved as much as she loved him. He couldn't get tangled up with Becka, no matter how strongly his body reacted to her presence. A list of other problems aside, if things went badly with her, it could cause a wrinkle in someone's relationship with Edith. Whether it was his or hers would depend on which of them Edith decided to blame.

It wasn't worth the risk.

A calculation he likely wasted his time making, because he was pretty sure Becka was more likely to chew broken glass and spit it at his feet than she was to look at him with anything other than casual contempt.

He realized she was still staring at him, waiting for a response to whatever she'd said when he wasn't paying attention.

"What?" Grayson jerked his gaze away from her legs, desperate to stop looking at her only to find his attention settling on her chest instead.

Shit.

His mind went blank. He had no idea what they were talking about. Whatever it was had flown straight out from between his ears somewhere between noticing the eyeliner and when his gaze had landed on her breasts. All he could do was hope she hadn't noticed him looking.

"Ruffles?" Becka shook her head, looking nearly as confused as he was. "Didn't you say you wanted to try to win her over? You can try but you can't rush her. She's nervous and if you try to push it..."

"It'll make it worse." Thoughts re-centered on the topic at hand, he nodded. "I get it."

"I'm only agreeing to this because it seems to make Edith happy that you're here, and I don't want Ruffles to be nervous every day because there's a man in her house that she doesn't trust."

"Makes sense." He let the words linger until he was sure she knew he meant more than just the dog. It was pretty clear to him that Ruffles wasn't the only one that didn't trust him, and he wanted to ask if Becka had an asshole in her past as well, but he knew neither of them were ready for her to answer that question honestly.

Or any other question, really.

Because she hadn't done much poking into his personal

business, but that also meant he had no reason to ask her anything personal, either. It was as though she had done her best to get him to stay for Edith's sake, and then drawn a thick, red, uncrossable line between them.

The silence grew, broken by the waves and the indignant cry of a seagull but not by words as they both seemed to realize they'd run out of things to discuss. It was the longest conversation they'd had since he'd arrived, not counting the argument they'd had about his bedroom—which he was still angry about, but that was beside the point—and he was searching for something else to say when she cleared her throat and gave him a brilliant customer service smile.

"I've got to take Edith to a doctor's appointment, so I need to go and make sure she's ready. You should come, too, and start getting familiar with her health needs. She has to take a lot of medication these days, but I'm sure you'll get the hang of it in no time."

"Oh." A sudden light went off in his mind. "Is that why you're mad at me all the time? You think I'm going to come in and take your job?" He laughed, relieved that he'd figured out the source of animosity between them. "No, you've misunderstood. I don't plan to stay any longer than I need to. I just want to make sure Grandma Edith is set up properly. I thought you knew because you were the one that was so insistent that I stay. I swear, it's not going to be—"

"Are you serious?" The smile, fake as it had been, dropped from her face, leaving behind a far more hostile, if admittedly confused, expression. Beside her feet, Ruffles growled. "You're still planning on taking off as soon as you get the chance?"

"Whoa." He took an involuntary step back as she leaned forward, once again seemingly unaware of how small she was and her natural disadvantage. "I never said I was going to stay indefinitely—"

"You're a real piece of work, Barlow." She pushed her way

past him, the height difference between them suddenly insignificant when she threw all her weight into her shoulder as she went. He stumbled back another step, stunned at how quickly the first positive interaction he'd had with her had gone south.

"Stay away from our dog." She tossed it over her shoulder as she went, practically running with Ruffles hot on her heels. She was definitely pissed, but unless he was very much mistaken, there had been more than a little hurt in her tone. He didn't know what he'd done wrong, but he hadn't done it on purpose.

They both loved Edith, and he was willing to apologize if it meant putting some peace back in place between them. It had been nice, for the whole two minutes it had lasted, and he thought he might like her, if she'd give him half a chance.

"Damn it." He took off after her, long legs an advantage she couldn't escape from, and managed to get a hand around her wrist before she could start ascending the stairs. "Wait just a minute."

She turned on him, eyes flashing—were those *tears?*—as she yanked her arm out of his grasp. "Wait for what? For you to explain to me what's so great about the other places you've been that you can't stay here and be with Edith after all this time? Go ahead. Explain it."

He knew she was protective of his grandmother, that she was just doing what she thought was right, but he didn't know the answer to those questions. It was enough to take the breath out of him and suddenly he was too tired to fight with her. She couldn't know what it had been like, not really, and she was in no place to judge him. He'd been hard enough on himself and he didn't need her help in feeling like shit for doing what he had to do.

"Those places weren't here." He dropped her hand, stepping back and carefully avoiding the barking dog running circles around his ankles. "And all I ever wanted was to be far, far away from here."

"That's pretty apparent." If he was hoping for sympathy—and maybe he had been, at least a little bit—it seemed she had none to give as she left him standing there, bitter words echoing between them.

Chapter Six

Becka

He hadn't even asked about the doctor's appointment. That was the point Becka focused on later, when they'd seen the doctor and started heading to the diner for lunch, when she started to feel guilty for the way she'd talked to him down by the beach. Sure, she'd been a little snappish, bordering on downright rude, but he'd deserved it, damn it.

She'd been walking along the water's edge with Ruffles, enjoying the sun and the breeze, when he'd sauntered out, distracting her with his bare feet and loose shirt and that sculpted face. Those eyes of his had been boring into her soul, even though he'd been too far away for her to make out the ever-changing color. Ruffles had gone tearing across the small beach like she was trying to protect Becka from the devil himself, and he'd looked so panicked, so adorable and vulnerable as he'd scrambled to figure out what to do, that she had let her guard down around him. Hell, she'd even politely pretended not to notice when he was staring at her tits.

A mistake.

Clearly.

Not surprising, considering letting her guard down was exactly what she'd spent two weeks trying very hard *not* to do. His pretty face and charming smile had kept her on her toes, but she'd known that whatever was going on in that thick little Barlow brain of his would lead to nothing but trouble. And, as usual when it came to distrusting men that were too good looking for personal comfort, she'd been right. A few minutes of conversation and a polite smile from her had been all it took for him to admit he was planning on running off again.

If it had been purely up to her, he could have left the day he showed up, but she hadn't been able to handle the look on Edith's face when she'd realized he wasn't intending to stay. Becka wasn't exactly a gentle person, despite what people tended to assume about a woman with a short stature and feminine look, but she had a soft spot for Edith. Watching the little light of hope in her eyes flicker out had been more than enough for Becka to step in and bully him into hanging around.

She'd thought things were going well since then. Edith was happy. Grayson had settled in. Becka had managed to keep him at a polite distance that didn't invite conflict or questions. All was well in Barlow House.

Until this morning, when he'd come along and dropped a bomb on Becka's perfectly curated peace. He was still planning to leave, and, what's more, he hadn't even cared enough about his own grandmother to ask why Becka needed to take her into town for a doctor's appointment.

Becka knew it was just a check-up and Edith's health was improving steadily now that she didn't have George in her life, but *Grayson* didn't know that. How could he know, when he was so busy worrying about himself that he hadn't even thought to ask about anyone else? His attitude was selfish and irresponsible and he needed to be punished.

She was going to over salt his breakfast in the morning, just to watch him suffer. It wouldn't change anything, but she was pretty damn sure it would help her feel better.

Edith hummed a little under her breath from the passenger seat when Becka pushed a hand through her hair, wincing as her fingers caught in the tangled strands. She'd brushed it after she'd come inside from the beach, but it was freshly windblown again after making the trip back and forth from the doctor's office to the car.

"What's wrong?" Edith's question was patient, maternal even, but there was enough determination in the tone to make it known to kids and grandkids alike that it wouldn't be easy to wiggle out of.

Becka tapped a finger on the steering wheel of Edith's sensible gray sedan—she would have preferred driving her own car, but Edith wasn't fond of her yellow VW bus—and tried anyway.

"Nothing."

It was an obvious lie, her voice rising at the end in an embarrassing little squeak, but Edith waited in silence as they drove, keeping her thoughts to herself as they passed the post office and the bakery. A dozen little businesses with their faded signs, most of them with ocean themed names and color palettes. Not much to look at in the colder months, but it got pretty busy in the summer, with tourists driving up the coast to catch a peek at the rocky cliffs and tumultuous sea.

There wasn't much to Widow's Point, but it was still Becka's favorite place to be. Not just because it was where Edith was, though her attachment to this surrogate grandmother of hers had been nearly instant and surprisingly strong, but because it was the closest Becka had ever come to being part of a real community.

It wasn't like the little scraggly group of buildings where she'd been raised amidst a congregation of brainwashed zealots masquerading as a town somewhere in rural California. No, to her this place felt different, like the people here really tried to look out for each other when they could. Maybe it was because of her proximity to Edith, who was involved in what felt like every aspect of town life, or maybe that was just what normal people did when they lived and worked so close together and in such small numbers.

She slowed down as they passed the elementary school, cruising just under the reduced speed limit for the campus that housed everything from kindergarten to high school. The small buildings were painted the blue and white of the school's sports teams, and there was a mural on the gym wall with a silly looking octopus wearing a goofy grin that looked out over the football field with its sagging metal bleachers.

Becka didn't think an octopus was bad, as far as high school mascots went, but somehow this one only had seven legs, and she wasn't sure anyone else had ever noticed the mistake. According to Edith, that mural had been there for decades, painted fresh every year, and if the citizens of Widow's Point had never noticed, Becka wasn't about to tell them now.

Most of them were here from the cradle to the grave, and though it was a running town joke that everyone was trying and failing to get out, all Becka wanted was to fit in. To not be viewed as the weird one, the outsider, any more than she already had been in her life.

Okay, so it wasn't *perfect*—her lips turned down in an involuntary frown as they passed the sheriff's office and Edith gave Sheriff Levine a stiff wave. They still had their problems like any other town, but it was leagues above the life Becka had experienced growing up. She'd know what it was to be isolated, to have no one to depend on, and she'd promised herself a long time ago that she'd never go back to that.

A spouse and kids of her own was out of the question as

far as she was concerned, but she could still make a life for herself here. She could find other relationships, ones with people that didn't hurt you and try to gloss it over while they demanded your forgiveness. She'd had enough of that shit from her own family and what she had seen happen to Edith.

George had certainly been no prize and Grayson ...

It wasn't that Becka minded doing her job. She genuinely *liked* taking care of Edith ... protecting her, caring for her, taking her to doctor's appointments and late lunches and making sure she had everything she needed. Becka didn't resent a single moment of it, but did Grayson not see what he was missing out on by not being there for his own family even now that he was back and it was right under his nose?

Edith had let her stew in silence as they drove, saying nothing as they passed through town and parked in front of the diner. It wasn't until Becka had turned the car off and started looking around for her purse that Edith spoke again.

"Does it bother you that much?" It was hardly more than a whisper, her voice so quiet that Becka could hardly hear her.

"Hmm? What?" Becka was distracted, her mind still running over the morning's confrontation with Grayson, and the doctor's adjustments to Edith's medications after her check-up—she really should try to get Edith to drink less wine, though Becka doubted Edith would listen—and just about everything else but the question she'd been asked.

"Grayson." Edith paused, and though she was as composed as always, she weighed her words before she continued. "Does it bother you so much that he's here? You've been ... different since he moved back in."

"Oh." Her attention firmly captured now, Becka tried to compose her face. She knew how much Grayson meant to Edith, and she didn't want her personal issues with him to cast a shadow on their time together, especially since Grayson was determined to keep it short. "No, it doesn't bother me that much. I just don't like that he left you alone and let you worry for so long."

She gave Edith's hand a reassuring pat and tried to keep her expression and tone neutral. Edith was a worrier, for all that she pretended not to be, and the more she suspected bad feelings between them, the more she'd be determined to mediate. Better to let her think all was well than to suffer through who knew how many well-intentioned rounds of meddling.

"That's all?" Despite her age and soft expression, her blue eyes were piercing and Becka resisted the urge to look away. "I know you don't believe it, but Grayson is a good boy. He's never been one to speak about things that he shouldn't."

"Oh." Becka's heart jumped hard in her chest, and she glanced around quickly, suddenly realizing Edith's concerns were not about her relationship with Grayson, but about his new proximity to secrets they'd agreed no one but the two of them would ever know. She, too, would rather not speak of it. Inside a car with the windows rolled up in a mostly empty parking lot wasn't exactly a likely place to be overheard, but any chance was too much of a chance, in her opinion. "Best not to think about those things."

Edith nodded at the reminder, her serene expression suddenly teetering between fear and understanding. "What if—"

"I wouldn't have pushed for him to stay if I was worried about any of that." Becka wiped the sweat from her palms on her skirt covered thighs. Some things were meant to be left undisturbed, but she was confident—at least as much as any person could be—that Grayson was not among the few people with the capability to kick over their particular hornet's nest. He had no interest in the past and they had no interest in sharing, and a sensible arrangement like that, one that suited all parties, was no cause for concern. "I want you to be happy."

"How would I be happy if anything happened?"

"It won't happen and you two will have a nice visit." Becka grabbed her purse, her smile tight and final. "Simple."

"You always say that." Even after Becka had pushed the driver's side door open, Edith didn't reach for the handle of her own door. Instead, her hands remained folded in her lap, fingers twisted in the loose fabric of her pale blue skirt. It was the only sign of her nerves, but for Becka, it was impossible to miss.

"Have I ever been wrong?" Becka reached across the car to untangle her hands and push the door open herself. "You know I haven't."

Edith only shook her head, but she got out of the car and let Becka lead her into the building, waiting quietly to be escorted to a booth. The same waitress as always guided them to their seats, and Becka took a moment to subtly appreciate the view of a beautiful woman—not the late season tourist she'd almost had a date with—and her softly swaying hips as they followed her through the nearly empty dining room. It was nothing but a superficial distraction—everyone in Widow's Point seemed to be straight as an arrow or pretending to be—but even that didn't last long.

Catherine—affectionately referred to as Cat by Edith and absolutely no one else—had been their waitress for almost every lunch they'd had in the diner since Becka had moved to town. She knew their favorite spot, their drink orders, and their favorite lunch special by heart. She had them seated and their drinks already on the table before either of them could get their thoughts fully sorted or their emotions under control.

A problem not helped at all by the arrival of Sheriff Levine.

Becka spotted him first, unable to miss it when the front door swung open and he swaggered through the entrance like he owned the place, which he decidedly did not. She was never happy to see him but knowing damn well he'd followed them here left an especially bitter taste in her mouth.

There was a lot Becka could say about this man in particular, but the most notable thing about him, apart from his size, was a devoted sense of punctuality and routine.

He ate lunch at the diner daily, but not this late in the day. He was typically here at noon, which meant his arrival this late in the afternoon was far less likely to be for the purpose of filling his stomach, and far more likely to be for the purpose of poking his nose into other people's business.

Their business, in particular.

Becka said a quick prayer—a habit of her childhood she'd never completely been able to get away from—and swore under her breath when God didn't make both her and Edith immediately invisible. Sheriff Levine took one long look around the nearly empty dining area and settled his gaze right on them.

Shit.

He barely acknowledged Catherine—a quick smile that didn't reach his eyes and a shake of his head when she offered to find him a seat—and then he was walking toward their booth, covering ground too fast with long, purpose driven strides. The badge on his chest gleamed under the dim overhead lights.

Double shit.

Becka hated him.

She hated *cops*.

Her parents had raised her to view them with suspicion, and she'd done enough sketchy shit since they'd kicked her out to be wary in a way that was based less on paranoia and more on genuinely existing arrest warrants in another state. She didn't realize her hand had come to rest in a death grip on the handle of her mug until Edith's warm palm covered it, her touch soothing but firm enough not to be shaken off. Before Sheriff Levine could reach them, the message was conveyed quickly and without the need for words.

The smile pasted on Becka's face hid the frustrated breath she pushed out from between gritted teeth. At best he wouldn't notice anything amiss, at worst it would be nothing more than a stiff tension. Edith's message was clear. No more violence, no matter how badly the bastards deserved it, and especially not him, especially not here, in front of so many witnesses.

No matter what he did, no matter what he said, she had to use her words and mind her manners, which was going to be one hell of a challenge.

The whole protect and serve thing he had going on was bullshit. She'd known that since the first time the cops had tossed her back at her parents after a brief stint in a shithole foster home, and every interaction she'd had with Sheriff Levine had reinforced the lesson. Still, Edith was worried about her landing her ass in jail, so she'd sit and smile and not stab their unwelcome guest in the leg with her fork.

Even if it was spectacularly tempting.

"Ladies." As far as greetings went, this one had never sounded less pleasant than it did on his lips, but Becka held the muscles in her cheeks immobile, her face frozen in a facsimile of a polite and welcoming expression. He stood at the end of the table, gaze sweeping over Edith and lingering on Becka in ways that made her skin crawl. "Nice to see you."

"Patrick." Edith returned the greeting, but she didn't ask him to sit. He seemed flustered for a moment, tapping the hat he'd removed at the door against his thigh as the silence became awkward and then uncomfortable. Edith finally spoke, her ingrained manners eventually overcoming the warning looks Becka was shooting in her direction. "What brings you in today?"

"I just happened to see you drive by a few minutes ago," he pulled over a chair and sat beside Edith, apparently abandoning the need for an invitation, "and thought I'd drop in to talk to you again about George."

"Hmm." Edith picked up her drink and busied her mouth with the straw. Talk less, listen more. She tended to ramble when she was nervous, and Becka had drilled that mantra into her. Luckily for both of them, it seemed to have stuck.

"Well," he plowed on despite her lack of response, "I remember I told you back when it first happened that I thought the whole thing was a bit strange." He drummed his fingers on the table, his hat abandoned beside Edith's waiting set of silverware. The way his body leaned toward Edith made Becka have second thoughts about stabbing him. It wasn't fair for him to use his size to intimidate someone like her. She was small enough to be easily pushed around and after living with George for so many years, it was hard for her to be so close to any man without fear.

Becka could see the tremble in her hands as Edith set the cup back on the table and the simmering anger in her gut flared back up into a roaring flame. She'd promised Edith not to hurt him, but there was more than one way to choose violence.

"I do seem to recall you saying something about that, Sheriff." Unlike his quiet and conspiratorial tone, Becka's raised voice carried across the diner. "You came by the house the very next day, if I remember correctly. Hardly seems fair to ask Edith to remember much about it, though, since her husband had just died and all."

He sputtered, face reddening as people turned to look. To most, it would probably have looked like he was embarrassed, but Becka recognized that look in his eyes. Oh, he *was* embarrassed, as she had intended for him to be, but from that root sprang its companion blossom. Rage. In men like him, the first was rarely seen without the second.

With the hand closest to him, she trailed a casual finger down the side of her glass, collecting condensation on the tip. Her other hand inched closer to her fork.

Seemingly aware of their audience, the sheriff did nothing but recline against the back of his chair and appraise her with barely concealed resentment. "You have a good memory, Miss Simmons."

Becka waved a hand, dismissing the observation as though it was a compliment she hadn't earned. "It was a particularly difficult day for all of us. Edith was a bit lost in her grief, you understand? It was my job at that time to take care of her and to make note of what needed to be done."

Seeing an opening, he jumped on it. "That's exactly why I wanted to talk to her again now that her head has cleared a bit." He jabbed a finger in Becka's direction, aggressively stressing his point. "It's been a couple of months, and I'm sure she's adjusting to her sudden loss."

Edith listened as they talked about her like she wasn't there, head swiveling from one to the other and straw still in her mouth as they played a game of cat and mouse that would have been hardly discernible to an uninformed passerby.

"We've done all we can to look after her health and mental well-being after the shock of it all," Becka confirmed. "What is it, exactly, that you wanted to talk to her about?"

Becka settled back against her seat, watching the crease form between his eyebrows as he realized that she had not only drawn far too much attention to their conversation, but she had also maneuvered him into dealing with her, instead of with Edith directly.

Catherine arrived with their food before he could answer, some of the attention in the diner dissipating as she handed the women their plates and then disappeared again. Sheriff

Levine waited for her to move out of earshot as he chewed on his bottom lip, probably trying to think his way back into a more favorable position. The movement wiggled his ridiculous mustache like an oversized, gray caterpillar. The fuzzy kind. How he expected anyone to take him seriously was simply beyond Becka's comprehension.

No one moved toward the food on their plate as the sheriff continued. "I just wanted to ask about her health." *Lie.* "See how things were going out at Barlow House." *Lie.* "Ask if there was anything either of you remembered being out of place the night he died?" *Ah, there it was.*

Becka ticked off her answers on her fingers, pleased to see him unable to take his gaze away from the movement of her hands, and off of Edith's stricken face. "One, she just had a check-up at the doctor and she's doing well. Two, Barlow House is Barlow House. What could possibly have changed? Three, no. There was nothing unusual about it, aside from the death of a beloved husband."

Sheriff Levine looked like he wanted to ask more about George's death, but he got distracted, as she'd hoped he would, by the answer she'd given to question number two.

"Nothing has changed?" He looked from Becka to Edith and back again. "Have you... I mean, did he not..." He stopped mid question, as though unsure how to proceed.

"Have we not what?" Becka bit down hard on the inside of her cheek to stop the amusement from showing on her face. "He who?"

"Well, I just thought ..."

"Yes?"

"Did Grayson not come out to Barlow House?" He spat it out quickly, like mentioning his name was somehow the betrayal of a secret.

"Grayson?" Becka drew her brows together and tipped her head like a curious cat as Edith choked quietly on her drink and sprayed water through her nose and onto the tabletop. She accepted the napkin Becka offered, though neither of them had looked away from the sheriff's gobsmacked expression.

"Grayson," he repeated. Slowly. As though slowing it down would somehow make the name more comprehensible. "George and Edith's grandson." He looked at Edith, baffled, but she had fully turned her attention to the spray of water and he got no reaction from her.

"Ohhhh." Becka drew the syllable out to comic lengths. She twirled a piece of her hair around her finger, batted her eyes at him with as much innocence as she could fake without it becoming offensive. "*That* Grayson. Of course, he's there. Where else would he be?"

There was a throbbing vein in the sheriff's forehead and for a moment, she was disappointed that there were so many witnesses. If they had been alone, his temper might have blown his head clean off his shoulders. As it was, he glanced around, one eyelid still twitching, and nodded absently. Not agreeing with her, he simply didn't know what else to do with his body.

"I see." He clearly wanted to say more but was at a loss of how to pursue the conversation further. She was being deliberately difficult, but everyone was listening to their conversation and accusing her of pretending not to understand just to irritate him would be viewed as very rude. She was still considered new here, no one really knew her yet, for all they knew she might actually be as lacking in intelligence as she currently appeared to be.

Becka eyed him, her expression carefully bland, as he tried to gather his thoughts. He had fallen into the same trap as countless men before him. He'd assumed she didn't have three brain cells to rub together and then had been undermined entirely when she'd embraced the assumption and delivered far more than he'd bargained for. Apart from the possibility of alienating their attentive audience, to confront her would be to admit she was smarter than he'd given her credit for, and as much as he wanted to call her on what was clearly exaggerated foolishness, his pride wouldn't let him.

It seemed she wouldn't need that fork after all.

"Well." Becka took a bite, puffing out her cheeks to show it really would be too inconvenient to try to talk to him and eat at the same time. "Thanks for stopping by, but I really do need to get Edith home as soon as we're finished here. It's almost time for her meds, you know?" Tiny bits of food flew across the table as she spoke, her words unable to bypass the chewed contents of her mouth without making a mess.

Sheriff Levine brushed at his sleeve, finally admitting defeat in this battle, though the thunderous expression on his face gave her little hope that this would be their last encounter. He was determined to get to Edith and start hammering her with a bunch of bullshit questions and Becka wasn't about to let that happen.

After all the years Edith had been with George, she had been through enough already, and the Sheriff sure as hell hadn't done anything about it. If he'd put half as much effort into protecting the rest of the Barlow family from his favorite piece of shit Barlow man as he did skulking around trying to ask Edith irritating questions ... Well, maybe there wouldn't have been any need to ask. The situation with George would have been handled long before he washed up on that beach.

Since the sheriff had ignored what was happening, George had sat in that house terrorizing everyone in reach until he'd gotten exactly what he deserved. That's what happened when nature was allowed to run its course without intervention from the people that were meant to protect the vulnerable. Her hippie-wanna-be parents had been wrong about pretty much everything, but they had been exactly right about how useful the average cop was to their citizens.

The sheriff pushed to his feet, went back to tapping his hat on his thigh, though with less confidence this time. "Edith, you let me know if you think of anything."

"Will do." She smiled at him around the straw in her mouth, her singular contribution to the conversation saccharine sweet and infuriating. "Nice to see you, Sheriff."

"Miss Simmons." He gave an extra aggressive tap of the hat to punctuate the acknowledgment but he was already turning away before she could say anything else. Not the most polite goodbye she'd ever experienced, but less hostile than she had truly expected.

"Pig." She muttered it under her breath, loud enough for Edith to hear her but no one else.

"Becka." Edith's tone was shocked and she glanced over her shoulder twice before leaning across the table to whisper loudly. "You can't say that."

"It's true." She held up a hand to stop the rest of the scolding that she knew was coming. Edith hated Sheriff Levine, but there were lines of propriety that she was simply not prepared to cross. "But I won't say it if you don't want me to."

"Thank you." Now that their unwelcome guest had gone, Edith returned her attention to her lunch. She dismissed the entire incident just that quickly, pushing it out of her mind over a glass of lemon water and a salad. It was a trick Becka recognized, one she and her sister had relied on often when they'd been stuck at home dealing with their own little version of hell on earth. When it was too much for you to deal with, you just ... didn't. You forced it down. Pushed it out. Didn't think about it and certainly didn't have any feelings about it.

Sometimes, when you were weak enough, you even ran away from it, Becka acknowledged, familiar hurt slicing through her at the thought. She twisted Payton's necklace between her fingers, no closer to forgiveness than she had been all those years ago. Becka wished she could leave her anger in the past, but that was impossible, so she pushed the memories away, turning her attention back to Edith.

"He'll be back. The sheriff, I mean." Becka hated to worry her, but Edith needed to know the truth so she could be prepared.

"I know." Edith reached across to pat her hand without looking away from her salad. "But we don't have to worry about that today. Eat. Thinking too much will ruin your digestion."

"We could take a long vacation and hope he forgets about it," Becka teased. "Just the two of us. We could go somewhere warm. Florida maybe? What do you think?"

Edith finally looked at her, a light laugh shaking off the last of the tension at the table. "And leave all of this?" She twirled her fork through the air, indicating the restaurant and probably the town outside, as well. "I could never."

Becka thought that was probably true. Edith's whole identity was wrapped up in Widow's Point and Barlow House. She wouldn't know who she was without those things. Without these people.

"You're right." Becka clinked her glass against Edith's, the tinkling ring echoing as she drained the glass and let the water soothe her throat and the knot in her chest. "You're always right."

Chapter Seven

Grayson

The moon cast long shadows on the walls of Barlow House and Grayson wondered what his grandmother would think if she knew he'd taken to wandering the halls at night. He'd spent hours moving silently from room to room, so he figured she might have taken him for a vengeful spirit or a prowler if she'd stumbled across him in the dark.

His time at home had been going well until his confrontation with Becka on the beach. Since then, she'd been ignoring him, Edith had been unaccountably preoccupied, and suddenly he was alone in the house again the way he'd been when he was young. The familiarity of the feeling paired with the location must have done something to his brain, because now all he could see when he closed his eyes was George's face.

Twisted in anger, impassive in judgment, bloated and rotting after being washed in from the sea. Not exactly images that let him get the kind of sleep that actually felt restful, so what was the point? Instead, he'd lain on his bed, staring at the ceiling, and getting progressively hungrier as the night passed.

George had always enforced strict rules about who was allowed to be where and when, including an absolutely inflexible lockdown of Grayson's bedroom at nine pm. Not even trips to the bathroom were permitted, unless under dire circumstances such as illness or injury.

So, the first night he'd been plagued with loneliness and George's phantom presence, Grayson had stayed in bed until the sun came up, hunger gnawing on his insides but too afraid to get up. The second time, bolstered by years of having complete control over his own life and the absolute certainty that George wasn't waiting in the shadows to punish him for his transgressions, he'd cracked open the door, slipped out and down the stairs, and into the kitchen like a starving wraith.

Making that sandwich had been the most terrifying moment of his life right up until Becka had thrown open her bedroom door as he was creeping back to his own room, letting light spill out across the space between their doors and catching him in the act of being where he definitely wasn't supposed to be.

He'd jumped so hard he'd almost thrown the sandwich at her face.

"Everything okay?"

His heart had been trying to beat its way out of his chest, and she had been standing there, half dressed in an oversized T-shirt and a pair of boy short underwear, hair a tumbled mess over her shoulders and yesterday's mascara smudged around her eyes.

"Hmnnng."

She'd given him the once over at the sound that wasn't quite a word—raising an eyebrow when she caught him staring at her naked thighs but still leaving him grateful that at least that time it hadn't been her chest—and then shrugged.

"Next time you make a run downstairs for midnight snacks, bring enough to share."

He'd fumbled in his pockets, looking for the cookies he'd hidden away—taking food out of the kitchen was another rule broken—and finally pulling a crumbling chocolate chip from the front left pocket of the cardigan he'd thrown on before wandering the halls. He held the cookie out in her direction, suddenly embarrassed.

To his surprise, she took it, undaunted by the lateness of the hour or the stray piece of lint she plucked from the side. She shoved it into her mouth in one giant, impractical bite, grunted a barely coherent thank you, and shut the door in his face.

He'd been wandering the house every night since then, hoping to catch her alone and ask her what the hell that had been about. She wouldn't talk to him during the day or he'd have asked then, but she'd barely looked at him since the day she'd taken Grandma Edith to the doctor, barely even willing to answer him when he'd sheepishly asked how the appointment had gone. She was obviously still mad about something. Okay, maybe she *had* noticed him staring at her chest when they were on the beach, but she apparently didn't hate him so much that she'd turn down his pocket cookies.

Nor had she said a word about the oddness of his wandering the house at night in his pajamas, casting no judgment on his comfortable house slippers or that threadbare old sweater with big front pockets.

There had to be more to the situation than what met the eye, because the only guess he'd come up with as an explanation was that she'd simply overlooked all of that because he'd given her sweets. Becka seemed far too complicated to be won over by something so simple.

And so he wandered, hoping for a glimpse of her and refamiliarizing himself with the house he'd grown up in. It was different late at night. Stiller. Quieter. Spookier than he remembered.

He'd spent hours now poking around the big rooms, looking at the pictures Edith had taken to hanging on the walls. Him. His parents. His grandparents.

The forced smiles made his stomach tighten and his chest ache as old familiar anxieties came back to haunt him. If his bed hadn't been full of nightmares—and the hallways so potentially full of attractive women with naked thighs—he would have stayed in it, instead of walking the halls of a cursed house and letting it taunt him with its ghosts.

Every room in this house held some terrible memory for him, and if it hadn't been for Edith needing him so much, for Becka ruthlessly hemming him in with his obligations, he might have fled as soon as the nightmares started, no matter what promises he'd made. He wasn't too proud to break his word, and his ego would not have been enough to hold him here.

He'd abandoned his grandmother once and though he still felt bad about it every day, he knew that time had not changed him. When things were difficult or frightening or sometimes even just inconvenient, his first urge was to run. He did not cling to anything hard enough that it could not be left behind and he would not be bound to a place of pain when there were better options elsewhere.

The passage of time had not changed George, either, from what Grayson could tell. He hadn't asked directly, reluctant as he was to bring up the past, but if Edith's behavior and the passing remarks she made were any indication, George had remained the same until the day he'd died. She'd feared him until God, or the sea, or his own rotten karma had taken him out of this world.

Grayson wondered how much Becka knew about their past, about what life had really been like in this house, or if

George had managed to hide it from her. She seemed like a smart woman—protective and observant—but George had a lifetime of experience showing only the cards he wanted you to see. If things with Edith had gotten bad enough that he was willing to risk hiring a live-in caretaker for her, he surely would have had a plan.

Though, now that he thought about it, Grayson wasn't entirely sure how George could have hidden it from Becka entirely. Maybe he had simply been willing to bet that he could control and intimidate Becka the way he had everyone else in his life.

Grayson snorted, the sound echoing down the empty hallway as he approached the library. If he had been a betting man, and he'd been asked to choose who would come out on top in a war of wills between George Barlow and Becka Simmons, his money would have been on Becka.

George had been cruel and manipulative, but there was something about the way Becka held herself—or the set of her chin or the light in her eyes—that made him absolutely certain she was more stubborn than he'd ever been. She was stronger and braver than Grayson, too. He doubted she'd ever taken a punch lying down or run away from a fight.

Grayson had taken quite a few punches—and kicks and shoves—without fighting back and that had been before he'd run away. He was a coward, a fact he'd admitted to himself long ago, even if he'd never spoken it out loud to anyone else.

Well, anyone except for George.

Grayson turned the corner into the library, scanned the long rows of neat shelves and the old book spines and the carpets, worn from so many years of people passing the same routes between the furniture. It had been here that George had first knocked him down.

His grandfather had just come off a night of drinking and laid his hands on Edith again. Grayson could still hear the echo of her soft sobs even now, the years between doing nothing to soften the memory of the sound or Grayson's anger. He'd wanted to help her, to stand up for her. Instead, George had knocked him on his ass with one punch, lip bleeding and pride shattered.

"Get up." It had been a challenge, spit between clenched teeth, carried on whiskey-soaked breath. "You think you're man enough to stick your nose in other people's business? Get up!"

Grayson figured he must have been about twelve at the time, well used to George's backhand or his belt but still unfamiliar with his fists. He'd been terrified. Too scared to move. Too scared to fight back.

"Then admit you're a coward."

He didn't know how long it had taken for him to speak or how many blows George had landed in the meantime, but when he was able to form the words, he'd said whatever George wanted to hear.

He'd also never tried to step between his grandparents again.

Edith had never seemed to blame him, but Grayson blamed himself. He carried the loathing around with him, but he'd never gotten up the courage to be anything else than what he'd been that night. A coward. Unable to help and unworthy of love.

He dropped his body into George's favorite chair, let the thrill of that transgression chase away some of the negative thoughts he'd been dealing with the last few days. Such a small act, this tiny disobedience, but George had never let anyone sit in this chair.

The view was admittedly pretty nice. The chair faced the wide window, revealing the waves and the full moon that hung overhead. There was a polished wood table just in front of him, neatly stacked with books and a chessboard, a game partially played frozen and waiting for someone to come back and finish it. Grayson plucked a piece from the board and rolled it between his fingers.

Black. Tall. Not a horse. Possibly a king or a queen. Not that he'd know the difference between them. George had never bothered to teach him to play. Maybe he'd taught Grayson's father Thomas, at some point, but after raising a child and having all that effort wasted … He'd been disinterested in Grayson as anything other than a body to discipline.

Grayson rarely allowed himself the luxury of wondering how life might have been different if it hadn't been for the car crash that had taken his parents, but it was hard to think about the ways being raised by George had molded him, without also considering whether Thomas had been the same. Had he gotten George's temperament or Edith's?

Neither of them had been willing to tell him much, and while the townspeople of Widow's Point spoke only good things about Thomas, they also spoke only good things about George, so they weren't exactly reliable sources of information.

"Already stole your daily ration of cookies?"

Grayson's heart jumped so hard he was surprised it didn't come all the way out of his chest, his body lifting from the chair with such force it practically levitated off the cushion. "Fuck!"

Becka's laugh was loud and only a little mean, and though he knew he'd made quite a scene, he glared at her anyway as she sauntered over with a grin plastered across that mouth of hers.

"It's just me." She sank onto the couch opposite him, the moonlight shadowing her face as she wrapped her arms around her drawn up knees and wheezed at his overreaction. "What the hell, man?"

"You can't sneak up on a person like that!" It wasn't like he'd been *scared* or anything. It was just that she'd materialized out of the darkness like some kind of rumple-haired ghost. She was even sleeping in a black shirt and underwear, the only things visible in the darkness had been her head and seemingly disconnected limbs.

One hell of an image, that was for sure.

"Oh, come on. It wasn't that bad." She finally stopped laughing and held her hand out expectantly. "Cookie?"

"You could go to the kitchen and get your own." He sounded petulant, not a mark in his favor, but he was already digging in his pocket for her cookie. "What are you doing here so late at night, anyway?"

Probably not looking for him the way he'd been looking for her. He knew that. But it was nice to see her, all the same. Maybe it was because he was lonely, maybe it was the skin of her legs in the moonlight, maybe it was just that he'd developed a kink for being bullied by very short people.

She popped the whole cookie in her mouth again—disgusting and fascinating but impossible to look away from—and tried to answer him around a mouthful of stolen dessert. What came out was flying cookie chunks and undecipherable noise.

"What?"

She swallowed hard and tried again, more successfully this time. "I couldn't sleep. Didn't know I'd run into you here, but since I did, I'm glad you came prepared. You?"

He figured that when she said *prepared,* she meant *with a pocket full of cookies.*

"Hungry, I guess. Couldn't sleep. Whatever." He was still turning the chess piece over and over in his hands, and he had to resist the urge to shove it under the chair cushion before she noticed that he'd been in here ruining his grandfather's last game. It hadn't occurred to him before, but she might think he was being disrespectful of the dead.

She already seemed to hate him, no need to make it worse.

He held the piece in his hand, unsure of what to do with it as the night settled in around them. The library was silent except for the sounds she made, a little hum of satisfaction as she chewed the rest of her cookie, her relaxed body practically melting into the couch as she tipped her head back and closed her eyes.

Sure she wouldn't notice, he took the chance and hurried to put the piece back, but she spoke without ever looking at him.

"He played all the time."

Caught, but reassured by the bland nature of the observation and her sleep laden tone, Grayson tried to respond without letting his embarrassment show. "He did when I was a kid, too."

He hadn't really talked about George since he came back, except for the short conversation with the sheriff the first day he'd arrived, and he wasn't sure how he felt about it now. He tried to change the subject. "You play?"

She shook her head, eyes still closed. "Never learned how. I just come in here to read and smell the books."

"Me too." He was wondering what kind of books she read when she suddenly lifted her head up, face alert again, and pushed to her feet. "Uh ..."

"I'll be right back." She disappeared to the other end of the room, her footsteps carrying her at faster than usual speed, like she was on a mission. It only took her a couple of minutes to come back, a book in her hands that hadn't been there when she'd left. "Here."

She tossed it at him and he caught it on instinct, his hand closing around it, obscuring the cover before he'd gotten a good look. Once he had, it felt like she'd hit him on the head with a big rock.

"Where'd you get this?" He traced the worn colors, the

faded letters of his name where he'd pressed the pencil into the title page years and years ago. "I thought I'd lost it."

"Edith said you used to love books, had a bunch I guess, but George tossed out most of them. She found that one and had stashed it in a drawer or whatever in case you ever came back. I think she'd forgotten about it, so I wanted to make sure you got at least one back."

Grayson nodded, still trying to process the cruelty of his grandfather throwing his books away. He'd suspected, but it was different to hear it confirmed.

"Was he a world class asshole back then, too?" She was watching him as he examined the book in his hands, and for all the emotion in her voice, she might as well have been talking about the weather. There was no sympathy in it, but no malice either.

It should have made him angry—George was his grandfather, after all, and a dead one at that—but instead some of the ache in his chest faded a bit. He didn't owe Becka the way he owed his grandmother, so he didn't have to worry about her reaction to whatever he said. On top of that, if she knew what kind of man George had really been, then he didn't have to worry about offending her like he would if he tried to talk about this with anyone from Widow's Point.

They all thought George had been, if not a hero, then at least an all-around good guy. Coming along now to tell them he'd been a wife beater and a child abuser probably wouldn't go over too well.

"He was always an asshole." It felt good to say it out loud, though he did glance over his shoulder after he said it, still a little superstitious about running into George, alive or as an angry ghost, as soon as the words left his mouth.

She held out her hand, waited for him to supply her with another cookie. Before she stuffed it into her mouth, she said, "I figured as much. People like him don't usually change."

"No, they don't." He took a bite out of one of the remaining cookies, chewing and swallowing before he spoke the way a polite person—not Becka—would do. "You already knew all about him before you asked, didn't you?"

At that, she cracked open one eye, looking Grayson over as he sat in a chair that didn't belong to him, with food in his pockets he couldn't resist the urge to hide. "Maybe. Does that bother you?"

"Yes ... No." Neither option was entirely the truth. As much as he hated anyone knowing how badly he'd allowed himself to be treated, it also felt good to talk to someone about it that didn't have their own George-related baggage and feelings. "Maybe."

"Do you want to talk about it?"

"Do you want to tell me why you've been avoiding me since that day on the beach but suddenly want to get all up and cozy in my family business?"

"Ah." She shoved a hand through her hair, wincing when it tangled. She seemed to make a habit of that, one he found both foolish and endearing. "Well, I haven't exactly made it a secret that you haven't done a good job of taking care of Edith. You didn't even ask about her doctor's appointment, which is just ... I don't know, man, it was shitty to not care enough to even ask about her health. And *then*, like you haven't been gone long enough already, you're planning on running off again at the first opportunity."

None of this was new information—she'd said it to him before—but this was the calmest and most concise way he'd ever heard her express it. Without so much anger to tangle up her messaging, it was clear that she was doing her best to look out for Edith. She blamed him for hurting someone they cared about, and though Grayson knew that might not be entirely fair, feelings like that usually weren't.

They came from your heart, not your brain.

"True." This time he held out a cookie without prompting, grateful it gave them something to do while they tried to work this out. He needed to stay far away from her thighs and other assorted sexy bits, but they did need to get along while he was here for Edith's sake. "But that doesn't explain why you decided to stop being mad at me long enough to chat about George."

"Oh no. I'm still mad at you." She kicked her feet out to land on the table between them, stretching into the motion like a cat and drawing all his attention to the bits he wasn't supposed to be looking at. "I just like having my midnight snacks personally delivered."

"Convenient," he agreed. "And George?"

She grew still, bit down on the corner of her lip as she thought about it. Was she trying to come up with a lie? Trying to decide if she was going to answer at all?

"I know what it's like to be the kind of kid that has to hide food," she said at last. She reached for the necklace she always wore, spinning the locket on its short chain. Another habit he'd noticed. She tended to play with it when she was feeling upset about something. "I know what it's like to creep around. To be scared. To be hurt."

She waited then, probably expecting him to object or try to cover it up and nodded when he didn't. She'd figured it out on her own or Edith had told her. Either way there was no reason to deny the truth.

The library slipped back into silence again, a bubble that wrapped them in a small intimate moment he wasn't sure he was ready for. He was aiming for a truce and nothing more.

"I'm sorry." What else could he say? It wasn't enough, nothing ever was, but he had nothing else to give. "No one should have to live like that, and I'm sorry you know what it feels like."

"Yeah, well, we're not about to sit here and start trading

childhood horror stories and bonding over our scars, if that's what you're thinking." The momentary softness had vanished from her eyes and she tilted her chin at him, the window of vulnerability replaced with her customary combative stance. Had he said something to upset her, or was she reluctant to let him see her weaknesses? "I just wanted to know why."

"Why?" He stared at her, dumbfounded. "You want to know why he was an asshole?"

"No." Based on her expression, if she'd had anything in her hands, she might have thrown it. As it was, her hands flexed, little fists that he knew she wouldn't hesitate to use if the need arose. It was subconscious with her. He knew she didn't think she was going to have to start swinging, but her body didn't feel safe without the option. "I want to know why you left. Why did you take off out of here and abandon Edith to deal with all of it alone? Why didn't you come back for her, even after all this time?"

"Are you serious?" Grayson laughed, shocked by the question and bitter about the answer. Of course she'd managed to hit him right where it hurt the most, but if she wanted to get into it, he was willing. It wasn't like anyone else had ever cared enough to ask or even been close enough to him to know about it.

He'd spent all his life running away and putting up walls, and here was this tiny fearless woman, bulldozing over the top of him with her assumptions and her questions and her total lack of acceptable boundaries.

"I'm dead serious." Becka still hadn't looked away, hadn't flinched when he raised his voice. "You seem like a decent guy. Why didn't you come back for her?"

"She would never have left."

Chapter Eight

Becka

After several weeks, Becka had to admit that living with Grayson was actually not half bad. He was quiet, picked up after himself, and the more he relaxed into living there, the funnier and more pleasant he was to be around.

Things had been tense between them in the beginning, but she liked to think they had started to hit their stride the night she'd caught him sneaking cookies into his bedroom. It had been such a familiar scene. Guilt all over his face and his pockets full of off-limits food. How often had she and Payton made that same illegal midnight run, risking devastating consequences to fill the emptiness in their stomachs? Too many to count.

Seeing him there like that, his willingness to share his ill-gotten gains, had given her a little bit of something to think about. She'd still spent the next few days avoiding him, watching from the sidelines as she tried to figure him out.

He'd handed out Halloween candy to groups of kids without ever losing his smile, and Edith had looked happier than Becka had ever seen her as they celebrated her first holiday free of any of George's rules and restrictions. Grayson had bought extra chocolate just for Edith, and Becka felt her heart soften.

It was dangerous territory, starting to think he might be a decent guy. She'd been fooled by George at first, too, a mistake she was determined not to repeat, even as she worked to understand what kind of person his grandson really was.

He *had* left Edith, he'd never denied it, but his explanation that night in the library did make some sense, even if she was still deciding whether to fully believe it.

Edith was part of Widow's Point and it was part of her. It would have been hard enough convincing her to risk it all leaving George. Could Grayson have convinced her to leave the house and the town behind? The more she thought about it, the more Becka wasn't sure.

She'd had her mind made up about him since he'd arrived, and feeling some of that anger fade, made her wary of him in a different way. It wasn't a good idea for her to start getting soft around him, even if he wasn't as bad as she'd originally thought. He hadn't actually left yet, but he was still planning to leave, and when he did, she'd have to be there for Edith. There wouldn't be time for her to have her own feelings hurt because she'd decided to like him.

The best she could do was indifference and since that night, they'd settled into a truce of sorts. Not exactly friends, but roommates without any hostile intentions. An improvement, if only barely.

"Hey!"

She caught the flying candy bar an inch from her face as Grayson walked in the front door and tossed it at her without any further warning. The wrapper crinkled as she looked down, chocolate and coconut.

A risky choice but one she appreciated.

"What the hell?" There was no heat to it, more like confused amusement, and she was already tearing it open, the wrapper between her teeth and words muffled.

"We were out of coffee so I ran into town." He was chewing his own candy already, as guilty as she was, despite it being before nine am. "Figured I would buy some snacks since we ate all the cookies."

"And you brought this instead of going to the bakery?" She clucked her tongue at him, ready and willing to shame him for his poor decision making. "When in doubt, always go to the bakery."

He seemed to still for a moment before setting the bag down on the nearest table and digging around inside until he found the new package of coffee beans. "I was in a hurry. Being out of coffee is an emergency, you know?"

"You can buy coffee ..." she let it linger, waited for him to turn to face her, "... at the bakery."

"Fine!" He threw his hands up in surrender. "I admit defeat. Next time I'll go to the bakery."

"Tell Henry that I sent you and he might give you an extra donut." She was already imagining it, the sweet glaze and soft, fluffy fried dough. "He likes me."

"Henry Schmidt?"

"That's the one!"

Something flickered across Grayson's face, unreadable and gone in a flash. There was no evidence of it in his casual, curious tone. "Is his dad not running the place anymore?"

"Nope, his parents retired a few years before I moved here and took off for Florida." She crossed her arms and looked at him with mock seriousness as she followed him toward the kitchen. "You've got to catch up on your gossip, Barlow."

She'd thought Edith had caught him up on everything already, but it seemed she'd missed a spot with the bakery and the Schmidt family. It was bound to happen, of course.

Even in a small town, it was impossible to keep track of everyone.

"Hmm." He wasn't paying her any attention, his focus back in the bag as he searched for something else. After a few seconds, he pulled out a shiny red bag and beamed at her triumphantly.

"What is that?"

"Bribery." He threw open the junk drawer and dug around until he found the scissors to cut the top off the bag. "If it works on one, then it will probably work on the other."

"Works on one?" She had no idea what the hell he was talking about. "Who are you bribing? What's in the bag, Grayson?"

"I'm not telling you." He gave the bag a hard shake, got the contents rattling around as loudly as possible. "It's about making friends, you know? You've got to be prepared to make sacrifices, to do what you have to do, even if it's humiliating."

"I really don't know what you're—"

Becka stepped out of the way just in time as Ruffles came running down the hallway and into the kitchen as fast as she could go. She overshot the turn by the cabinet, slid across the tile until she bounced off the opposite wall, and came to a skidding halt at Grayson's feet.

"Treat?" His smile was wicked as he pulled a treat from the bag and held it where she could see it. He crouched down at her level, giving the bag another little shake when she started to back away. Tiny growls still rumbled in her chest, but he definitely had her full attention. "I bet you can even take it from my hand without biting me, right?"

She did, indeed, take it from him, after which he turned to Becka and said simply, "See? Bribes! A few days of this and I bet she'll be happy to see me every time."

"She'll also be considerably thicker in the middle." Becka rolled her eyes, but there was something to be said for a man that was willing to work to earn the trust of a dog. She stepped closer, hovering over them to make sure Ruffles was still going to mind her manners once the food was gone. He'd stop handing out treats eventually, and Becka wasn't entirely sure he'd get out of the encounter with all his fingertips intact. "Just make sure you're taking her out for exercise and that she doesn't get sick from getting too many treats."

"Got it." He put the bag away, out of reach of Ruffles' still sniffing nose. "No problem at all."

Becka tried to take a step back when he pushed to his feet suddenly, his full height far too aggressively in her space as he towered above her. Her retreat was brought up short by the corner of the countertop digging into her back, and she was still close enough to feel his warmth against her chest.

They'd been living together for over a month, and they'd never been this close. She could see the little flecks of blue and gray color in his eyes, feel his breath on her cheeks, smell the scent of his cheap shampoo. Her muscles locked, unable to back away and unwilling to push forward, to go through him, to escape.

She'd known since the first time they'd locked eyes outside the diner that there was something between them, some kind of purely physical attraction that neither of them was keen to act on. Once they'd realized the connection between them, how deeply involved they both were in Edith's life, they had both set that feeling aside.

It had been a silent, mutual, common-sense decision that had had them using Edith as a buffer, dancing about their shared home always more than an arm's length away from one another. She'd wrapped her anger around her like a shield and pretended not to notice all the times she'd caught him looking at her, that lingering gaze of his taking its time sweeping over her legs or across her chest.

Now she was pinned under it, heart pounding in her ears,

blood rushing through her veins. The words she needed to say —excuse me, please just let me step around you—were trapped. Her nerves left her with a suddenly thick tongue and dry mouth.

It wasn't like anything had changed. He'd *been* attractive. She distinctly remembered noting that exact thing when he'd first arrived. Yet somehow, standing close enough to him that she could see the smattering of freckles across the bridge of his nose, it was as though she had never really looked at him before.

Now things were less tense between them, and he was being so nice to the damn dog and he was just standing *so fucking close* ... She wasn't sure when her eyes had settled on his mouth or when his hand had come to gently circle her wrist, but it was impossible to move away.

"Becka?"

She jumped at the sound of Edith's voice, and she didn't think it was her imagination that he jumped, too. He jerked his gaze away; shoulders hunched and face pink as he dropped her wrist like it was on fire.

"I'm in here." Becka only had to clear her throat once for her voice to be loud enough to carry and by the time she had, Grayson had bolted to the other side of the kitchen as fast as he could without making it obvious that he was running from her.

It was a good thing Edith had called out when she had, otherwise ...

Otherwise what? Becka's stomach flipped, anxiety and anticipation dueling it out as she considered the possibilities. She didn't think she'd imagined the sexual tension. He could have kissed her. Worse, *she* could have kissed *him*. That would have gone over splendidly. The last problem she needed to be dealing with right now was cozying up with Grayson.

Apart from her solid wisdom against trusting him too

much or getting too attached, she knew exactly how that kind of relationship progressed. You started out rightfully hating a man on sight and then the next thing you know you're kissing in the kitchen and then crawling back to your own bed in the middle of the night to avoid the morning walk of shame.

No one involved in this situation could have said any of that was a good idea, but there was more at stake here than her pride or even her relationship with Edith. There were reasons, damn good ones, that she had determined from the beginning to keep herself away from him, and though she'd let him charm her out of some of her defensiveness, she could never let things go any further than this tentative truce they had built.

She'd just have to go back to not looking at him. They could both pretend that awkward moment had never happened, and it would be a simple case of no harm, no foul.

Resolute in her determination and with her mind firmly made up, Becka turned back to Grayson, hoping to give him a short, casual dismissal as she went to search for Edith, who had yet to appear. The look on his face knocked the breath clean out of her. Whatever he was thinking, there was a fire in those eyes. This was a bit more than a few stolen glances at her tits.

That had been amusing.

This was terrifying.

A man fumbling a little over being attracted to her was one thing. It was unthreatening, maybe even a little cute. A man she absolutely and without question needed to keep her distance from? One looking at her like the only thing keeping him from tossing her into the bed and keeping her there for days was his grandmother being under the same roof? That was another thing.

A far more dangerous thing.

Especially when a tendril of want unfurled low inside her and heat rushed to flood her cheeks, her chest, her ears ... Her brain had common sense. Her body had only ill-advised desires. It didn't take a genius to figure out which one was winning.

"Stop looking at me like that." She sounded peevish, the petulant and irritable note in her tone unfamiliar to her ears even as she tried to tell herself he wouldn't notice.

She got to keep her delusions, as Edith chose that moment to finally appear in the kitchen, an unreadable look on her face as she zeroed in on Becka and tried to force a smile.

"Grandma Edith?" Grayson, too, must have noticed something off about her, because his attention immediately shifted to her as she walked into the room.

Edith ignored him completely, the entirety of her focus on Becka as she stopped walking and cupped Becka's cheek in her hand. "You have a visitor."

"A visitor? Nobody visits me here. I swear, if it's that fucking pig cop again, I'll—" She never finished the threat, all thoughts of the sheriff disappearing like a puff of smoke as her sister hesitantly followed Edith into the room.

Becka's hand flew to the necklace at her throat, the familiar metal in her hand the only thing grounding her as shock set her adrift, leaving her floating in a fog of disbelief.

Payton, still nearly a mirror image of Becka even after all this time, looked painfully out of place in the gentle splendor of Barlow House. Her clothes were disheveled, perhaps from days spent traveling to get here from wherever she'd been, and her hair was still damp from the encroaching autumn rain.

She wasn't even wearing a jacket, Becka noted in annoyance. Just standing bare armed and bedraggled in the kitchen, dripping water from her wet hair all over the floor.

Becka had long ago stopped hoping she'd ever come back, only for her to pop up out of the blue. "Of course." All her effort went to controlling her rage, and she still couldn't keep the disappointed anger out of her tone. "You would just show up here one day without calling. No explanation, no justification. Just *bang*," she gave the countertop an accompanying slap, "and here you are. I can't believe I spent so many years wondering what happened to you, if you were okay, and you just—"

The rant died in her throat, the words dissolving as her mouth dropped open. Payton's hand rested on the noticeable curve of her stomach, a worried pinched look between her brow that Becka had never seen before.

"What the fuck?" It flew out of her mouth, aimed directly at the irresponsible big sister she loved more than anything else in her life. The one who'd hurt her more than anyone else could have possibly done. "Is that what I think it is?"

"Becka." It was quiet, a warning that didn't carry any farther than the distance from Grayson's mouth to her ears, but she shook it off. Possibly decent guy or not, he had no right to stick his nose in this. She ignored the voice in her mind that tried to remind her how deep her nose had been in his relationship with Edith. This was different. He barely knew Becka and he didn't know Payton at all, so it wasn't like he knew what the hell he was talking about anyway.

Maybe it wasn't right for her to raise her voice at a pregnant woman but goddamn it, how could Payton do this? Show up after all these years with no attempt at keeping in touch and not because she'd missed the little sister she'd left behind. No, it was because she needed something. Why else would she have turned up now? In the condition she was in?

Payton seemed to draw in on herself under Becka's caustic tone. "It's a long story, but I suppose the short version... Yes, it is what it looks like. I'm pregnant. About six months, I think."

"You think?"

"Well ..." Payton shuffled her feet, eyes on the floor. To the outside observer, it probably looked like she was the younger sister and Becka the older. "That's what the doctor said at my first appointment, based on my last period."

She gave Grayson a sweeping, uncomfortable look from beneath her lashes as he pretended to look through them like he hadn't heard a word. He had to be nearing thirty and Payton, two years older than Becka, was in her late twenties, but they were both blushing like teenagers in a sex ed class. Becka wasn't sure why that irritated her, only that it did.

"And at the other appointments?" Becka wanted her to get on with it, spit out what she'd come for and leave. She'd wanted her sister back, but not like this. If Payton only cared about her when she needed something, Becka figured she could go right back to wherever she'd been this whole time.

"There weren't any others." It came out in a rush and Payton took a small step forward, half straining toward Becka and half hiding behind Edith. "I couldn't stay there, Becka. Not with him. I wasn't safe and if he knew about the baby—"

"I don't even know what you're talking about." Becka held up a hand, giving her head a small shake to keep Grayson from trying to interject to ask a question of his own. She could see enough out the corner of her eye to know he'd opened his mouth and then closed it again. "Do you mean your boyfriend? What was his name? Alex?"

Payton shook her head. "No, I haven't been with that guy in ages. The baby's father is … someone else."

"Someone else." Becka repeated, taking in the news that the boy Payton had left her for wasn't even the one she was running from now. "What happened to Alex?"

"We broke up." Payton shrugged, her expression turning more miserable by the second "I was a teenager back then. I've been with Jared for years."

"Jared." Becka tested the name, lip curling over the instant dislike it inspired in her. "The father."

"Yes."

"Whatever." Becka rubbed her temples, headache building as she tried to figure out what to do. Payton was older but they had always looked enough alike that people frequently mistook them for twins when they were children. Now, Payton seemed to have finally aged. There were already fine threads of gray in the dull strands of her hair and lines of worry at the corners of her eyes.

Despite the round fullness of her stomach, she had none of the healthy glow Becka had always thought pregnant women should have. She seemed frail and dangerously thin. Her skin was sallow and her cheeks were pale, except for the dark circles under her eyes it was as though all traces of life had left her.

Even her lips had no color.

Either the pregnancy was not going well or the stress of her situation had taken a heavy toll on her body. Either way, it was clear she was in dire need of help. Becka felt herself wavering, the years of conflicted feelings bending under the weight of love and responsibility.

"Please, Becka" Payton almost reached out a hand before thinking better of it and dropping it back to her side. "You're my sister."

It was the wrong thing to say. There was no way for Payton to know that, of course, but nothing else she could have come up with at that moment would have been as damaging. Where had that attitude been, Becka wondered, when Payton had run off? If she'd remembered then that they were sisters, she could have prevented so much of Becka's suffering.

Instead, Becka had been forced to stay there alone, her own wits and an endless supply of rage all that had kept her going. It had sustained her—though barely—long enough for her to burn their bullshit church to the ground and escape, but Payton couldn't have known that Becka would make it out.

The memory was bitter and so was the look on her face.

Becka could feel it, though she couldn't control it. The flared nostrils. The downturned mouth. The tension in each little muscle. She didn't want any of this, or any of those memories, and she didn't appreciate Payton coming around and digging it all up again, no matter what situation had prompted her arrival. Becka was on the verge of telling her so, maybe even kicking her out of Barlow House—okay maybe not *actually* kicking her out because Payton *was* her sister, even if she had left her—when her disordered thoughts were interrupted again.

"Becka." This was a plea, not a warning, and it did not come from Grayson this time, though he looked worried. It was from Edith. Becka could easily have ignored Grayson, in fact she did it daily, but the same was not true for Edith. "Let her stay. If not for her sake, then for the baby's. That's your little one, you know?"

"What?" Becka's gaze snapped back to Payton's stomach, Edith's words unlocking something she hadn't considered. Payton's baby was her responsibility, no matter what Payton herself had done. It wasn't just a situation that had driven Payton to look for her now, after all this time, it was a child, one that also needed her. Becka knew that, of course she did, it was just that she hadn't had time to work it all out yet. There was so much hitting her at once. There were too many new facts, too many complex emotions for her to keep up and be rational.

How was she supposed to think anything through in these conditions?

"If she's not safe where she came from, it's only right for her to stay here." Edith stepped in when Becka hesitated a moment too long, still trying to process her complicated feelings about Payton's sudden arrival and the revelation that she was going to be an aunt. "We have plenty of room, don't we Grayson?"

Grayson

Now that Becka's brain was catching up with the rapidly evolving situation, there was a blooming protectiveness in her chest for her sister's unborn child. Did they need to ask Grayson anything? Edith had already said it was fine for Payton to stay, and now he would come along just like his grandfather had, or Becka's father had, and change everything until it was ruined.

Alarm bells in her head were ringing, some warning her against this man and his presence, the dangers he might present to the child she now needed to keep safe, and others trying to reel her back, reminding her that Grayson had done nothing wrong and did not deserve the cutting resentment swelling inside her.

Years of finely honed anger and survival instinct were suddenly at war with her rational mind, and there could be only one outcome. What were Grayson's feelings in the face of a child's wellbeing? She conveniently forgot that a moment ago, she had been thinking about kicking Payton out herself.

That had been before she had fully had time to think the situation over.

Now that she had, she gripped her anger, irrational as it was, and wrapped it around her like a protective cloak. She had lashed out before Grayson could say another word.

Chapter Nine

Becka

"No one asked you for your opinion, Barlow."

His eyes widened at the venom in her voice and Becka heard Edith take a deep, shocked breath from behind her. Payton was the only one that didn't seem all that taken aback by the sudden anger, her only response a slight tightening of her hand where it rested against her stomach.

"Listen, I was just—"

She had no intention of hearing what he was "just" about to do. Whatever truce they had tentatively built, whatever unusual awareness had passed between them a moment before, it was nothing compared to the need to defend her family from a man she didn't entirely trust.

There was too much at stake for her to let him interfere.

The little voice in her head, the logic that spoke against the developed instinctual anger, reminded her that losing Grayson would inevitably hurt Edith, but she was too far gone to listen. The part of her that knew she'd regret hurting him like this once she'd calmed down, had been drowned out by her own fear.

"Save it." Adrenaline was already pumping. Heart pounding. Breath coming hard and fast even though she was standing still. Her palms were sweaty and she could feel her body blooming as it puffed up with rage. Every muscle poised, ready to spring. Every thought in her mind was focused on him, her tongue sharp and ruthless. She was prepared for battle, verbal or otherwise. "You have no say in this. Edith already said she could stay."

He frowned at that, further heightening her defensiveness with his dour expression. "I wasn't going to... What do you mean I don't have a say?" Whatever his first point had been was swallowed as the full meaning of her little barb hit him.

"I mean, you don't have a say in what happens here. You took off, remember? Why do you think you'd be able to come back here now, after all this time, and have your opinion count for jack shit? Shut up. Get out. Stop bothering people you obviously never cared about in the first place just because you've decided to go on a power trip in a house that doesn't belong to you."

Each word was a blow, carefully aimed at the soft spots. His insecurities. His guilt. His fragile relationship with his grandmother. She watched, vicious and satisfied despite the guilt she knew she'd feel later, as his mouth fell open slightly in hurt and surprise. It was better, no matter the cost, to hurt him before he had a chance to hurt the rest of them.

She watched, leaned in as he sucked in a breath and clenched his teeth. It was impossible to miss the anger that flashed in his eyes, the way it contorted his face, and she braced for it, her fists balled and ready to swing until ...

He turned on his heel and fled, carefully sidestepping the rest of them to be sure his body didn't bounce off Becka's shoulder as he passed or brush against Payton's stomach under her threadbare blue maternity top. Edith stretched out a tentative hand, her expression as fragile as Becka had ever seen it, but he evaded that as well. In seconds, he was gone. The peace they had found in the kitchen that morning lay shattered in his wake.

Ruffles snorted inelegantly from her place at Edith's feet and trotted after him, scrambling as fast as her short legs would carry her and shooting a judgmental glance at Becka as she went.

Payton whistled, long and low, and raised a brow as Becka swung around to face her. She didn't step back but Becka saw the worry in the way she gnawed a loose piece of skin on her lower lip and brought her other hand up to rest on her stomach beside the first. "Well, I see some things haven't changed."

"Shut up." Seeing Payton react as though she had to protect her unborn child in the face of her own anger, Becka felt a flush of heat and shame rise up the back of her neck. "You know I would never hurt you or the baby."

"Well." Edith cut in before either of them could say anything else, cheeks puffing out as she blew a steady breath out through her teeth.

Becka figured that interruption was probably a good thing because she'd seen Payton's hesitation. There had been a moment there where Becka wasn't sure what her sister was going to say. Did she truly think that Becka might take her anger out on the two of them? Sure, she had a temper, and of the two of them she'd been the one most likely to fight back when their parents had been violent toward them, but that wasn't the same thing.

Was it?

Becka's gaze drifted toward the door where Grayson had disappeared and fought to ignore the first wave of guilt and regret. She'd work through all that stuff later, after she'd dealt with Payton.

"Why don't we get you settled upstairs?" Edith's voice was still pleasant, with no outward sign of upset in her words or her controlled expression. Becka still felt uneasy. Edith was the perfect hostess, as always, and she wouldn't show it now even if she was unhappy about what had just happened with Grayson. Still there was a stiffness in her movements, a shortness in her glance, that told Becka they would be having a private conversation later.

One that Becka would do just about anything to get out of since it would inevitably lead to her having to apologize. Even when she knew she was wrong, Becka *hated* apologizing.

They both followed obediently as Edith led the way out of the kitchen and across the house. Becka frowned a bit as they passed her room, and Grayson's across the hall, to the last bedroom, the one farthest from the stairs. It would make more sense for Payton to stay in the room across from hers, but that would mean asking Grayson to move again.

After the way they'd bumped heads the first time, when he'd realized she'd taken over his old room, and now the confrontation in the kitchen, it was unlikely he'd budge this time. Not unless Edith asked him herself and the ramrod straight posture of Edith's spine told Becka it was best not to bring it up.

They were quiet as they walked, but no sound could be heard in Grayson's room, and Becka wondered if he was still at home at all. Maybe he'd left. A little spark of fear flashed in her heart—maybe she actually *had* driven him away—but then she remembered Ruffles running after him. The dog was nowhere to be seen now, and surely he wouldn't have taken her if he planned to leave for good.

Besides, they couldn't have been more than a few minutes behind him, and he wouldn't have had time to pack already.

No sound coming from the bedroom was probably a good sign. If he was in there, tossing clothes into a bag and tripping over a stubborn dog, they would surely have been able to hear him.

Of course, she told herself she only cared about *that* because his leaving would certainly upset Edith, maybe even to the point of not letting Payton—or even Becka herself—stay in the house anymore. That thought honestly hadn't occurred to her, and Becka nearly tripped over her own feet as she reached the door to what was apparently going to be Payton's new bedroom.

It wasn't even the thought of having to start over finding a place to live while having to take care of an extra person and prepare for the arrival of a brand-new baby, it was the thought of having to take care of an extra person and a brand-new baby without Edith.

She had long since gotten used to the idea of Edith being there for her. They helped each other, supported each other, loved each other in a way Becka had rarely encountered in her life. The only other person who had ever come close had been Payton, and in the end, even Payton had abandoned her.

Just like Grayson had done to Edith.

What would she have done, how would she have felt, if Edith had turned Payton away? Driven her out, the way Becka had just tried to do to Grayson? No matter the reason, it would have hurt her deeply.

Damn it.

She really owed Edith an apology, too.

One apology was bad enough, but two? Make no mistake, Becka fully acknowledged that she could be a total bitch, but she rarely fell into it accidentally. It was usually a calculated choice, and one from which she was unlikely to back down. On the rare instances she felt a real apology was necessary, it stung her ego.

Still, she would make an exception every time for Edith and it was more than worth swallowing her pride to mend their relationship if she had damaged it, no matter how unintentionally.

"Do you have any bags?" Edith had opened the door and turned on the light, stepping aside so Payton could take a few hesitant steps into the room and turn in a slow circle. "We can bring them up from the car for you."

Payton shook her head, lifting the small gray bag she wore settled against her hip. The strap crossed her upper body, wedged itself between her breasts, pulled tight like she was afraid someone might try to steal it. It was larger than a normal purse but not quite big enough to qualify as anything else. Obviously full but not overflowing or bulging at the seams. "This is all I brought with me, and I don't have a car. I walked here from town when the trucker I caught a ride from dropped me off in front of some diner."

"Jesus, Payton, you hitchhiked here? Pregnant? What if something happened to you?"

Payton didn't seem to notice the seething anger and worry in Becka's questions. Her eyes were watery and her smile was pasted on, just enough to be polite and show Edith she was grateful. "Didn't have much choice. It's not like he was going to let me bring the car."

"Why don't you sit down?" Edith guided her over to the bed, somehow managing to be incredibly tender and absolutely forceful at the same time. Payton sat without question and Becka wondered if she realized how little choice she'd had in the matter. One simply did not say no to Edith on the subjects of care and hospitality. It was a terrifying talent Becka quite admired. "Tell us what happened."

Payton glanced uncertainly at Becka as Edith patted her hand.

"How did you even find me?" This was the most pressing

question in Becka's mind. She'd spent a couple of years trying and failing to find Payton, and she couldn't imagine what had led her big sister, not just to Widow's Point, but to Edith's actual front door.

"I guess it wasn't so hard once I figured out where to start." Payton winced and looked down at her hands as she started to fidget under Edith's gentle patting. "I went to Mom and Dad's first."

Becka's mouth fell open, her bottom jaw hanging comically for several seconds as she tried to organize her scrambled thoughts. "Mom and Dad know where I am?" It came out as a high-pitched screech and Payton winced again, rubbing her ears as she glared at Becka.

"No."

"You just said—"

"I said I went there first. I was desperate to get the hell away from Jared and I didn't have anywhere else to go." She held up a hand when Becka opened her mouth and fixed the no-nonsense, older sister look on her face that had always kept Becka under control as a kid. "I know what you're going to say and you're right. It was a terrible idea to go there, and I won't ever go back."

"Good."

"But," Payton said over her, "while I was there, I found a box of old pictures."

She reached into her bag and pulled out an old photo of two young girls in front of an old yellow VW bus. They were at some beach in California and neither of them could have been older than six. This was from their early years when their parents had been at worst neglectful. Before they'd gotten sucked into the lies of a glorified snake oil salesman who'd promised them salvation in exchange for their money and their children and their sanity.

"You took it when you left."

"Hmm?" Becka tried to pull herself out of the memories. "The bus?"

"Dad was still bitching about it when I asked what had happened to it." Payton picked at a piece of skin on her thumb, lost in thought as whatever had happened when she'd gone home played out in her mind. "He loved that car more than he ever loved us."

"Yeah." It wasn't even a close comparison really. It was part of the reason she'd taken it, a little extra insult and injury on the way out, though not the only reason. "I lived out of that thing for months when I left."

"How'd you know he wasn't going to report it stolen?"

Becka grinned, the question one she'd pondered herself for a while before settling on a single unavoidable truth. "Dad? Call the cops?"

They both laughed. He'd rather have his house, his car, and all the contents of both stolen than deal with the police.

"Anyway, I figured you probably had a plan and you'd been forging his signature for years for permission slips and free lunch applications. I had a friend with some access look up vehicle registration information for yellow VW buses on the west coast. This is your listed address on your driver's license."

Becka was actually impressed. It was the kind of thing she would have done herself if Payton had left any clues behind. In fact, once she'd turned eighteen, she'd managed to get the bus's title changed over to her name by pulling some strings of her own. The friend of someone who owed her a favor had a brother that worked at the DMV. Their parents had given them very little, but the ability to work around and outside the system did occasionally come in handy.

"Nice work."

Edith coughed, a small sound that was less about clearing

her throat and more about reminding them of her presence and her general disapproval of casually breaking the law.

"Sorry." Becka stood up a bit straighter and put on a more serious face. "Now that we know how you found me, why don't you tell us what happened? Why'd you show up now?"

It took a few minutes for Payton to answer, and before she did she turned her hand over in her lap, no longer letting Edith gently pat her arm but gripping her palm to palm, as though she could draw strength from the contact.

"I was able to put up with it, when it was just me," she didn't specify what *it* was, but a quick glance between Becka and Edith was enough for each to confirm they both already knew, "but what about the baby? He was just... God, he was just always so *mad*. It didn't matter what I did or what I said. I was always wrong."

"Why didn't you—" Payton shook her head and Becka fell silent.

"He pushed me down the stairs." The explanation was deadpan, like Payton had been rehearsing the story so she could get through it without emotion. "We were walking up the front porch steps and I was carrying in groceries, and he pushed me. I couldn't even catch myself and I landed on my stomach so hard." She looked up at Becka, pain etched in the faint lines beside her eyes. "I was lucky. I wasn't showing yet and it didn't hurt the baby, but what if it happened later? What if he hurt our child because I wasn't strong enough to stop him?"

"Does he know?" Edith looked pointedly at Payton's stomach. She was already showing but no one knew how long ago she'd left him.

"No." Payton shook her head, and her tone was more resolute now than it had been at any other time since she'd arrived. "I couldn't tell him. He'd never let me go if he knew. No matter how far I ran, he'd find me. I'll be lucky if he doesn't chase after me now, even though he thinks it's just me that left him."

Becka pushed a hand through her hair, pulling it through the tangles and wincing at the tug on her scalp. How many years had Payton been with that son of a bitch? How long had he been abusing her with no one there to stop it?

"Well, he can't ever find out." Edith was calm, a perfect balance to the rage simmering in Becka. "You'll just stay here with us and we'll help you get back on your feet. Widow's Point isn't such a bad place, name aside. You can find a job and even an apartment later on, if you want to."

"That's fine." Becka was nodding along, but she was only half listening. "You do what you need to do to get set up here. Just tell me where that," she glanced at Edith and swallowed the profanity on the tip of her tongue, "where *Jared* is right now. Seems like we need to have a few words with him about the way he treats women."

"No." What little color there had been in Payton's face drained away. "You can't do that."

"Why are you trying to keep me from getting to him?" Becka was exasperated, already pushed to the end of her rope by everything else that had happened since Payton had shown up in her kitchen. All she wanted to do was protect her sister and the baby. She hadn't been there to do that since Payton had run away and look what had happened to her. Payton had always been softer, more vulnerable. Without Becka as a shield, she'd gotten hurt.

Besides, Jared deserved to get smacked around a little and Becka figured she was just the right woman for the job. Payton suddenly trying to defend him from the consequences of his own shitty actions didn't sit right with her.

"I'm trying to protect *you*." Payton reached for one of Becka's hands, clinging to her as Becka refused to meet her eyes. "Don't you know how lucky you've been? Dad told me what you did before you ran off. You could have been arrested. You could have gone to jail. You can't take those kinds of risks!"

"You're willing to let him get away with it, to suffer no consequences whatsoever? To just run away and leave everything behind and then not even care what happens after? You are such a coward—" Becka snapped her mouth shut. She knew she'd gone too far, her anger getting the best of her. She huffed, frustrated, and turned toward the door. It was best for both of them if she left for now. Got some fresh air and some distance. There would be time to come back and apologize later.

She made it no farther than the doorway, her feet stopping almost of their own accord when she caught sight of Grayson, standing motionless in the hallway, one hand on his doorknob and a haunted look on his face.

There was no way he hadn't heard her. The word, coward, felt even dirtier now. She hadn't meant it, not really. Not for Payton and maybe not for him, either. In either case, she certainly hadn't meant for him to hear it. It had been a weapon thrown out carelessly, and it had landed on him, even though he hadn't been her target. Collateral damage.

It wasn't an excuse.

Becka knew firsthand that sometimes those blows were even worse. The hatred wasn't even aimed in your direction, but still it took you down. It added a layer of humiliation somehow, that the hurt hadn't even been intentional. How weak must you be, to be knocked out by a punch that wasn't even meant for you? To be brought to tears by words spoken to someone else?

Grayson turned the knob and fled before she could stop him, the door clicking closed quietly behind him. He didn't have the decency to slam it, slinking away instead like an injured child. Her guilt tripled.

"It seems you owe him another apology." Edith's voice came from just behind her, and Becka knew she'd seen the whole ugly thing.

"It seems I owe everyone an apology today."

"Best get started then" Edith ran a fond hand over Becka's arm, the warmth of it a balm against the harsh truth of her words. "No sense in putting it off. The longer it waits, the worse it will be."

Chapter Ten

Grayson

The knock at his bedroom door was too polite to be Becka.

It wasn't like she made it a point of knocking on his bedroom door, but he knew on instinct that if she did, it would be far more confident than the three timid raps he'd just received.

Grayson pondered that a bit as he unfurled his body off the bed and shuffled without enthusiasm toward the door. If it had been Becka, she likely would have knocked the door half off its hinges.

Instead, it was Edith standing in the doorway, alone, which was equal parts unsurprising and disappointing. It wasn't like he really expected Becka to apologize, somehow it didn't seem like walking back on the shit that came out of her mouth was really her style, but it would have been nice to hear it, all the same.

"Grandma Edith." They both stood awkwardly, her on one side of the line and him on the other, both unsure which way they should move. She'd never really bothered him in his room, not even when he was a child. "Do you want to come in or ..." He drifted off unsure what the other option might be.

"Would that be all right?" She peeked around him, taking in the little bedroom with its rumpled bedspread and too full laundry basket.

"Uh, sure. It's fine, just sit anywhere, I guess." He waved an arm, indicating the bed or the single chair, set off in a corner by the window.

She chose the chair, perching delicately on the edge and angling her body to keep herself facing him as he sat on the corner of the bed. The room hadn't been furnished with visitors in mind—people in the guest room didn't typically receive company sitting on a borrowed bed—but she made the uncomfortable seating arrangement as normal as possible.

"I wanted to talk to you about Becka and her sister." She spoke with all the calm authority of an accustomed host. Leader of countless community boards and planning committees. The woman she had always been when his grandfather wasn't around. Silk laid over hard steel.

"There's no need." He shook his head and ignored the irritated tilt of her head. It was easier to pretend not to notice when he wasn't looking directly at her, so instead he watched the lazy clouds floating outside the window. "I know what you're trying to say and there's no reason to get into all that. I wasn't trying to kick a pregnant woman out on the street for Christ's sake."

"I'm well aware of that." She lifted an elegant brow when he snapped his attention back to look at her. "I know very well that you're not that kind of man. Becka knows it, too, in her heart. It's just that—"

She paused, lips twisting into a small frown.

Grayson filled in the rest. "It's just that she fights first and thinks second."

"Something like that." Edith shrugged and moved on, skipping forward to the next point she wanted to make. "It's not personal and not a comment on how she views your character. What she went through as a child, well, I suppose you'd understand it better than most people, but she handled it a bit differently."

"With her fists?"

Edith's laugh was dry. "She has a short temper, but I don't think you have anything to worry about. She's protective of others, even more than she is of herself. Once she takes you in as part of her family, there's nothing she wouldn't do for you. I think you're closer to being there than you realize."

"It certainly didn't feel that way this morning." It was impossible to keep the petulant tone from his voice. It wasn't just the incident in the kitchen. It was the way she'd frozen in the hallway when she'd realized he'd heard her conversation with her sister. It wasn't just Payton she thought was a coward. It was him, too.

"If it wasn't true, she'd come after you with more than just her words."

"How the hell did she end up working for you anyway? She doesn't seem like the kind of person George would have let under his roof."

Edith's smile faltered for a moment. "I think that was pure luck. She'd just moved to town, and he knew my health was getting bad enough that he needed help around the house. I guess he thought it was best if it was an outsider, someone whose word wouldn't hold much weight with the people in town if she started telling tales about what happened here."

That was exactly the sort of calculating decision George would have made, and Becka's eccentricities would actually have helped in that regard. She didn't have the attitude of a local, and it would have made it that much easier to convince everyone she was a liar, maybe even a troublemaker or a thief.

Whatever he had to do to discredit her if she started talking about abuse.

"He underestimated her."

"Hmm?" Grayson pulled himself out of his thoughts, not sure he'd understood what Edith had said. "What was that?"

"Nothing." Edith shook her head and waved a hand to dismiss his question. "Just thinking out loud." She stood up, having apparently said what she needed to say. "Becka will probably come looking for you. Maybe not today but soon. It's not easy for her to apologize and though I know you don't owe her forgiveness; it would mean a lot to me if you could at least hear her out. Her heart is in the right place."

"That mouth of hers is in the wrong place." Grayson muttered it under his breath, but his heart wasn't in it. Truthfully, despite his problems with Becka and her bad attitude, he was glad she and Edith seemed to be able to lean on each other.

It had been a long time since he'd had that kind of relationship with anyone. He'd refused to make a home or a family and his life had become empty. He'd gotten exactly the life he'd built for himself, but it still ached sometimes.

Becka didn't seek him out the rest of that day, choosing instead to spend most of what remained of it in the room down the hall. He heard her slink past not long after Edith left, and she came down to the kitchen at dinnertime only long enough to take two plates and disappear again.

It was right that she had chosen to devote her energy to making up with her sister first. He told himself that over and over again. Her focus being on someone else didn't mean she was less willing to mend her tentative relationship with him, just that he was predictably less of a priority.

Hell, they were barely even friends.

He'd known that, had been just fine with it really. What was the point of getting too close with her when he was just going to leave soon anyway? It was best for everyone if they maintained a polite, amicable distance. Yet seeing the proof of it now, no matter how much sense it made, pissed him off.

One sexually charged moment in an empty kitchen didn't make them anything special to each other, but it didn't stop him from staring hard at the wall beside his bed most of the night, conflicting feelings churning in his gut. Even late-night stolen cookies didn't help settle him, and he was bitterly disappointed that she didn't open the door to her room and take the ones he'd grabbed for her.

He ate those, too, and it gave him a stomachache.

The sun was up, and he was still staring at the wall when a short knock on his bedroom door pulled him from his thoughts. It was still a bit early, but he'd expected his grandmother to follow up with him after yesterday. She'd want to come in again and ask him if he'd spoken to Becka, which he hadn't, so it should be a short talk.

He threw the door open without doing much more than tossing on a T-shirt and running a quick hand through his hair. On the other side was a woman who looked quite a lot like Becka, if Becka was a few inches taller and pregnant. She looked up at him with wide, surprised eyes—blue instead of Becka's rich brown—and then flinched away from him when she saw his expression.

"Sorry!" She stepped back, used an awkward laugh as a shield as he tried to resist the urge to reach out and steady her. He could tell it would only make it worse, so he kept his hands to himself and shuffled back a few steps, letting her get her distance and her balance. "Becka wanted me to ask you, well, we're going out for breakfast? She thought you might want to go?"

That was surprising. Her odd version of an olive branch, apparently, after everything the day before. She hadn't been willing to face him herself just yet, or maybe she thought he'd be more likely to accept the invitation if it came from someone else.

"Is Edith going?"

Payton looked uncomfortable, her job was done and she was already inching toward the stairs. "We asked her, but she said she'd rather stay here. We're leaving in about fifteen minutes, so I guess if you want to go, you can just meet us downstairs." With that, she fled, disappearing down the hall and then down the stairs, leaving without even the echo of her footsteps as evidence that she'd been there.

Fifteen minutes later, hair combed and wearing real pants, Grayson was downstairs in the driveway, leaning against the side of Becka's yellow bus. He had a newer, nicer car parked right beside it, but he just knew she was going to insist on driving, and he'd already decided not to make a fuss about it. Not in front of Payton. Whatever she'd been through, and it wasn't hard to guess at least some of it, she was half terrified of her own shadow and maybe of him in particular. No sense in causing another conflict that might upset her.

Payton was made from different stuff than her hot-tempered sister, but when she came out the door a few minutes later, her only reaction to his presence was a brief hesitant pause and then a polite smile. Maybe she wasn't as fierce, but she was still tough in her own way.

It took him a few seconds for his brain to catch up—he still wasn't fully awake yet—but when he did ...

"Wait, are you going to breakfast in your pajamas?"

They were having a rare, if slightly chilly, sunny morning, but still, both women were wearing brightly patterned pajama pants with tennis shoes and thin jackets they hadn't zipped up yet, the fronts opened enough to show him the T-shirts they wore beneath didn't match. The clothes on Payton were tight enough over her hips and stomach that he knew they were borrowed from Becka, and it astonished him that she owned two full length pairs of pants to sleep in. All he'd ever seen her in were those damn little shorts that left very little to his overactive imagination.

He supposed he'd be seeing less of them now that the air was starting to get colder, which would certainly help him keep his eyes—and hands—to himself. Not that she didn't still look attractive. Even in vividly colored, mismatched pajamas, she was one of the most beautiful women he'd ever seen. In fact, the way that top hugged the curves of her—

Becka coughed, the sound pointed and unnatural, and he snapped his attention back to her face. Both women had come to a stop directly in front of him, and he hadn't noticed because he'd been too busy staring at her chest again.

Well, it was only half his fault. He wasn't the one walking around with a pair of perfect breasts. And that wild hair. And those lips on a face that always looked like she was on the verge of committing some act of great passion, and she was still deciding if it would be violence or lovemaking. Whichever it was, it bubbled constantly beneath the surface, an ever-ready, endless pool of emotion he could only stare at in wonder.

He hadn't felt that deeply about anything since George had beaten the idea of saving his grandmother out of him, and Becka walked around with it effortlessly. Happy to hand it out to anyone and everyone without any concerns at all about consequences. It was as breathtaking as it was frightening.

"I guess this means you're coming with us to grab breakfast?" It was Payton who broke the silence, her assessing look passing from Grayson to her sister and back again.

"Might as well." He tried to make it sound as casual as possible and gave Payton his friendliest, least intimidating smile. "I'm hungry, too, right?"

"Get in the damn car." That was from Becka, her whole demeanor prickly and unwelcoming. So much for that apology.

He resisted the urge to be an asshole in return, Payton's presence a buffer that kept him from biting back and reminding Becka that she was the one that had invited him on this little morning adventure.

"Sure." He had the satisfaction of watching a confused crease form between Becka's brows when he responded to her waspish tone with relaxed ease. Huh. He'd been bribing her with snacks since that fight they'd had in the library a few weeks ago, but he added this new bit of information to his arsenal. She expected him to fight her, and doing the opposite seemed to throw her off balance.

Interesting.

He thought about adding a wink to it as he walked by, but she'd already snorted and stalked away, leaving him and Payton standing on the passenger side while she went around to the driver's side door.

"You sure know how to push her buttons." Payton was side-eyeing him, a look he recognized from his grandmother during his teenage years. The look grandmothers, mothers, aunts, and older sisters gave you when they were speculating about your love life. "Are you two—"

"No." He cut in quickly, already worried about what Becka might do if she heard he'd even entertained the thought of sleeping with her. Their tentative truce had already been seriously rocked by everything that had gone down the day before. No need to add any more complications.

"Okay, I was just wondering. You know, because of the way she looks at you when she thinks no one else is watching." Payton chuckled a little when Grayson's jaw dropped and opened the door to the front passenger seat without letting him say another word.

He'd have to find a way to talk to her in private later. Find out exactly how Becka looked at him. He walked around the back of the bus in a daze, every thought in his head preoccupied, and almost ran into Becka.

She hadn't gotten in like he'd assumed she had, instead she'd stopped in front of his door, waiting to see if he was going to come around or get in on Payton's side, which he might have done if he hadn't been so distracted.

"So, listen, about yesterday ..."

"What?" He struggled to pull his thoughts together, registering first the furrowed brows and scrunched nose of her expression. He wanted to reach out and tug on the ends of her hair, to feel the softness of the strands between his fingers, but he was still a little mad and she clearly had something to say, something she found deeply unpleasant, even if he had no clue what she was talking about.

"Yesterday." She bit out, mad again already about having to repeat herself. "You remember yesterday, don't you? The day before today?"

The sarcasm shook the rest of his brain loose, and memories flooded back in. "Yes, I remember."

"Well, you know, I'm..." She huffed, cheeks puffing out as she shoved a hand through her messy, windblown hair. She was a cranky mystery wrapped in bitchy enigma, but even then he liked the look on her face when she was struggling, the little crinkle of her nose as she tried to work up the courage to say whatever was on her mind. "I'm sorry or whatever, okay?"

"I—"

"Yeah, I know." She suddenly wasn't looking at him, gaze flitting almost everywhere except his face, and her hands, usually so still, were moving restlessly, almost desperately trying to emphasize her points. "I was a bitch. I shouldn't have said any of it, probably especially that bit at the end. I know I get worked up sometimes and stick my foot in my mouth like a dumbass."

"I—"

"But I don't like apologizing even if I am wrong, though, so if you're gonna make this hard for me—"

"Becka, stop."

She clamped her mouth closed, eyes widening at the commanding tone that was so out of character for him.

"It's okay." Maybe that wasn't entirely true, it wasn't *okay* exactly, but it wasn't as big of a deal as he'd thought it was yesterday. Not when she was looking at him, all flustered and trying so hard to do the right thing without sacrificing too much of her ridiculous pride. He honestly thought he probably meant it when he followed that up with, "I forgive you."

"Oh." She shuffled her feet, looked down at her toes like she couldn't think of anything else to say. "Well, get in the car then. Let's get some breakfast before Payton gets cranky. She's always been a jerk when she's hungry."

It wasn't the most polite apology he'd ever gotten, but Grayson slid into her backseat feeling like a man who'd just struck gold.

Chapter Eleven

Grayson

"This is where we're going for breakfast?" Grayson felt like he'd been hit in the stomach by a champion boxer, heavyweight division. In fact, he didn't think the current champ could have knocked the breath out of him any faster than Becka's sharp turn—Jesus Christ, who'd taught this woman to drive?—into a far too familiar parking lot.

"Donuts." Becka seemed to think this was a perfectly good explanation and had already thrown the bus into park and started wrestling with the seat belt buckle. The car was in good shape for its age, but it seemed that once that particular belt was fastened, it was reluctant to let her go. Fortunately, that fight kept her occupied long enough for Grayson to get his facial expressions and runaway heartbeat somewhat under control.

It hadn't occurred to him to wonder where the women were planning to eat. He'd assumed they were probably intending to drag him to the diner or the weirdly fancy coffee shop someone had opened across the street from the small grocery store. He'd heard they carried a few pre-packed pastries along with their offerings of lattes and macchiatos.

Pretty much the exact opposite of what you'd find at the bakery. You'd be lucky to have cream and sugar to soften the acrid taste of black drip coffee, but the pastries—muffins, croissants, and, yes, Becka's precious donuts, couldn't be beat. His stomach rumbled and his mouth watered. He absolutely did *not* want to go in, but as long as he had no choice, he might as well fill his empty stomach.

"Come on, Barlow, get a move on." Becka had finally managed to free herself and was standing at the front of the bus beside her sister, both of them rubbing their arms in the brisk wind. "You can't keep a pregnant lady waiting when she's hungry."

"I'm coming." It would be worse, probably, to have to explain his reluctance than it would be to just go inside. Besides, the glass front of the building with its painted designs kept no secrets. He'd been inside often enough to know that there'd never been a car pulling into the parking lot that had ever escaped the notice of the person behind the counter.

Henry's car, many years older but just the same as Grayson remembered it, was parked in its usual spot at the far end of the lot, beneath the old tree they'd climbed as kids. If he was here, he would be working the register. If he was working the register, then Grayson might have already been spotted.

It would definitely be worse to turn tail and run now, no matter how tempting it was. After all these years, there was no way for Grayson to face him, and no way to avoid it.

He should have stayed in Indiana.

It was too late now to run, so he climbed out of the car, took his jacket off, and handed it to Payton. Both women were shivering—the trees around Barlow House had shielded them from far more of the brisk November wind than the open parking lot they were in now—and he thought for a moment a strange look had crossed Becka's face as he handed the jacket to her sister.

Still, after watching Payton zip it up and get lost in the excess fabric, her rounded belly disappearing beneath another warming layer, Becka gave him an approving nod. He'd known Becka longer, but manners were manners. Children and pregnant women first and all that.

The bell above the door rang happily as Becka shoved it open, a wide and mischievous grin on her face that Grayson had never seen before. The place was empty—there was very little seating and most patrons grabbed their breakfast to go—and she took advantage by throwing her arms out wide and shouting, "Good morning, Henry! I'm back and I demand apple fritters."

"Welcome to The ..."

Bakery.

The last of the greeting trailed away into silence as Payton and Grayson walked in behind Becka.

Henry was behind the register—exactly where Grayson had known he would be—and the years had done nothing to change him, except perhaps to make him somehow even bigger than he had been as a teen. Tall, blond, and broad, he'd been a star athlete and ace student. He should have been arrogant but he'd never let it go to his head, remaining charming, likable, and funny. He'd been everything George had always wanted Grayson to be. The shining example of masculinity and achievement that had been thrown in his face all his life.

Anyone would have forgiven Grayson for hating him, but it was simply impossible to hate Henry. They'd been friends, at the very least, for as long as Grayson could remember. Right up until he'd skipped town without telling a soul.

Henry didn't look as angry as Grayson had feared he would, but his voice was stiff and unfriendly, his eyes glazed with shock. He had to have known Grayson was back in town —news like that traveled fast—so he was probably just dumbfounded that Grayson had the audacity to show up on his doorstep like the last twelve years of silence between them didn't exist.

Becka's confident smile faltered, replaced by confusion and hesitancy. Whatever kind of welcome she'd come to expect from Henry, it wasn't this awkward, nearly robotic response.

"Henry?"

The sound of his name seemed to pull him out of the daze he'd been in, and a more relaxed smile replaced the wooden one. "Sorry, Short Stack, I was caught up in my thoughts. You always demand apple fritters, but not usually with company?"

"Stop calling me Short Stack, asshole." The worry on Becka's face melted, replaced by a warmer, more affectionate expression that made Grayson's stomach twist. It wasn't like it was the first time he'd seen a woman get friendly with Henry, but it was the first time it had made him feel this uncomfortable. It was hard to put his finger on exactly what caused it, but he didn't think any of the possibilities were good.

"Gonna introduce me to—" Henry was clearly looking at Payton, his focus intentionally not including Grayson, body angled away from him just enough to be exclusionary without being obvious, and Becka perked up even more.

"This is my sister, Payton. She's older than me, so obviously my parents had to have a second try to get it right."

Payton lifted a brow at the dig, and her answering barb was just as sharp. "I think what my darling baby sister means to say is that I was so perfect as a child that they wanted another just like me. They were, unfortunately, disappointed."

Henry chuckled, a look of appreciation crossing his face at her quick rejoinder. "Nice to meet you, Payton. Are you going to be in town for—"

"Wait, we almost forgot the prodigal son." Becka's arm shot out, her finger pointing straight at Grayson, who was doing his best to remain invisible and hoping the floor would open up and swallow him whole. "The missing Barlow, returned after all these years from wherever the hell he's been. This is Grays—"

"We've met." Henry's tone was flat enough for Becka's smile to wobble again. "It is a small town, after all."

"Oh." Becka looked at them, suddenly reading the tension in the room, her hand coming up to rest against her lips. It was obvious that it hadn't occurred to her that this might be a problem. Grayson figured that his coming home had made Edith so happy that Becka hadn't ever stopped to think that his welcome would not be so assured everywhere.

"I can go." Grayson did his best to lighten the tension with an easy smile and a careless shrug, ignoring the heat of embarrassment that he could feel on his face and neck. The lighting had always been shitty in The Bakery, so maybe no one else would notice. He was already backing toward the door. "I didn't mean to intrude."

A muscle worked in Henry's jaw and Payton took a quick, almost imperceptible step closer to Becka. Most people wouldn't have noticed, but Grayson knew exactly how that kind of discomfort felt, and Henry had spent years watching him hide in the same way. One look between them was enough to come to a silent agreement.

Personal grievances could wait.

Henry blew out a frustrated breath, hands up to show he wasn't holding a grudge. "Nonsense. Grayson, you'll stay and have breakfast with Short Stack"—he ignored Becka's pissy huff—"and her sister. It's on the house today to celebrate your homecoming. I'm sorry for my bad manners. It's been too long since we've seen you around. Took me a bit by surprise is all."

Grayson imagined that it had.

They'd have to deal with that at some point, but for Payton's sake, it wouldn't be today. He went along with Henry's suggestion, settling in at a table not far from the front counter and listening absently to the women talk to Henry and each other. No one was paying much attention to him anymore, and he used the time to look around and drink his coffee from a chipped mug that looked like it hadn't been replaced since the business opened.

Not much else had changed, either. Though the words on the windows were more faded, "The Bakery" was still painted across the wide windows of the building's front in deep red block lettering. The small tables were still the same white Formica. The chairs were still the same cracked red vinyl. Both were unchanged from who-knew-when, but still serviceable. When he'd heard Henry had taken over running the place, Grayson had hoped he'd made some updates to the décor, finally done something for himself instead of living for the approval of his parents, but Henry, like so much about this town, seemed stuck in time, unable to move forward.

Whether that was a comfort or an inconvenience probably varied by person and how well they liked the place to begin with. It was true that Henry had never really liked the way his dad ran the family business, that he'd always wanted to update things and make some changes, take some risks, but Grayson was reminded again how little he knew about this place these days. Maybe Henry's dad was still making some of the behind-the-scenes decisions from his sunny spot in Florida, and Henry himself was only responsible for the day-to-day operations.

Once, he would have thought it impossible not to know what was happening in his best friend's life, but that had been a lifetime ago. He'd thought he'd gotten used to the sting of not knowing since he'd run away, but looking at it now, seeing Henry and The Bakery ... He had never gotten over it. He'd just stopped paying attention to the void it had left behind.

He snuck a quick look at Henry and found him looking at Payton. The look on his face was enough to soothe Grayson's initial irritation about the way he'd interacted with Becka earlier. A man interested in a woman romantically wouldn't be looking at her sister like that. It surprised him until he remembered Payton was wearing his coat. Her pregnancy was completely undetectable once she'd been swallowed up in a jacket that was several sizes too big.

Well, wasn't this just turning into a royal cluster fuck?

He wasn't sure what Henry had been up to since he'd left town, but it was a safe bet that he wasn't married—a subtle glance was enough for Grayson to confirm he wasn't wearing a ring and probably wasn't hitched up to his high school girlfriend anymore—and someone needed to tell him about Payton's situation before he stuck his foot in his mouth and embarrassed himself.

Grayson was staring off into space, trying to figure out how to work the topic around to Payton's expectant condition while Henry was still close enough to overhear, when the door to the back swung open. A teenager walked in, untying a red apron and paying the rest of the room no attention at all.

"Hey, Henry, listen, I've got to get out of here a little early today. My math teacher has it out for me this semester, I swear. You wouldn't believe the grade I got on—"

Henry chuckled when the kid fell silent and pushed turquoise bangs away from a face with too much black eyeliner. Apparently, they didn't get too many strangers coming in at this time of day.

"Who are you?" The kid wrinkled their nose like they'd smelled something unpleasant. Immediately on the defensive, the attitude was plenty rude. Grayson didn't blame them, though, being even a little different in a town like Widow's Point put one hell of a target on your back. You learned quick to protect yourself, and that meant keeping your back up.

"Customers." Henry didn't seem upset at the kid's question or the tone. He was calm and unruffled as he plucked the red apron out of the kid's hands. "You know Becka already, and the other two are special guests of hers."

It hurt that he didn't introduce Grayson as a friend, but he tried to keep it off his face as the kid turned back with renewed interest. "Oh, well, I'm Elliot."

"And?" Henry hadn't moved at all but it seemed like he leaned into the question, his presence stronger as he waited for an answer.

"And I'm sorry I was rude." A quick puff of breath moved the fallen bangs back out of their eyes. "It's a bad habit and I'm working on it. Happy now?"

The last question was directed at Henry, who rolled his eyes. "We'll talk about it later. Get out of here and try to pass your math class this semester, please."

Grayson was trying to figure out an age for the kid, running possibilities through his mind. He was pretty sure he hadn't been gone that long, but maybe the kid's mom was Henry's girlfriend or something. Thankfully Payton asked what he was too embarrassed to bring up himself.

"Cute kid." She smiled at Henry, a look that was a lot nicer than Becka's and seemed to have Henry a bit star struck. "Yours?"

"What?" Henry blinked twice. "The kid?"

"Yeah." Payton waited—Grayson waited too—for Henry to put his head back on straight. Someone really had to tell him.

"No. Well, maybe. Kind of?"

Payton laughed and exchanged a confused look with Grayson. "I'm afraid I don't know what that means."

Becka took pity on him, looking between him and her sister like she was finally catching on to what was happening to poor Henry. "He means Elliot isn't his kid, but they live with him."

Grayson caught her use of the word *they* to describe Elliot and made a mental note of the kid's preferred pronouns so he wouldn't accidentally be an asshole in the future. Out loud he asked, "Girlfriend's kid?"

Henry looked at Grayson when he asked the question, but he answered more in Payton's direction. "Elliot lives with me because it's safer. I'm sure you're the last person I need to tell, but not all parents—or grandparents—are decent people."

"Oh." Payton looked like she was thinking about it hard. "You can do that?"

"You can if their parents aren't trying to take them back. I guess I could have done things more formally through the state but all they wanted was for their kid to be out of the house. When I showed up for their things, the parents handed everything over without a fuss."

"I can't believe they'd just throw out their own child."

Payton and Henry were lost in their conversation, with Henry explaining more in depth about how easy things were when you lived in a small town where no one cared at all about what you did with a kid like Elliot. Their parents didn't want them, and living with Henry kept the cops and the teachers from having to get involved. As long as no one went missing and they had food and clothes, that was good enough.

Grayson thought it was probably one of the few cases where their negligence was actually to the kid's benefit. Better to be taken in by someone like Henry than be a ward of the state and bounced around all over the place. He'd met plenty of those kids after he'd run away, and the horror stories they had were as infinite as they were painful.

"Cat got your tongue?"

"Hmm? Oh." He hadn't realized Becka was looking at him, her chin was resting on her palm and her eyes narrowed in speculation as she watched him think. "No, I just wasn't paying attention."

"It doesn't seem to bother you." She seemed surprised but he had no idea what she was talking about. Whatever it was must have been a point in his favor since her voice was unusually soft. Almost tender. "Elliot. I mean, you don't seem to be mad that Henry took them in."

He frowned, trying and failing not to be insulted by the insinuation. What the hell kind of person did she take him for? Did she really expect him to be mad that an old friend of his had opened his home to a child in a bad situation?

She held up a hand, obviously tipped off by the thunderous expression he could feel forming on his face. "Hey, I didn't say there was anything wrong with what Henry did. It's just that George didn't exactly take it this well. He stopped coming in here altogether and told me and Edith we weren't allowed to, either."

Of course he had. Grayson felt some of the anger drain out of him, at least the anger he'd felt toward Becka. What was left was shame and resentment. It was bad enough that George had been a monster to his own family. It was somehow worse when he did it to other people.

"I'm not my grandfather." He didn't mean it to come out the way it did. In his head, it was flat. A simple statement of fact. Out of his mouth, it was aggressive, a challenge he'd thrown at her feet. He was daring her to contradict him.

Becka's face—always so expressive—registered her shock. "Did I say you were? I've thought many things about you since we met, a lot of them less than flattering, but I never thought for a minute you were anything like him."

"Then why did you seem surprised when I didn't react to Elliot the way he did?" Some of his anger had faded, but he thought he was entitled to at least a little bit of an explanation.

She actually had the decency to look a little embarrassed. "I didn't mean it like that. It's just that I've seen enough people react badly to things like that, that I can never be sure who's going to be normal about it and who's going to be ... well, like George. We're all a little protective of Elliot."

"You're a little protective of just about everyone except me." Grayson didn't mean it as petulantly as it sounded, and something indiscernible flashed across her face before he rushed on, trying to get to his point without having to address that telling slip up. "Maybe just try to keep in mind that I don't generally make a habit of kicking puppies or stealing candy from babies."

She took a deep breath, cheeks still an embarrassed pink. "Yeah, I'll try to do that."

Chapter Twelve

Grayson

Edith was nothing if not persistent.

It had taken her all these weeks of hints and gentle nudges, followed by several not-so-gentle nudges, for her to finally get Grayson to the cemetery where his grandfather was buried.

They'd come together on a day when the skies above were gray and the ground damp beneath a steady drizzle, creating the perfect atmosphere for Grayson's thoughts as he followed her to the family plot in the back. The new headstone stood out against the rows of older slabs. Among those more established plots were many that represented the final resting places of ancestors he'd never cared much about, but also the relatively recent ones belonging to his parents.

Thomas and Anna Barlow.

He'd come here sometimes with Edith as a kid, sat beside those stones as she'd mourned their loss, her broken heart obvious even to a child. Her grief then had been real, written in the lines of her face, evident in the strain in her voice.

Perhaps he'd expected something similar when they went to visit the place where George had been buried, but if he had, Grayson was surprised to find her outwardly indifferent. Her face was impassive as she stood beside her husband's grave—not one sign of a tear or the stricken expression of a grieving wife could be seen—and if he could see anything at all in her expression, it was only satisfaction that she had done her duty.

Grayson knew she'd stop bothering him about it now. He hated this place, with its neat rows of tombstones and carefully trimmed grass, but coming to stare at a cut gray rock that bore his grandfather's name had brought Edith some peace of mind. Making the appearance would stop the town tongues from wagging, and that was enough for her.

He could feel the eyes of curious onlookers on his back. Even a small-town cemetery like this one was unlikely to be completely deserted—especially since Edith had chosen a time when they had the greatest odds of being spotted by others who were also paying their respects to the dead—and news would travel fast to the rest of town.

How Edith did it, he simply couldn't fathom, but she knew exactly what to do and when to do it, if the object of the game was to manipulate societal convention to her own will. She was a formidable opponent in the realm of gossip or social position. Her choices were never obvious, but always effective.

They'd brought flowers for the grave, pink carnations that she had chosen herself. It was perfectly respectable on the surface, something a grieving widow would do, but Grayson knew George had hated pink and hated carnations. It was a slap in the face, a subtle act of revenge for the years she'd spent being married to him. Grayson thought it was an excellent choice, and he smiled a little, triumphant and grim, as he placed them on the rain drenched marble of the tombstone.

"You never deserved her." Grayson kept his voice down, low enough even Edith couldn't hear him. He was sure

George's spirit wasn't here, but on the off chance the bastard could still hear him, he wanted to make his position clear. "You never deserved any of us."

When he'd left Widow's Point as a teen, his primary emotion toward George had been fear. He'd carried that with him in all the years since, his constant and unwavering companion. Since he'd come back, though, that had changed. Without the ever-present threat of violence hanging over his head, he'd had time to breathe, time to think.

His feelings had shifted, leaving him less room for that old terror, and far more room for anger and disgust. This man had never been worthy of having Edith as his wife or Grayson as his grandson. They were stronger than him, but they were also loving, compassionate, and forgiving. Each of them was better than George had ever been, in a dozen ways, both big and small.

They had owed him nothing in life and they owed him nothing in death.

Coming back to Widow's Point had been truly helpful, if only because he'd been forced to start facing the past he was always trying to escape from. He supposed you had to go through the fire to get to the other side, something he'd been avoiding for far too long, running from his problems, as always.

It was a good thing he'd been bullied into hanging around, or he would have given into the urge and missed out on all the healing he'd done. George's death had been the catalyst for his return, but it was staying that had brought out the biggest changes in him. George dying had brought him home, but Edith's steadfast love and Becka's obstinate and unyielding presence had done much of the rest.

Actually, it surprised him how much of his current peace he could trace back to that little hellion and her terrible attitude.

She'd refused to let him leave. Refused to let him hide or run from his feelings. She'd teased him mercilessly and stolen his snacks and given him hell every day since he'd come back. He'd tried every trick he knew to wiggle out of it, from bribes to arguing to simply running away, but she'd refused to budge and now he was closer to being free of George than he'd ever been.

He doubted it had been intentional on her part—it was more likely just being in close proximity to someone who'd rather fight her demons than flee from them—but he was still grateful. Her words in The Bakery echoed in his mind, when she'd assured him that he wasn't anything like George. It had been a silent worry, one he'd feared he'd never be able to shake, and it had been banished in an instant beneath her honest assessment.

He wouldn't have been able to believe anyone else, but if there was one thing he'd come to trust in these past weeks, it was Becka's tendency to tell the truth, even if he wished she wouldn't. If she thought he was anything like George, she would have said so to his face. She wasn't the kind to sugarcoat her opinions. If she said he wasn't, then he wasn't.

It really was that simple.

Grayson knew he should be happy but looking back... So much of his life had been wasted on that fear, on one man and his reign of terror. Time he'd never get back, years he couldn't redo.

He patted the tombstone, putting on a good show for the passersby as they filed it all away for the evening gossip rounds. "I hope you find no more peace in the next life than you gave me in this one."

His voice carried a little more this time, and he knew Edith had heard him when she let out a soft gasp of surprise. He glanced at her over his shoulder, afraid he'd hurt her with his honesty, but there was no judgment there. The only thing he could see in the blue of her eyes was the same mixture of pain and anger that he felt himself.

He stood up, offered her his arm to lean on. "Ready to go home?"

Most of the onlookers had lost interest, and it was only Grayson that was paying close enough attention to notice how tightly she held onto him as they walked back to his car. She really was getting a bit frail. It was easy to forget, especially since her attitude these days was feistier than he'd ever seen it. George had only agreed to hiring Becka in the first place because of Edith's declining health.

It was a grim reminder that his time with her was limited. That was one more thing he wanted to blame George for, but how could he? Sure, he was the reason Grayson had missed all those years with her, but wasn't he still planning to leave her behind again?

His plans, so firmly set from the time of his arrival, seemed less appealing by the day, which confused him. Didn't he want to leave at the earliest opportunity?

Somehow, the answer wasn't clear in his mind anymore.

He made small talk with Edith during the drive back to Barlow House and he kept up his end of the conversation when the house's current four residents all sat down together to eat dinner, but his mind was elsewhere. Too much had happened in too short of a time and he hadn't had a chance yet to puzzle it all through.

It was well after midnight when Becka found him in the library, slouched in his grandfather's chair with a mostly empty glass of whiskey in his hand. It was his third, or possibly his fourth.

He hadn't gotten drunk since he'd gotten the news about George, and he wasn't sure why he was doing it now. Maybe it was because the trip to visit the cemetery had made him sad about losing so many years or made him question what he wanted out of his future. Maybe it had made him feel guilty about leaving again.

He wasn't sure what it had made him feel, exactly, but he was sure it felt bad. He was sure it had brought up a lot of questions he didn't have answers to.

It wasn't like he thought he'd find those answers at the bottom of a bottle, but maybe he'd feel a little better as he looked.

"Barlow, what the hell are you doing?" Her voice sounded too loud in the late-night quiet, a little angry and a little amused, but mostly just confused.

"Hmm?" He closed one eye and tried to focus on one of the spinning faces in front of him. They were all staring at him, but only one of them really belonged to her. He wondered absently if she'd be upset if he was looking at the wrong one. "Nothing."

"Nothing?" She pointed at the glass. "That doesn't look like *nothing*."

"Ah, you mean this?" Her expression didn't soften even a little when he held it up and looked at it like he'd never seen it before. Tough crowd. He figured that should have earned a little chuckle from her, at the very least.

"Don't play with me, Barlow. Are you seriously sitting alone in the middle of the night getting shit-faced?" She sounded disappointed, her arms crossed over her chest as she looked down at him, and the sigh that followed the question was deep enough to empty the lungs of a deep-sea diver. Where did she hold all that air? Was it kept in special reserve for when she thought she needed to sound extra upset with him? "What if it had been Edith that found you in here like this?"

"It's not like she's never seen a drunk man before." Grayson wiggled the glass at her, shaking it until the ice clinked. "Besides, I'm perfectly willing to share."

"She's seen plenty." The tone was pointed enough to have him dropping his arm, smile fading even before she continued. "I'm sure she doesn't need to see another, especially another Barlow."

He surged forward, amber liquid sloshing until it poured onto his hand and the carpet below. "What exactly is that supposed to mean? I thought you said I wasn't anything like my grandfather?"

She pointed a threatening finger at him, unwilling as ever to de-escalate an argument. "It doesn't matter if you're like him or not like him, don't you think it's a bit of a painful reminder for her? Why don't you take your drunk ass back to your bedroom and sleep it off?"

He stood up, frustrated and annoyed because even though he hated to admit it, Becka was right, damn it. He *should* have realized how upsetting it might be for Edith to come across him drunk in this room in particular, where George did most of his drinking, and all the memories it might have pulled up for her.

The movement was too quick for him, all the blood rushing out of his head as he pushed to his feet, and he wobbled a little. It had been meant to be intimidating, the alcohol giving him a little too much courage and bravado, but she had to reach out for him to keep him from falling on his face. One hand on his arm, the other on his waist to steady him.

And just that quickly, she was too close.

They hadn't been in proximity to each other like this since that day in the kitchen. Since Payton's timely arrival had given them both time and reason to step back and cool their overheated thoughts. He didn't know about Becka, but he'd dreamed of that moment more than once, always pulled from a deep sleep just before he lost complete control of himself and pressed his mouth to hers. Sometimes, when he first woke up, he could almost taste her, it had been so close.

And now she was blinking up at him with that same damned expression. Oh, yes, he recognized that look. The confused line between her brows and the way her eyes darkened as she tried not to let her gaze linger on his mouth.

A moment ago everything had been normal between them —maybe even a little worse than usual—and now she was clutching his arm and he'd suddenly found her so much closer than he'd expected. How could he have known she was going to be looking at him like this again? That the very face that haunted his dreams would be within kissing distance of his mouth?

The first time she'd been this near, it hadn't lasted longer than a moment, just enough time for him to see the bewildered flick of her gaze turn to panic, before she stepped back. She'd pulled away back then, first putting a foot of distance and then a whole house worth of space between them.

He knew she wanted to do that now, could see it in the way her chest lifted as she sucked in a breath and prepared to flee, and his hands were already raising to stop her. If he hadn't been a little drunk, he probably would have caught her before she could slip through his grasp.

Instead, she took a clumsy half step backwards and collided with the bookshelf behind her. It blocked off her escape route and he pushed forward, his hands closing around her arms to stop her from shifting to the side and escaping around him. His heart thudded painfully as she brought her eyes to his. They made the same realization at the same time.

There was nowhere for her to run.

She was trapped.

"Grayson, I—"

He closed the space between them and pressed his mouth

to hers. Her lips were parted, more in surprise than welcome, but he didn't delve into her warmth despite the temptation. It was quick, a darting thing that barely let him feel the heat of her before it was over.

She raised a hand to her mouth, fingertips settling where he had been as she stared up at him. "What was that for?"

"For?" He tightened his grip on her arms, worried that she'd bolt if she got the chance. He was half drunk and dazed from the warmth of her skin, and she wanted him to answer questions about his motives? "Hell if I know."

"What?" She blinked at him, lashes fluttering as she tried to process what had just happened. "You can't do that. You can't just kiss me out of the blue like that and then not even be able to explain yourself. What the fuck is wrong with you?"

A good question and not one that he had any easy answers for. He didn't know what he'd hoped to accomplish with it, truthfully he hadn't given himself the chance to think it through, all he knew was the urge to do it had been stronger than his will to resist. His body trembled, guilt slamming into him as he belatedly realized his error, as she blew a shaking breath out from between clenched teeth. "You're right. I don't know what I was thinking. I'm sorry. I'd blame it on the whiskey but—"

Her eyes flashed, brighter and sharper than the blade of any knife. "Don't you dare. Don't you even think about just ... just ... *kissing me* and then making it seem like something you didn't want to do in the first place."

He pushed a hand through his hair, ignoring how close to her body the sweeping movement brought him because he still hadn't moved back from where he had her pinned against the shelf. "You wanted me to kiss you?"

"I—" She ran her tongue over her lips, her hand dropping away to fist at her sides. "No. No, of course not. But if you're going to do it, then don't insult me by making it seem like it was unpleasant. Like it was a mistake."

"It *was* a mistake." He vaguely registered that what he'd meant, *'I shouldn't have kissed you while half drunk and without your permission'* and what she'd likely heard, *'I didn't like kissing you and don't want to do it again'* were two very different things, before he was forced to catch her fist as she started to swing it toward his stomach. His little fighter didn't have much room to gain momentum with such a small space between them, but he didn't want a punch in the gut when it was swimming with so much alcohol. *"But,"* he emphasized the word, leaning into it as she tugged on her arm, "that doesn't mean it was unpleasant."

"So, you got drunk." She ticked off his sins on her fingers, leaving them up as she went as a visual reminder. "Then, you kissed me without my permission." Another finger. "Which was an accident." Another. "And you liked it, but it was still a mistake? Have I got that right?"

"Yes?"

"That makes no sense!"

He was too drunk to keep up with all of that. Still, he'd be damned if he admitted it to her. "It makes as much sense as you wanting me to *want* to kiss you but not wanting me to *actually* kiss you."

She made a small, frustrated sound at the back of her throat, nearly a growl, that caused him to raise an eyebrow. Always so angry, so defensive, so unwilling to bend or admit she might be as wrong as he was. Ridiculous. Her attitude was, of course, but his response was just as bad. Why did her stubbornness, her prickly and unyielding and infuriating personality, make him want her more?

She tried to punch him again, but he caught it even more easily this time.

"Quit it." He tugged her arm up, wrapped his fingers

around her wrist as he secured it against the shelf just above her head. "Do you always have to be this difficult?"

"Yes." She was as unapologetic as always and, though he knew he deserved it this time, he still sighed.

"Please." He dropped his head until his forehead rested against hers, suddenly tired of the bickering and the bartering and the constant restless unease between them. "Can we have just a few minutes where things aren't like this? We might actually like each other if we weren't constantly at each other's throats."

She stopped struggling, her body softening against him unexpectedly. It was more than he'd anticipated he'd get from her, and he let himself get lost in the details of the moment. The soft hair brushing against his cheek. The floral scent of her shampoo. The soft skin of her wrist. Through the whiskey haze, he was sure he'd never been more relaxed, more content than he was now.

It lasted just long enough for her to bring one leg up and stomp down hard on the top of his foot. "Damn it, Becka!" He hopped on his other foot, nearly landing on his ass when she pushed by him with a derisive snort.

"If you want to get handsy with me, Barlow, next time try it when you're sober and not acting like a jerk. I can't guarantee it'll work, but I promise your odds will be better. Go back to bed and sleep it off before you hurt Edith's feelings."

With that she was gone faster than she'd arrived, leaving him struggling with a foot that just might be broken, a still fuzzy head, and a bulge in his pants he hoped like hell she hadn't noticed when he was rubbing himself all over her.

It was always one step forward and two steps back with them, every bit of progress swallowed by a foolish mistake or some conflicting bit of trauma and now look how things had ended up! She was probably more pissed at him than she'd ever been, and he couldn't even pretend to be the injured party. He was lucky she hadn't done worse than stomp on his toes and throw a few half-assed punches.

All these weeks, he'd tried so hard to stay away from her. He'd kept his distance, tried not to notice how attracted he was to her, and as soon as he'd lost the slightest hold on his inhibitions, all he'd wanted to do was drown in her.

Fuck!

He flopped back down on the chair he'd vacated, shifted uncomfortably when the new position proved uncomfortable in his current state of arousal. Every time he tangled with her, it was a fucking disaster, but he couldn't deny wanting her anyway. Common sense didn't stop him from looking at her, and now it seemed it couldn't stop him from touching her, either.

Living so close to her, being around her like this, was a ticking time bomb. He just wasn't sure if it was her fiery temper or his repressed desire that was going to explode first.

Chapter Thirteen

Becka

What the hell had she been thinking?

That was the question that kept Becka on edge for days after her run-in with Grayson in the library. She'd gone looking for him, which was the first and possibly worst of her mistakes. She'd let her heart be softened by his ready acceptance of Elliot at the bakery, and when he'd come home from the cemetery with that gloomy look on his face ...

She'd waited until the house had gotten quiet, the shadows long and the air still, except for the sound of the ever-present rain on the windows, and she'd gone looking for him. She'd gone to the kitchen first, and when she'd found him in the library, her pockets had been bulging with cookies. His favorite. Chocolate chip.

Seeing him lounging in there with his hand wrapped around a glass of George's whiskey, it had knocked the breath out of her. He'd looked so much like George at that moment. The face, the posture, the bleary-eyed gaze when he'd caught sight of her.

She'd been confused at first, then worried about Edith, her growing fondness for Grayson warring with her concern about how his grandmother might react to seeing him that way. Shooing him along to his room had seemed like the best way to deal with all those problems—keeping him out of Edith's sight and her own—but he'd responded with an uncharacteristic show of his own temper.

He'd always tucked under when she'd pushed at him, always let her have the last say as he gave in to her greater show of force. Suddenly finding herself backed against a bookshelf with his lips pressed against hers had been startling. She'd poked the bear a few too many times, and even though she knew him well enough to know he'd never actually hurt her, she had been holding her breath for a second there.

Because it had surprised her, clearly, and not for any other reason.

Certainly not the reasons he'd come up with. The audacity of that man was simply mind blowing. First, he kissed her. Then he acted like he hadn't even wanted to kiss her. Then he'd somehow concluded that she'd actually liked it.

Pfft.

Except for that one moment when he'd had his forehead resting against hers, when she'd found herself softening just a bit in his arms, she'd been absolutely unaffected by the whole thing. The only part of her that had been shaken at all had been her pride.

The number of dreams she'd had since then that involved spontaneous library nudity and hot, passionate sex had been entirely coincidental. Nonetheless, those dreams did make it hard for her to be in the same room with him without blushing like a schoolgirl with her first crush. He couldn't seem to keep his eyes off her, and she absolutely could not meet his gaze without her face burning and turning a humiliating shade of cherry red.

As a result, she'd started practically running from the room anytime he entered and she was fairly certain, if the hurt looks he kept throwing her way were any indication, he thought she was still mad about what happened. It would have been easy enough to dispel that misunderstanding, but she'd rather he thought she was holding a grudge than admit the truth.

"You're spending a lot of time hiding in your room lately." Payton faced her down across the kitchen counter, one brow raised in inquiry as she chopped vegetables for their dinner. She was a good cook and a better baker, skills that would come in handy now that Thanksgiving was practically upon them and Christmas was just around the corner.

Becka kept her own hands busy, trimming fat from a plump chicken breast and trying to keep a subtle eye out for Grayson as she did so. He had a bad habit of sneaking in so quietly she didn't realize he was there until he was practically within arm's reach, a place she definitely, positively did not want him to be.

"I don't know what you're talking about." The lie rolled over her tongue, years of sisterly relations making it easy to deny, deny, deny, anything that might be held against her later.

"Hmm." Payton dipped her head to hide a smile. "If you say so."

"I do say so." Becka waved the knife she was holding, forgotten in her hand. "Why would I be hiding? What could I possibly have to hide from?"

Edith didn't look up from the book in her hand as Becka's knife blade flashed, but her brows creased, sensing trouble with whatever psychic skills mothers had. She was seated at the table with a glass of wine as the younger women prepped dinner, looking completely at ease. "Careful."

"Sorry." Becka went back to trimming her chicken, making faces at her sister as she did. This was a happy moment. The kind of domestic family harmony she'd always dreamed about as a kid.

She'd have to be out of her mind to risk disrupting this just to get a taste of a grumpy Barlow. It was a good thing she'd come to her senses and stomped on his foot instead of sinking into him the way she'd almost done.

Unaffected.

Aloof.

Completely and utterly cold.

That's what she had been and what she would remain. There was too much at stake for her to let it all go to hell over a moment of weakness. She had more control over herself than that.

Didn't she?

Becka had no time to ponder that question, because Payton chose that moment to announce, "So, I think I might get a job."

"What?" Becka blinked at her, the chicken in her hand forgotten. Payton had only just gotten here, only a few short weeks had passed since she'd shown up looking like she was on death's doorstep and now she was already trying to get a job? Wasn't Becka already paying for her necessities? Maybe there was room in the budget for her to also get some spending money each week...

Payton laughed. "Close your mouth, Becka. It's just a job. I need money for baby stuff, don't I? It's not like I'm trying to move out already."

As if Edith would have let her. Payton would have to have closed her eyes to reality entirely if she couldn't see how thrilled Edith was about her being at Barlow House and the chance to have a baby around the place again. She'd quickly become very fond of Payton and Becka knew the feeling was mutual.

So what was going on in Payton's head, that she'd come to this sudden decision?

Becka squinted at her, evaluating the healthy bloom of color in her cheeks and the rosy glow of her skin. She did look much better than she had a few weeks ago—the safe, stable environment had done wonders in just a short time—but there were still worry creases at the corners of her eyes and Becka still caught the lingering look of sadness on her face when she thought no one was looking.

"I don't know ... "

"Edith, please tell my sister that having her own money and a purpose in life is good for pregnant women."

Edith nodded, eyes still on her book. "Of course it is, dear. Just nothing too stressful, you understand? Nothing that keeps you on your feet all day or anything like that."

"Where is she going to find a good job in this condition?" Becka puffed out her cheeks, grateful to have a topic other than Grayson to think about but irritated with Payton's stubbornness. "No one is going to want to hire someone that's going to need maternity leave in a few months. Especially not now, when all the summer temp work is over."

"She could always try The Bakery."

Becka jumped, only narrowly missing taking a chunk of her thumb off with the knife, when Grayson's voice chimed in from way too close to her ear. How the hell had he managed to sneak into the kitchen without her seeing him? She'd only been distracted for a few seconds.

"The Bakery?" Payton tipped her head and considered it. "That might work. The guy who worked there seemed nice enough."

"Henry's a good guy and his family owns the place." Grayson was standing between the rest of them and the door, his mouth curved in a knowing grin. He was talking to Payton, but his gaze was fixed on Becka. "He'll treat you well."

Becka turned back to the cooking. It didn't matter if he was trying to keep her in the room. She was busy, so it wasn't like she'd be able to leave anyway.

Smug bastard.

"It is a funny name, though, isn't it? Just 'The Bakery'. That's not very inventive." Payton chatted on, seemingly oblivious to the undercurrent of tension in the room.

"That's a Schmidt for you." Edith finally looked up from her book, eyes twinkling. "Henry's great-grandfather started the business, and rumor has it, he said that's what everyone else was going to call it, anyway. No need to think of a fancy name."

Becka had heard the story before, but it was still worth a quiet chuckle. It was a practical choice and one she could easily imagine the current generation Schmidt making. Henry, too, was a blunt and sensible fellow. A good man. Maybe Payton working at The Bakery was a good idea, though she hated having to give the points to Grayson for thinking of it.

"I just wonder..." She caught Grayson's gaze and said meaningfully, "How will he feel about the pregnancy?"

She knew Grayson had noticed the way Henry was looking at Payton that day. Becka was Henry's friend now, and he had been Henry's friend at one point, too. They both knew him well enough to know he'd been knocked more than a little off kilter as soon as Payton walked in the door.

Finding out she was pregnant was bound to be a shock, and Becka didn't want him to say anything that might hurt Payton's feelings. Henry *was* a good man, better than most in Becka's opinion, but he also tended to be overly blunt at times. Something she was betting Grayson knew, as well.

Payton asked, "Do you think he wouldn't hire me?" as Grayson and Becka shared a look that turned into a silent argument. The library incident was forgotten as they each tried to get the other to bend first.

In the end, it was Grayson that shook his head at Payton and assured her, "I'll go have a talk with him first. It might help to pave the way a bit, make sure he's expecting it when you come by."

That seemed to please her and she thanked him before giving her attention back to her vegetables, apparently content that the matter was in good hands.

Becka was beaming about winning their little game of mental tug of war when Grayson turned to her and mouthed, "You owe me."

Like hell she did. Henry was his friend first, so it was only natural he should be the one to handle this, wasn't it? She tossed her head, stubborn and difficult to the core, then turned away when his eyes flicked down to her lips, his expression suddenly hotter than it had been a second ago.

The conversation with Payton had served as a distraction, but as soon as that had been dealt with, he'd gone right back to his previous bullshit. Now he was looking, and she was blushing, just like before.

Couldn't he keep his mind out of the gutter? He needed to stop thinking about that kiss—if one could even call it that, with it being just a barely there whisper of contact—and he *definitely* needed to stop thinking about kissing her again. If *he* was thinking about it, then *she* was inevitably going to be thinking about it, and how was that fair?

She plopped the chicken into the pan and tried her best to ignore him. Just because he couldn't control himself, didn't mean she had to be just as bad. It was in everyone's best interest if she maintained her current stand-offish attitude. Still not interested, thank you very much, and if she could still feel the hot caress of his eyes on her back, well, that wasn't proof of anything.

$$\text{Chapter Fourteen}$$

Grayson

I f there had been an award for 'Best and Longest Lasting Holder of Grudges', that title would undoubtedly have gone to Becka. Grayson had tried everything he could think of since that kiss in the library and none of it had made a bit of difference.

He'd brought her chocolate from town, and she'd given it to her sister and criticized him for not stopping by The Bakery to talk to Henry like he'd promised. He'd tried to stop by her door at night with pockets full of cookies, but she'd kept it stubbornly and firmly closed. Hell, he'd even tried picking fights with her on purpose just to get her to speak more than a few words to him, but even his most irritating comments seemed to roll off her without so much as a flicker in her expression.

In short, he was getting desperate.

The longer she ignored him, the less he cared about common sense and good judgment. All the reasons he'd been so determined to avoid getting involved with her were nothing compared to the intense and growing desire to be near her in any way he could. He wanted her, and he'd worry about the consequences when they inevitably came knocking.

He'd taken to loitering around Edith anytime he wasn't working, hoping being close to her would force Becka to come around. She couldn't ignore Edith, and as long as he was right there, it gave him an excuse to talk to her, too. It worked for a few days, until Becka got wise and shifted most of her tasks to Grayson's working hours and asked Payton to help out more whenever he was around.

By the start of the second week, not only was Becka outsmarting the new system, Edith herself had started to get annoyed.

"Grayson, darling, why don't you go into town today?" She was buttering toast at the breakfast table, her tone sweet as ever, but the firmness of the suggestion was unmistakable.

"Oh?" He pretended ignorance, scooping up a forkful of scrambled egg and looking at her with all the innocence he could muster. "Did you need something?"

She was, as always, unflappable, her answering smile placid. "No, not exactly, but you did promise to talk to Henry for Payton, didn't you? I'm afraid she's been getting a bit restless these days, stuck in the house with nothing to do."

He glanced at Payton, seated to his right and absentmindedly nibbling on a piece of bacon. She had been dropping subtle hints about him going, and he truly did feel guilty that he hadn't done it yet, it was just that the idea of having to face Henry again ... Well, he supposed he couldn't put it off forever and he'd been unsuccessful in his attempts to hint to Becka that she should go instead.

There really wasn't much point in staying next to Edith for another day. His current plans to get Becka to talk to him could be considered another failure, so he might as well handle the situation with Henry and try to come up with something else.

"No problem." He pretended not to notice that Edith looked intensely relieved. "I'll get ready to go after breakfast. Make a list if you want me to pick anything up for the house while I'm out."

He snuck half a piece of his own bacon to Ruffles before he left the table and made a mental note to pick up more dog treats. He still wasn't her favorite person in the house, but a steady supply of bribes had bought them a steady truce.

That was the first stop he made when he drove into town, but he was man enough to admit he was still trying to delay the inevitable, so he didn't feel any shame at making several other stops after that.

Thanksgiving was less than two weeks behind them—how Becka had managed to get through the entire day, fancy meal and everything, while ignoring him, he still had no idea—but the town was already heavily decorated for Christmas, lights and garland wrapped around all the lamp posts and every store front shimmering with a festive display. Grayson wasn't foolish enough to wish for snow—it didn't quite get cold enough to turn the endless rain into anything more solid—but they were settling into temperatures that kept them bundled in their jackets and sipping coffee or hot chocolate most mornings.

He poked around several little shops downtown, enjoying the Christmas music every store seemed to be playing and the feeling of being recognized by people he hadn't seen in years. It had been a couple of months since he'd come back to Widow's Point, but he'd spent most of that time hiding away at Barlow House, only coming into town when he'd had no choice.

His spontaneous shopping trip brought him face to face with a lot of townspeople that had heard rumors of his return but hadn't seen him for themselves yet. They all wanted to tell him how much he looked like his grandfather and how sorry they were for his loss, but more than that they wanted to shake his hand and welcome him back.

He'd spent a long time being a nobody, a face in the crowd that was forgotten even before it was gone, but since he'd come back, he was once again that Barlow boy everyone knew. Not long ago, he'd been worried about what that might feel like, but this felt less like being part of George's legacy and more like being in the place he belonged.

It was getting to him, he admitted, and the longer he stayed here, the more appealing it became. As he tackled the demons of his past, Widow's Point seemed less like a comfortable, familiar cage and more like a home.

It made it easier than he'd anticipated to waste an afternoon and head just about everywhere in town except The Bakery, which suited him just fine. He bought a book for himself and then started picking up Christmas presents for the others. A soft little baby blanket in many shades of pastel for Payton. A bottle of her favorite wine for Edith. And for Becka...

He had no idea what to buy for Becka. This was a problem, because he'd specifically bought items for everyone else in the house, including the dog. Not having a gift for her would not be doing himself any favors if he hoped to win her over.

He was still contemplating his options when he looked up to find his path on the sidewalk blocked by a familiar face. "Afternoon, Sheriff."

"Grayson." Sheriff Levine clapped a hand on his shoulder. Dressed in full uniform today, instead of the civilian clothes he'd been wearing the last time Grayson had seen him, he looked more like the giant from Grayson's memories. If his hair and hideous mustache hadn't turned so white over the years, it might have been possible to pretend the last decade hadn't happened at all. "Haven't seen you in town much since you came back."

"I do most of my work from Barlow House," Grayson reminded him. "Not much need to come in unless I have shopping to do." He lifted the bags in his hands as a demonstration and the sheriff leaned forward to get a look at the contents.

"Looks more like you're shopping for a sorority house than for yourself." He chuckled at his own joke, trailing off into silence when Grayson didn't join him. "I'm just saying, there's more to Widow's Point than just places to work. You could come into town and have a drink with the boys the way George used to do. Might do you some good to get out of that house every once in a while. God knows, you're probably hen-pecked half to death every damn day."

Grayson was speechless. Hen-pecked? What the fuck was that supposed to mean? "I don't have any idea what you're talking about."

"It was bad enough with just Edith and that housekeeper, but I heard your grandma's even let some other girl move in? I gotta tell you, kid, I don't know what Edith's thinking these days. She was always such a fine woman when George was alive and since he's passed, it's like she's lost her mind. I think that housekeeper is a bad influence on her, if I'm being honest."

Housekeeper? Grayson assumed that was referring to Becka and there was something about Sheriff Levine's tone that made him uneasy. Besides, it wasn't like she was a newcomer in town. She'd worked for George and Edith for months before Grayson had ever come home, so it was a safe bet that they'd been introduced. He should know her name, or at least her proper job title.

"I—"

"I'm telling you, something about that whole situation just

isn't right, and I've been saying so ever since George passed. If you know what's good for you, you'll put your foot down as the man of the house and take control of whatever's going on there."

Grayson opened and closed his mouth, teeth clacking together. He knew he should say something, but his mind was completely blank. What the hell kind of weird rant was this? He'd known deep down Sheriff Levine probably wasn't a good person—years of close friendship with a man like George tended to give off a certain impression—but it was the first time the man had dared to speak this openly in front of him.

The worst part of it was the way he seemed to assume Grayson would share his shitty opinions, like it was the easiest thing in the world to take for granted. Was it because he was a man? Or because he was a Barlow?

"I'll keep it in mind." He wanted out of this conversation as quickly as possible, so he kept his tone neutral, though his ears were still buzzing. "I've got to finish this up and get back to work for the day."

"Sure." Sheriff Levine didn't seem to have noticed Grayson's stiff expression or the lack of warmth in his voice. "You just let me know when you're up for it and we'll have a boy's night at the bar."

By 'the bar' Grayson assumed he meant after hours at the diner, since that was the nearest thing they had in town. He still liked the name of the place and he'd thought a few times about asking Becka if she'd like to go and have a few drinks at some point, but with Sheriff Levine?

What he thought was, *I'd rather chew gravel.*

What he said was, "Yeah, yeah. Will do."

He wouldn't, but there was no point in arguing with him about it. That kind of attitude was too firmly ingrained to be changed, and it would be a waste of his breath to try. It was disappointing, sure, but not surprising.

He dropped his bags off at the car after giving the sheriff a final farewell wave and getting the hell out of there. The weather had turned colder while he was shopping and the overcast sky looked like it was about to start spitting rain again, but he could still put off the talk with Henry by a few extra minutes if he walked the three blocks instead of driving. There was a decent chance he'd end up rain soaked and cold to the bone, but the risk of pneumonia was a small price to pay, in his opinion.

Fortunately for him, luck seemed to be on his side. The first few fat drops of rain started to fall as he pushed the door open, the bell above his head ringing its happy peal, and there were already several customers lined up at the counter. Henry spotted him immediately, his brows creasing, but nothing could be said until he'd dealt with the line first.

It gave Grayson a few minutes to sit at a table by the window and observe. He let the familiarity of the place, the smells and the sounds and the unchanging routine, soothe his nerves. If he was going to stay here longer than a few months, and it looked increasingly likely, then they'd have to deal with each other eventually. At least Payton had given him an excuse to come by. It would make his visit less awkward, give them something else to discuss to smooth the way.

"All by yourself today?" Henry was as blunt as ever when he finally had time to make his way over to Grayson's table, a cup of shitty coffee in each hand. He kept the black one, apparently oblivious to the acrid taste, and passed over the one he'd laced heavily with cream and sugar. He continued without waiting for an answer. "Brave of you."

"I'm on a mission." Grayson took a sip and winced. Even the extras couldn't hide the taste. He'd long since been convinced there was something wrong with Henry's taste buds and it was obvious that was another thing that hadn't changed. "Edith sent me."

Some of the irritation cleared from Henry's expression. However hurt he'd been all these years since Grayson had left town without leaving a trace, he'd never take it out on Edith. "What's going on? Is she all right?"

"She's fine." Grayson waved a hand to dismiss the concern and the edge of anxiety in Henry's expression relaxed. "It's just that she's hoping to ask a favor and I got voted in to be an errand boy."

Rain was running in rivulets down the window, scattering the light from outside in strange patterns across Henry's face as he contemplated. Grayson knew better than to push. When Henry was ready to speak, he would. Eventually, he said, "If she wanted a favor, she should have sent Becka."

Grayson wasn't offended and lifted his coffee cup in mock salute. "I tried to tell them." No fewer than ten times, in fact, but who was counting?

"Why didn't she?" Henry was calculating, green eyes shrewd as he tried to figure out what lurked beneath the surface. "Send Becka, I mean?"

"Well, it's about Payton." Grayson got no further into the explanation than that before Henry's attitude softened quite a bit. The furrowed brow and bracketed mouth disappeared, replaced by a more youthful looking enthusiasm.

"Oh? Well, then she definitely should have sent Becka. What the hell does Payton have to do with you?"

"She wants a job—"

"Done." Henry leaned back in his chair and shook his head. "That's barely a favor. I could use the extra hands anyway."

"*And*," Grayson emphasized, trying not to get off the subject despite being incredibly tempted to pry more into how his childhood best friend became a surrogate father, "we wanted to make sure you understood the special circumstances involved before you agreed."

"Special circumstances?" That dimmed a few of the stars in his eyes. "What special circumstances? Is she on the run from the law?"

"Not quite." Henry's guess was closer than Grayson would have anticipated and he shrugged when Henry's brow shot up in surprise. "On the run from an ex-boyfriend. Real abusive piece of shit, from what I understand."

"That's hardly what I'd consider—"

"She's pregnant." Grayson dropped the bomb, flatly cutting Henry off before he could say anything else. "Which means she's going to need maternity leave in a few months and she's not really looking for anything, romantically speaking, right now."

Henry blinked at him twice, looking exactly like what Grayson imagined robots would look like in the future when they were uploading new data. He could practically see the spinning circle on Henry's forehead.

Update in progress.

"Oh."

"Yeah." Grayson downed the rest of his coffee, wished immediately that he hadn't, and pushed the empty cup across the table. "So, that's it. That's why they sent me. I guess Becka figured it would be easier if this was a man-to-man sort of conversation."

Henry shook it off, regaining his composure with a self-depreciating grin. "Well, it's certainly not the most embarrassing conversation we've ever had, is it?"

Grayson snorted. He'd spent years trying to push that memory to the back of his mind. "At least this time you're the one in the hot seat."

"Oh, come on, it wasn't that bad." Henry threw a paper napkin at him and some of the empty years between them fell away. "It's not like it ruined our friendship or anything."

It had been a close call. Henry had handled it well enough,

that first precarious year of high school, but finding out his best friend was in love with him, and being a straight guy in a small town, had been a lot for him to deal with.

He could easily have dropped Grayson like a hot potato, decided it wasn't worth the risk to his spotless reputation. Grayson would have understood that, especially knowing what he did about Henry's relationship with his parents. Their love had been conditional, entirely dependent on Henry's successes and how well respected he was as their son.

Instead, Henry had weathered the worst of Grayson's broken heart with compassion and ruthlessly put down any rumors that might have caused him a hard time.

They sat in companionable silence for a while, listening to the rain hit the glass, until Henry couldn't take it anymore. "Why'd you leave, man? You didn't say shit to anybody. No forwarding address. Changed your phone number. It's like you didn't even want me to find you."

"I didn't." Grayson met Henry's shocked look without flinching. "I didn't want *anybody* to find me."

"What happened?" Henry was unmovable, and Grayson knew there was no way through without a full explanation. After all these years of wondering, of living with the loss and the unanswered questions, there could be no return to any kind of friendship without filling in the gaps.

"George happened." Grayson shook his head before Henry could interrupt. "I know, he was always doing something fucking awful, but it was worse that time. He, uh, well..."

Henry waited him out, letting him compose his thoughts without pressing him to hurry up and spit it out, though it sure looked like he wanted to.

"He figured it out. That I had feelings for you, you know?" Grayson couldn't resist the urge to fidget, tapping his fingers on the table and the edges of his coffee cup while avoiding Henry's gaze. "I don't know how, maybe he was just making wild accusations because we were always hanging out together. Maybe he just said it to be an ass, and I denied it a little too hard or something..."

The only sound for a moment was the drip of fresh coffee from across the store and Grayson's shuddering sigh.

"He was always doing that kind of shit, you remember? He did the same thing with Grandma Edith, always accusing her of cheating on him. Anyway, whatever it was, when he figured out it was true, he lost it. He'd beat me plenty, but never like that. I thought he was gonna kill me."

"It was because of me?" Henry looked stricken, his face pale. "It's not like, I mean, we never ... It was just feelings. It's not like we ever did anything." He'd never made Grayson feel guilty for his feelings, but Henry had never reciprocated them, either. It was clear he didn't understand George's over-the-top reaction to such a one-sided crush, but then Henry had never been able to understand George about anything.

There was too much heart in Henry and too much hate in George.

"I tried to tell him you were straight, that nothing would ever come of it." Grayson could still hear the way his teeth had cracked together after the punch that had followed. "It wasn't about that, though, not for him. He was afraid someone else would find out, that I'd be an embarrassment to the family."

"He was always an ass." Henry said it with such feeling that even Grayson had to laugh. It had never been a secret that Henry hated that old man and in all the years they'd been friends, he'd rarely ever set foot in Barlow House.

"I had to get out." Grayson steered the conversation back to the topic at hand. As much fun as Henry had dunking on George, Grayson needed him to understand that he hadn't stopped being his friend all those years ago because he stopped caring about him. "I wanted to tell you, but I had just had all of this place I could take. I needed a fresh start and a clean slate."

Most of it had been George and some of it had been needing space to get over the last of his feelings for Henry, but in the end that last fight with George had been the straw that broke the camel's back. He'd shoved a bunch of his shit in a bag and climbed out of his bedroom window before the blood finished drying on his chin.

Henry sat for a few minutes, his fingers drumming a steady beat on the tabletop. He seemed to be taking it all in, letting Grayson's explanations fill in the gaps for him. "Yeah," he said after a while. "I guess I can see that."

That was as close to forgiveness as Grayson was likely to get and he nodded, drained of everything except a profound feeling of relief. Maybe they'd never be close again, but at least there wouldn't be any lingering hostility or bad blood between them. Grayson had long since gotten over any romantic feelings he'd once carried, but he didn't want those memories shadowed with animosity or misunderstandings.

"So..." Having apparently decided they'd talked enough about the past, Henry moved on to the next subject without even pretending it was connected to the first. "You and Becka, huh?"

Chapter Fifteen

Grayson

The women of Barlow House were in the kitchen when Grayson came home. He could hear them all the way from the front hall, the sound of bright chatter interspersed with peals of laughter echoed through the rooms and the hallways.

It was the sound of harmony and home, something Barlow House had rarely ever been host to, and he was reminded starkly of the conversation he'd had with the sheriff that afternoon. How could anyone think he'd prefer to be back in town, sitting at a crowded bar with a bunch of men and their stale cigarette smells and spilled beers, than in a comfortable home, all decorated for the holiday and full of festive cheer?

How much did they hate the women they had at home to think that was a logical choice to make nearly every day? Sure, Grayson understood the occasional need to hang out with a friend—he'd been reminded how enjoyable that could be once he'd gotten over the initial awkwardness with Henry at The Bakery—but the way Sheriff Levine talked about it was particularly gross.

Do you find the presence of women in your house intolerable? Come get drunk with a bunch of dudes instead! What a way to think about people that you were supposed to love. Mothers. Daughters. Wives. It turned his stomach, and Grayson was apparently not the only one that had noticed the man's attitude toward women or the way he talked about them.

The rest of his conversation with Henry had been eye opening to say the least.

Grayson's shoes squelched on the tile until he pushed them off and tossed them to dry on the rack beside the coat stand. Every inch of him was drenched and cold. He'd been lucky enough to avoid the rain on his way to The Bakery, but not so lucky on the return trip to the car.

Instead of heading to the kitchen, he climbed the stairs to his bedroom, leaving wet footprints and newly formed puddles in his wake. He'd only been half serious earlier about the possibility of catching pneumonia, but now he was afraid he might have jinxed himself.

He'd spent too long away from this part of the world, forgetting how cold and wet the weather was and how long the rain lasted. The time away had made him thin skinned and his current wardrobe wasn't up to the task of keeping him dry in these conditions. He'd been trying to make do with what he had, but with months left to go, he was going to be forced to admit defeat. At some point soon, he'd need to waterproof himself as well as possible for the rest of the season.

It wasn't like he'd been lounging around in warm southern states all these years—though he had made a few stops in those places and soaked up the sun before the summers became too brutal to tolerate—but the Pacific Northwest brought a new meaning to the word *damp*.

Maybe he could convince Becka to make a day trip with him. They could do some shopping in the nearest decently sized town, pick up the supplies he needed and a few neat surprises for Payton. Maybe a bassinet for the baby or the fancy stroller/car seat combo they all knew she'd been eyeing online.

He frowned as he pulled a dry shirt over his head, because as much as he wanted Becka to go with him, to use the excuse of the trip to finally break through the barrier she'd put up between them, she was extremely stubborn. She'd probably insist on ordering the baby stuff to be delivered to the house just so she could avoid being stuck in the car with him. God forbid she be forced to share a meal with him or something.

The thought of a meal made his stomach rumble, and he headed back downstairs to hunt through the kitchen looking for a late lunch. Now that he was warm—he'd rummaged through his stuff to find his only long-sleeved T-shirt, an old pair of gray sweatpants, and his thickest socks—his body was reminding him exactly how long it had been since he'd eaten breakfast.

The room went quiet when he walked in and he waved a hand at the group seated at the table. "Don't mind me! I'm not here to eavesdrop on ladies' time. I'm just hungry." He had his head buried in a cabinet before he even finished talking, looking for a snack to hold him over while he cooked a meal.

"It's not *ladies' time*." Edith's words were muffled by the cabinet around his head, but she seemed to be laughing at him. "We were just the only ones here. You can join us if you want, once you find something to eat."

There was already an open bag of chips in his hands, but he was still digging through cabinets and searching shelves of the refrigerator. He hoped the sound he made could be considered an agreement, but it was garbled around a mouthful of half chewed nacho flavored tortilla chip.

He started pulling out the stuff he needed to make a sandwich—nothing wrong with a quick classic when in a rush—as the rest of them turned back to their conversation.

"You haven't given any thought at all to names?"

Payton made a low humming sound, and Grayson glanced over his shoulder at the table, undeniably curious. It had always seemed like such a weighty decision to him, having to pick a name for another person, something most people kept for a lifetime, while knowing nothing about them. He'd always thought it would make more sense to let the kid pick their more permanent name once they got closer to adulthood—hell he was pretty sure some cultures did exactly that—but until that caught on, parents were dealing with one hell of a burden.

"Jared always said he'd want to name a kid after him if it was a boy but—"

"No." Becka cut her off, and Grayson's attention shifted to her when she spoke. She looked away quickly when their eyes met, her cheeks pink as she turned to Payton with a frown. If he hadn't known better, he would have sworn he'd caught Becka looking at him several times since he'd come in, but she hadn't acknowledged him once. "I think we can do better than that, don't you?"

"You mean you don't think I should name the baby after his father?" Payton's tone was sarcastic, but Becka didn't rise to the bait. She had already looked away, distracted again.

Payton waved a hand in front of Becka's face, trying to regain her attention, and Grayson realized she was looking at him again, but not at his face. He glanced down, sure he'd find out he'd spilled something on the front of his clothes, but there was nothing there. Just his black T-shirt and gray cotton sweatpants.

But Becka's face was still pink and she was still looking at him every few seconds as the conversation behind him plowed along, various names being discussed and discarded for one reason or another. It didn't make any sense to him. Maybe she'd come down with something and was running a fever. He'd have to ask Edith to keep a closer eye on her for a few days.

Grayson put the sandwich he'd made onto a plate and took a seat next to Becka at the table, relieved some of the flush on her cheeks seemed to fade once he'd sat down. Good, it wasn't like he didn't have enough to worry about when it came to her.

He wasn't sure how much Becka knew about Widow's Point and its occupants, but the conversation he'd had with Henry at The Bakery was still fresh in his mind. Henry had playfully mentioned Becka, having clearly picked up on some of the tension between them, but then the conversation had turned to Grayson's run in that afternoon with Sheriff Levine ...

The teasing look on Henry's face had faded away almost instantly.

"I know the sheriff was a friend of George's and he fully believes that means he's gonna be friends with you, too, but if you're willing to take a bit of advice from me—"

"Who else would I take advice from?" Grayson was joking, trying to lighten the mood, but Henry had been deadly serious.

"I mean it." He leaned forward in his seat, gaze keen. "Not just about not being friends with him, about staying away from him in general. We were pretty young when you left, not always let in on the adult gossip, especially being who we were.

You were George's grandson and I was the town's star athlete, so we were some of his favorites, you know?"

Grayson shook his head, perplexed. "I really don't know."

"He was nice to us." Henry laid it down in its ugliest, roughest truth. "In a way he wasn't nice to people he considered less deserving. He's been tossing his power around on people in this town for as long as anyone can remember. Anyone he thinks of as weak, undesirable, or an outcast gets bullied with the full weight of his badge, and the women have it even worse."

Grayson didn't have to ask what 'even worse' meant, so he focused on the rest of Henry's explanation. "Does he, uh ... Is Elliot safe?"

"They're fine." Henry crossed his arms, the bulge at the bicep even more prominent now than when they were teenagers. "Levine doesn't mess with me or what's mine."

A wise decision if Grayson had ever heard of one. Not only did Henry have just as many generations of family born and raised in this town as the sheriff did, he was also younger, bigger, and more intimidating. Pissing Henry off wasn't a smart move, even for someone as influential as an elected government official.

"But you need to keep a close watch on your house," Henry continued, "and on everyone in it."

"My house?" Grayson echoed. "Why?"

"He's been paying too much attention to Edith and Becka since George died." That explanation didn't make much sense to Grayson, but Henry was more than willing to fill in the gaps. "He seems to think something fishy happened the night George died, at least that's what he keeps hinting at to everyone who'll listen. I don't think he actually believes it, to be clear, but he wants people to think he does."

"Okay?"

"He's been sniffing around Becka's heels since she moved

to town, but she was out of reach because of George. Now that George is gone ..." Henry sighed, and Grayson knew he wasn't going to like whatever he said next. "If he can put a little pressure on them, maybe get Edith and Becka to believe he's trying to implicate one or both of them in George's death, he's got pretty significant leverage."

"You think he wants to blackmail her into sleeping with him." It wasn't a question, not when he could see so clearly how it fit with the sheriff's personality and his behavior since Grayson had moved back, but Henry nodded anyway.

"Exactly, and if you believe the rumors, it's not the first time he's done something like this."

Grayson believed them, all right, and now he figured it was his job to make sure that the bastard kept his hands off Becka. And not *just* Becka, if he was being honest. He was a Barlow. This was practically his town. George may have taken that as some sort of sick permission to do whatever he wanted to whomever he pleased, but Grayson had learned better than that from Edith. He had a responsibility, not just to the house and his grandmother, but the town and its people.

He hadn't fully decided whether he wanted to stay, but he wasn't going anywhere until he'd pulled Sheriff Levine off his pedestal and made him pay for what he'd done.

Fighting back was out of character for him, but he figured it must be contagious. Too much time spent around Becka, with her ready fists and eager tongue. She was barely standing over five feet tall and looked like a good wind might carry her away at any moment. If she could stand her ground over every tiny little inconvenience, both real and imagined, surely he could dredge up the courage to do it when it counted most.

"What do you think, Grayson?"

"Hmm?" He realized he'd stopped listening to the conversation and now all three women were looking at him expectantly. Apparently, someone had asked him a question and he had no idea what was going on. "I, uh—"

"Baby names," Becka supplied, snapping her fingers to indicate he should hurry up. "Classic or unique? Classic is better, right? It's safer! Everyone knows a kid is gonna get picked on more for having a name like Turpentine Blackberry than if you go with something more standard. Sure, the Bobs and Deborahs of the world aren't exactly memorable, but it's better than the alternative."

"Is it?" Grayson was trying to imagine what life would have been like if his parents had named him Bob and found the idea ... unpleasant.

"Give me one downside to having a perfectly normal classic name." Becka crossed her arms, combative as usual. "You can't because there isn't one."

"You share a name with countless other people," Grayson argued. "At least some of whom are probably detestable. Think of the person you hate the most and imagine sharing a name with them."

"How often do you think that happens?" Becka tossed her hands up, obviously exasperated by his refusal to see things her way.

"Give me a name, then." He would not be intimidated by her, and besides, the more he got her all worked up, the more attractive the flush of adrenaline was on that pretty face of hers.

"Abigail."

Payton and Edith watched in amused fascination as Becka shot back the challenge, both sets of eyes moving from her to Grayson as they waited for his response.

"First grade recess and she threw dirt in my face." He thought her name was Abigail. Maybe it was Amanda? Not that it really mattered. He smiled, enjoyed the way Becka's teeth clenched. "Next."

"Andrew."

He pretended to give it some thought. "I waited tables with a guy named Andrew. He was a complete sleaze to the women who came into the restaurant and he stole tips."

"Evelyn."

"High school math teacher." This one was actually true, and his revulsion was real. "Enough said."

"Patrick."

"Sheriff Levine."

"Oh." She sat back in her seat, the light of combat fading from her eyes. He didn't miss the subtle glance she flicked at Edith, either. "I didn't realize. I guess most people don't call him by his first name."

"Do you have something against him?" Edith was looking at him intently. "He was friends with your grandfather, after all."

The air in the kitchen was suddenly stifling as she waited for his answer, and Grayson tried to decide how much to reveal to them. All he had to go on was Henry's word, and even if it was true, would telling them about it cause them unnecessary stress?

Just because Edith had started to settle into a life without George didn't mean she was fully ready to cast aside everything that had been part of their lives together. What if she didn't know what Sheriff Levine was really like and still harbored some fondness for him? If he'd kept it hidden from Grayson back then, had he also managed to hide it from her? Let her believe George had deceived him, as he had deceived so many others?

"Nothing personal." Grayson thought Edith looked a bit relieved and felt he'd made the right decision. "It's just that a lot of people dislike the police on principle. Like math teachers or lawyers or cafeteria lunch ladies." Painting with that broad of a brush wasn't exactly fair, but it covered up for his slip of the tongue.

Payton seemed to be the only one that had been oblivious to the tension of the moment before, and she shrugged. "Seems like no one pays much attention to his first name, but I agree with Grayson, anyway. Isn't it more fun to have a name that's special?"

"I don't think so." Becka was pouting, her lower lip pushed out in a way Grayson had never seen before. She really hated losing.

"Then you can name your own kid something boring." Payton didn't seem concerned about Becka's pouting face. Apparently, it wasn't her first time encountering this particular side of her sister. "Go really wild with it and give us an Agatha or a Richard. We promise not to call him Dick... at least not to his face."

Everyone laughed except Becka.

"I'm not having kids."

There was not a trace of humor to be found on her face, and Grayson would know, because he searched for it. The pout of the previous moment was gone, and in its place was the resolute expression he knew so well. The one she wore when she'd dug in her heels and would not be moved by any force this side of heaven.

"Why?" Payton was staring at her sister like she'd never seen her before, her expression perplexed.

"You think everyone has to have them?"

Payton's mouth snapped shut at Becka's sullen tone. "Of course not. It's just ... " She looked to Edith for help, an uncertainty in her expression that she rarely had when it came to Becka.

"You seemed so excited about Payton's baby." Edith tried for tact, wading in to mediate the unexpected situation. "I think perhaps we just didn't know you felt so strongly about not having any of your own."

Becka, arms already crossed, lifted her shoulders closer to her ears, drawing her body protectively around herself. "Payton is different. She came out of our parents' house wanting everything they hadn't given us. Home. Belonging. Family. The whole thing."

"And you?" Grayson couldn't help it. No one had told him exactly what Becka and her sister had gone through as kids, but he wanted to know how she'd handled it, how it had affected her. Why had the two of them come from the same situation and yet become so different from one another. "You didn't want the same thing?"

Becka hesitated and Payton stepped in to fill the void. "Becka's priorities have always been a bit ... different from mine."

"In what way?"

"She burned it down."

"What?" Grayson was sure he'd heard incorrectly but no one disputed it, not even Becka herself. What the hell was Payton talking about?

"She burned down the weird church my parents went to," Payton explained. "And stole their car." She let that information settle for a moment—Grayson noticed he was the only one surprised by this so apparently Edith had already known—and then twisted her lips into a wry smile. "Becka's not exactly the sentimental family type."

"Oh, bullshit." Now Becka did react, dropping her arms and leaning forward to put her elbows on her knees. "I've got nothing against the idea of family. You're here, aren't you? You and the little next generation nugget you're carrying? Not to mention the rest of the people in this house. You can't tell me you don't think of this as some kind of family."

Payton had no answer to that, and Grayson shared a look

with Edith. It did seem like they were forming a strange, slightly broken family unit but Becka was the first one to say it out loud.

"I'm just saying, after everything I've been through, maybe I shouldn't be a mom. Maybe I don't want to be, which really seems even more important. I don't have to take the risk of passing along all my fucking problems to some innocent kid that doesn't deserve it."

Grayson found himself nodding in agreement. Wasn't that part of the reason he'd never let himself get close to anyone in all these years? All he knew was how to survive in a messed-up household. He had no practical, healthy skills, for parenting or otherwise.

Surprisingly, though Payton and Edith both looked like they had objections to her logic, Becka stabbed an aggressive finger at him when she noticed him on the verge of agreeing with her. "Not you."

"What?"

"I see you over there." She gestured to where he was sitting as though that might clear up his confusion. "You don't agree with me because, unlike me, you have a good reason to have kids. You have Barlow House and Edith."

"What does that have to do with anything?" He looked around the table, but everyone looked as confused as he felt. They were no help at all.

"You have a legacy!" Becka stabbed the finger at him again. "You have something for new generations to inherit. And don't you think Edith deserves great grandkids?"

He'd been prepared to argue the first point—the house was hardly a reason to have kids he wasn't sure he wanted— but he was brought up short when she mentioned Edith. He'd taken so much from her. Did she deserve to see him with kids of his own? A new generation to keep the Barlow name going? He'd never considered it before.

Edith jumped in, "Now, that's not fair to Grayson. He doesn't owe me anything," but Grayson had stopped listening. He could very clearly recall the moment in the library when he'd realized she'd practically adopted the whole town after he'd run away. He'd left a void in her life, years of emptiness and isolation. He'd been afraid and he'd let George run him out. Grayson had been missing his own lost years, but he wasn't the only one that had suffered.

Didn't he owe her whatever he could do to make amends?

Chapter Sixteen

Becka

Rain pattered against the windows, and the darkening sky beyond had been gray all day. Becka had never been particularly fond of rain, but she'd learned to deal with it since coming to live with Edith. She basked in the sun as often as possible, and when it wasn't shining, she'd learned to find her joy in other places.

A wet hike through a green and rain-drenched forest. A wind-swept walk along the beach in her favorite waterproof jacket and colorful, polka dotted rain boots. A warm blanket and a cup of coffee as she read a favorite book in the library.

Since George had died and the library had become more of a shared space than his private domain, she'd even added some candles. The kind that smelled like vanilla or warm oatmeal cookies. It added a bit of a cozy vibe that she'd appreciated more and more as the cold set in and the days grew wetter, grayer, and shorter.

She grabbed a cookie—Grayson's gift from the bakery the last time he'd gone to town—and snuggled down deeper into her blanket. The storm wasn't going to distract her from finishing the book in her hand. It was a gripping thriller, blood soaked and fast paced, and she was on the last chapter. As long as she had enough light to see the words on the page, everything else could wait.

It wasn't just that she wanted to find out the answer to the mystery—she was pretty sure she'd figured out the murderer early on—she also needed the distraction. Something to keep her mind busy and off the way Grayson had looked walking around the kitchen in a pair of gray sweatpants.

It had been borderline indecent and if it hadn't been for the perplexed looks he kept sending her when he'd caught her staring, she would've easily believed he'd done it on purpose. After she'd given him the cold shoulder for so long, determined not to fall into the temptation of him after that kiss he'd stolen, he'd been getting desperate. If he'd known the power those pants held, he probably would have been wearing them every day and then she'd really be in trouble.

Ever since that night in the library, he was always looking at her like he wanted to bury himself in her body, get lost in the taste of her, fuse himself with her soul and never be forced to walk the earth alone again for the rest of his life. It was as arousing as it was unsettling and it was her own determination that was keeping them both on the path of sanity.

She was the only one capable of logical thought, and she was clinging to it by a fraying thread. Each time she was forced to be in his presence she could feel it wearing thinner. Her only defense was unreasonable animosity to keep him at a distance and the knowledge that letting go of that would be a disaster for both of them.

Every time she wavered, something happened to remind her why she had to stand firm.

Sure, she'd been contemplating sneaking into Grayson's room after lunch that day and peeling those sweats off with her teeth, but then the whole table had erupted into chaos when she'd said she didn't want kids. She'd seen the way he'd looked at her, the lines that had formed into creases on his forehead as he'd tried to process it, just as she'd noticed Edith's sudden stillness.

If they were a family, and Becka believed that they were, then how could they not take Edith's feelings into consideration? They both loved that old woman and they both owed her as much as they could give of the happiness to be found in the world.

Becka knew if she slept with Grayson and feelings got involved, that might be even worse than things between them ending badly and him leaving because of her. There simply was no way for them to do anything but avoid each other, because all other roads led to someone getting hurt.

Becka would not be responsible for that. She would not be the reason Edith lost her grandson again or the reason he didn't have babies for her dote over.

She had to hold the line.

Not interested.

Damn it.

Two more cookies disappeared in quick succession, lost to her angry chewing as she reread the same page again for the third time. It looked like she'd been wrong about the murderer in the book, which added another annoyance to a rapidly growing pile.

Under her feet, Ruffles stopped snoring and jumped up. In a flash, she was out the door and down the hall, but Becka didn't pay much attention to her. Grayson had gone to the store for Edith, and he wasn't back yet. More than likely, Ruffles had heard his car pulling up the driveway.

She didn't think anything else about it until she heard faint shouts from outside. It was hard to be sure over all the wind and the rain, but it sounded like Grayson.

Becka was up and at the window faster than she'd ever moved in her life, the book discarded on the floor and her face pressed to the glass. She could barely see in the dark—just a long curve of beach and churning sea—but the second shout was much clearer.

It was definitely Grayson.

Fear and adrenaline had her down the stairs in record time and she threw the back door open still barefoot and wearing nothing but a thin sleep shirt and cotton pajama pants. She was soaked to the bone and freezing before she'd even left the back porch. By the time she'd made it down the long stairs to the beach, her toes were numb and her teeth were chattering.

Gusting wind whipped her hair around her face, stinging where it lashed against her cheeks, and stole her voice as she cried out for him. She knew he was here, but she couldn't hear him over the storm and couldn't see him in the dark, rain swept night. If she'd been thinking properly, she would have shoes and a flashlight, but she was too afraid to turn back and get them.

What if the added time was too much and he was lost to her completely? Was she going to find him dead on the same beach as his grandfather? Or would he get washed out to sea, never to be seen again?

She stumbled forward, feet in agony as she tripped blindly over rocks and driftwood, and screamed Grayson's name. From the dark, something bolted in her direction, a shadow that launched itself at her ankles before she could react.

This time, her scream was one of terror.

A familiar body jumped at her knees, paws scrambling as it tried to climb into her arms. All the fight drained out of her as she bent down and scooped Ruffles into her embrace. Her heart had pounded nearly all the way out of her chest and she couldn't hold back her panicked laughter.

"How the hell did you get out here?" She rubbed Ruffles'

fur and tried to cover her as well as she could with her T-shirt. "Have you seen him? Where is he?"

She barely finished asking the question, desperately scanning the beach for signs of movement, when Grayson, too, ran out of the darkness and skidded to a stop a few feet in front of her. His hair was soaked and rain ran off him in rivulets, but at least he was wearing a jacket and shoes.

The worry on his face deepened to confusion and then anger as he looked her over, taking in her soaked pajamas and ending on her bare feet.

He didn't ask a single question or waste his breath scolding her for her foolishness. Before she had time to even guess at his intentions, he had stomped over and swept her up in his arms, bridal style. She carried Ruffles and he carried her as the three of them made their way back up the winding wooden staircase to the back door. Only then did he look down at her, standing in the dimly lit kitchen hesitating like he couldn't decide where to go with her next.

The options were limited, but when he turned toward the stairs and their bedrooms, Becka started fighting to be put down. If he took her there, the next step would be trying to peel her out of her clothes and she couldn't let that happen.

"Here is fine!" She wiggled until he set her down, still clutching the shivering dog to her chest. "We just need some towels."

A muscle in his jaw worked, but he didn't argue, and a moment later he disappeared in the direction of the laundry room. He knew where they kept the extra towels, so he wouldn't be gone for long, and Becka knew she had preciously few moments to compose herself.

She wiped at the water on her face with her free hand, but without putting the dog down there was nothing she could do about her tangled hair or the puddle that was forming rapidly under her feet. The house was much warmer than outside but they were both still shaking, Becka's teeth still clacking so hard it hurt her head, and she felt nothing but relief when he came back.

His face was set, and his movements were rough, but the towels he'd brought were warm from the dryer and Ruffles sighed and snuggled in as soon as Becka wrapped her up.

"Thank you."

"Don't." He was practically vibrating, as he wrapped the second towel around Becka, but his voice was soft. "Get changed, get dry. Then we'll talk about it."

She didn't have to be told twice.

A quick shower at the hottest setting and a fresh pair of pajamas brought the color back to her skin and the feeling back to her toes, but she still limped down the stairs a little while later. It was a good thing he'd carried her earlier, her feet were scraped up and sore after her little run on the beach. She tried to pretend it was fine when she got back to the kitchen, but Grayson narrowed his eyes at her and she knew he'd seen it.

He'd taken the time during her shower to take off his jacket and shoes, towel dry his own hair, and he looked warmer and more relaxed as he slid a freshly brewed cup of coffee across the table to land in front of her. At least she thought he was more relaxed, until he sat in the chair across from her and crossed his arms. "Explain."

The coffee cup was hot, and she busied herself wrapping her fingers around it just so, trying to keep her body warm and delay answering him at the same time. "Explain what?"

"Becka, if you don't tell me what you were doing on that beach with no jacket and no shoes in the middle of a rainstorm, I swear to God—"

"It was your fault!" The look on his face had her scrambling. "I heard you outside, screaming, so of course I came out to find you. What else was I supposed to do?"

"Ruffles got out." He said it slowly, like he was talking to a particularly difficult to deal with child. "I went out to find her."

"Well ..." It was a perfectly logical explanation and certainly one she should have at least considered before jumping straight to serial killers or bear mauling. "How was I supposed to know that?"

His eyebrow twitched and she had a sudden perverse urge to laugh. She swallowed it down before it could escape, sure that would be the thing that pushed him over the edge he was obviously clinging to.

They settled into a strained silence, both of them drinking their coffee and trying not to meet each other's eyes. She really ought to leave, finish her drink and disappear back upstairs before she could spend any time at all thinking about what it had been like being carried back to the house with his arms around her and her head nestled against his shoulder.

"So ..." He coughed a little to cover the awkwardness and glanced at her out the corner of his eye. This was the longest she'd been in a room alone with him since the library and he didn't seem to know what to say to her. "Becka, huh? Is that short for Rebecca or ... uh ..."

She snorted and lifted her cup to her lips. Poor man had absolutely no game at all and he was lucky he was so damn cute. There was still water stuck to his eyelashes and she wanted to wipe it away with her thumb, but she was afraid to touch him.

"Nope, just plain old Becka." Everyone had always assumed it was a nickname but Rebecca was too long and stuffy for her parents' tastes. "I've been a disappointment my whole life."

"Why?"

She glanced at the clock on the wall. Only ten o'clock. Still well within the respectable time for two adults to sit at the table in their own kitchen and have a perfectly normal, not at all sexually charged conversation. "Well, I guess everyone always thinks it's a nickname and they look at me funny when they find out it isn't."

"Do you ever wish your parents had given you the longer name instead?"

She chuckled and tightened her grip on her cup. "I wish a lot of things about my parents, but I guess if I ever thought about it, that one would be pretty far down the list."

He looked a bit lost at that, like he'd forgotten for a second that he wasn't the only one with a fucked-up childhood.

"Besides, I like classic names, but maybe not famous ones."

"Famous?" Relief and curiosity played out across his features as he leaned forward, eager to get her talking and make this chat less strained. It brought his lips that much closer to her, and Becka leaned back an equal amount.

"You know?" She waved her hand in a circular motion, watched his eyes for signs of recognition. "The book? Rebecca?"

"I think it's a movie, too."

"Hmm." She nodded. "More than one, but the new one is trash. Anyway, like you said, who wants their name associated with something outside of their control like that?"

"It must be a pretty good book, though, right?"

She pursed her lips and looked at him with one eyebrow raised. "Sure, but Rebecca's not the main character, is she? And I don't like those Gothic stories, anyway."

He seemed surprised. "Somehow I figured you would. Aren't they kind of dark, a bit creepy? That sounds like the kind of thing you'd enjoy."

Becka's grimace was exaggerated enough to make him laugh. "With all those heroines fleeing perfectly good old houses in the middle of the night? In flowing nightgowns? Please, you know me better than that."

"Perfectly good but *haunted* houses."

"Most of them aren't even actually haunted!" Her palm struck the table hard enough to rattle the coffee cups. "It's always the memory of some former wife or a housekeeper with a grudge."

"So what would you do instead?"

She knew he was laughing at her, but she played along anyway. "You can always fist fight a housekeeper. That lady was old enough to be her mom and you're telling me one good punch wouldn't have sent her packing?" She made a rude *pffttt* sound and waggled her fingers dismissively. "And as for the memories... I'm stronger than the bad dreams in any house. I don't run away."

He tipped his coffee cup at her, in acknowledgment of her point. "Didn't Payton say you burned down the church your parents went to? Want to explain that?"

Becka gripped her necklace, wishing Payton had kept her mouth shut about certain things that she didn't want everyone to know about. She wasn't ashamed of it, but she knew other people weren't likely to understand that particular decision.

"There was nobody in it! It was just a broken-down building they used as a front for whatever weird grifter shit they were up to that week." She sniffed and looked away, picked at a piece of skin on her thumb. "Besides, that was about sending a message."

That set him off again, and soon he was laughing so hard he was clutching his side and struggling to catch his breath. "I'm sure it sent a message, all right."

"It's not that funny."

"You should have seen your face when you said it." He wiped actual tears from his face and jumped to his feet when she pushed her chair away from the table and tried to stand . "Okay, okay! I'm sorry. I won't laugh at you anymore."

He had a firm grip on her arm, and a hard tug wasn't

enough to get him to let go. She faced him, brows knit and harsh words already forming on her tongue and found herself entirely too close to him again.

This time there was no shivering dog in her arms, no drunken blunder to ruin the mood, no well-meaning grandma to walk in at just the right time. There was just her and him and not enough space between them.

Time stopped and then stretched, both of them frozen in that breathless second as they each waited to see what the other would do next. She wanted to step back, to pull herself back to sanity, but before she could move, it was already too late.

He'd been reckless before, but polite. This time, almost to make up for it, he wasted no time on niceties. His hands were cupped under her thighs, lifting and separating until he had hoisted her up and pressed her against him. Her legs had nowhere to go but around his waist, and before she could do anything more than wrap her arms around his shoulders and hold on, he'd already caught her bottom lip between his teeth. He nipped just to the point of pain, tugged her mouth open, and plundered with a silken tongue.

All her good intentions went up in flames.

She clung to him, fingers tangled in his hair, as every fantasy she'd ever had about kissing him got blown out of the water by the sheer overwhelming reality of it. His mouth was hot and greedy, consuming her as his hands kneaded the flesh of her thighs.

There was no excuse for it, and she knew she'd regret it later, but when she rocked her hips and rubbed her core against him, felt the hardness waiting for her and heard the way he moaned in response, the consequences seemed far away and insignificant.

Maybe she could have a taste of it, just a little. Just enough to satisfy her curiosity without crossing the line too much.

She didn't realize he was moving until her back collided with the front of the refrigerator, glass bottles inside knocking together as he used the hard surface to help hold her up. One hand now free to wander over the rest of her body, he wasted no time pushing up the loose shirt she was wearing. Long fingers skimmed over her stomach and found her breast as she arched into him.

He found her nipple as she finally tore her mouth away from his and sank her teeth into his shoulder, stifling the words she wanted to say by taking it out on his body. If she asked him to carry her up the next flight of stairs, there would be no coming back.

There were limits to what he could take from her in this kitchen, but if he got her behind closed doors...

God, she wanted him behind closed doors.

He abandoned her nipple to cup her breast, squeezing in rhythm with the motion of his hips as he dry humped her against his grandma's refrigerator like a man possessed.

"I want you," he rasped, the words hitting her straight in the gut with a punch of desire. "Becka, please, let me ..."

Maybe there *wasn't* a limit to what she'd let him do to her here. There should be—rationality and a fully developed sense of shame should have created a limit—but she was reaching for the waistband of his jeans before she'd fully decided to abandon decency.

The creak of a floorboard down the hall hit them both like a bucket of cold water.

"Someone's coming."

She didn't need him to tell her that, but she was grateful for his quick reflexes. He'd practically tossed her halfway across the kitchen and was already standing with his back to the room, one cabinet open like he was languidly looking for a late-night snack.

Becka slid into a seat at the table, grabbed the nearest

coffee cup and hoped whoever came in didn't notice how swollen her lips were or the tangled furrows he'd left behind in her hair.

She'd lied to herself as long as she could. Living in this house with him was dangerous, no matter how cautious she was. No amount of self-control was enough to defend against a passion like that.

Not interested, my ass.

Chapter Seventeen

Grayson

Payton's arrival the night before had been the worst thing that had ever happened to Grayson. Tired and hungry, she'd barely paid attention to them as he tried to pretend his dick wasn't hard enough to cut diamonds.

He'd experienced plenty of hardship in his life, but nothing had upset him more than watching Becka dart out of the kitchen as fast as she could without rousing suspicion, knowing damn well she'd been seconds away from letting him fuck her against the front of a refrigerator in full view of God, his grandma, and anyone else who happened to wander by.

Sure, Payton had saved them from committing a mistake they likely would never have recovered from, but at what fucking cost?

He shoved a bite of bagel into his mouth and tried not to glare at the back of Payton's head as she rummaged in the cabinets looking for her own breakfast. It had been bad enough being forced to return to the scene of the crime and finding her here instead of her sister had only added insult to injury.

Where the hell was Becka?

He just had to sit here, staring at that refrigerator and thinking about how good she tasted, all by himself? She didn't even have the decency to come down and sit beside him and suffer in equal parts? That was unfair and he was not going to take it lying down. If he was going to come out and face the rest of the household and pretend to be unbothered, then damn it, so was she.

He was about to abandon his shitty bagel to climb the stairs to find her and drag her down to breakfast, when Payton plopped down beside him.

"Bad morning?"

"What?"

She'd curled into her chair, wrapped in an oversized sweater and holding a cup of steaming tea. "You look ... cranky." She used a finger to draw a circle in the air in front of his face, and he realized he was scowling as he stared at her.

"I'm fine." Realizing he was scowling only made the scowl deeper, but he would not acknowledge it.

"Sure, sure." He caught a glimpse of a smile before she hid her mouth behind her teacup, but all hell broke loose before he could ask her what that was all about.

Ruffles jumped up and started barking as a firm knock sounded on the front door. They weren't expecting company, and Grayson waved to Payton, indicating for her not to get up as he went to answer it.

All that talk with Henry about the sheriff had made him paranoid.

He opened the door a crack, peeking cautiously through the opening and then blowing out a relieved breath that ended in a quiet laugh when the person on the other side lifted several boxes of baked goods.

Grayson threw the door open wide and stepped aside for Henry. "What brings you all the way out here?"

"I had some free time, thought I'd come by and deliver some pastries, maybe have a quick chat with Payton about that job." Henry didn't wait for Grayson to lead the way, the few visits he'd paid to Barlow House in the past having apparently been enough for him to remember where the kitchen was. He was halfway down the hallway already.

"Just thought you'd save her a trip into town, huh?" Henry's face was as innocent as it was possible for a man's face to be, and Grayson didn't buy it for a second.

"What is causing all this noise so early in the morning? Ruffles, stop barking." Becka was coming down the stairs as Henry walked by, rubbing the sleep from her eyes. She was still in pajamas and at least half her hair was falling out of the bun she'd slept in. "Oh, hey, Henry."

"Morning, Becka."

Grayson swept Ruffles up in a tight grip and handed her over to Becka, still struggling and barking like she had the first few days he'd lived here. "Glad to see it's not just me she hates."

"I did tell you back then that she hates men." Becka tucked her under an arm and headed back up the stairs. "I'll keep her with me while I get dressed."

"Hey, Becka ..." He glanced over his shoulder, trying to make sure Henry was out of sight. "About last night—"

"I don't know what you're talking about, Barlow, and even if I did ... It won't happen again." She left him at the bottom of the stairs, staring up at her retreating back and trying hard not to pull out a handful of his own hair in frustration.

Damn the woman and her fluctuating, mercurial moods.

He was debating the wisdom of following her up, invading the space of her bedroom until she agreed to talk about what had happened like a fucking adult, when Payton came rushing down the hall from the kitchen.

"You didn't tell me someone was coming over!" She pushed each word out from between clenched teeth and jabbed him with a hard elbow as she shoved her way by him on the way up the stairs. "I am wearing Becka's oldest and most disgusting pajamas, for fuck's sake."

"I didn't know he was coming ..."

It was a waste of breath. She was gone before he finished half a sentence, leaving him standing there with his mouth open, just like her sister.

He went to the kitchen to look for Henry, hoping at least one person in the house would be reasonable, but found him standing at the kitchen counter with a puzzled look on his face.

"You okay?"

Henry blinked at him for several seconds before answering. "She just ran off."

"Payton?" He waited for Henry to nod, grateful he wasn't the only one out of sorts and having problems with women so early in the day. "I think she went upstairs to change."

"Oh." Henry pursed his lips and stared at the door. "Do you think she'll be gone long?"

"A woman getting dressed can take anywhere from five minutes to five hours, depending on the day and how much she likes you." Grayson grinned. "I don't think she'll be gone long at all."

"Hey." Henry grabbed his chest and dramatically pretended to be wounded. "That hurts my feelings, you know?"

Grayson flipped open the lid on a pastry box, permanently abandoning his shitty bagel for better fare, and rolled his eyes. "In all seriousness, though, do you remember what I told you? She's not only very pregnant, she's also freshly out of a bad relationship."

"I know what you told me." Henry crossed his arms, all

traces of humor gone from his expression. "I'm still interested, but only when—*only if*—she's ready and interested in me. It's not like I'm going to be an ass about it. If all she ever wants to be is friends, then that's fine with me."

The two of them stared each other down over the boxes of donuts and croissants before coming to a silent understanding built on years of history and a shared fondness for the women of Barlow House.

Grayson would let it go, and Henry would behave himself as a gentleman that could be trusted with something as fragile as Payton's healing heart. If she wanted him, Grayson wouldn't stand in the way, but if Henry ever pushed her more than she was comfortable with, Henry would have to answer to Grayson for what he'd done.

They both sat at the table, at ease with each other again.

"You sure you're willing to take on being a dad?" Grayson trusted him, but it didn't mean he was going to give up the chance to needle him a little more, especially after Henry had given him such a hard time before about Becka. "It's a big responsibility."

Henry shrugged, unbothered. "I've already got Elliot."

"That one came mostly grown," Grayson reminded him. "Babies are different."

"Always wanted kids." Grayson didn't remember Henry ever mentioning it before but there was a set look in his eyes that made it impossible to doubt him. "If she wanted them, I'd probably be willing to give her a half dozen more."

"Don't let her hear you say that." Grayson held back a laugh and looked over his shoulder to make sure Payton wasn't in earshot. "She's uncomfortable and not exactly keen on the idea of doing the whole thing again."

"Just the one is fine, too."

Grayson shook his head and looked at Henry in disbelief.

"You don't even really know her. Aren't you jumping into this a little too quickly? You don't even know if she likes you."

It was a very reasonable argument and one that fell on the least attentive of ears.

"Sometimes you just know." Henry was as serious as Grayson had ever seen him. "You can feel it right here." He rubbed a hand against the center of his chest, knuckles digging into his sternum.

Grayson remembered that feeling, the tightness in the chest, the shallowness of his breathing, the first time he'd laid eyes on Becka. It hadn't improved in the months since.

He sighed, unable to argue any more against Henry's flawed logic. As long as he was treating Payton respectfully and didn't scare her with his weird woo woo love stuff, the rest of it was between the two of them.

"So, did you tell them?"

"Hmm?" Leave it to Henry to change the subject mid-conversation and leave everyone else scrambling to keep up. "Tell who? Tell them what?"

"Becka and the others." Henry looked at him impatiently, like he was the one causing problems. "About the sheriff?"

Grayson grimaced. "It may take her a few more minutes to get dressed, why don't we take a quick walk on the beach while we wait?"

Henry lifted a brow, but he followed Grayson's lead and didn't say anything else about it until they were far enough away from the house that the chances of being overheard were effectively zero.

"Well?"

"No, I didn't tell them," Grayson admitted. "I didn't want to worry them, and besides, if you were so worried about it, why didn't you tell them?"

Now it was Henry's turn to grimace. "I wasn't sure they would believe me."

"Why wouldn't they? You've gotten along with Edith, and you seem to be pretty friendly with Becka."

Henry held up his hands with a laugh when he heard the slight bitterness in Grayson's tone. "Calm down. I thought we just established Becka isn't the sister I'm interested in?"

They had, but Grayson still didn't like the easy way Becka and Henry seemed to get along, not when he'd had to work so hard for every bit of progress he'd made with her. He'd never really been the jealous type, and the feeling was both novel and uncomfortable.

"Anyway." He would not be discussing that issue any further. "Why wouldn't they believe you?"

"It's got nothing to do with me and everything to do with the sheriff." Henry glanced back at the house with an unreadable expression. "Becka might give the idea some thought, at least, but Edith has known him most of her life. How would she feel if I suddenly showed up and started throwing those kinds of accusations around?"

"If you could prove he'd been saying those things, hinting around about George's death, what alternative explanation could there be? Either he has an ulterior motive, or he actually thinks they committed a murder." Grayson shook his head, the idea of it incomprehensible. "Could you imagine?"

"Them committing murder?" Henry hesitated a moment longer than Grayson thought was reasonable before shaking his head. "I guess not."

"Did you actually just think about it?"

"Did you really *not* think about it?" Henry was just as serious, the tone incredulous even in the face of Grayson's rising confusion. "Sheriff Levine probably doesn't actually believe they did it, but that doesn't mean the idea itself isn't worth considering."

Grayson found he'd involuntarily curled his hands into fists by his side. "You think my grandmother is a murderer?"

"I think Edith went through a lot during the years she was married to George, and Becka is not the kind of person to let something like that go. It's not in her nature to live in that house and let him abuse someone she cares about and do nothing to stop it."

Grayson had always been able to count on Henry to hand out the blunt truth even when it hurt, but it felt like he'd been hit in the gut with a hammer. Every word of what Henry had said was true, and suddenly her voice from the night before was playing through his head...

"That was about sending a message."

He turned away from the house, shifted his gaze to the beach where they'd found his grandfather's body.

"I ..."

"Don't get all weird about it." Henry clapped a hand on his shoulder in a silent show of support. "I may have given it some thought, but I don't think she did it."

"Why not?"

Henry laughed and some of Grayson's fear ebbed away at the sound. "She wouldn't have come up with some convoluted scheme to make it look like he drowned. If Becka had killed him, they'd have found him at the bottom of the stairs with her footprint on his chest."

That much Grayson could admit was true. She was many things, but subtle was not one of them. She fought back first and asked questions later.

"But you did just say she wouldn't have stood by and let George lay hands on her."

"Looking back on it, I don't think he did." Henry rubbed a hand over his chin and laid out his argument calmly. "Edith wasn't doing particularly well health-wise in the months before he died, and Becka hadn't been living with them very long. I think it's possible he actually hadn't been as violent with Edith so Becka may not have known what he was normally like."

"She knows." Grayson wanted to give her the benefit of the doubt, but she'd told him herself that she knew George was abusive.

"But did she know then or did she find out after he died?" Henry shrugged like he wasn't sure of the answer himself. "I think the more likely option is that Edith came clean after George died, because she felt it was safe for her to finally talk about it."

They'd walked the whole beach and back again, and Grayson found himself back at the foot of the long staircase. Last night he'd carried Becka up those stairs, held her and protected her and ended up nearly losing himself in her.

He had no choice but to believe Henry's explanation for how things had happened back then. There was no way he could live with himself otherwise. The relationship between him and Becka had always been complicated, but something major had just shifted between them—and within him—with all the force of a hurricane. Now, he had to believe she was innocent, for his own sake.

Because it wasn't just that he wanted her body, though he'd have given everything he owned for another taste of her. No, that wasn't it at all. He was beginning to suspect his desires encompassed more than just the physical, as illogical as he knew it was.

Becka was mean, irrational, and confrontational. She lacked the ability to do even basic introspection. Hell, she probably still hated his guts. None of which made a difference in the way he was starting to feel about her, and that was the real problem. That was why he needed Henry to be right about her.

After all, what kind of man fell in love with a murderer?

Chapter Eighteen

Becka

Payton working at the bakery meant one less person in the house for Becka to use as a human shield between herself and Grayson. A shield she desperately needed as the weeks passed by and the tension between them remained near the boiling point.

She'd given up lying to herself about her own desires, and she was aware of the way he watched her, the little excuses he found to be near her or touch her as often as he could, but she was no closer to giving in. Arousal had become an almost constant companion, ready to settle like a heavy flame in the pit of her stomach any time he was in the same room with her, but she was determined to keep from jumping with both feet into a disaster of her own making.

Successfully managing not to be in a room alone with him was tricky, and he was pouting, but what else could she do?

Becka ignored the looks he'd been sending her all morning, just like every morning since she'd nearly done the unthinkable and stared out the window at another gray and dismal day.

"You should come into The Bakery later." Payton struggled into her jacket, a frustrated frown forming as she tried to zip it around the width of her expanding belly. "Nobody except me has gotten out much lately, and I'm worried you're all turning into weird little woodland hermits."

"It's cold." Becka took pity on her and helped with the zipper, confident Henry would help with it when it was time to come back home again. "Nobody wants to go out in this weather, if they can help it."

"It's only going to get colder, so you should get out and do something while you can." Payton sighed when Becka stuck her tongue out and turned to Edith instead. "Come on, don't you want to see something other than these same walls?"

"Too cold for my old bones," Edith declared, "but I agree about the rest of you. Payton is at least getting some fresh air and exercise. You're too young to be cooped up in the house like this every day."

Before Becka could protest again, Grayson cut in. "We'll go." His smile was aimed at Edith, pure innocence and reassurance. Becka wanted to kick him and that was before he said, "I'll drive us."

"I don't want—"

"Good." Edith's tone was not one that invited further discussion and Becka bit back the rest of the retort. "Bring back something sweet for me, will you, dear?"

"Of course." Grayson's pout had disappeared entirely, the glum expression he'd been wearing like a mask gone in the blink of an eye. "Anything for you."

A few hours later, Becka let them bundle her up into her warm wet weather clothes and shove her into the passenger seat of Grayson's sensible sedan. She'd considered throwing herself down the stairs to create an injury serious enough to avoid being in a car alone with him, but decided in the end that a fifteen-minute car ride was better than several weeks in a cast.

She regretted that decision as soon as he pulled out of the driveway.

"Are you warm enough?" He fiddled with the buttons on the dash, adjusting the temperature and the radio, turning on the heated seats. She was sure he thought he was being nice, but all she could smell was the subtle scent of him beside her, and all she could see was the graceful way his hands moved.

Each flex of his fingers caused the veins to move beneath the skin and she had no idea why he was asking her if she was warm enough. It might be cold outside, but she was burning up. At this rate, she was likely to spontaneously combust before they even made it to The Bakery.

When did his voice become that deep? When did his gaze get that possessive?

She was going to smother Payton in her sleep for causing this mess, just wait and see. Not enough to kill her, of course. Just enough for her to see the error of her ways a bit.

"Becka?"

"Hmmmm?" She hoped he hadn't noticed how much that had sounded like a moan and barely resisted the urge to cover her cheeks with her hands. She was blushing. She was absolutely sure of it.

Humiliating.

"You okay?" He seemed torn between genuine concern and amusement, casting frequent looks at her while trying to give enough attention to the road that he didn't crash the car into a tree.

"Fine." If she didn't get out of this car, she was going to find herself in his lap doing unspeakable acts and enjoying every second of it. "Why do you ask?"

The last word ended on a croak and she briefly considered

sticking her head out the window. Maybe the rain in her face would have the same neutralizing effect as a cold shower.

He chuckled and the sound made her clench her teeth and rub her thighs together. He probably noticed, he seemed to notice everything else, but she couldn't help it. It provided some relief and she was getting desperate.

She almost jumped out of her skin when he casually reached across and put his hand on her knee. There was a layer of denim between his palm and her skin, but she could still feel the heat as he gave it a gentle squeeze that made her insides catch fire.

Her whole body reacted to the contact as she hissed out a ragged breath.

"Barlow?" She tried to ignore the way her leg moved instinctively to let him in, but he took full advantage, his hand sliding around the side of her knee to creep up her inner thigh. "What the fuck are you doing?"

They were already driving by the houses on the outskirts of town, less than five minutes from their destination but he was unhurried and unashamed. "Touching you."

"Stop doing it." She flapped her arms at him, trying to shoo him away like a pesky seagull, but her leg was trembling and opening beneath his gentle persuasion.

Talk about mixed signals.

He shrugged and pulled his hand away. "If you're sure that's what you want."

Of course it wasn't! Anybody with eyes could see how badly she wanted him to do more than just touch her. He was doing this on purpose.

Bastard.

Any more of that and she would have been an incoherent mess, not just in his lap, but begging him for all the things she kept insisting she didn't want. He knew she was being a hypocrite and he couldn't understand why, so he'd begun a calculated campaign against her.

Touching just so, here and there when she was least expecting it and pulling away just when she was on the verge of giving in. He was building her up, keeping her in a constant state of unfulfilled need, all while acting like he was the one suffering.

Not just a bastard, a *sneaky* bastard.

She hated him and his hot hands and his plush lips and his all-consuming kisses ...

The car hadn't even fully come to a stop in The Bakery parking lot before she'd thrown open the door and jumped from the passenger seat like the hounds of hell were on her heels. She hit The Bakery door with so much enthusiasm it bounced off the opposite wall and Payton looked up from behind the counter with her mouth open in shock.

"Are you okay?"

"Fine, fine." Becka laughed, high and strained, babbling to fill the awkward void. "Of course I'm fine. Why wouldn't I be? Are *you* okay?"

"Uhhh ..."

The bell above the door rang again when Grayson walked in, calm and collected like nothing at all happened between them. He lifted a brow at her when she made a choked noise, but otherwise didn't acknowledge her at all, turning to Payton instead with a warm smile.

"I see you managed to talk Henry into putting up some Christmas decorations in here." Grayson pointed at the small tree in the corner and strands of red garland hung at the edge of the countertop. "First time for everything, I guess."

"Just in time, too." Payton looked pretty proud of herself for getting him to do the minimum. "He said that old Mr. Schmidt didn't like it, which is why they'd never done it, but with me and Elliot ganging up on him, he didn't stand a chance."

"That's putting it mildly," Becka muttered. She was pretty sure Henry would bulldoze the whole place down if Payton suggested it.

Grayson bent down to look in the case at the day's offerings, turning his attention back to the business at hand and telling Payton. "Edith sent me with a list of stuff to bring home, so if you don't mind, I'll just hand that over first while we're trying to decide what to order."

Payton nodded, her confused gaze moving from him to Becka as she took the list from his hand. "I'll start boxing this up and get you both some coffee."

It didn't take them long to decide and Grayson sat down at a table near the register as soon as they'd ordered, his expression bored as he waited for Becka to join him. "If you get a few minutes while we're here, grab Henry and have a seat. We came all this way for you, so the least you can do is have a donut with us. If he won't let you take a break, let me know. I'll rough him up for you."

Payton rolled her eyes and started pouring coffee into two white ceramic cups. "Please, Henry hardly lets me do anything here. He's set me up with a stool back here and only lets me get up if I have to. I'm collecting a paycheck, but it's barely a job."

"As it should be." Henry came in from the back, arms laden with a tray of fresh muffins for the case in front. "What kind of boss would I be if I let you work yourself to the bone in your condition?"

She snorted and smacked him on the arm. "I only let you get away with pampering me like this because you do the exact same thing to Elliot."

"Big softie." Grayson shot him a teasing grin that Henry received good-naturedly, but there was an undercurrent to it that had Becka wondering, not for the first time, if there was something more than met the eye to the relationship between the two of them. Edith had told her about their childhood friendship, but sometimes the way Grayson looked at him ... Well, it would explain some of the falling out between him and George.

He'd been a homophobe if she'd ever seen one, and if he thought his only grandson was carrying a romantic candle for another boy ... She hesitated to think of what he might have done to Grayson.

It piqued her curiosity and her desire to understand better the man who'd so thoroughly captured her attention, but she'd been too afraid to ask. The friendship between him and Henry was too newly rekindled, too vulnerable. She didn't want to bring up anything that might trigger painful memories for them.

Still, she watched closely as they talked, happy to have some distraction from her runaway sexual response from a few minutes ago. Based on what she could tell from their conversations and the way they behaved around each other now, if Henry had ever had feelings beyond friendship, they were long gone. He only had eyes for Payton these days.

As for Grayson, he did seem to have a lingering fondness that seemed deeper than what might be expected, but if he'd gotten his heart broken at some point, he seemed to be more over it than not.

The hot glances he kept sending her way, even when Henry was right there, were more than enough to prove he was interested in her now, regardless of how he might have felt in the past.

Not that she was worried about it, of course, because she was not going to sleep with him.

Not at all.

Definitely not.

She swallowed hard and realized she'd spent several minutes just staring at his lips while he talked. Not a single word of what he'd said had made it past her ears to her brain during that time, which somehow made it worse.

What the hell was wrong with her?

Payton laughed at something Henry had said, her head tossed back and a pink glow on her cheeks, and Becka knew she wasn't the only one smitten. Widow's Point seemed to grow the kind of men the Simmons sisters liked. Tall, handsome, vaguely obsessed and kind of annoying.

At least Becka knew she was in over her head and was fighting against the current. She was pretty sure Payton hadn't figured it out yet. She thought she was still drifting along on calm seas.

The bell above the door jingled again and the happiness on Payton's face vanished like smoke in the breeze.

Chapter Nineteen

Becka

"**J**ared!"

Becka was on her feet as soon as she saw the look on Payton's face, fists ready and adrenaline pumping. She hadn't needed to hear his name to jump into action, but knowing who she was facing, and why Payton had been so frightened by merely seeing him walk in the door, ramped her up by a few more dangerous degrees.

She'd never met Jared but after only a few seconds in his presence, she was ready to make sure he never walked out that door again.

The bastard had hurt Payton. He'd laid his hands on her in violence and a potential prison sentence wasn't enough to keep Becka from fantasizing about putting him six feet under for a well-deserved—and permanent—dirt nap.

He took a few steps toward their table when he spotted Payton and Becka put herself in his path, sizing him up as he came to an awkward stop just outside of punching range. Smart on his part, if a bit of a disappointment for her.

He was lean and wiry, just a bit taller than Grayson, but with none of the easy grace. His face might have been handsome at one point, but the years had carved lines into the skin beside his eyes and the corners of his mouth. Not the kind that softened an expression with evidence of past joys, but the marks of unkindness and dissatisfaction. It was like he'd worn a scowl, a cruel frown, for so long his skin couldn't remember what a happy face was supposed to look like.

Even when he smiled, it sat unnaturally on him, a mockery of genuine happiness that made the observers around him so uncomfortable that Becka wanted to wipe it off him. By force if necessary. It made her skin crawl.

"Payton." He'd seemed genuinely surprised to see her when he'd first walked in, but he recovered quickly, glancing at Becka and the others before trying to slide around to catch Payton's eye. "I've been looking for you for months. I had to hire an actual private detective to track you down and he couldn't get any closer than just this fucking town. I've been staying at that shitty motel for days, baby, just hoping I'd run into you eventually."

Becka personally thought that sounded like he needed a hobby or maybe a real fucking job. Payton said his dad owned some kind of construction company, but Jared lived off his handouts, choosing to be a leech on the family money instead of making any meaningful contributions of his own. It apparently gave him plenty of time and disposable cash, because here he stood, being a menace even after months of Payton going out of her way not to be found.

"Go away." Payton was hiding behind Becka, scooting further behind her and closer to where Henry was sitting. Becka wasn't sure if she'd already explained the situation to Henry directly or if she was just betting instinctively that he'd help her, but either way ...

"Can I help you?" Henry's tone was pleasant, customer

service voice on full display, but Becka could feel the hostility emanating from him as he got to his feet. If all he knew was that Payton was uncomfortable, it was enough for him to be seconds away from tossing the source of that discomfort out on his ass.

"I'm just here to see Payton."

Payton turned her head aside, buried it in Henry's shoulder, and Becka got a front row seat to the change in Jared's expression. That ugly smile slipped, and the monster beneath flashed in his eyes before he could get ahold of himself.

"Payton doesn't want to see you." Becka lacked Henry's subtlety and was unable to hide the naked aggression in her tone. "Take yourself out of here before I take you out. Don't stick around town, either. Go home. Forget she ever existed and move on with your life."

He laughed and visibly took in her slight frame from head to toe. It wasn't the first time someone had underestimated her because of her size and it wouldn't be the last, but she made sure they always regretted it.

She reached behind her, groped across the top of the table until she found the handle of a coffee cup, and tightened her grip on it in preparation. He wasn't leaving with her sister, and if he had any ideas to the contrary, she was happy to show him in hot liquid and shattered ceramic just how wrong he was.

"Who the hell are you and why do you think it's any of your business what I do with my wife?"

Everyone froze, the word 'wife' hitting with the force of a nuclear bomb. Henry exhaled loudly enough for even Becka to hear him, but he didn't move away from where he stood, Payton still tucked in the protected space beside his body.

Becka took a half step forward, all bristle and no apology. It didn't matter if he was a boyfriend or a husband or the goddamn king of England. He had no right to her if she was unwilling.

"I'm her sister and if you don't move your ass out that door right now—"

"Becka." Grayson's hand covered hers where it gripped the coffee cup behind her back, his voice low and soothing like he was trying to calm a frightened wild animal. "Let Henry handle this."

"Like hell." Since they'd been friends she'd come to adore Henry, trusted him as far as she was able to trust a man, but with her sister? With Payton and the baby's entire well-being? Of course not. No one would love her sister, care for her and protect her, as well as she could do it herself.

She gave a firm tug, hot coffee splashing over both of their hands, but Grayson refused to let go, and before she could wrestle free, Henry had untangled himself from Payton and pressed her down into a seat.

He stepped out in front of Becka, calmly making himself the first line of defense, but in those few seconds, Payton's stomach must have been visible in the space between their moving bodies.

"What the fuck?" Jared's eyes were locked on her face, fury causing the brackets at the side of his mouth to deepen. A vein in his forehead throbbed and Becka started wrestling with Grayson again over possession of her coffee cup. "You're pregnant?"

"I—"

He didn't let her speak. "You dumb bitch."

"You will not speak to her that way." Henry stood between them like a brick wall, the only sign of emotion on his face the working of a muscle in his lower jaw.

"Shut up." Jared grabbed the nearest empty chair and shoved it across the room where it collided with a table and clattered to the ground, landing on its side and rolling away.

Payton flinched and Grayson had to get out of his seat to grab Becka's arm.

If it hadn't been for the steel vice of his hand on her bicep, she would have been in the middle of committing assault before that chair stopped rolling.

Jared was predictable, oblivious to the danger he was in and solely focused on intimidating the woman that had escaped from him. "You think you can do that? That you can just leave me and take my fucking kid with you? Or is it not mine? Were you already fucking someone else?"

He sneered as he asked the question, throwing it in her face, an accusation of infidelity to smear her reputation in front of others and embarrass her. She was already crying, one hand on the top of her stomach and the other pressed to her lips, when he rolled his eyes and muttered under his breath. "Useless whore."

"It's not yours."

Payton sucked in a loud breath, a wet hiccup punctuating her shocked gasp when Henry stood in front of her abuser and lied to his face.

"What did you just say?" Jared's jaw dropped and it was clear he hadn't been expecting that. "What the hell do you mean, it's not mine?"

"The baby isn't yours," Henry repeated. "It's mine."

Becka and Grayson stopped fighting, mouths open, and Payton was silently looking from one man to the other with tears still dripping from her chin.

"That can't be ..." Jared looked like he was mentally counting the months, trying to guess from the size of Payton's stomach how far along she was, and comparing the dates. "It can't be yours."

He didn't sound at all sure of himself.

"Care to make a bet on that?" Henry took a step forward and then another, each bit of lost distance highlighting how much taller, how much broader, he was than his opponent. Jared took a step back and Henry's calm exterior cracked just enough for his lips to turn up into a mocking smile.

"The baby is mine." He was backing Jared toward the door now, keeping a steady forward pace like a cat chasing a panicked mouse. "Payton is also mine."

"She is my *wife*."

"I don't give a damn what you think she is or what she used to be." Jared's back hit the closed door but Henry kept coming. "What she is now and will be in the future is all I care about. If she wanted to still be your wife, she would have left with you, but she didn't."

He finally stopped a few paces away, and watched dispassionately as Jared swallowed hard, his face pale and covered in a fine sheen of sweat.

"Do I look like the kind of man that would let a spineless, weak-kneed, self-important prick put his hands on what belongs to me?" Henry reached out and plucked a nonexistent piece of lint off the shoulder of Jared's shirt. When he shook his head wildly, Henry nodded. "Good, then we understand each other. Go. Run. And whatever you do ... don't come back."

Jared finally managed to pull the door open enough to slide his body out through the crack and they all watched through the wide front windows as he ran across the rain-swept parking lot and fumbled the keys trying to get into his car.

He peeled out of the parking lot, tires squealing, and disappeared from sight.

"Well." Henry walked back to the table and crouched down in front of Payton, quiet concern creasing his brows as he tried to get her to look at him. "Are you okay?"

She wailed and threw herself into his arms, sobbing and hiccupping too hard for anyone to understand what she was saying. The rest of them shared a confused look and Becka shrugged. She was her sister, not a mind reader, and the sounds Payton was making barely resembled human speech.

"What a mess." Becka grabbed a napkin off the table and started wiping coffee off her fingers, moving on to Grayson's once she'd finished her own without thinking about it at all. She'd burned them both, and she frowned at the pink splotches on his skin. "What the hell was that about? His wife?"

Grayson stood still and let her hold his hand, not struggling as she poked at the burns that were already turning into painful looking blisters.

"To hell with the wife thing," he said, ignoring Becka to interrogate Henry instead. "Your baby?"

Payton was ignoring them, but Henry didn't look at all embarrassed. "What? Do you want him coming around again? Trying to harass her and stick his nose where it doesn't belong?"

"It *is* his baby," Grayson began and Becka tossed his hand away, her already surging adrenaline kicking into overdrive.

"Fuck that." She was practically snarling in his face despite the height difference between them. If she had to stand on tiptoe to get her point across then she'd damn well stand on tiptoe. She had no problem with that. "He gave up the right to be part of their lives when he became a danger to them."

"I'm not disagreeing with that." Grayson ran a hand up her arm, back in placating mode. "I just don't know that we can keep him away with a boldfaced lie and a little intimidation."

Heat was rising under her skin where he touched her and she found herself struggling not to be distracted from her murderous thoughts. "Maybe we should try a lot of intimidation instead of just a little, and I can break his legs."

She saw Grayson and Henry make exasperated eye contact over her shoulder, but she wasn't kidding. If they didn't come up with a better plan, she had a handy baseball bat ready to deal with him.

"Maybe we should call the sheriff." Grayson looked like he'd rather swallow a live toad, but when she glared at him, he shrugged helplessly. "I think we have to have a police report if we're going to get a restraining order."

"No." Payton managed to pull herself out of Henry's embrace enough to shake her head. Her face was puffy and her red rimmed eyes were still overflowing with fresh tears but she looked ready to fight Grayson herself. "We can't call the police."

"Why?"

"They won't do a damn thing." Becka already knew exactly what Payton was thinking. "Even if you filed the report and somehow got the judge to give you a restraining order, who's supposed to enforce it? Sheriff Levine?"

Payton looked at Grayson and asked flatly, "Do you expect him to show up and protect me?"

"Maybe not, but I don't think we have a choice." Grayson looked at Henry, and they both turned to look at Becka. "Do you?"

Becka hated giving in, but she couldn't think of an alternative, either. As far as backup went, the sheriff's office was all they really had, especially out at Barlow House. All they were asking him to do was his job, so it shouldn't be that complicated. Payton took a little more convincing, but eventually, they put in the call and then waited in tense silence for Sheriff Levine to show up.

In the end, they were forced to admit they should have listened to Payton, though she resisted the urge to do more than lift her brows in a way that clearly said, *I told you so,* when Sheriff Levine spent less than two minutes listening to them explain what had happened, before declaring there was nothing he could do. The Bakery was a business, open to the public, and Jared had left without damaging anything or hurting anyone.

Technically, he hadn't broken any laws.

"Nothing he can do?" Becka thought about throwing a coffee cup at the door Sheriff Levine had just walked out of but refrained when she remembered she'd be the one that had to clean up the mess. "Such bullshit. Couldn't he at least talk to him? Give him a warning about harassing her since he admitted he followed her all the way to Widow's Point?"

Grayson was sitting back in the same seat he'd left when Jared arrived, chewing on his thumbnail and staring at the door. "I don't know enough about these things to be sure what he can do," he admitted.

Henry shook his head, disgust written on every line of his face. "It's like everything else in Widow's Point. What he *can* do depends on what he *wants* to do. Sure, the asshole hasn't broken any laws and maybe the sheriff isn't technically supposed to try to run some stranger out of town, but he doesn't have any problem throwing his weight around when it suits him. He uses that badge every day to intimidate people he doesn't like or protect the ones he does. The only reason he isn't helping us now, is because he's not going to go out of his way to protect a woman, especially a woman from Barlow House."

Becka had no idea what the hell that bit about Barlow House was supposed to mean, but she didn't have time to figure it out before Payton, who'd held up well enough while they were waiting for the sheriff, burst into noisy tears again. Now that they were alone, it seemed all the emotion had hit her at once.

Becka would have rushed over, but Henry was closer. He went to work immediately trying to dry Payton's tears and Becka changed direction, walking over instead to straighten the fallen chair that Jared had thrown. It had been a terrifying few minutes, but they'd been lucky there was no one else in the bakery to witness it. She only knew Jared through Payton's stories, but she doubted having a few more sets of eyes on him would have changed his behavior.

The last thing Payton needed was her new start in this town getting tainted by gossip and if anyone had heard Jared calling her his wife and then seen the way Henry was tending to her—how familiar and intimate their interactions were—it would have caused plenty of problems for both of them. Small towns had plenty of small minds and words like "adultery" spread fast and with weighty consequences.

Becka jumped a little when Grayson cleared his throat, still anxious after the chaotic scene they'd just been through. She hadn't realized he'd gotten up and moved to stand so close to her. All her attention had been on her sister.

"Sorry." He wrapped an arm around her and she let him, leaning on him for a few seconds before he said, "It's still about an hour before Elliot shows up for the afternoon shift. Why don't we get out of here and let the two of them talk this out?"

She nodded, but it took them a minute to catch Henry's eye to indicate they were leaving, both of them waiting awkwardly to the side and trying not to interrupt as he finally got Payton to stop crying. They both heard the words "delusional" and "not his wife" as Payton began passionately explaining the situation to him.

If he had been anyone other than Henry, they might have worried, but with him there was no need. Whatever level of entanglement existed—or didn't exist—between her and Jared, he would help her sort it out.

When they finally did manage to get Henry's attention long enough for Grayson to tip his head in the direction of the front door, all they got was an absent wave to dismiss them. Becka was pretty sure they could have slipped away unseen and neither he nor Payton would have remembered they were supposed to be there in the first place.

Grayson's arm never left her as he guided her out of the building and into the passenger seat of his car. Now that the threat had passed, Becka was tired and aching, her muscles sore from the tension she'd held in her body and the adrenaline high she'd been riding. Now that her brain had decided it was safe to do so, all the fight was draining out of her, leaving only exhaustion in its place. It was warm in the car and Grayson turned the radio to something quiet and soothing, letting her relax without demanding conversation from her.

She stared out the window as they drove home, her hand wrapped around Payton's necklace.

Chapter Twenty

Grayson

There was no one else in the world that could cause him so much worry and distress. How could one person inspire such conflicting emotions? One moment he was considering pulling the car over to the side of the road so he could drag her into his lap and devour her, and the next he was terrified, convinced she was going to go to jail for assault. What the fuck had she been thinking?

She'd gone from calm to violence in about half a second. It had been stunning to witness, especially as someone that firmly believed he knew her well and was prepared to deal with all the hostility she had to offer.

Apparently, he'd been wrong about that.

What he'd believed to be hostility directed at him had been nothing more than a passing shadow of annoyance in comparison to what he'd seen her about to unleash on the unsuspecting—but extremely deserving—fool who'd walked into Henry's bakery like he owned the place.

Or at least, like he owned Payton.

It was a good thing Henry had been there to help handle the situation. Grayson didn't think he could have dealt with the ex *and* managed to keep his hold on Becka at the same time. For such a small woman, she was unusually strong and kind of slippery. It was like trying to wrestle an eel into a pillowcase. If the eel was hot and you were maybe a little bit in love with it.

Possibly.

Grayson rubbed a rough hand over his face and wondered what the hell was wrong with him. Any reasonable person would have looked at her behavior and decided at the very least to stay far, far away from her. They probably would have started giving at least a little thought to the idea that she might actually have had a hand in the somewhat mysterious death of his grandfather. A death that had happened right under her nose, giving her the means, motive, *and* opportunity.

The fact that he wasn't doing either of those things and was instead loitering in the hallway beside her closed bedroom door—one she had closed behind her as soon as she'd disappeared inside—proved what he had already come to suspect. He was too emotionally invested in her to think rationally about the situation.

Maybe he was just a glutton for punishment—a real possibility considering the way she treated him and how ridiculous it was that he had grown feelings for her in the first place—but the more he thought about it, the more Henry's assessment made sense to him.

If Becka had wanted George dead, there wouldn't have been any doubt she was responsible for it. She probably would have signed her name on the corpse's forehead. Added a little smiley face just so the cops knew she had no regrets.

She was plenty capable of doing the deed, but was she capable of acting with restraint? Of plotting and biding her time? Henry didn't think so and Grayson was inclined to agree with him.

Besides, no matter how unhinged she'd been at The Bakery, seeing her standing in front of her sister like some kind of protective arch angel had been one hell of an experience. He should have been reevaluating his willingness to live in the same house with her, and instead he'd been fighting down his own desire.

She was dangerous—how much was debatable but still— and he was more than willing to risk whatever consequences might come his way as long as it meant he got to roll her under him and...

Nope.

Not the right time for that line of thought. Not when she was clearly still upset and vulnerable.

She'd been quiet all the way home, her hand clenched around that necklace she always wore, like it was giving her comfort. He'd wanted to ask her about it, because it was clearly important to her, but she hadn't given him the chance.

As soon as he'd turned the car off, she dashed for the front door, grumbling as she went and ignoring everyone's attempts to speak to her. He knew she was in a bad mood when she didn't even stop to smile at Edith.

Whatever she was feeling about the events of the afternoon, she clearly wasn't in a sharing mood. By the time he'd made it inside and stripped his jacket off, she was already up the stairs, her bedroom door closed firmly behind her.

He'd knocked, but she hadn't answered.

That had been over an hour ago and he hadn't heard a peep out of her since. Not even the sound of Ruffles barking when Payton came home from The Bakery, shaken but still willing to give them a weak smile, had roused her from her sanctuary.

All he could do was sit and wait.

Which was what he was doing—playing a game on his phone and listening to the sound of endless rain on the roof—when Payton came up the stairs carrying a tray with two plates on it.

"I brought dinner." She handed it over when he'd gotten to his feet. "Maybe she'll open the door if you have food."

"Any idea why she'd so upset?" He tipped his head toward the door and hoped she would be willing to answer. Payton was often reluctant to talk about her history before she'd come to Widow's Point, and Grayson had a strong feeling that whatever was bothering Becka had something to do with their complicated pasts.

She was quiet for a moment and Grayson got the impression that she was weighing how much to reveal. After a few contemplative minutes, she said, "I don't know how much she's told you ..." She looked at him inquiringly and Grayson shook his head to indicate it had been practically nothing. "Well, I'm sure she'd prefer to tell you the specifics herself when she's ready, but our parents were ... not the best. I was older, but Becka was the one that always tried to protect us. I was a runner, a hider. Appease when possible and flee when it isn't. Becka was my last line of defense when all that other stuff didn't work."

That certainly explained a lot of Becka's behavior, if she'd always felt that not only her own safety, but the safety of others, depended on her willingness to fight whatever threats she encountered. Since it seemed that was often her own parents, there probably wasn't a limit to who or what she was willing to take on.

"I don't like to talk much about what happened to me. Not with Jared or with my parents, either."

Grayson had gathered that much already. Whatever bits she'd chosen to share seemed to have been for Becka and Edith only. She hadn't shared any specifics with him and neither had the others.

Payton continued, "Neither does she, but I would imagine that she's pretty angry right now. At me for choosing a man like Jared and at herself for not being there to protect me."

Grayson nodded. "She does blame herself for everything, doesn't she? She thinks it's her job to take care of everyone else, keep them all safe. She's as bad as the damn dog."

Payton laughed, genuine humor brightening her face. She looked so much like Becka, but softer and less brittle. He was hit with a wave of brotherly affection.

"She really is, but I doubt she would appreciate the comparison. Truthfully, I feel better and safer with the two of them around. I may not be much of a fighter, but her efforts are never wasted on me."

Grayson laughed, too, but he was a little jealous that whatever they had been through, they had been lucky enough to have each other.

"Hey can I ask you a question? You don't have to answer." Grayson tightened his grip on the tray. "Do you know the story behind that necklace she's always wearing? It seems like it matters to her a lot, so if it's personal, you don't have to tell me."

"Necklace?"

"The little gold heart? I think it might be a locket. It's usually under her shirt, but sometimes when she's upset she pulls it out and holds onto it."

"I guess I hadn't noticed." Payton looked a bit stricken, her face paler than it had been a moment before.

"Like I said, if it's personal ..."

Payton smiled, seeming to push away her sadness. "It was mine. I left it for her the night I ran away."

"Oh." Well, that explained her attachment to it and why she kept it tucked away out of sight. She seemed to have forgiven Payton, mostly, for leaving, but maybe she wasn't ready yet to talk about it with her. Not ready to face those memories.

"Don't tell her you told me," Payton instructed. "She doesn't like to share those kinds of things. Nothing that makes her look vulnerable."

"Yeah, I noticed." He winced as he realized he'd stuck his foot in his mouth by asking. "Sorry for bringing it up."

"I'm glad you did. I probably wouldn't have ever known about it otherwise."

"Well." Grayson cleared his throat, trying to smooth over the sudden awkwardness in the conversation. "I guess I should see if she'll let me in before dinner gets cold."

"Just let yourself in." Payton shrugged at his surprised look. "She'll get over it."

He was already trying to juggle holding the tray and opening the door, grateful when Payton brushed him aside to turn the knob.

He expected Becka to start yelling the second the door cracked open, but everything was dark and still inside. Maybe she was asleep?

"Take care of her, okay?" Payton's expression was unusually serious and it occurred to him—belatedly—to wonder why she'd brought the tray to him instead of taking it herself or giving the responsibility to Edith.

"Uh ..."

She seemed to read the question on his face. "Because you were the one sitting outside her door for the last hour."

Well, he supposed he couldn't argue with that, but as Payton walked away and left him standing with his mouth open and his dinner going cold in his hands, he made a mental note to ask her not to mention that particular detail to Becka. She'd never let him live it down if she knew he'd been hovering over her.

Once inside the bedroom, it took him a minute to make a clear space on her desk for the tray—it didn't help that he couldn't really see in the dark and her room was a cluttered mess—but once he'd gotten that handled and kicked enough discarded shoes and unwashed shirts out of the way to make a path, he sat down on the bed next to her.

She didn't move as his weight dipped the mattress, or when he brushed a stray strand of hair off her cheek. Actually, if it weren't for the steady rise and fall of her chest and the warmth of her skin, he might have thought something more upsetting than a power nap was happening.

Apparently, she was a deep sleeper.

He took the opportunity to examine her face, so soft in sleep, so much more open than he was used to. Her lips were slightly parted, and the necklace she usually hid was resting in plain sight on her chest.

The sight of it tugged at his heart. Everything about her was so much more than it seemed. All her strength, all the bluster, and it concealed such a gentle soul. One who loved too hard, and gave too much, and protected everyone even when it hurt.

He was in love with her. Not possibly or probably, but definitely and against his better judgement.

He sighed.

He'd have to figure out what to do about that later, for now, her dinner was getting cold.

"Becka." He leaned over, his face getting closer to hers as he tried to see if she was stirring. Her eyelids didn't even flicker, so he tried again, louder this time. "Becka."

Still nothing. He sighed and poked softly at her cheek with each new syllable. "Bec-ka. Wake. Up."

Nothing.

"Becka!"

"What?" She came awake in an instant, her eyes meeting

his and her fist connecting with his face just as he realized he was far too close to her. There was no recognition in her expression until *after* she'd clocked him.

"Damn it!"

"Sorry." She sat up and rubbed her eyes, staring at him with creased brows and a frown. "What are you doing in here, anyway?"

"I was bringing you dinner." He watched her scan the room and spot the tray on the desk before sniffing the air like a hungry puppy.

"What'd you bring me?" She was still suspicious—he couldn't really blame her since she'd woken up to him not just in her bedroom uninvited but also inches from her face—but the smell must have been intriguing.

"No idea," he admitted with a shrug. "Whatever Edith and Payton made. I think it might be pot roast."

"Payton's home?"

Dinner forgotten, she threw the blanket off, narrowly missing tossing it directly onto his head, and tried to climb over him to get off the bed.

"Hey!" He pushed her back down. "She's here, and she's doing fine. I'm under specific instructions from her to make sure you eat this before you go running off to play superhero again." A slight exaggeration, but he assumed Payton would forgive him.

Becka made a pouty face and threw herself back against the pillows, arms crossed and nose crinkled. "Fine."

She should have looked petulant, like a toddler throwing a tantrum, but Grayson thought she was adorable. Let her pout. It wouldn't stop him from feeding her anyway.

He was half afraid she'd bolt for the door when he got up to get the tray and he was ready for her to try, but to his surprise, she stayed put. She spent most of the time glaring at the back of his head, but at least she wasn't fighting him.

He set the tray on the bed between them and didn't object when she ignored the plate that held her actual dinner and grabbed a pastry instead. Crumbs fell on the front of her shirt and the sheets, but he didn't complain about that, either. She was a human tornado, mess following in her wake, but now wasn't the time to nitpick about what could be easily fixed with a few minutes of cleaning.

"You're okay, right?"

"Mmmm." She didn't look at him and he couldn't decide if the noise she made was supposed to be agreement or contradiction. She picked at the pastry with her fingers, breaking off little pieces to plop into her mouth.

"Becka." How was he supposed to know what to do, if she wouldn't look at him or talk to him? She'd had plenty of spirit when she was trying to forcibly pry a coffee cup from his hand and now she was acting like some kind of shy, shrinking violet. "Look at me."

She threw the pastry down and they both watched it bounce on her lap. "Why? So you can lecture me about how I shouldn't have behaved that way? Try to get me to apologize?"

Ah.

There she was.

His little monster, with all her teeth and sharp claws.

"I'm not doing it," she finished, and he assumed she meant apologizing. It really was hard to get her to say she was sorry, and he'd come to consider himself lucky to get the few he'd gotten already.

"I don't expect you to." That got her attention and he lifted a brow when her shocked gaze shot to his face. "He hurt your sister, and he was trying to do it again."

"You..." Her face was stunned, but typically mulish. "You tried to stop me."

"I tried to stop you from going to jail," he corrected, shoving a bite of roast into her mouth with his fork and watching her chew it as fast as possible so she could argue with him again. "Henry was right there, and I was right there, and there was no reason for you to hit that man in the head with a cup and go to jail."

"He deserved it." She still had a mouthful of food—her cheeks were puffed out and she was looking at him like an angry chipmunk—but she was predictably not going to let him get in the last word. He picked up the fork again and shoved another bite in on top of the first.

That would keep her busy for a while.

"He absolutely deserved it, but that doesn't change the consequences that would fall on you if he called the cops, now does it?"

She glowered, but there was no way to speak without spitting half chewed potato onto her mostly clean bedspread. Grayson smiled, victorious, and a vein in her forehead throbbed.

"Anyway, in the future, let's save the coffee cup smashing portion of our itinerary for times when we don't have other, less punishable, options, shall we?"

She flipped him off, and he pretended to be offended. "That's hurtful, you know?"

"Good." It came out garbled, only half intelligible around the portion of food she'd yet to swallow, but he understood the intention. If anything, she got even madder when he laughed.

"Has anyone ever told you how fucking cute you are?" She went rigid when he leaned over her crossed legs and kissed one puffed out cheek. Shocking her into stillness hadn't been his intention, but it was a pleasant side benefit, so he quickly reached around and kissed her other cheek.

She swallowed the rest of what was in her mouth, wincing from the size of the bite, and eyed him with renewed suspicion. "What was that for?"

She'd asked him that before, but this time he was sober and he had a better answer. "Because I wanted to."

Her eyes softened and her lips parted, open just enough for him to know she wanted to speak but hadn't found the right words. Instead, her tongue darted out, the flash of pink leaving behind a trail of glistening moisture.

It would have been easy to push it at that moment. He'd been doing enough of that since he'd almost had her last time, teasing and tempting her every time he got the chance, but he didn't reach for her knee or lean in any closer.

She was like a bird, hovering at the edge of his hand. If he reached for her, it would spook her, and she would fly away. If he scared her badly enough, she might never return. But if he stayed still and let her make the decision herself, she might land exactly where he wanted her.

So he waited, still and patient, not daring to move or even breathe as she made her choice.

Chapter Twenty-One

Grayson

He watched as her eyes dropped to his lips and stayed there. This was no passing, accidental glance. All of her attention was focused directly on him as she calculated the risks and her own desires.

She knew he wanted her, and he'd made sure she wanted him, too. After weeks of doing his best to tempt her, the tension between them was too thick for her to deny it. Maybe he'd walled her into a corner, and maybe he should feel bad about that, but he couldn't find it in him to care. If this was what it took for him to finally have her, he wouldn't go into it with regrets already formed. No sense borrowing tomorrow's trouble's today.

His heart was hammering when she slowly leaned forward, placing one hand down on the bed to support her weight, and laid her lips against his in a chaste kiss. She lingered for a moment, neither of them moving, as Grayson slowly closed his eyes and let a wave of vicious triumph course through his veins. It was too early to celebrate—he still remembered exactly what had happened last time and how close he'd been to the prize when it was ripped away from him—but her mouth on his felt like one hell of a win.

A pleased hum came from somewhere deep in his chest when she sighed against his mouth, her tongue darting out to quickly taste the seam of his lips. They were hanging above some precipice, both acutely aware that one wrong move would send them tumbling into the void, both trying to move carefully, patiently, without demand.

He opened his mouth, used his tongue to guide them until her lower lip was situated between his teeth, and bit down softly, a gentle pressure that freed an answering moan from her. A tiny, controlled sound that told him how tightly she was holding on to keep herself from falling apart.

She pulled her mouth away and pinned him with those luminous brown eyes. "Grayson, I—"

He hoped whatever she'd been about to say hadn't been important. If she'd been planning to tell him she'd changed her mind, using the last bit of sanity available to her, it was too late. Hearing his name—his real name, not Barlow like every time before—was enough to shatter the self-control he'd been hanging onto so desperately.

Before she could finish that sentence, he had her face with one hand and the back of her head with the other, catching her in a firm grip and he plundered her mouth with his own. Any worries he might have had that she'd think it was too much, too fast were swept away by the voracity of her kiss in return, the way she fisted one hand in his hair and the other in his T-shirt, the low moans spilling out of her that were neither dainty nor controlled.

His name had been like a match tossed on a pile of kindling and now they were both going up in flames. With what little brainpower he had left, he took a moment to be grateful she was as ready for this as he was. There was no need to try to rein himself in when she was right there with him, demanding more with every step.

She was reaching for his pants before he'd even gotten her shirt off, pulling a surprised laugh from him as he reached under her clothes to find one already hardened nipple that seemed to be waiting for his touch. Her nimble fingers worked open the buttons as he pushed the fabric of her top out of the way and pulled that nipple into his mouth.

That ripped a sharp gasp out of her and earned him a retaliatory stroke of his dick through his pants that made his hips shift uncontrollably closer to her. If he'd had any rational thoughts left, he would have lost them at that first touch, and by the time she'd managed to properly get enough of his clothes off to get her hand wrapped around him, he didn't have enough blood left in his head to think about anything but how good it felt.

Weeks of dreaming and fantasizing had given him plenty of time to think about what sleeping with Becka might be like, and he'd guessed she'd be wild and untamed and perfect, but somehow he still hadn't managed to dream up anything quite like this.

She was wholly devoted to getting what she wanted, all of her being focused on where his hands and mouth touched her, on where she was gripping him, those slender fingers working over his body with just the right amount of pressure, just the right amount of speed.

"Damn it." He pushed her hand away and shoved her over until she was splayed out on her back, hair a tousled mess and lips turned down in confusion. "You're going to have this party over before it's started if you keep that up."

Her face brightened and the frown was replaced by a pleased grin when she picked up his meaning. She was already reaching for him again, evading his attempts to keep her hands away from his body.

"Patience." It came out a strained hiss as her fingers grazed the hot skin of his dick again, but he was determined not to let her win. Even if she did seem willing to turn this into some kind of strangely erotic wrestling match. "Hands off, Becka."

She pouted but went still enough for him to press a fevered kiss to her mouth and another to the column of her throat. It wasn't until he made his way down over her breasts and over her stomach that she finally figured out his intentions, but when she did, she let her knees fall open without shame.

He'd had moments where he wanted to taste her more than he wanted to keep breathing and he was ready to worship at the altar of her body for not making him beg for the privilege. He closed his mouth around her, tongue working to find the sensitive spot he knew would make her whimper in that way he couldn't get enough of, and she arched her back at the sudden sensation, practically bowing off the bed until he had to hold her down with an arm across her hips.

Not only did she whimper, but she also whined and panted and called out both his name and God's before he finally let her go, both of them dripping from her arousal and his skilled attention.

Her legs were shaking and he kissed the skin of her inner thigh before working his way back up her body to settle his weight between her legs. There was nothing he wanted more than to drive himself into the wet heat of her pussy, but a tiny alarm in the back of his mind had started ringing and he knew if he went ahead with it, she might hate him forever.

"Becka, look at me." He waited for her to open her eyes, keeping her chin pinched between his thumb and his finger to help her focus on his face. "I think we might have fucked up."

The blissed-out haze cleared from her face. "What?"

He cleared his throat, feeling like an awkward and unprepared teenager all over again. "Do you have protection?

Here, I mean? I should have thought about that before, but I didn't actually expect to get this far. It's not a big deal if you don't, we don't have to—"

She put a finger on his lips to stop him from rambling. "Top drawer of the nightstand."

He leaned over to rummage through her drawer, necessity winning out over his concerns about her privacy. "Do you usually invite people back here to, uh ..." He was going to fuck her down the hall from his grandmother's bedroom, but he couldn't imagine anyone else doing it.

"No." She smacked his arm, but she was still pressing kisses to every part of him she could reach, her hands wandering and her eyes glazed. "You don't expect me to carry the whole box around in my purse do you?"

"Good point."

He finally found what he was looking for—did she ever clean this damn room?—and after a few quick seconds of fumbling, he was more ready than he'd ever been in his life. He settled back between her legs, his body fitting against hers like it was made for just such a union.

Still, he wanted to be sure she was as ready as he was, pausing at the last second as sweat beaded on his brow and every instinct urged him to bury himself in her heat. "Now?"

"Yes." It came out on a rush of air, her hands digging into his hips as she urged him to abandon caution and throw his good sense to the wind. "Now."

He lost his ability to hear anything else as he lined himself up and sank into her with one steady stroke. There was only her heat, that perfect fucking wetness, and a tightness that made him sure he'd somehow earned a ticket to paradise on earth.

When he finally managed to regain some use of his senses, he realized she was being a hell of a lot louder now that he was fucking her than she had been when he'd only been using his mouth.

"Shhh ..." He nuzzled his face into the skin of her neck as he tried to get her to be quieter. He could probably solve the problem by being a little gentler, but he would rather the whole house hear her than change one single thing about the way they were moving together. "Do you want everyone to know what we're doing in here?"

She shook her head back and forth but did nothing to change the volume of her pleasured moans, her logic not matching up with her ability to follow through.

Well, he could help with that.

He pressed a hand softly over her mouth to stifle the unending stream of noise, careful not to cut off her breathing as he did so. "There, now you can be as loud as you like and no one but me can—"

Her sharp teeth sank into his palm, cutting him off as he swore instead and yanked his hand away. Every time he thought she couldn't surprise him any further, she pulled a new stunt that left him stunned. "Did you just *bite* me?"

She seemed to find that funny, which at least meant laughter replaced the other sounds she'd been making. Hushed giggles shook her whole body and made him grit his teeth at the way her pussy tightened around him.

"That's funny to you?" He caught her mouth in a punishing kiss, both of them trying not to laugh as he pressed his lips into hers with too much force. He'd already left a trail of fingerprints and bruise-sucked skin, so he figured if she was going to object, she'd have done it already. She might be small, but she sure as hell wasn't fragile.

To hell with it.

If the whole house knew, then they knew, he wasn't going to let it stop him. He cupped one ass cheek in his hand and lifted her other knee up over his waist until he was pressing even deeper into her. The amusement faded from her face, rekindled desire taking its place.

He set a softer pace this time and tried to enjoy just being inside her, finding all the places that made her breath catch until she was writhing under him, her hands clutching at his back as she tried to urge him on with her body.

It didn't take long until she was close. He could tell by the changes in her breathing, the tension in her muscles, the way her body clenched around him with each thrust. "One more time," he coaxed, despite knowing damn well she'd given him three already when he'd had his head buried between her legs and she was probably balancing a fine edge between pleasure and overstimulated pain.

He had no problem admitting he was a greedy bastard when it came to her, and he could already tell how much he loved watching her come undone under him.

"I can't."

There was an uncomfortable whine in her voice, but he knew she was reaching for it. He kept rocking into her at the same lazy pace, circling her clit with his thumb, letting her take as much time as she needed and fighting to keep his own climax at bay.

He could go as long as she needed him to, her pleasure the only thing that mattered to him at all. "You can do it." He kissed one corner of her mouth and then the other. "One more. Give it to me. It's mine."

He must have said the right thing, because within moments they were both being swept away on the force of the orgasm that ripped through her body. Her eyes closed as it broke over her and with the benefit of being inside her this time, being able to feel her pleasure as she lost herself to it, he was unable to hold himself back anymore.

A few more strokes and he, too, was carried away into

mindless ecstasy, aware of nothing but the way it felt to be one with her, his hands in her hair, his teeth on her skin.

It was the softly whispered, "Oh *no*," that pulled him out of his daze. He hadn't even had time to pull out of her yet. He'd still been floating on a rush of endorphins that had turned his muscles soft and put a self-satisfied smile on his face.

He'd assumed Becka was feeling similarly and her panicked little whisper, the absolute regret contained in those two little words, pulled the rug right out from under him.

Oh no?

Oh, shit.

He knew she'd enjoyed it. He'd heard all the feral noises she'd made, felt the spasms of her inner muscles as she'd come around his cock. He had the teeth marks on his shoulder and the nail tracks on his back from her trying to get him to go harder and faster and give her more, more, *more* ...

So if that wasn't the problem, then why was she shoving him off her and scrambling over him to get out of bed, taking the blanket and all his hopes with her?

"I ..."

He waited for an explanation, carefully removing the condom from his rapidly softening erection as he did so, but she wrapped the blanket around herself, covering the nudity he'd been so damn eager to see, and shuffled her feet like she was embarrassed. Was that it? Could it be that she was ashamed for some reason? He didn't think they'd done anything particularly strange, but he had no idea what kind of experience she had.

He tried to put her at ease, extending his hand to welcome her back to the bed and giving her his most reassuring smile. "Becka, I—"

"We shouldn't have done this."

"I—" He was trying to wrap his mind around what was

happening and how quickly things were falling apart, but she wouldn't let him get a word in.

"I think you should go." She tipped her head toward the door and stepped back, putting more space between them to clear a path for him to get there. "I don't mean to be rude, but I think you should definitely sleep in your own room tonight."

"Did I do something wrong?" He felt like she'd punched him in the gut, all his soft parts rolling and rebelling as the pain hit and spread out in a shockwave that started just below his heart and ended at the tips of his fingers and toes. "I just don't understand."

"There's nothing to understand." For a moment he thought there was a wet sheen to her eyes, like there were unshed tears ready to fall, but then she blinked and her gaze was cool and direct. It must have been a trick of the light and nothing more, because when she continued, her tone was flippant. "We had a good time, but that's all there is to it. I think we both know this has the potential to get complicated —just think about how Edith would feel—so it's best if we tuck it away into the history books and move on."

He hesitated and she narrowed her eyes at him. "What? You can't do that? I mean, we are both adults, right? It's not like every quick fuck has to mean something."

It wasn't like he'd bared his heart to her, but he hadn't expected to have even this tossed back in his face. Why he'd gone and fallen in love with this particular woman, he had no fucking clue. Just looking at her face, that cold and detached expression, was enough to remind him that she'd always been this way.

It hadn't been a deception on her part, but a miscalculation on his.

He'd thought he could ...What? Wear her down? Soften her up? Convince her to go to bed with him and then she'd suddenly be emotionally available? Whatever he'd thought, it clearly hadn't worked and he was the one that was going to have to suffer for that mistake.

She didn't say anything else to him as he got out of bed, tossed the condom in the bedside trash can, and pulled on his clothes. The blanket in her hands hung loosely from her body and left her shoulders bare, but it might as well have been a shield, impenetrable and made of cold iron instead of soft, well-worn fabric.

He turned back at the door, wondering if he should say something, but she looked away and refused to meet his eyes, so he left without another word, closing the door quietly behind him.

Chapter Twenty-Two

Becka

He'd barely spoken to her for more than a month. Hell, forget speaking to her. He'd barely looked at her and immediately fled whatever room she entered. The stubborn jackass hadn't smiled at her at all since he'd left her bedroom.

Not one time.

Not even when she'd cried opening the book he'd bought her for Christmas, still stacking it under the tree with everyone else's gifts even though he wasn't speaking to her.

And it was driving her mad.

Okay.

Sure.

Fine.

She'd been a bit heavy handed that night, said some things that she *probably* could have said in a nicer, friendlier way... Who was she kidding, that she *definitely* could have said in a nicer, friendlier way, but *come on*, what did he think was going to happen? That he was going to get one little tumble in the sheets with her and all her reservations about the situation were just going to disappear?

Having one lapse in judgment didn't mean she was ready to give up sanity completely and the way he'd been looking at her, she'd half expected him to drop to one knee on the spot and ask her to marry him. He probably wouldn't have gone through with it, but could she be sure?

Who knew what kind of shenanigans were going on in that brain of his! Certainly not her, which was why she'd panicked and sent him packing before she'd had time to think about it, or he'd had time to do something ridiculous.

It had been impulsive, but the right choice.

She'd believed it then and she believed it now, so why did she feel so damn *guilty* about it? Every time he refused to look at her or practically ran out of a room at the sight of her, she had to fight the urge to throw herself at his feet and beg for forgiveness.

Foolishness.

Even if she did, it was unlikely he'd accept her apology, so why humiliate herself like that for no reason? Even if she didn't have Grayson and his friendship anymore, at least she still had her pride. That was something, right?

Right?

Besides the cold comfort of her last remaining shred of dignity, her only consolation in all of the mess she'd made was that he hadn't left. Those first few days, she'd thought he might. He was so hurt, so angry, she'd feared he'd leave and never come back. She really might have been the thing that pushed him away from his home and from Edith, just like she'd feared, and she couldn't imagine what the hell she'd been thinking letting things get this far.

And despite all of that, reason and logic and consideration for everyone's feelings aside, she missed him and could think of nothing else but the way she'd lost herself in his arms. He'd rocked her to her core, pulled reactions from her, physically and emotionally, that she hadn't thought were possible. She was fighting herself every single day to keep from asking him to do it again, a moral failing that would likely see her spending eternity boiling in the devil's special hot tub.

It was weakness, plain and simple, and she hated it.

"Are you still pouting?" Payton was sitting beside her on her bed, tucked in under several layers of blankets until only the top of her head was visible. Becka had tried to kick her out twice—she had her own room just down the hall—but she'd refused to budge.

Becka thought about actually kicking her, abandoning the idea only because kicking a pregnant woman, even a sister, would likely raise the temperature on the devil's hot tub by at least a few degrees. "I'm not pouting," she said instead, clearly pouting as she sulked on the bed with her arms crossed.

She hadn't told Payton about what happened between her and Grayson, but sisters had a very annoying habit of being able to tell when something was off about you, and Payton had been hounding her almost every day since.

"You say that," Payton nudged Becka with one foot and Becka clenched her teeth, "but you clearly are. Tell me what happened or I'm not leaving."

"Fine, then you stay here and I'll go sleep in your room instead." Becka abandoned the bed and the nest of blankets to the most irritating sister in the history of the universe and stalked toward the door.

"Come on, Becka." Payton didn't chase her—who would abandon a warm spot on a cold night in the middle of winter—but she did roll her eyes and sigh dramatically. "You can run but you can't hide."

"Watch me."

It was a perfect closing line, delivered with just the right amount of sibling condescension, and Becka was still congratulating herself over it when she opened the bedroom door, turned to leave, and ran straight into Grayson.

Literally.

She collided with his chest as she flounced out the door and he had to catch her to keep them both from falling. One minute she was on top of the world, spitting winning quips and refusing to be bullied by Payton, the ever-present menace of her life … and the next she was back in the arms of the one man she could not have, enveloped in a strong grip and surrounded by his warmth and his scent and …

He straightened her up, set her back on her feet, and let go of her like she burned him.

"Watch where you're going." Half the warning came from behind an already closed door, that was how fast he'd discarded her and made his way to the safety of his own bedroom.

It was right.

It was logical.

It was exactly the way she wanted him to treat her …

And only Payton's curious presence behind her kept her from banging the door off its hinges as she tried to get him to come back out here and … and … and do something.

Anything.

Talk to her.

Hold her.

Take her back to bed—his, hers, whichever was closest—and make her forget all the reasons they shouldn't be there.

A hysterical laugh bubbled up in her throat and she fled to Payton's bedroom before it could escape. If Payton thought she was acting oddly now, she couldn't imagine what kind of harassment she'd be subjected to after having a mini mental break in the hallway, in full view of everyone in the house and their endless curiosity. Better to keep a tight lid on the turmoil and handle that shit when she was alone and no one could see her.

She didn't even bother turning the lights on in Payton's room, just tossed herself down on the bed and screamed into Payton's pillow. The whole damn bed smelled like springtime from Payton's perfume and it was colder over here in the corner of the house.

Becka made a mental note to buy Payton some more blankets, both for her and later for the baby. Payton hadn't complained, but just in case. No reason for her very annoying, bedroom stealing, far too perceptive for her own good sister to be cold. After a few minutes—buried under Payton's blankets and waiting for the heater to come on—she fell asleep.

She rarely dreamed and was a deep sleeper, so when she jerked awake sometime later, she was confused and disoriented. Something must have woken her, but the room was perfectly still and the only sound she could hear was the incessant rain on the windows.

It was Payton's room, so she wasn't as familiar with it as she was her own, but her first scan of the shadows didn't reveal anything that looked out of place. If it hadn't been for the sick feeling in her stomach, she would have believed it must have been a rare clap of thunder that woke her. But thunder didn't wake her with nausea in her stomach and her heart pounding in her chest. She was uncomfortable, on edge, adrenaline surging to meet a threat she couldn't see.

There were few options that came to mind about why someone might have come in and left again when they saw her sleeping—Payton trying to trade rooms, Grayson coming to find her but changing his mind, Edith needing help but then going to someone else instead—but none of those would explain her paranoia, either. Something was wrong, all her instincts were screaming, and if she'd learned anything about survival, it was that it was always better to move and look foolish than stay and get hurt.

She slipped from the bed, attuned to all her senses, and tried to creep toward the door.

A floorboard creaked under her weight—damn this unfamiliar room and its loud old floors—and something moved in the shadows beside the window. She froze, her breath and even her heart standing still—and a bright flash of lightning from outside revealed the silhouette of a man.

He lunged and she bolted like the devil himself had shown up to collect her for that hot tub appointment, bare feet scrambling against the floor, nails digging into the door as she fought to turn the knob. She should have been screaming, of course she knew that, but it was stuck somewhere inside her, and all she could do was try to bite back a silent sob as whoever was in the room with her grabbed her by the back of the neck and flung her down.

If this had been her room, she would have known where every potential weapon was, the baseball bat under her bed, the scissors on her desk, the heavy vase beside the window, but this was Payton's room and as Becka crawled across the floor all she found was a fine layer of dust on the hardwood.

Not even a discarded shoe.

Damn Payton and her tidy tendencies.

Fine.

Becka would have to make do with her fists, then. She didn't know who this motherfucker was, but he'd made the mistake of his life.

He grabbed her by the hair and pulled her to her feet, then grunted in pain when she hit him with a right hook that broke his nose with a satisfying crunch. Blood splattered across the front of his shirt and she followed it up with a knee to the groin as he cursed under his breath.

"You bitch."

That voice was familiar, but Becka couldn't place it. The memory stayed just out of reach as she broke free from his grasp and ran toward the door again. She'd just managed to turn the knob and pull the door open when his next words stopped her dead in her tracks.

"You're not Payton."

Ah.

Now she knew exactly who he was, and all thoughts of escaping, of finding help and ending this before it got completely out of hand, disappeared from her mind.

"Jared." She was already turning back, practically snarling with rage. He had broken into their house, crawled in through Payton's window, and laid hands on what he thought was a pregnant woman.

Fuck running.

Fuck finding a murder weapon.

Becka was going to tear his throat out with her teeth and watch him bleed out at her feet. Some people deserved to die, and he'd elected to buy a ticket for the express lane to hell.

She'd already jumped, thrown herself at him like a wild animal, when a pair of familiar arms snatched her out of midair. Instead of hitting Jared—lucky bastard—she fell back against Grayson's hard chest.

"Get out of here," he commanded. He was watching the intruder and didn't take his eyes off Jared even when he shoved Becka behind him and out into the hallway.

"Damn it, he came here for Payton." She wanted to push back inside, but the look on Grayson's face kept her outside the room. She'd always had the impression he was the kind of man to turn tail and run when things got tough, but now ... Maybe he'd outgrown that teenage urge, because he seemed to be poised on the edge of picking Jared up and tossing him out the second story window.

"I know what he came for." Grayson finally flicked a quick

glance at her, gave her the barest smile. "Go to my room, get my phone off the desk. Call 911 and tell them we had a break-in. Then go to your room and stay in there. You don't come out and neither does Payton, understand?"

She wasn't sure if he was trying to keep her safe from Jared or keep Jared safe from her, but she did as he asked, his phone pressed to her ear as she slipped into her bedroom and found Payton sitting on her bed.

Even under the mound of blankets, even in the dark, Becka could tell she was shaking.

"It's all right." Becka crawled in beside her, pulled her into a comforting embrace as she dealt with the 911 dispatcher.

"Are they coming?"

Becka nodded and Payton stopped shaking, but the feeling of relief didn't last for long. Grayson walked in a few minutes later, his expression thunderous. "That son of a bitch."

"What happened?"

Grayson flung an arm out, his tone equal parts angry and confused. "He jumped out the damn window and took off."

"Is he crazy?" Becka had spent a lot of time looking out her own window. It was not a short fall and the ground below was hard and rocky. "He's lucky he didn't die."

"He's lucky you didn't kill him." Payton pulled the blanket all the way up over her head until only her face was visible. "What the hell was he thinking, actually breaking into the house like that?"

"I guess he couldn't stand the thought of you being happy without him." Men finally getting the break-ups they deserved always had some of the worst feelings about it, in Becka's experience, and they usually didn't back off without a fight. She'd hit him pretty good and that knee to the privates had probably not felt so great, either, but she wasn't sure it would be enough to keep him away permanently. "We should see if Edith would mind letting Ruffles sleep in your room for a while and we're going to check the outside of the house and figure out how he managed to get up there in the first place."

"I think the days of driving to work alone are probably going to have to stop for a while, too." Grayson looked contemplative, like he was running over ideas in his mind. "I'll drive you into town and Henry can bring you home."

"Don't you think that's a bit much?"

Becka cast her gaze at the ceiling, frustrated beyond all possible belief. "He was in your bedroom. He attacked me because he thought I was you. There's no telling what might have happened if it had been you in there and you couldn't fight back."

Payton didn't look happy, but she didn't argue about it anymore.

Grayson caught Becka's attention and nodded toward the hallway. Surprised, she told Payton to lay down, "*Rest*," and then followed him out.

"The sheriff will probably be here any minute." He stepped away from the door, trying to make sure Payton couldn't hear him. "I need to go down and deal with them. Check on Edith. Call Henry."

"Sure, I can help—"

He pulled her into his arms, roughly pressing her against his chest, and only then did she realize he, too, was shaking. "If you ever do anything like that again, Becka, I swear—"

"He was—"

"I don't care!" He shook her, his hands like steel bands on her arms. "Do you know how scared I was when I heard all that noise? And then, I come out here to find you going back in there! Just casually about to die or commit murder! You don't have to love me, but can you at least consider how it would make the rest of us feel if we lost you?"

She heard it. That word, *love*, piercing her heart at a hundred miles an hour, but she set it aside. That was a problem for her to deal with in the future. Right now, she just needed to calm him down.

"I was only trying to protect her."

In the moment, it had seemed reasonable, but now she was being held against him like she was fragile, or maybe like he was, and it didn't seem so reasonable anymore. It seemed selfish and impulsive. Fighting to get away from him was one thing, charging back in instead of running for help was another.

She was no longer the last line of defense.

Payton had other family now—hell, they both did—and now that they weren't alone in their struggles, Becka putting her life at risk when she didn't have to had the potential to hurt the ones she cared about.

She could see it for the first time, understand it even, but if she was honest, she wasn't sure if she could have made a different choice in the moment. The urge was too ingrained. She'd lived a lot of life with that as her most natural response, and it wouldn't be easy to change it.

"Protect her." Grayson still hadn't let go of her, his face buried in the crook of her neck. "Just don't forget to protect yourself, too. You don't have to fight all these battles alone."

Becka lifted her arms and turned his awkward hold into a proper hug. "I'll try to remember next time."

He nodded against her neck, gave her one last hard squeeze, and turned to leave. The blue and red lights of an approaching cop car were climbing the walls, and they had run out of time.

Becka stood in the hallway, taking the few remaining seconds she had before they called her down to give her statement and using it to rub her chest. Her whole body was sore, but the ache in her heart hurt the most.

Chapter Twenty-Three

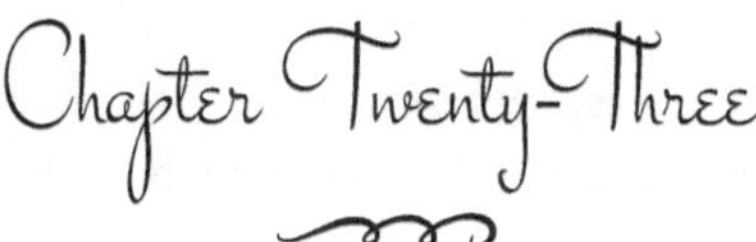

Grayson

Sheriff Levine was walking a fine line.

On one side were the possible pitfalls of doing his job. Real, tangible consequences, like hurting the feelings of a known abuser or violating his personal code against helping people he didn't like.

On the other, was Grayson punching him straight in his smug little face.

Somehow, he managed to straddle the narrow border between the two by pretending to do something about the break in while really not doing a damn thing at all. He was going to *'take their statements'* and *'look into the incident'* and *'keep an eye out for potential problems'* whatever the fuck that meant, but since there was no culprit on hand and it was his word against theirs about whether Becka's injuries had been caused by Jared or someone else ...

Well, according to the sheriff, his hands were tied.

The fact that he said that and then acted like they should be grateful he was there at all made Grayson second guess his decision not to punch him. It was definitely Becka's influence rubbing off on him, but he wasn't upset about that anymore. Sometimes people did, in fact, deserve to be on the receiving end of a manual attitude correction, and society's rules about not providing it might actually be the problem.

Widow's Point as a whole would have been better off if someone had decked Sheriff Levine a few decades ago, but maybe it wasn't too late.

"What's got that look on your face this morning?"

Edith's question broke into his thoughts. He'd come down early, hoping to catch her alone over her morning coffee, but now they were sitting in silence while he glared at nothing in particular and snuck part of his breakfast to the grateful dog.

"Just thinking about last night," he said, looking her over again to make sure she looked unaffected by the chaos that had erupted under her roof.

Sheriff Levine had been unhelpful at best, but Edith had been a rockstar. Once the sheriff's rapid fire knocking on the front door had woken Ruffles, her barking had roused Edith, who had promptly taken control of the situation with Payton and Becka upstairs.

She'd calmed Payton and tended Becka's wounds with brisk determination and an unwavering calm that was admirable. Sometimes, looking at her now, it was hard to remember all the trauma she'd been through, but she held her own in uncertain situations with a poise that could only come from years of dealing with the worst life had to offer.

Which was why, when she slammed her coffee cup down on the table hard enough to chip the bottom, Grayson felt his eyebrows climb so high on his forehead they basically became part of his hairline.

"I can't believe Patrick came all the way out here just to stand in the driveway and twiddle his useless thumbs." She was irate, glaring out the window like the water outside had offended her personally. "A stranger broke into my home. He hurt one of my girls and would have done God only knows what to the other one if he'd gotten the chance."

"I know."

"It's unacceptable."

"I agree." Grayson wasn't sure what else he could say to calm her down. He knew she was right, just as he knew that nothing they could say would change the sheriff's attitude toward Payton's situation. They were on their own when it came to Jared until they could provide undeniable proof of his wrongdoing.

As far as Sheriff Levine was concerned, Jared was just a man trying to get back a runaway partner and a pregnant one at that. He couldn't officially approve of Jared's behavior, but he was going to give him the same calculated blind eye that he had always given George.

Edith was brooding silently, so Grayson turned his attention to Ruffles, begging at his feet as she always did in the mornings. He held her piece of bacon hostage and said in a stern tone, "You have to do a better job of keeping the house safe at night if you want breakfast bacon. It's your job to bark when intruders climb in our windows."

She tipped her head and looked at him without remorse.

"Fine." He gave her the bacon and she took it over to her spot beside Edith's chair, her use for him gone the minute she'd gotten what she'd come for.

"Are you sure you don't mind her sleeping in Payton's room?" Edith had gotten quite attached to her spoiled little dog, and he worried she would be lonely.

"Of course." Edith patted Ruffles on the head absentmindedly, still lost in her own thoughts. "Keeping Payton safe is the most important thing right now and my room is just too far away from that end of the hall. We didn't hear anything until the sheriff showed up."

Grayson was nodding along, also only half paying attention to their conversation as he prepared his mental list of things to check on the outside of the house—how the hell *had* Jared gotten up there anyway—when he heard her mumble under her breath.

"Useless pig."

"Grandma Edith!"

Her cheeks immediately turned a fiery red, but her expression was obstinate. "Well, isn't he? Are you going to sit there and tell me he's not?"

Grayson shook his head, bewildered. If anyone was, it was definitely Sheriff Levine, but he would never in a million years have thought those words would come out of his grandmother's mouth. "What the hell has Becka been teaching you?"

Edith folded her hands in her lap and looked primly down her nose at him.

"A lot of things, if we're being quite honest, and most of them are things I should have learned a long time ago. Patrick never kept me safe, and he won't do anything worth a damn to keep Payton safe, either. What does that make him then? He's not worthy of my respect, try as he might to demand I give it anyway."

Grayson took a breath and puffed out his cheeks. She was right, but hearing her talk like this, he felt like he'd been hit over the head with her coffee cup. Where had this come from all of a sudden?

"You're right." It was important that he acknowledged that. His surprise was not synonymous with disapproval. "I just didn't expect you to be so ... blunt about it. You're different than I remember. Different than you used to be. I'm not sure if it's because of Becka or because George—"

He couldn't quite bring himself to say the word 'died' in front of her, but she knew exactly what he meant. She covered his hand with her own and gave it a squeeze.

"It was a relief," she admitted.

Grayson was unsurprised to find no trace of grief in her tone or expression. "I don't know what kind of person it makes me—he was my husband, after all—but I was happy when he died."

They'd been avoiding this conversation all the months since he'd come back, both of them afraid to speak the truth about their feelings, afraid the other would be horrified to learn that they held no sadness in their hearts for George's passing. Grayson was glad they'd finally come far enough to be honest with each other. It was one more of the chains keeping them captives of the past that had been broken.

"It was a relief to me, too, though I don't think I realized it at first." He gave her the gift of his own truth and felt the weight lift off his shoulders. He was tired of carrying that secret around with him, of the burden of it weighing him down.

He swallowed hard, felt the expectant silence give him permission to voice the rest of what had bothered him for decades. "I'm sorry I wasn't there for you. Not just the years I was gone, but before that. I should have done more to protect you back then."

She made a noise, a small, wet sound somewhere between a laugh and a sob. The tears that had been clinging to her lashes, finally spilled over to run down her cheeks. "You shouldn't be apologizing to me for that. I was an adult, and I was the one who should have been protecting you, just like I should have protected your father before that. It's just—"

It was just ... Grayson knew there was no way to finish that sentence. It was a million different little things and nothing at all. She'd been afraid. Broken. Battered. Unable to see a way out or a path forward. She'd been unable to save herself and helpless to save anyone else.

George had made sure of that.

But now, George was gone, and they were here. Both of them different, more whole, than they had been while he was alive.

"Let's be grateful for what we have now." He handed her a napkin and patted her hand as she dabbed delicately at the tear tracks on her face. "We're not the same people we were then."

Edith laughed and choked back a sniffle. "No, I certainly am not. Becka's seen to that, hasn't she?"

That was putting it mildly.

"She's certainly given us an example to follow when it comes to standing up for ourselves and the people we care about, hasn't she?" Grayson remembered the look on her face the night before. All the terror she must have felt had turned to rage when she'd realized the identity of their intruder. "I don't think there's anything she wouldn't do. I thought I was going to have to pry her off of Jared last night."

"Hmm." Edith's smile, so open and vulnerable the moment before, became stiff. "She really does go all in."

She really did and, unfortunately, everyone knew it. He'd told himself he wasn't going to worry the rest of the household by sharing the ridiculous rumors the sheriff had been spreading about George's death, but seeing Edith hesitate like that ... She already knew Becka had a reputation for solving problems in the most direct way possible. It wouldn't come as all that much of a surprise to her that other people had noticed it, too.

Since Sheriff Levine had been pissed when he'd left the night before, it might be better to make sure they were prepared in case he stepped up his hate campaign.

"Actually, uh, I'm not sure if you're already aware, but it

seems the sheriff is going around town telling people that he's a bit suspicious about what actually caused George's death."

Edith froze, her expression void of all possible emotion for several seconds. He wasn't sure what was going on inside her head and she seemed determined to give him no clues. When her reaction came, it was a noncommittal, "Oh?"

He'd expected some kind of feeling from her, but she gave him nothing else.

"I just thought you should know." He waited several seconds before continuing, but there was still no visible reaction to his words. "I probably shouldn't have kept it from you, but I didn't want to worry you."

"Then why are you telling me now?" The question was blunt and her gaze when it met his was direct and controlled. There was none of the worry he thought she'd have. None of the timid fidgeting or rush to provide alibis or explanations.

He was unsure how to feel about it, but decided that she probably just assumed he, of all people, knew better than to suspect Becka of murder.

"When Patrick was here last night, he was pretty heavily focused on Becka, and he made a few jabs about her using violence to protect her sister. It seemed like he might be trying to imply she could have used that same method on other problems, like he was building up a case against her, even if it's just in the court of public opinion."

Edith's only reaction was a small, "Hmm," like she was taking it all in and trying to make sense of it, so he continued.

"And not only that, he also stormed off when he left last night because Becka told him exactly how she felt about him refusing to do anything to help Payton. He's wound up, and I want to be prepared."

Edith held up one hand to stop him from talking and rubbed her temple with the other. "Wait, if I'm understanding all of this correctly, you mean he's probably going after Becka?"

Grayson explained Henry's theory as quickly as possible and watched Edith's eyes widen with shock before narrowing to dangerous slits. It was obvious she hadn't considered this, and now that she had, she was even angrier with Sheriff Levine than she had been already.

"I'll pass the warning along to Becka, and we'll see what we can do about damage control. It wouldn't be right for anyone to get the wrong idea about what happened to George just because Becka wants to keep her own sister safe."

"I trust you completely when it comes to handling town gossip," Grayson assured her.

She smiled, pleased with his flattery, her tension vanishing like it had never existed in the first place. "As you should. No one is better at it than I am."

"To be honest, though, I'm not sure how much weight people have given to the rumor, anyway." That was something Grayson had only really started to consider recently. The sheriff had been running his mouth for months, but no one in town was giving anyone from Barlow House the suspicious side eye. Becka and Payton, maybe even to a lesser extent Grayson himself, would have been low hanging fruit for the gossip mill, but they were protected by the power of Edith's unsullied and formidable reputation. "I don't think anyone really believes anything unusual happened to George."

"Not even you?"

He lifted his cup to his mouth to hide his smile. "No, not even me. I considered it, I guess, when Henry first brought it up. Becka *is* a little ... well, anyway, Henry was quick to change my mind."

"He doesn't think she's capable?"

He laughed out loud at that. "She's more than capable, but

she couldn't hide it. Becka doesn't have shame about that kind of thing, does she?"

"Maybe not," Edith fiddled with the handle of her coffee cup, unaware of his assessing gaze, "but I'm surprised you discount her so easily. She has a strong sense of self-preservation. It's one of the things I admire about her the most."

"Do you wonder?" He cleared his throat, suddenly uncomfortable. "If you think she could have, do you wonder if she did?"

Edith shook her head slowly. "No, I don't wonder. I'm probably more certain than anyone in the world that she didn't kill him."

Grayson relaxed, glad Edith had come to the same conclusion that he had, though less certain about why she believed it. Before he could ask her, Ruffles jumped up and ran down the hall. They could hear Becka and Payton talking as they made their way to the kitchen, and he let the subject drop.

It didn't matter why Edith knew Becka was innocent, it only mattered that they were all on the same page and ready to face the sheriff as a united front if it came down to that. Grayson hoped it wouldn't, but he didn't count on the sheriff being reasonable.

He'd already let one man hurt the woman he cared about —a fact that he was painfully reminded of when Becka came into view and he got a full glimpse of her scraped knees and bruises in the daylight—and he wasn't about to fail her twice.

Still, despite the wounds, her morning smile was bright and without regret. Beside her—arms linked with Becka's as though afraid someone might try to pull them apart—Payton was healthy and without any outward signs of having been touched by the violence before. She and the child she carried were safe because Becka had reacted without a single thought for her own safety.

Grayson had been so mad at her the night before, he'd been on the verge of trying to shake some sense into her, but looking at the two of them now, he knew she'd never be able to make a different choice. She was a weapon and a shield for the ones she loved, and it would be up to him to make sure she never had to put her life on the line again.

Assuming, of course, that she ever let him close enough to do the job.

The past month had been torture. He'd tried to keep busy, to keep his mind off it, and the events of the night before had eclipsed his concerns about the current state of their relationship, but being battered didn't stop her from being beautiful. He wanted to scoop her up and run away with her, carry her off to somewhere private and convince her with his mouth that she'd made the wrong choice, that it was a mistake to deny their feelings for each other.

She'd probably knock him brainless with a heavy bottomed pan if he tried, which was the only thing that had stopped him from attempting it. He'd thought about it every day since she'd chased him out of her room, still smelling like sex and her perfume, but a hearty dose of caution and concern for his own health had always stopped him just shy of actually doing it.

Instead, he'd avoided her at every opportunity, trying to give her the space he thought she wanted and hating every minute of it.

"Grayson?"

He looked up to find her standing over him, a concerned crease between her brows and her lower lip—God help him—caught between her teeth. "Yeah?"

"Can I ..." She glanced sideways at Payton and Edith, made

sure they were involved in their own conversation before finishing. "Can I talk to you? Privately?"

"Sure." He didn't know how he managed to answer her in a normal voice when he was screaming inside, but he followed her out of the room, surprised when she passed the living room and continued up the stairs. For a moment, he thought she was taking him to her bedroom—can't blame a man for hoping—but she turned at the library instead.

They always seemed to end up here, and he sat down in his grandfather's chair as she paced in front of the window and tried to get her thoughts together. He was in no hurry, so he let her take her time, content to just be in the same room as her for more than a few minutes without feeling the need to run away.

She came to a stop in front of him, abandoning her pacing to plant both feet and face him head on. "I just wanted to say thanks for last night. For helping Payton, you know?"

He blinked twice and said, "Uh ..."

It wasn't like he'd had any specific idea what she'd wanted to talk to him about, but somehow, if he'd been forced to guess, that would not have been it. Gratitude was so impersonal, so generic. Couldn't she have said that downstairs in front of Edith and Payton?

She shifted from foot to foot, nervous in a way that didn't make any sense to him at all, as she continued in a rush, "I mean, I probably could have handled it on my own, but I guess I'm glad I didn't have to."

"Okay." He said it slowly, drawing the syllables out as he tried to figure out exactly what message she seemed to be trying to convey. She was looking at him like there was something special hidden between the lines, but he wasn't getting it.

"I'm glad you were there." She tugged at the bottom of her

T-shirt, twisting the fabric around her finger. "Specifically, you know? I wouldn't have wanted anyone else."

"Oh." He ran through the implications of that while she continued to stare at him expectantly. She was glad it had been him. She wanted him around. It softened, unexpectedly, the line she'd drawn between them. "*Oh!*"

Relief washed over her face when he seemed to get it, and she smiled at him, teeth flashing in a wide grin. She was fucking terrible at communicating her feelings, and he wanted to laugh, but he knew she'd be pissed if he did.

"Yeah, so I just wanted to let you know that and—"

"Nope." He was up and out of the chair before she could finish her sentence, one hand wrapped around her wrist to keep her from escaping. "Not getting away that easily. Come back here."

For once, she seemed happy to comply and let herself be drawn into a tight hug, her head tucked under his chin as he held her. It was going to be a battle every step of the way with her, and God only knew when he'd manage to work his way back into her bed again, but he was going to wear her down one day at a time until she was ready to admit that this was where she belonged.

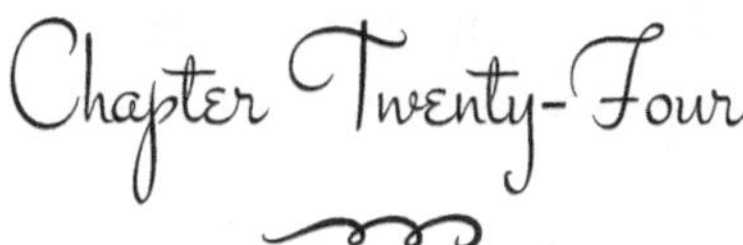

Chapter Twenty-Four

Grayson

Midwinter was always Grayson's least favorite time of year. Maybe it was the slump after Christmas or just the gloomy weather, but he could never seem to shake off the bad mood that gripped him between the holidays and the first warm days of spring.

He'd been wandering around Barlow House and Widow's Point for months now, so there was nothing new to see there, and while he'd made it back to a place of peace with Becka, she wasn't yet welcoming him in any kind of romantic—or potentially distracting—ways. He didn't want to push her too hard and have it backfire like the first time, so she wasn't doing a thing to help keep him occupied.

Payton was busy with work and preparing for the baby, and Edith had threatened to make him sleep outside on the deck if he didn't stop bothering her.

In short, he was bored out of his mind.

He took the first day with somewhat decent weather, stuffed a raincoat in his back seat, and took the highway out of town and up the coast. It wasn't exactly a five-star vacation, but it got him out of the house and seeing some fresh scenery for the first time in ages, a fact that he couldn't possibly have appreciated more. He would have paid any price to be out under the gray sky with dark green forest flying by outside the windows, and not spending another minute locked in that house.

Fresh air, a little classic rock on the radio station, plenty of places to stop the car and stretch his legs as he poked around nearby towns or wandered a bit through a local park. He stopped for lunch at a random mom and pop type place and had a decent burger with soggy and questionable fries.

All around, he thought he'd done a pretty good job slaking his wanderlust without actually packing up and hitting the bricks. A skill he was going to have to hone if he was planning on sticking around permanently.

The only thing that might have made the drive better was taking Becka with him, but she'd gone with Payton for her doctor's appointment, apparently planning to follow that up with a birthing class now that the time for that was getting nearer.

Maybe by the next time he felt the itch, she'd be ready to tag along, arguing with him about the safety of putting her bare feet up on the dash and singing out of tune with her terrible choice in music. That would really be a perfect day.

It wouldn't hurt to bribe her with promises of coffee or sweets along the way, so he kept an eye out for places that she might like to stop. Fancy little coffee shops and corner bakeries with prettily painted signs. He even spotted a few bookstores he thought she'd like to see and imagined how pleased she'd be if he surprised her with a visit to a quaint little place like that.

In fact, he spent so much of the day thinking of her, that when he finally made his way back to Widow's Point, at first he thought he was imagining her car parked in the diner parking lot.

It wasn't until he watched her come out the door, hands full of takeout just like the first time he'd seen her, that he knew she was really there. He was already getting ready to turn in when he spotted Sheriff Levine coming out the door behind her, and realized his squad car was parked beside her yellow bus.

Grayson had a sick feeling in his stomach, and that was before she walked toward the driver's side door of the bus, the sheriff right behind her, and he lost sight of them. He threw the car into park before the wheels stopped turning, seatbelt unbuckled and door open in record time.

He came around the bus from behind and found Becka pinned between the still closed driver's side door and the sheriff's broad body. He wasn't touching her—she had the takeout held up in front of her like a shield—but he was closer than he had any reason to be and the badge on his chest was the only thing that stopped Grayson from punching first and asking questions later.

Judging from the look on her face, Becka felt similarly.

"I think I can handle getting things home without any help." There was a smile on her face, but the warmth didn't reach her eyes. "I've done it plenty of times before."

"I'm trying to be friendly." Sheriff Levine shuffled forward another half step, scooting in closer as he tried to reach around her and grab the door handle. "No need to be so stiff about it."

The movement brought him down to her level, his face almost touching the skin of her neck, and Grayson's palms itched with the urge to grab him by the back of the uniform and haul him off her. Instead, he did the next best thing and infused his voice with a friendly warmth at odds with the cold anger churning in his gut.

"Becka, there you are!"

Sheriff Levine jumped back like he'd been shot in the ass, his face flushed—with anger or embarrassment, Grayson couldn't tell—as he snapped his head around to find Grayson closing the distance between them.

He quickly put himself in the space the sheriff had just vacated, his arm coming up to rest around Becka's shoulders as she blinked at him, her mouth open in surprise. He winked at her, just out of Sheriff Levine's line of sight.

She had no idea what he was up to, but she was a quick thinker and when he said, "Edith called and asked me to stop by on my home. She said you'd been gone a long time and might need my help." She nodded and played along.

"Oh, right." She smiled at him and lifted the takeout she was carrying a little higher, acting like maybe he hadn't noticed she was holding it. "I just made an extra stop. Didn't feel like cooking dinner, I guess."

"You should call next time you're running late." He gave her a wolfish grin before adding, "Okay, babe?"

She lifted a brow at the 'babe' but in front of the sheriff there wasn't anything she could do except give a cheerful little laugh and glare daggers at him.

Sheriff Levine coughed, clearly unused to being so ignored when he was standing so close.

Grayson looked up like he noticed the man standing there. "Oh, Sheriff Levine, how are you doing?" He stuck out his hand and forced Sheriff Levine into an awkward handshake. "I didn't see you there. It seems I only have eyes for Becka these days."

"I didn't realize you two were ..."

"That's because we aren—"

"We just started dating." Grayson still had his arm around her shoulders, and he cut her off with a warning squeeze. "You know how it is. If we didn't keep it a little quiet, it would be all over town before we'd had time to decide if we really liked each other."

Becka wrapped her arm around his waist and leaned into his embrace, a happy smile on her face as her hand on his hip was pinching hard just out of sight. "It's just all so new, you know?"

"Well." Sheriff Levine didn't seem to know what to say to that. "You *have* been living together for months."

"Separate bedrooms." Grayson could see his mind working, already trying to find a way to turn the situation to his advantage and made sure to cut him off before he could get any bright ideas. "You know Edith, eyes like a hawk and her morals are unquestionable. Isn't that right?"

He looked down at Becka and almost laughed out loud at the sugary sweet expression on her face. She was every inch the loving girlfriend on the surface, but her nails were digging holes into his torso. It was comical despite an unusually high chance of scarring.

"Of course." She turned to Sheriff Levine and her voice was just as nauseatingly sweet. "The whole town knows she'd never step a single toe out of line, don't they? And who would dare do anything under her roof? Not me."

A vein throbbed in Sheriff Levine's forehead and Grayson was sure he'd gotten the message that they weren't just talking about where he and Becka spent their nights. Edith's reputation wouldn't just shield a young couple against accusations of living together in sin. No, his little smear campaign was running into the same problem and not only did the occupants of Barlow House know about it, they also knew how poorly it was going.

"I wouldn't do anything, either." Grayson laughed, a dry chuckle with little warmth. "No sense in going against Edith, is there Sheriff? I'm afraid I'm not that brave. Wouldn't want to turn the whole town against me for upsetting her."

"No, I guess not." Patrick looked uncomfortable, like suddenly he'd rather be anywhere but there. "I should probably get going. Just wanted to check in on Miss Simmons, here, but it seems she's in good hands."

"The very best," Grayson assured him.

"Well ..." He finally backed away and Grayson felt Becka take a deep breath beside him. "Let me know if anything else happens out at Barlow House."

"Will do." He gave Becka another warning squeeze, sure she was about to open her mouth and make a sarcastic remark about how he hadn't done anything helpful the first time they'd called him. "Have a good evening, Sheriff."

Sheriff Levine only grunted an acknowledgment as he rounded the end of the bus and disappeared, presumably headed back to his car and off to find someone else to harass.

Grayson blew a deep breath out of his nose and let his arm drop from around Becka's shoulders a split second before she stomped down hard on his toes.

"Damn it!"

"Dating?" She was already trying to shove her key in the door lock, hands shaking and still full of takeout. "You told the town sheriff that we're dating. That's just really great, Grayson. Great plan. Now, how do you suppose we explain that to Edith and my sister?"

He plucked the keychain from her hands and opened the door himself, trying to put most of his weight on his uninjured foot. "I was trying to be helpful. He doesn't seem like the kind of guy to take no for an answer unless it comes from another man, and he definitely *is* the kind of guy to haul your ass off to jail for trying to defend yourself. Maybe, instead of being so... so... so *you* about it, you could just say "*Thank you, Grayson*" or "*Good job saving me*"—he mimicked her in a high falsetto that made her eyes narrow to warning slits—and when we get home you can tell Edith and Payton, oh, I don't know ... *the truth*."

"You want me to tell them the truth?" She tossed the takeout on the passenger seat and turned back to face him, newly empty hands already fisted and settled on her hips. She was obviously pissed, more than half ready to brawl right there in the parking lot, and gorgeous. "Fine, why don't we go home and tell them the full story, then? Hmm? We can tell them how I let you dry hump me in the fucking kitchen or maybe how I pulled you into my bed and let you fuck my brains out that one time? I think that would go over spectacularly."

"Maybe!" She had a unique way of getting him so riled up he lost all common sense, and he was teetering on the edge of it. Anger and desire twisting in a coiled knot in his stomach. "Maybe, while we're at it, we should add some new fuel to the fire? What do you think about that?"

"Yeah, why don't we—" Her angry expression vanished, confusion knitting her brows. "Wait, what?"

Too late.

He already had her backed against the side panel of the bus, only her open door shielding them from any curious gazes that might happen to be looking out the diner windows. She sucked in one furious breath before his hand tangled in her hair, the other going to her hip to hold her in place.

He hadn't tasted her in so long and as soon as her mouth opened to him—that angry breath turning into a fucking *moan* that almost brought him to his knees—he dived in. For a fiery little hellcat, her mouth was soft and sweet. He wanted to experience all of it, memorize the velvet heat of her tongue and the gentle give of her lip beneath his teeth.

His hand moved down to her thigh, dragging it up to rest against his waist. She was so short he knew she had to already be pushed as far on tiptoe as she could go with her other leg. Hell, he wasn't sure she was even touching the ground at this point, but it didn't matter. She was pinned between him and the bus, his body completely covering her as she wrapped her arms around him and tried to climb him like an eager koala.

"Get in the fucking car." He didn't know where he found the strength to pull away from her, to slam the front door shut and pull the back door open, but he knew if he let this continue the way they were going, there were going to be a few indecent exposure charges in their future.

Well-deserved and probably worth it, but why take the chance when she had a car that was practically designed for the kind of activities he had in mind?

"I—" She was looking at him, lipstick smudged and cheeks flushed—but he didn't think she was really seeing him. Her body had overloaded her mind, desire taking away her capacity for rational thought.

He loved her like that, all the fight softened just for him and turned into a vulnerability he wanted to drown in. "Get in the car, Becka." He nudged her toward the open door—he could smell her, that dusky floral scent that haunted his dreams—and for a moment he thought he'd won. She took a half step sideways, and he thought that she was going to say to hell with common sense and self-preservation, to hell with decency and modesty and all that shit, but the flash of headlights from the road cut across the front of the diner.

A car pulled into the other side of the lot—thankfully they'd come in from the wrong direction to see anything happening on Grayson's side of the bus—but the intrusion of voices and the slamming of doors was enough to pull Becka out of her trance and back into reality.

"Fuck." She gave him a little shove, just enough to give her a few inches of space, and ran a hand through her tangled hair. "You've lost your mind. Do you know that?"

"Yeah."

What else was there to say? He knew damn well he'd been

seconds away from fucking her in a parking lot, right in front of the front door where their privacy would have been more illusion than actual protection. Forget steaming up the glass, he'd have made plenty sure the whole bus was rocking well enough for everyone and their dog to know what he was doing to her.

"You're not going to apologize?"

He snorted even though he could tell she was serious as all hell. "Why would I apologize? I'm not the least bit sorry. In fact, *you* are currently the only thing stopping me from doing exactly what I was trying to do a few minutes ago."

"You're ... You ..." The sound she made was half groan and half scream of frustration. "I'm going home."

"Fine, but when you get there I hope you know that I haven't pushed for anything because I was giving you time to think things over., But not only am I not going anywhere, I have every intention of you ending up back in my bed again. Permanently."

"Permanently?" She'd climbed into the driver's seat after slamming the back door shut again, and she slapped a hand on the steering wheel. "What the fuck does that even mean?"

"Figure it out, Becka." He took his chances, gripping her chin hard and pressing a bruising kiss to her already swollen lips. "When you do, the door to my room is always open."

He didn't give her a chance to respond—she was just going to spit more curses at him anyway—and shut the car door in her face. She stared at him through the dirty window, mouth open in comical shock.

That was fine with him. He'd given her plenty of time to stew it over already, afraid to make a wrong move and send them back to square one again, but she was clearly content to sit right where they were forever, and he couldn't have that.

It was time to start pissing her off again and see what happened.

Chapter Twenty-Five

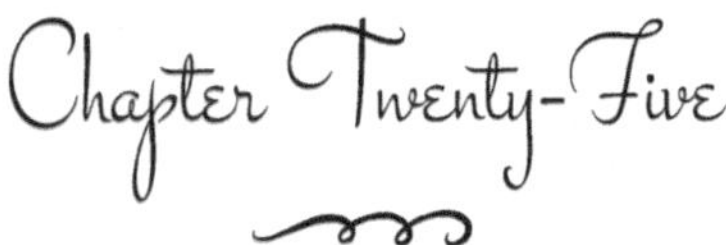

Becka

It was clear from the look on his face when he opened the door that he hadn't actually expected her to show up.

She'd spent a few hours in bed, tossing and turning and trying to ignore the persistent ache between her thighs before she'd given up and tossed her blankets off in a huff. There was more than her pride on the line, so much more that she was risking just being at his door at one in the morning, but it had still rankled, the heat of embarrassment climbing her cheeks as she'd waited for him to answer.

But then, he'd pulled the door open blurry-eyed and wild-haired and with that gorgeous mouth of his hanging open just a bit in surprise, and all that ceased to matter. It was worth it. Worth wrestling with all the doubts and having to swallow her own ego, to see him looking as off kilter and unsure of himself as she was.

She'd leveled the playing field again and it felt so good.

He'd caught her off guard at the diner and she didn't like being a step behind in any game, but especially this one.

Scoring a critical hit was a rush and, emboldened, she pulled a hand from her pocket to reveal a tidy stack of chocolate chip cookies. "I brought a little peace offering. Mind if I come in?"

He was still staring at the cookies, blinking sleepily as he tried to figure out what the hell was going on. Becka upped the wattage on her smile, hooking a finger under his chin and lifting until he was forced to meet her eyes. "Grayson?"

"Huh?" He ran a hand over his face, gave his head a shake to clear the sleep from his mind. "Yeah, yeah, sure. Come on in."

She slipped past him, noting he liked to keep the room pitch black and silent when he was sleeping. He even kept the curtains drawn tight and if it wasn't for the light spilling in from the hallway, she wouldn't be able to see her own hand in front of her face.

At least he kept a tidier living space than she did. She was able to make her way from the door to the curtains—drawing them open enough to still be able to see his face in the moonlight when he closed the door behind her—without tripping over clothes and shoes discarded on the floor. She'd always meant to learn to keep her spaces cleaner, but she didn't seem to have his discipline.

When he'd first come back to Barlow House, that trait had irritated her. She'd thought he was stuck-up and pretentious. Now, it was endearing. He was still a stuck-up pain in the ass, but he'd never looked at her with condescension. Even when she was at her most unlikeable, he'd found something about her to keep him coming back again and again.

Okay.

Fine.

So, there was a good chance that in the beginning most of his motivation had been that he liked looking at her tits... He was a man, after all. She could probably forgive him for that. Actually, she could probably forgive him for a whole lot more than that, as long as he continued to look at her like he'd done outside the diner.

Like he was doing now.

Like he wasn't sure he'd be able to keep breathing if he wasn't touching her.

Still, he hadn't moved from his spot by the door, following her path across his bedroom with nothing but his eyes. His hands were loose fists at his sides, like he was trying to keep from reaching for her and that was the only way to control his own arms.

The heat banked low in her belly, leftover from having him all over her in the parking lot a few hours earlier, grew hotter with the first rekindled flame of desire.

She loved his hands.

She wanted them on her.

She wanted them *in* her.

Air whistled through her teeth as she drew in a ragged breath. Patience. No matter what she wanted or how badly she wanted it, there were a few things they had to talk about first. A few decisions she'd made while she'd been in her bed, not sleeping, that she needed him to know about.

Then, once the technicalities were handled, she'd let him use those hands to ...

Nope, not helping.

Business first.

Coming on his fingers, a delightful, pleasurable second.

She shivered at the thought, and his brow creased with worry. "Are you cold? Here, I have a blanket or a ... shit ... a jacket."

He'd tripped over the edge of the bed and stumbled a bit in his hurry, and she brought a hand up to cover her smile. He was so fucking adorable in his big ass, overly eager golden retriever way.

"It's fine." She coughed to cover a laugh and took a few

steps closer to stop him from ripping the blanket off his bed. "I'm not cold."

"Okay." He'd been so confident outside the diner, brash and sure of exactly what he wanted, but she'd pulled him out of a dead sleep and hadn't said much to him since, so he stood in front of her, flummoxed and directionless. "Did you, uh, did you just come to bring me cookies?"

"No, but you can have them." She passed most of them to him, physically picking up his hand to press most of the stack against his palm. There were only two left when she was done and she took a bite out of one immediately, the crumbling sweet sugariness of it giving her a little boost to finish what she'd come for. "I actually came to talk to you."

He sat down on the edge of the bed, still holding his uneaten stack of cookies in his hand. "I'm all ears."

"Right, well ..." To be honest, she'd mostly skipped this part in her mind when she was planning this whole thing. It had been easy to imagine what came first—get cookies, knock on door, convince Grayson to let her talk—and what came after—hot, mind blowing, casual sex—but not so much the part in the middle. She figured she'd just wing it and the right words would come, but now she was here, and the words were definitely, well, *not coming*.

"Becka?"

"Yeah." She puffed out her cheeks and ran a hand through her hair. "Right. So, I've been doing some serious thinking—" He didn't interrupt her, but she didn't think she liked the way his eyebrow shot up. She might be impulsive, but she *did* think ... sometimes. "And what I was thinking about was what you said earlier at the diner."

Now *that* got his attention and he sat up a little straighter on the bed, his eyes locked on her as she paced nervously across his bedroom floor. "Oh yeah?"

"Yes." She could do this. Really she could. "I think I should probably start by saying thank you *and* I'm sorry. You were right and I overreacted. Sheriff Levine is a problem and you were only trying to do what you could to keep him away from me, which I should have been grateful for instead of acting like that."

He leaned forward and put his elbows on his knees, the intense gaze he'd had locked on her since she'd arrived finally softening as the conversation took a turn to something less sexually charged. "I don't know if Edith told you, but you need to be careful around him. So much more careful than you might think. He's done his best to get this town to think—"

"I know." This was the part she was most afraid of and fear, the sharp twist of it in her gut, quickly doused her arousal. It felt like a basket of snakes was wrestling in her stomach, and she fought back the urge to be sick. "That's something else I wanted to talk to you about."

"You have a lot to say tonight."

She nodded, ignoring the teasing in his tone. "If I'm going to end up in your bed before I leave this room, we have things to discuss."

That shut him up quick. He waved a hand, inviting her to continue. "By all means, please discuss away."

She went back to her pacing, wringing the bottom of her pajama top with sweaty hands. "Let's just say, hypothetically, that the town believes Sheriff Levine and it comes down to his word against mine? What would you do?"

He frowned. "I don't—"

"Whose side would you be on?" she clarified. Those snakes were trying to crawl their way up her throat now and she pressed a hand to her neck to still the reflexive spasm of the muscles there.

"Yours." There was no hesitation at all. "I'm always on your side."

"Okay." She nodded, breathed a little sigh of relief. "And

let's just say, *hypothetically*, that maybe he's not entirely wrong about some of those accusations. Would you still be on my side?"

He blinked at her while the seconds ticked by.

"Hypothetically," she repeated.

"Uh ..." He blew out a deep breath. "Well, I guess I'd still be on your side. Are you trying to tell me you killed my grandfather?"

She laughed, the sound of it high and humorless. "Of course not. That would be crazy, right? No, definitely not. I was just worried that, at some point, he might be able to convince you that I did, and then ... Well, I just needed to make sure, you know? That even if that happened, you wouldn't—"

He didn't believe her. She could tell by looking at him right at that moment, he believed she'd killed George. Now it was actual vomit climbing the back of her throat, the burn getting worse as it got closer to her mouth.

She was going to throw up on his carpet. She was going to lose it right here in front of him and—

"I don't give a shit."

"What?" She stared at him, and it took several seconds for her to realize her mouth was hanging open. Her teeth clacked together when she closed it too hard, an ache spreading across her jaw from the force. Better than puking at his feet, but she was still in shock.

"Hypothetically, Becka, I don't give a shit if you killed him." He shrugged like they were discussing the weather. "I didn't care when you told me you burned down your parents' church and I don't care about this."

"He was your grandfather."

"What he was to me, biologically, doesn't change the fact that he was a terrible person." His flat, factual tone had her shaking and there were tears forming on her lashes. "I've picked up enough little tidbits here and there to know your parents and that wacky ass cult they raised you in were also pretty terrible. If you want to go burn down some more of their shit, just let me know. I'll drive."

"But—"

"Nope." He emphasized it, putting a little extra pop in the 'p'. "I'd prefer it if you tried not to kill anyone in the future, but mostly that's just because I don't want you getting hurt or going to jail."

She took a shaking breath. None of this had gone down the way she'd expected and it seemed he'd come to his own conclusions about a few things, but it could have been worse. Actually, now that she had a little time to think about it, she could see that this was probably for the best.

"Okay." She took a few deep, calming breaths. "I can live with that."

"Great." His smile was a little wicked at the edges, and it was clear his mind had gone straight back to the gutter.

"Not yet." She held up a hand to hold him off and tried not to laugh when he groaned and fell back to lie on the bed.

"There's more?" He was pouting. She didn't have to see his face to know, because she could hear it in his pathetic whine. "You're killing me here."

"Just one more thing."

"Fine." He sat back up and she could see that she'd been right. His lower lip was actually stuck out in a little pout. She'd have to bite it later, just because she could.

Assuming, of course, that he was agreeable to her final condition. He wasn't going to like it, but she needed to make her position clear, so there couldn't be misunderstandings or hurt feelings between them.

"This isn't a permanent thing." She moved her finger back and forth in the air between them, drawing a line from him to her to indicate which *thing* she was talking about. "I know you said earlier that you wanted it to be, but I can't do that."

"Why?" She didn't find any of the anger she expected in his question, just calm curiosity, and a patient expression. "I don't understand."

"I can't make promises like that and ..." She shook her head and rushed to finish the rest of it. "And I especially can't make them to you, because then, when it ends, and your feelings are hurt, things fall apart. We'd hurt Payton and Edith and I can't do that."

"Becka, there's no reason it has to end—"

"I don't know if I want children." She cut him off, her gaze on the floor but her tone stern. "Maybe, someday, I might change my mind, but what if I don't? You're gonna let Edith down? Abandon your duty to Barlow House?"

There was silence for so long she finally glanced up, worried he'd somehow fallen asleep, only to find him staring at her like he couldn't believe what she was saying had actually come out of her mouth. It made her a little angry, a little defensive. It's not like she was being unreasonable.

"I'm already bending more than I should to even be here." She lifted her chin, stared him down. "And it's not like I think you love me or anything like that. I just need you to know that there can't ever be anything serious between us. So, if you just agree to never getting any weird ideas about us, we can stop all this talking and ..."

She flicked her gaze, full of intention and inuendo, to the bed beside him.

His expression was unreadable, but his tongue darted out to wet his lips and her knees went weak. If he didn't agree to this, she didn't know what she'd do. She wasn't sure she had the strength to leave without tasting him again.

"Just a little casual fling, then?"

She didn't trust herself to speak, so she dragged her gaze away from his lips to meet his eyes and nodded slowly.

"Deal." He didn't smile, the serious expression remaining on his face, and he didn't move to come and pull her into his arms like she'd expected him to.

"Grayson?"

"If you want it, you're going to have to come here." He looked at the ground just in front of him, the little patch of floor where he wanted her to stand.

Damn him. He'd been chasing her for so long and now that he'd caught her, he wanted to make her prove it was her idea this time. No chance of saying later that it had been a mistake. No backing out and acting like she hadn't made a conscious choice.

She hissed out a breath, but there was no way she was leaving now, not after coming this far. If she could manage to swallow her pride enough to come to his bedroom, she could swallow it enough to walk to his bed.

The first step took all her willpower, her face hot and embarrassment churning in her stomach, but each one after that was easier and then she was in his lap. One leg on either side of his hips, her core pressed to the hard evidence of his arousal and her lips slanting across his waiting mouth.

The tiny flame of her desire, nearly extinguished after all that talk, erupted into an inferno.

She was going to have him. Right now and then again and again, as many times as it took for her to get her fill of him. There would be time later to linger and savor the feast, but this time she was a starving woman presented with a full meal, and all she could think of was getting more, of satiating the hunger that had plagued her.

He seemed to feel the same, tugging her shirt over her head with such force that she thought she heard it rip and then tossing it aside. Cool air hit her skin, but his hand was already cupping her breast, his thumb skating across her nipple, and she was too hot to care how cold the room was. She could have been drifting along on an ice floe in the Arctic Sea and still been warm enough just from his touch.

She rocked her hips against him, felt that spark of electric pleasure, and heard him groan from deep in his chest. There was something about that sound, about knowing she had caused it, that drove her almost mad. Everything else ceased to exist and all she wanted was to pull that noise from him again.

The muscles in his stomach jumped when she reached between them, lifted the hem of his T-shirt and let her fingers work their way beneath the waistband of the sweatpants he was wearing as pajama bottoms. The gray ones that she liked so much. No underwear underneath, just hot skin and a hard cock practically begging for her touch.

She tugged the waistband down, wrapped her hand around the throbbing length of him, and caught her breath at that next perfect little moan.

Oh, *yes*.

That was exactly what she wanted to hear.

She wanted to hear it again.

And again.

And again.

She stroked him, dipping a few fingers in her mouth first to catch some moisture to ease the glide, his noises telling her when to go faster or harder or give a little more attention to the tip. Neither of them was in a hurry to get him anywhere close to the edge—they were just getting started—but it was obvious he was enjoying it and soon her hand was coated in wetness just from the persistent precum dripping down his shaft.

When she thought he'd had as much as he could take without putting an end to their fun a little too early, she brought that wet hand to her mouth, her eyes locked on his as she used her tongue to clean it off.

The sound he made this time was almost inhuman, less of a groan and more of a growl as he hauled her against his chest and kissed her hard, sucking at her tongue like he could take back what she'd stolen from him.

She was panting hard when he finally broke away from her kiss to lean back, his arms extended behind him to take his weight as he looked at her from under heavy lashes. His mouth was wet where she'd kissed him, a little pink on the bottom where she'd nipped him with her teeth, and she ran her tongue over her own lips just to watch the spark in his eyes.

Despite her parents' best efforts to raise her prim and shy, she'd had plenty of sex, but nothing had ever made her feel as deliciously dirty as the way Grayson looked at her. His gaze was moving over her body, the exposed chest and the stomach that was still twisted up with unsatisfied desire, and she had no urge to cover herself.

Let him look.

Hell, let him do so much more than just look. It was, for now, all his to do anything he pleased. She hoped whatever that was, he wanted to do it often and thoroughly. She still wasn't entirely sure she'd made the right choice, doing this, but if she was going to go to hell, she might as well enjoy the trip.

He squeezed her hip, ran a finger under the waistband of her flannel pajama bottoms. "Can we get you out of these? I need to see what's under them. I've been dreaming about it since the last time and I don't think I can wait any longer."

She stood up, sliding them down her legs as he took the opportunity to toss aside his T-shirt and work his own sweatpants off. They disappeared somewhere, tossed across the room with a flick of his wrist, and she was secretly a little bit pleased to see her messy tendencies were wearing off on him.

Then she stood at the edge of his bed, shifting a little from foot to foot as she took him in. He was glorious naked—all long, lean lines and tight muscles. She'd never liked a lot of bulk on a man and he looked like he might have been made just for her. Strong and tall, all that pale skin dusted with dark hair on his arms and legs, just a bit of it on the chest and stomach.

Perfect.

Even his feet were sexy.

Fuck.

She could feel the heat on her face and chest, but what was she supposed to do when confronted with a man who just might be God's gift to her personally?

Not look?

Pfft.

"See something you like?" He was grinning at her now, all smooth masculine confidence and she smiled back, just as willing to play along.

"Do you?" She hadn't missed that he'd been looking at her just as intently. Taking in her breasts and the curve of her hips, lingering on her legs. She was short and small, but full enough in the chest and ass that she'd never worried a man might find her lacking.

"Yeah." He licked his lips again, no shame whatsoever. "I like the whole package. You should bring it over here, let me get a little taste."

He didn't need to ask her twice. She climbed back into his lap and let him pull her close, pressing her tight against him so he could tug a nipple into his mouth while one hand slipped between her thighs. She sighed and spread her knees wider, letting him work his fingers in deep.

It was going to be a long night.

Chapter Twenty-Six

Grayson

She slept in his bedroom that night and most of the nights after, which Grayson thought was a pleasant surprise. He'd expected to have to fight her on it, especially after that spectacular speech she'd made about keeping things casual between them. Instead, despite her initial protests, it had been blissfully easy for him to convince her to take advantage of living together. Not just together, but so close he could almost feel her presence from across the hallway.

Payton and Edith both, by some unspoken agreement, pretended not to notice what was happening, and by the end of the first cold, wintry week, he didn't even have to ask anymore. They went to their own bedrooms as usual, hung out alone in their respective rooms until enough time had passed and the house had gone quiet. Then, Becka would open her door, tiptoe across the hall, and slip into his bed.

He didn't make the mistake of pushing for more when she'd already given him so much, but he *was* keeping his eye on the horizon. Progress between them, good or bad, would be made whether he planned for it or not. It was better to steer his boat in the direction he wanted it to go, than to get buffeted about by her stormy moods and the rapidly changing tides of her emotions.

He supposed, all things considered, that putting so much of his effort and energy into one beautiful, mercurial woman might be a mistake he'd come to regret, but he'd learned to live a simple life with relatively few needs. He had a steady career, a home, and three meals a day. Not much was missing or likely to change except her, and without her, the rest of it didn't seem to mean much.

He loved his grandmother, and he certainly enjoyed hanging out with Payton, but Barlow House needed Becka to feel like a home. His bed needed Becka to not feel empty. His heart needed Becka to feel whole and healed.

Maybe he was just a one-track mind kind of guy, but sometimes it felt like his entire body was tuned to the sound of her turning his doorknob. That was the only way he could draw her in, try to change her mind about their future. It wasn't just that the sex was mind-blowing—though it was—it was also that she was more willing to be open to him during those late-night hours.

She'd always been so closed off, so reluctant to talk about herself, and if he was quiet enough, when she was curled up in his arms in the pre-dawn hours, she'd tell him things he knew she wouldn't tell him at any other time. Some of it was trivial —her favorite color was green and she hated cooked carrots— and some of it was much more serious.

The night she'd finally opened up to him about her parents, about what it had felt like to be raised by people that cared more about their weird little cult than their own kids, she'd cried on his chest for an hour. Not that he blamed her.

Who sold off teenage girls to old men just because they were *church elders*, whatever the fuck that meant?

No wonder Payton had run away and taken her chances with some guy. Who wouldn't have done just about anything to get out of that situation? George had been bad enough. Grayson couldn't imagine what it had been like for the abuse to be sanctioned by an entire community so heavily invested in making sure you couldn't escape.

Unfortunately, that meant they'd kept a closer eye on Becka after Payton made it out, and she'd eventually taken matters into her own hands. If she hadn't, she'd probably be some geriatric asshole's domestic slave, popping out kids once a year and slowly losing her mind.

He wished she'd done more than burn down the church. He'd been so shocked the first time he'd heard the story, but he got it now. She'd told him back then that it was about sending a message, but he wasn't sure the destruction of one building was enough to properly convey *Get Fucked* to a whole congregation.

He'd briefly considered that he might feel better about the whole thing if he went all the way to California and tore her parents' whole house down with his bare hands, but then what would happen to Becka? Better for both of them if he stayed at Barlow House and poured enough love into her that eventually all that other stuff might feel like a distant nightmare.

Nothing could ever undo what they'd suffered, but spending the rest of their lives together in happiness might help them move on from it. He'd never believed in all that nonsense about the best revenge being a well-lived life, but knowing how much it would piss George off to see him happy and thriving did actually feel pretty good.

Maybe it would work the same for Becka. He certainly hoped so, though he hadn't asked her directly. Mentioning a future together was a quick way to undo all his carefully laid plans, so all he could do was wait and hold his tongue as he fell deeper and deeper in love with her.

Not exactly an easy task at the best of times and certainly not at times like this, when she had her pretty little mouth wrapped around his cock. She'd never believe him if he said it now, but how could he see her like this—all flushed and naked in the dawn sunlight—and not love her?

He tried his best to keep those three words out of his mouth, but he couldn't stop himself from talking entirely. There were plenty of other things to say, even if none of them were quite right. All the pretty phrases—*fucking perfect* and *don't stop* and *you look so beautiful like this*—would never be enough to really capture the depth of his feelings, but they were hardly a waste.

He could tell by the look on her face, the sparkle in her eyes that she liked it when he talked to her, when he told her exactly what he wanted. It had been one of the more unexpected things he'd learned about her since they'd started sleeping together, but that tough exterior was just a front.

She could deny it all she wanted, but he knew damn well she had feelings for him and beneath her prickly shell was a woman that craved affirmation. Nothing made her hotter than hearing how much she was wanted, needed, even loved in return. Luckily enough for her, he was willing and going to give her all of it, one bout of pleasure at a time.

Fucking his way to a love confession might not be the classiest plan he'd ever had, but it *was* a time-honored tradition, and if casting aside his pride allowed him to move closer to his goal... He couldn't say it with his words, but he could show her with his body.

He waited until he was teetering at the edge, and her cheeks and chest were flushed a fiery, needy red to wrap her hair around his fist and tug her mouth up to his own. The taste of his body lingered on her tongue, an erotic reminder of what she'd been doing with that mouth just a few moments before. His other arm slipped down around her waist to haul her up from her kneeled position on the floor as he twisted to press her beneath him on the mattress.

Becka had never been one for patience, and she tried to pull him close, parting her legs in invitation as soon as her back met the soft cotton of his sheets, but he had other, more wicked desires. He took advantage of the space she'd made between her thighs, working his way down to bury his face in the soft, glistening folds of her pussy.

He knew exactly what to do by now—there wasn't a single place on her body he hadn't mapped, not a single sound he hadn't memorized—and he used that knowledge against her, pushing her until she had climbed to peak twice. There was a fine sheen of sweat on her skin and her fingers were tight fisted, one in his hair and the other tangled in the pillowcase beside her head, before he pulled his mouth away.

He wiped the wetness from his chin with the back of one hand, while he moved the other, the one he'd used to stroke her until she'd clamped down around him like vice, to her face. She still looked a little stunned with her hazy eyes and softly parted lips...

Lips that opened to him without resistance when he dipped his fingers inside and let her taste herself on his hand. Never one to be outdone, she smirked up at him as she sucked the flavor away, running her tongue along each finger the same way she'd done his dick earlier in the morning.

He had been holding onto his control with every ounce of his being, but that look was more than he could bear.

She squeaked a little when he flipped her over to land on her knees with her face in the pillow—holding her still with one hand and slipping a condom on with the other—but her husky laughter as he pulled her up by the hips was clearly only meant as amused encouragement. He'd be the first to admit he was more than a bit rough and heavy handed with her—the hold he had on her as he drove into her from behind was going to leave marks on her hips and the perfect roundness of her ass —but she never seemed to mind.

In fact, he thought she enjoyed it, doing her best to provoke him every time they were together until he lost his control and fucked himself into her with no concern for anything but his own pleasure, and then tucking herself into his embrace with a contended sigh when he was done.

This particular morning was no exception and when her phone rang ten minutes later, she was lying half on top of him, with her ear pressed to his chest, listening to his racing heartbeat. She groaned at the early morning intrusion and swatted his hand away when he tried to grab her breast as she rolled over.

The happy afterglow on her face faded as she listened to whatever the caller was saying, and he was already sitting up when she slapped a hand against his naked chest, palm print stinging as she bounded out of bed.

"We've got to go." She was tugging on pants before both feet even hit the ground, hopping in a circle as she looked for her top.

"What?" He managed to get out of bed just in time to catch her before she fell over, one hand hooking under her elbow to hold her up and the other trying to get his warmest sweatpants tugged up his thighs. "Go where? Why?"

"It's Payton." She didn't stop by her room on the way out, heading directly down the hallway instead, half running down the stairs as she took them two at a time and left him fumbling in her wake. He only caught up when she finally made it to the front door, where she stopped to put a jacket over the top of her pajamas.

"Will you please tell me what is going on? Is she okay?" It

certainly didn't seem like she was, since Becka's face was about as pale as he'd ever seen it and he had to stop her from trying to leave the house wearing two different shoes.

"She's in labor."

"Labor?" He stopped pulling on his own coat to stare at her instead. That couldn't be right. He didn't know much about babies, but he did know she still had several weeks until it was officially time, and there was no way she should be in labor today. "Are you sure?"

Becka stopped long enough to look him up and down like she was wondering what kind of fool she'd fallen into bed with, and he could feel the back of his neck heat with embarrassment.

"Henry's taking her to the hospital now. He said she was already having contractions when she showed up at The Bakery this morning, and now they're less than five minutes apart, so we better get going."

Payton named her Finley.

Grayson thought that was a pretty good name for a baby, and everyone else seemed pretty pleased with it, too. Elliot had been the one to think of it, staring down at the new, pink-cheeked member of the family and suggesting a gender-neutral name might be a bit easier later if she realized she wasn't comfortable identifying as a girl. That seemed like a pretty good, forward-thinking idea, and since the baby didn't have an objection, it was all but official.

Finley Grace Simmons.

Born, February third.

Weight, five pounds and four ounces.

A few weeks premature but surprisingly healthy. The only concern anyone had expressed was that she was a bit on the small side, which, all things considered, was to be expected.

When it was his turn to hold her, Grayson decided that she looked like a small, wrinkly version of her mother, with a more serious expression. He couldn't remember the last time he'd held something so small and terrifyingly fragile. She blinked at him, big eyes a dark blue, and made a soft cooing sound. She smelled good, in that vague and indefinable way babies tended to smell, and he thought he liked her.

A good thing, considering he was currently engaged in a campaign to become her future uncle.

She'd certainly made a big entrance into the world, one that rivaled her Aunt Becka for drama. They'd all been total wrecks waiting for her to be born. The doctor had said a ten-hour labor wasn't bad for a first-time mom, but they'd privately agreed he didn't have the first fucking clue what he was talking about, especially Payton, who had spent almost the whole ten hours holding tightly to Henry's hand and promising anyone who'd listen that she was never going to have sex again.

Henry had taken it all—the bone crushing grip and the sworn abstinence—like a champ. He hadn't flinched when the hospital staff assumed he was the father, and Becka swore he hadn't missed a beat when the nurse asked him to hold Payton's leg while she pushed.

Grayson had missed that bit, and though he wasn't the only one who'd been cooling his heels in the waiting room, he thought his grandmother was probably more upset than he was about not being present for the big event. He didn't see the appeal personally, even if he did think most of Edith's annoyance came from being worried about Payton, rather than missing out on the birth.

Pointing out that she'd nearly not been at the hospital at all had not helped to calm Edith or her nerves.

He'd run out the door with Becka so fast they were halfway to the hospital before they realized they'd forgotten to tell Edith they were leaving. Becka had called her from the road and explain what was going on, promising to send Grayson back for her as soon as they could. He'd driven back to Barlow House to pick up Edith and Payton's—thankfully already packed—hospital bag as soon as he'd dropped Becka off in the emergency room parking lot. It was hardly an efficient way of doing things, but what could they expect when no one was prepared for such an early arrival?

Apparently everyone involved had panicked, so it had taken some backtracking and a bit of flustered rescheduling, but in the end they were all able to be there for Payton as she birthed their family's newest arrival, with Edith, Becka, and Henry all subtly trying to outdo each other.

Edith had made Grayson stop at the gift shop on the way to Payton's room and loaded him up with flowers and stuffed animals until his arms were overflowing, which was why Grayson wasn't surprised when she won the argument over who got to stay overnight with Payton and Finley in the hospital.

"Elliot's got to get home for school in the morning and you have a business to run." Edith was eyeing Henry over the top of Finley's head as he held the baby cuddled against his broad chest. "And besides, you and Becka were here all day, helping her through. You're both exhausted. Let me stay, and I can be up all night if I need to be. You all go home, get some rest, and come back tomorrow."

It looked like Becka wanted to argue more, but none of them were a match for Edith. She had them all out the door, and the baby firmly nestled in the crook of her arm, so fast they barely knew what hit them.

Henry shuffled out toward the parking lot—Edith was

right, he looked exhausted—with Elliot right behind him as Becka and Grayson stopped at the nearest vending machine.

"He'll be back first thing tomorrow." Grayson laughed a little at Henry's dejected expression and tipped his slightly shaken bottle of sugary soda at his friend's retreating back. "I bet he closes the whole bakery down for a few days."

"Hmm." Becka hummed as she made her selection. "I think so, too. I can see why you liked him."

Grayson tried not to let anything show on his face as he carefully unscrewed the bottle cap and took a drink. "He's always been a great friend."

"That's not what I meant."

"No, I didn't think so." Alarm bells were blaring in his head. He'd come too far, made too much progress with her, to have it fall apart now over someone who'd never felt that way about him in the first place. "Listen, I don't know what you heard—"

"I didn't need some small-town rumor to tip me off, Grayson." Her eyes were direct, but she didn't seem angry or disgusted. "I've got eyes, you know? I was just waiting for you to tell me. I'm kind of hurt you haven't yet, if we're being honest."

"Oh."

She shook her head and reached for his hand, giving him a tug to start him walking toward the parking lot. "Did you think I'd be jealous?"

Actually, that was a problem that hadn't occurred to him until that very moment but was suddenly a very real fear. "Are you?"

"Nah." She shook her head, still beautiful with tangled, sweaty hair and dark circles under her eyes. He'd never helped someone give birth before, but she looked like she'd been through the wringer. "He seems pretty firmly set in his attraction to the ladies, my sister especially. I don't think you're his type."

"Not at all." The moon was shining, glimmering off a parking lot full of puddles from another recent rain, and he kicked at one, sending spray flying out in front of them. Her hand in his was warm, and the air outside was cold enough for him to see his breath. "I still thought you might be upset. I've never ... Well, Henry was it for me, you know? I was never really into anyone else—another man, I mean—but I thought ..."

He didn't know how to tell her he'd been afraid she'd be disgusted by him and his feelings for Henry. No matter how many years had passed, he still remembered the look on George's face when he'd figured it out, and Grayson had always been too afraid to tell anyone else about it.

Becka stopped by the passenger side door of his car, her hand on the door handle but not doing anything to climb inside. "Do you remember what I told you about how I lived right after I left my parents? That I was basically homeless until I ended up staying for a while with the person I was dating at the time?"

He blinked at the sudden change of topic, but Becka usually had her reasons. "I think so? His name was Sam, right?"

"So close! *Her* name was Sam." Becka stared at him for several seconds but all he could do was open and close his mouth soundlessly. "She was my girlfriend."

"Oh." Not his best line, but he was busy putting together this information with all the little bits and pieces of stories she'd told him that hadn't quite made sense before now. "*Oh.*"

"Yep."

She grabbed his chin and pressed a quick kiss to his lips, then got into the car and closed the door, apparently oblivious to the years of turmoil and worry that she'd put to rest in one conversation. He'd carried that secret around all this time, ashamed of it and trying to hide it from the world, and now it suddenly didn't matter anymore. After all, who cared about anyone else's opinion? If it didn't bother Becka, then there was no one else with the power to hurt him over it.

"Well, I guess that clears that up." He spoke it out loud to an empty parking lot before walking around to open his own door, feeling lighter than he had in years.

Chapter Twenty-Seven

Grayson

"I think you did a pretty good job." Elliot held the baby and looked slowly from her to Payton and back again. "She looks like you, which is a pretty good thing, I guess."

Payton was in a good mood, the difficulties of labor already fading thanks to the rush of a new mother's love and whatever painkillers the nurses had given her. Grayson doubted it had been anything too strong since she was apparently trying to breastfeed, but she looked to be in good spirits for someone that had just pushed a whole person out of a very small space.

It was impressive, truly.

"She's beautiful." Payton sighed and took a drink from the cup Henry handed her, before giving them all a thousand-watt smile that even Elliot had to return. She'd been sad when she'd come to them, and it was clear everyone in the room was basking in her joyful glow. After everything she'd been through, she deserved to be happy and well cared for at this moment.

And well cared for, she definitely was.

Not only were Edith and Becka still hovering around her at every opportunity, eager to fluff a pillow or help her to the bathroom, Henry had been doting on her since he'd come back to the hospital, fetching her drinks and snacks, putting on her socks, holding Finley, changing diapers.

Payton may have been alone before, isolated and terrified in a relationship with a man that wasn't worthy of her, but she had a small army at her back now.

"She is beautiful," Elliot agreed, sliding an obvious glance at her and Henry. "You should have another one, don't you think? You can't have just one. What if she's lonely? Besides, I don't think you'd have to look too far to find someone willing to have some more kids with you."

Henry choked on his water and Payton turned a shade of red Grayson had never seen on a person before.

He had to give the kid points for getting their meaning across in the least subtle way possible. Like the rest of them, Elliot was clearly hoping for Payton and Henry to get together some day.

"Elliot." There was clear warning in Henry's voice but, typical of a teenager with an agenda, Elliot was completely unmoved by the threat.

"I'm just saying." Elliot shrugged like it was no big deal. "I don't see what's so bad about a little friendly suggestion."

"She *just* had a baby." Henry spoke the obvious like somehow Elliot might have missed it. "Maybe now isn't the time?"

Grayson expected that to be the end of it, but Elliot doubled-down, expression set and mutinous. "Hey, Finley needs a dad, I need a mom, and we all need more of these cute babies. I'm looking out for the wellbeing of everyone involved."

"Well, that's our cue." Grayson popped up out of his chair

before Henry could say anything else and grabbed Becka by the elbow. Edith was already halfway out the door, having reached the same conclusion at about the same time.

"We're just gonna leave you three, uh four, to figure this out. Remember we love you, and I've already called being best man at Henry's wedding so no picking someone else."

Payton somehow managed to flush an even deeper shade of red, her expression tense, and Grayson realized he'd gone a bit too far in his teasing. She *had* just had a baby, and it probably wasn't fair to put so much pressure on her to start thinking of anything but adjusting to being a mom.

He mouthed, "I'm sorry," at her before he left, and she gave him a tired smile in response. Henry already had Elliot mid apology of their own before Grayson had made it out the door, and he hoped the kid took it seriously.

"I give it six months." Becka pulled him to a stop not far outside the door, hooking her thumb to indicate the room they'd left behind.

"Six months?"

She nodded, looking around to see which way Edith had gone. "Until Elliot's convinced her to move in with them."

He hesitated. "Maybe, but as easy as it is for us to trust Henry and see that he'd be good for her, it may not be so easy for Payton. She's not as willing to take risks as you are."

Becka had no argument with that assessment, and they both turned their attention to looking for Edith. She was planning to stay with Payton overnight again, and visiting hours were almost over anyway, so he figured they could just say their goodbyes to her now.

And the sooner, the better, as far as Grayson was concerned. Now that they'd left the hypnotizing presence of an adorable new baby, he realized he was absolutely starving.

He was busy trying to work out how he could convince Becka that they needed to grab a burger on their way home, when she was stopped in the hallway by a nurse Grayson didn't recognize.

He'd seen plenty of them come and go from Payton's room, but this woman, with her vibrant red hair and tousled curls, was impossible to forget, and he knew he hadn't seen her before.

"Hey!" Becka stopped, her brief confusion giving way to recognition as the nurse pulled her aside with a bright smile. "I remember you. You were here last summer, right?"

"Yeah." Becka shot him a glance but Grayson didn't interrupt, thinking maybe Becka had brought Edith in for an appointment in a different part of the hospital. "It's been a while now. I'm surprised you remember me."

"I couldn't forget you." The nurse shook her head with a small laugh that told Grayson whatever she was thinking of was a fond memory. "That day you were in the ER is probably the hardest I ever laughed on the job. Most patients get loud when we have to pop a dislocated shoulder back in place, but I've never seen anybody come up with that many unique ways to swear. The doctor was almost laughing too hard to get the joint back in."

Having heard Becka's mouth when her temper was running hot, Grayson wasn't surprised the nurse remembered her, but Becka waved a dismissive hand. "I've come up with better, but that was the best I could do under the circumstances, with no one to hold my hand and all."

Grayson didn't know anything about this particular incident, but it still pissed him off to hear she'd been alone in the emergency room. If he had anything to say about it, she'd never face anything like that by herself again.

The nurse laid a friendly hand on Grayson's arm. "You should have seen her, throwing a fit about having to stay alone overnight after falling down a flight of stairs. She was the biggest baby because of that concussion."

"Oh, come on." Becka looked to Grayson for support. "Would you want to stay when you didn't have even one person to sit with you?"

Grayson wanted to agree, that he probably wouldn't have been happy about it, either, but she continued before he got the chance.

"Still, I shouldn't complain. Not knowing what I do now. Turns out, no one was able to be here with me because the night I was here was the night George died. Edith said she'd come, and she got mad at me for driving myself to the hospital in the first place, but of course she never made it."

The nurse looked back and forth between the two of them, her expression mortified. "I'm so sorry. I didn't realize ..."

"No need to apologize." Grayson cut in smoothly but the wheels in his mind were running at a million miles an hour. "He was my grandfather, and I can promise you he wouldn't have shown up for her even if he'd been alive."

"He's right." Becka nodded her agreement, and the nurse relaxed a little. "Besides, I wasn't hurt too badly. Nothing some ibuprofen and a little time didn't fix. See?"

She rotated one shoulder—presumably the one that had been dislocated—as though this was proof that the whole incident hadn't meant anything at all.

It meant quite a lot, though perhaps she hadn't realized it yet.

He kept quiet as they said goodbye to the nurse, as they found Edith to let her know they were leaving for the night, and as they made the drive home. There was one question tumbling over and over in his mind.

Why had Becka lied to him about killing his grandfather?

He woke up in his bed, wrapped around her with one arm tossed across her stomach and his face buried against the thin column of her neck. She smelled, as always, like flowers, and his heart was at ease.

He'd fallen asleep the night before still thinking about it, trying to process the lie he knew she'd told him and figure out why she'd done it. He might not have had all the answers but he had known a few things for certain.

The first was that she hadn't fallen down a flight of stairs, or, if she had, it certainly hadn't been on her own. That was exactly the kind of excuse George used to make up when he needed a lie to cover for the injuries he'd left on Grayson or Edith. The chances of her living in the same house as a known abuser and taking an accidental tumble down the stairs ...

The second was that Becka's hospitalization the night George died meant that she'd had the means and the motive, but *not* the opportunity. If there had been foul play, it must have been someone else that had done it.

Which brought him to the third thing that he absolutely knew without a doubt. She had lied to him about it when she "confessed" to doing it. Looking back on it, maybe it had been less of a confession and more of a line of questioning that had allowed him to draw his own conclusions, but the result was the same. He'd thought the woman he loved had committed a murder, and she hadn't done a damn thing to change his mind.

The only thing he didn't know—that he couldn't figure out no matter how hard he tried—was why she'd done it. She wasn't the kind of person to do something like that for kicks or even to drive him away, so she must have had a reason.

Now, looking at her sleeping face, he realized the answer had always been there, in plain sight. All he'd needed was a few hours of sleep to clear his mind and some time to really think about Becka. The answer was waiting once he remembered what kind of person he was dealing with.

What motivated her more than anything was love for the people around her. If she was taking the blame for something that had potentially disastrous consequences, and it was something she hadn't actually done ... Then she was protecting the person who had.

Once he'd put that together, it had been easy to stop feeling betrayed. He didn't blame her one bit for doing her best to cover for the only person in George's life who'd had means, motive, *and* opportunity.

He guessed George hurting Becka had finally been Edith's breaking point. He wasn't sure what she'd done to him— though slipping some sleeping pills into his drink before his evening swim would probably have done the trick and been hard to prove without an autopsy—but he was pretty proud of her for doing it. She'd been through so much and finally found the will to fight back against the monster who'd hurt her.

He knew Becka loved him, but when it came to trusting him with information that might have hurt Edith, she just couldn't do it. She'd backed out at the last minute, deciding instead of admitting to knowledge after the fact or covering for someone else, it was safer to just take the blame herself.

Who wouldn't love such a woman?

Someday she'd learn that she could trust him, that she didn't have to lie to him about those things. It was getting harder for him to be patient, but he could do it.

For her.

She opened her eyes when he pressed a soft kiss to the tip of her nose, a smile breaking like a wave across her face.

"Good morning." He moved from her nose to kiss both corners of her mouth, already reaching to lift the hem of her shirt and find the skin of her stomach. He'd been too preoccupied with his thoughts to have her last night, and he was already aching for her this morning.

"Hmm." She stretched up into his touch like a cat, a happy hum replacing the typical purr. "Good morning."

"I can make it a better one." He moved his mouth over her cheek, found the soft shell of her ear, traced it with his tongue until he felt her shiver.

"We don't have time for this." She was already pulling his shirt over his head, teeth nipping each inch of him as the fabric was swept away. Her words were saying one thing, her mouth was saying another. "Payton and the baby are coming home today."

"I can be so quick." He wanted to linger and taste her, but if all she was willing to give him was a morning quickie, he could do it. And not just for him, but for her, too. He could get her off in less than five minutes if she'd let him use his mouth. "Please?"

He punctuated the question with a flick of his finger across her nipple, chuckling when her legs parted for him almost of their own volition, her protests forgotten under the skillful negotiation of his hands.

As promised, he was quick, urging her to orgasm with his tongue and his fingers and then burying himself in her with reckless abandon. She was everything to him, all her broken pieces and sharp edges and brutal demands. He loved her and, though she didn't hear him, he told her so when he finally slipped over the edge into his own release, his face pressed against her shoulder and his lips mouthing his secrets against her skin.

Chapter Twenty-Eight

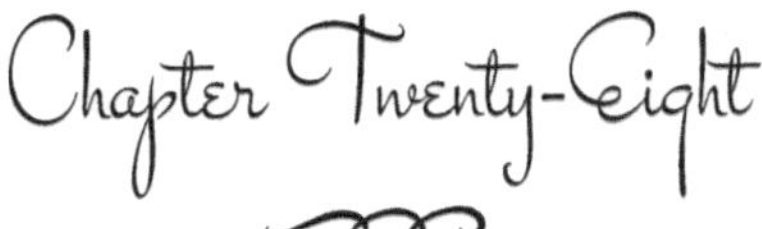

Grayson

Finley's arrival at Barlow House was an event to be celebrated, and they decorated the house in pastel-colored streamers that hung from every available surface of the living room next to more than a dozen balloons. Grayson thought they might have gone a little overboard when Becka insisted they bake and decorate a cake, but Edith was firmly on her side. One sternly worded conversation—Becka in front of him with her hands on her hips and Edith on the phone—and he'd been put in his place thoroughly.

They had heavily implied he should never be put in charge of deciding what events needed cake, and when Payton had come in the front door and her face had lit up with joy at the sight of it all, he was forced to agree.

He would have done much less, and he would have been wrong.

Having a baby was clearly the perfect reason for cake even if baking one with Becka had left their kitchen looking like it had been most recently used by a whole troupe of drunken monkeys.

Besides, Elliot had eaten almost half of it as soon as their little entourage had arrived. Feeding teenagers was no easy task, Grayson assumed, because Henry hadn't lifted a brow at the sight of the slice or how quickly it had disappeared. Grayson didn't think he'd eaten so much when he was young, but maybe it was because he'd always had George hovering over him, monitoring his every bite.

The memory threatened to ruin a happy occasion, so Grayson cut the kid another giant slice and then picked one up for himself. No need to linger in the past, when there were better times to be had in the present.

"Are you going to let anyone else hold that baby?" Becka was glowering at Edith, who was sitting with Finley in her lap and pretending not to notice. "You got to hold her all last night. It should be my turn."

"Shhh..." Edith held a finger to her lips. "She's sleeping."

"I should be the one sleeping," Payton cut in, stifling a yawn and handing the last of her cake to Henry, who was still hovering at her elbow, a constant and helpful presence. No one was sure exactly what conclusion the two of them had reached the day before about the status of their relationship, but it clearly hadn't changed the nature of his feelings for her.

"Do you want to go up? I can help you." Henry was already on his feet, setting her plate aside and ready to assist her as she climbed the stairs to her bedroom. "Becka said they got the bassinet all set up this morning, so they can bring Finley up with you?"

Edith frowned. "I don't think I should carry her up the stairs. I'm a bit clumsy these days."

"I can get her." Becka swooped in, an eager aunt with gentle hands and a baby stealing agenda. "Payton doesn't mind if I carry her, right?"

Grayson couldn't quite hold back a laugh. "I was going to ask if I could hold her, but I can see that will have to wait a day ... or several." He added on the amendment when he saw the looks on everyone else's faces. When it came to baby holding, he was clearly last in line. "I can wait, but don't think I haven't noticed how poor Uncle Grayson is treated."

Payton threw a couch pillow at him as Henry helped her out of the room, but something undefinable flickered on Becka's face as she stood there, holding Finley. He wasn't sure what that was about, couldn't think of anything he might have done to upset her.

"Are you okay?"

"Hmm?" She shook her head, pasted on an absent smile that did nothing to reassure him. "Yeah, fine. I'm just going to carry Finley up. I'm sure her mom is going to be impatient about getting her back."

She was gone before he could ask her anything else, leaving him and Edith staring at each other as Elliot tried to sneak a third slice of cake.

"That was weird, right?" He jerked his chin in the direction Becka had gone. "Any idea what's going on with her?"

Edith shrugged, a delicate motion of one shoulder that may or may not have been genuine. "Not at all."

Becka didn't come back down after giving Finley back to Payton. In fact, he didn't see her for the rest of the day and she didn't come to him that night. He thought maybe she was staying overnight in Payton's room to help—having a newborn certainly seemed like the kind of thing that was easier with two people—but even if that was true, why would she not have told him?

It simmered, her sudden withdrawal and his confusion, until after lunch the following day, when he was finally able to corner her alone in the kitchen.

"I thought we were past this." Not exactly his most subtle opening line, but it felt justified after she'd got up and left the day before with her weird attitude and no explanation.

"Past what?" She'd definitely been helping with Finley. There were dark circles under her eyes, and she wobbled a little as she turned in the direction of his voice.

He tried to be gentler and softened his voice as he approached her. "Hiding from me when something upsets you. We can talk about it, instead of doing this."

"I'm not doing anything." She tried to run a hand through her hair and puffed out a frustrated breath when she remembered she'd piled it up on her head in a messy bun. "Payton needs help and I'm helping."

"You are helping, I know that, but you're also not talking to me since yesterday and you were acting weird when they brought Finley home." He tried to reach for her hand, a familiar ache spreading through his chest when she pulled it away.

The way her expression closed off told him he'd hit too close to home for her comfort, but he was tired of her always doing that. She'd shut him out every single fucking time she had a feeling.

She didn't trust him with her secrets.

She didn't trust him with her emotions.

She didn't trust him.

Period.

It was like going back to square one with her again and again, and he was relying on the very last of his patience as he breathed deep a few times and tried to steer them back on course.

"Did I do something wrong? If I did, we can talk it over. I'll apologize—"

"You didn't." She didn't elaborate, leaving him stewing in

his own confusion as she tried to back out of the kitchen. "Payton's waiting, so I should—"

"Damn it, Becka."

That snapped her out of it, the vague look on her face sharpening in the face of his irritation. Good. He'd rather fight it out than keep getting her bullshit denials.

"Don't you curse at me." She was puffing up, her anger bringing her a few steps back in his direction.

"Then stop lying to me and tell me what your problem is." He didn't back down when she kept coming like a runaway freight train, coming to a stop only a few paces in front of him. She still looked exhausted, but adrenaline had her charging in and ready to do battle regardless.

Between that and his own hurt feelings, he had a strong inclination that they were about to say some things they'd both regret, but maybe then they'd get it all out in the open and could deal with it.

"Lying to you?" She poked him in the chest, emphasizing each word as she went. "It's not lying to you. I'm not required to share every thought in my head just because we're sleeping together."

"Is that all it is to you, then? Sleeping together?" He grabbed her hand, curled his fingers around it and brought it to his chest, warm and protected.

She tried to remove her hand, her teeth clenching tighter with each unsuccessful tug. "I told you, didn't I? I told you that was all it could be. We're not doing any of that sweet, homey, domestic shit. I'm not cut out for it, and I'm not getting married, and I'm not having any *babies*."

She spat it at him like it was a bad word, her face screwed up around unshed tears, cheeks hot pink with rage or embarrassment.

"First of all," he gave her captured arm a little shake to

make sure he had her full attention, "you're cut out to do anything in this world you want to do."

She started to argue and he cut her off, talking over her to finish his point.

"Second of all, if you don't want to get married or have babies, then we won't. But that doesn't mean I don't want to be with you. It doesn't mean that I don't love you, Becka.'

She sucked in a breath, her eyes so hot he was surprised they weren't shooting sparks. "Don't say that to me. You don't know what you're talking about."

"How do I not know? I know you hate your parents. I know you're willing to commit literal arson at the first opportunity if it suits your needs. I know you'll fight anyone, with no concern for yourself at all, to protect the people you love. I know you'll take a murder wrap to protect a little old woman who's not even your actual grandmother—"

She snatched her hand back—practically pulling the bones out of place to get it out of his grip—and pressed it roughly against his mouth to silence him. "Don't ever say that out loud again. What if someone hears you?"

He licked a broad stripe across her palm, satisfied when she made a disgusted face and pulled it away to wipe it on her pants. "What if you end up in prison? Did you ever think about that?"

She snorted and looked at him like he'd asked the most ridiculous question she'd ever heard. "Of course I have. You think I'd do it without thinking it through? Protecting Edith is more important."

"And that," he caught her face in his hand and pressed a quick, emphasizing kiss to her lips before she could back away again, "is why I love you."

"Well, just ... just ... just stop loving me then."

"Why?" She'd already pulled back, putting space between them, but it wasn't enough. He could see the tears she was trying so hard not to shed. "Do you not love me? I think you do."

"It doesn't matter!" Her voice rose until it was high pitched and desperate. "We aren't a good fit. You can tell me now that it doesn't matter if you have a wife and kids, but what about a year from now? What about five years from now? When you realize there's no one to leave this house to? When you realize Edith missed out on having your kids to dote on? You'll regret it then."

She turned and fled, leaving him no chance to try changing her mind, but he could tell this wasn't like her usual deflection. Becka was an expert at keeping him at a distance if that was what she wanted to do, but he'd never seen that look on her face before. She loved him, and she'd convinced herself that she couldn't be with him.

He loved her passion and that stubborn, bullheaded determination, but he knew once she was set on something, it took a miracle to convince her otherwise. As much as he hated to admit it, there was nothing he could say that was going to change her mind.

He left her alone for over a week, staying out of her way as she pitched in to help with Finley and hung out with Edith, and basically ignored him like they'd never shared a bed or all the details of their fucked-up lives.

Not long ago, he wouldn't have considered himself a patient man, but he'd been forced to learn to wait and watch for the best timing. Becka was never easy to deal with, and he had to admit that things went more smoothly between them —or at least with less yelling—when he had a plan and the restraint to wait for the right moment.

"Want a beer?"

Grayson opened one eye and looked up at Henry from where he was sitting, huddled in his jacket on the back porch as he watched the sun set over the bay.

"Sure." He pulled a hand out of his pocket and braved the winter's cold air long enough to grab the bottle and bring it to his lips. "Shouldn't you be inside wrestling with the rest of them over who gets to hold the baby?"

He set the bottle down on the table beside him and stuck his hand back in his pocket. Being outside to soak up some rare sunshine was probably good for him mentally, but he was damn cold with the wind blowing in off the water.

"Payton declared it was nap time and went upstairs to nurse." Henry sank down in the other chair and pulled his jacket collar up to his chin. "I didn't know babies slept this much."

"Me either," Grayson confessed. Edith swore she'd sleep less as the weeks went by, that she'd play more and be more active, but so far all Grayson had seen was a lot of sleeping, crying, and pooping. "Good thing she's cute."

"Looks like her mama.'"

Grayson nodded and the two of them settled into a companionable silence. Once, he'd imagined the two of them here, like this, enjoying the view from Barlow House's back deck and holding hands well into their old age. Things hadn't turned out quite that way, but he was happy that Becka and Payton were in their lives, that he'd found someone else to love and still managed to keep Henry as his best and closest friend.

If he could just somehow convince his feral potential romantic partner that she was better off with him than she was without him, that this house was meant to be her home, that his life was empty and meaningless without her, then things would have worked out just about perfectly.

He turned his head to ask Henry how things were going in his campaign to win over Payton, and if he'd finally talked her into moving in with him at some point, but shut his mouth with an audible snap when he heard Becka and Edith walk into the kitchen. The chairs on the back deck were positioned just out of sight of the large glass doors that connected the deck to the kitchen, which put him and Henry close enough to hear without being seen.

"I've never seen a kid eat so much." Becka was laughing, at ease with Edith in a way she rarely had been with Grayson. He wanted to hear her laugh like that around him. He wanted her to laugh like that for the rest of her life. "I don't know how Henry keeps groceries in the house."

"I'm sure he makes a trip to the store every other day." Edith was further from the door and harder to hear, but Grayson could still pick up on the affections he had for both Elliot and Henry. "That's what you do as a parent."

Grayson didn't catch what Becka said after that, but he'd bet good money it was one of her characteristic, noncommittal hums. She tended to do that when the topic of parenting came up.

"Of course, that's part of what makes parenting not the right decision for everyone." Edith continued as though she hadn't noticed Becka's lack of response. "Payton and Henry have it in them, but there's nothing wrong with those who don't."

"Did Grayson put you up to this?" There was a heavy dose of resentment in Becka's question but just as much resignation.

"I'm afraid I don't know what you're talking about, dear."

Henry's eyebrow lifted at the sugary, sweet tone of what was an obvious lie, and Grayson just shrugged. He was a guilty man, but he didn't think he'd ever deflected blame with such nonchalance. It was obvious they'd all underestimated her for years.

"Uh huh." Becka clearly wasn't buying it but no one, not even Becka, had the gall to contradict Edith to her face.

"As I was saying," Edith plowed ahead, a hint of laughter in her voice at Becka's surly tone, "it's up to each of us to choose what's best for our own lives."

"Until there's no more grandchildren for you to spoil and no heir to inherit this house. I can see how much importance this town puts on the Barlows—the family, the house, the whole bit—and you and Grayson are not an exception to that. You know how your reputation is here. How important your responsibilities are."

Grayson forced himself to stay in his seat when he heard her voice crack. He hated it when she cried, but she'd never listen to him. If anyone was going to get rid of the ridiculous ideas she had in her head, it was Edith. He had to let his grandmother work her magic if there was any hope of Becka coming to her senses.

"Oh, for goodness' sake." Grayson couldn't see her, but he knew Edith had just rolled her eyes. "You think I can't live without all that? Look at me, foolish child. How do you think I lived when Grayson was gone for so many years? When I thought I'd lost everything?"

"But—"

"Not only do I finally have my grandson back, I also have you and that sister of yours. Little Finley and Henry and Elliot. Every kid that's played T-ball in this town in the last ten years thinks of me as some kind of grandmother that pays for their uniforms and shows up at all the games. I'm not somehow without a family if you decide not to get married or have children."

"But—"

"What? Do you think I care about this old house? We can give it to Finley. If she doesn't want it, we can give it away for all I care. Do you know what does matter to me? You. What matters to me is you and Grayson and the rest of them. I want you to be happy, honey."

There was a loud sniffle, presumably from Becka, and Grayson motioned to Henry that they should try to sneak away without being seen. They could hear Edith talking as they crept toward the stairs.

"Don't let this place be the thing that keeps you from being happy. Sometimes you heal and you change your mind about these things, and sometimes you heal but you still don't want kids. Grayson loves you enough to let you decide."

After that, the rest of what was said was lost to the wind and the two men soon found themselves standing on the beach, cheeks and noses red from the bite of the cold wind on their faces.

"She sure as hell went to bat for you," Henry remarked, letting out a long whistle to show how impressed he was.

Grayson hunched his shoulders against the chill and shrugged. "I have to admit I asked her to do it. I knew Becka wasn't going to listen to me and someone had to get through to her."

Henry nodded and his expression was free of judgment. "Sometimes you just need a little help. At least you weren't too proud to ask for it." There was something about the way he said it, a little self-deprecating mockery, that let Grayson know he was referring to himself and the boost he'd gotten from Elliot.

Grayson wanted to reassure him that there was no shame in getting help without asking for it, either, that they were all happy to do what they could to help two people that were obviously meant for one another, but before he could, the sound of shouting and shattering glass drifted down to the beach.

Henry turned to look in the direction of the noise, but he was slower than Grayson, who was already running.

Shattered glass littered the living room floor, countless sharp, broken shards surrounding the gray rock in their midst. Wider than a grown man's palm and worn smooth by wind, waves, and the passage of time, it was an effective and frightening projectile when thrown hard enough.

Becka wiped the tears from her face and tried to pull herself together. One minute she'd been in the kitchen, facing off with a determined Edith, and the next they'd all been running in to see what had happened to their front windows.

As terrifying as home vandalism was, Becka thought this might be an improvement over her previous situation. Edith had pulled no punches, looking Becka directly in the eye when she'd asked if she *really* had so little faith in Grayson's feelings for her or if she was just looking for any excuse she could find to keep from having to admit she, too, had those feelings.

Given the choice, Becka thought she'd rather engage in some light hand-to-hand combat with a burglar than admit she was in love, but now it was too late to avoid the revelation and she had to deal with the burglar anyway.

Unfair.

Edith stood on one side of the room with her hand pressed to her chest and her normally serene expression now clouded with confusion and fear. Across from her, on the other side of the room, Payton held Finley in a protective embrace with Elliot standing silently in her shadow.

Henry and Grayson were around, somewhere, but it had been a while since Becka had seen them and there wasn't time to go looking. There were too many people here that needed protection. Too many people standing in the lingering echo of a violent act and looking for someone to come and save them.

"Get upstairs, find somewhere to hide and call the police." There was little room for argument in Becka's tone—she'd never been one to hesitate when shit went down and she didn't plan to start now—but Payton's brows creased even as Becka urged Edith in her direction.

"You can't be planning to stay down here!"

Becka stopped only long enough to grab a wildly barking Ruffles and shove her into Edith's arms, and then they were on the move again, not a moment too soon. The first shout came from out front—Payton's eyes flew to Becka's and they shared a moment of silent understanding—followed by the sound of another window breaking. There was a loud crash as the second rock hit the floor, and Becka gave Payton a gentle nudge to get her moving up the staircase.

"What I'm planning is to get you all settled in a safe place and then make sure he doesn't come inside until the sheriff gets here." Becka thought that was a perfectly reasonable explanation, and she was understandably upset when she had to push Payton up the stairs using gentle but impossible to resist bodily force.

Who had time to herd unruly sisters the way a dog might herd a runaway sheep?

"The sheriff?" Payton went up two more steps and scoffed directly in Becka's face. "You think he's coming to save us? That's your plan?"

Becka pushed her up the rest of the way, nudging her up to the second floor and a few steps down the hallway before answering. "I think he'll show up eventually and that someone has to keep that man away from you and the baby in the meantime."

It wasn't until she'd managed to get Payton down the hall in the direction of the room she shared with Finley, that Becka was able to make a quick stop in her own bedroom. When she emerged, she was holding an old baseball bat in one hand.

That seemed to calm Payton down, enough for her to at least take the baby the rest of the way to her bedroom without having to be guided along each step of the way. Edith and Elliot were already waiting, huddled together as they sat on Payton's bed. They were all together and as safe there as they could be anywhere. Still, Payton didn't close the door. "I know you can keep yourself safe," she paused long enough to wipe a tear from her cheek, "but please don't do anything you'll regret."

Becka grabbed the door handle and pushed it closed, ignoring Payton's indignant gasp as the wood clicked into place inches from her nose.

"I never regret it," she whispered. She knew Payton couldn't hear her, but it was a good reminder for herself that this wasn't the first time she'd faced down an asshole with a superiority complex and it probably wouldn't be the last.

When she didn't hear anything else from inside she called out, "Lock the door!" and waited for the click from within. Now that everyone—most of the people she loved and one dog that was in the process of barking the house down—were settled, it was time to deal with the real issue.

Her grip tightened on the handle of the bat as she took the stairs two at a time back to the ground floor. She'd hoped that getting his ass handed to him the first time he'd come looking for trouble would have been enough to keep him away, but men like him rarely learned their lesson the first time.

Not a problem.

She was all too happy to kick his ass again.

As she got closer to the front door, the garbled shouts, drowned out by the distance and the buffer of the house walls, became clearer.

"Get out here, you bitch!" Another rock crashed through the windows, a stray piece of flying glass hitting Becka in the cheek as she walked faster, her only thought shutting him up. "You think you can just keep my kid?"

Becka's fingers twitched on the bat in her hand, but she set her feet and assumed a protective stance just inside the door. As long as he stayed outside, she'd remain in the living room. The promise she'd made to Payton alone might not have kept her rooted in place but combined with the memory of Grayson's stricken expression the last time she'd tangled with Jared, it was enough.

"Go home, you woman beating piece of shit." She lifted her voice enough for him to hear her, but hopefully not enough for it to carry up the stairs to the others. "We've already called the sheriff, so you better get out while you still have the chance."

"You're not Payton." He stopped throwing rocks and she could hear him pacing back and forth in front of the door. "You must be that cunt of a sister she was always talking about."

"Guilty." She was going to win an award for patience and general good behavior for not ripping that door open and busting him straight in the kneecaps. "And you're the ex no one wants hanging around. She's moved on and I suggest you do the same."

"I'm not leaving without my kid." He stepped up to the broken window, peeking in through one of the holes he'd made, fingers hooked lightly on the broken edges of the glass. "I know she's had it by now."

"You don't have a kid." Not in any of the ways that mattered, anyway. Becka had heard enough about *parental rights* to last her a lifetime when she was waiting for someone, anyone with decency to come and save her from her own parents. That argument held no meaning for her as an adult. Fuck his rights. The only rights that mattered were Finley's and she had the right to not be dependent on some judge to see through Jared's bullshit.

If he'd wanted to be a father, he should have been a decent person, and his current behavior was not doing him any favors in changing her mind.

"You're still trying to convince me the baby belongs to that other guy?" Jared was too busy peering in the window, his disgusted gaze pinned unwaveringly on Becka, to notice the movement behind him. "We both know she's lying about that like she lies about everything else. No one but me would even want that trash—"

That was as far as he got before Grayson grabbed him by the back of the collar and spun him around. Henry's fist plowed into Jared's face with a crunch that made Becka wince, and he went down in a heap at their feet.

The bat clattered to the floor as she ran to open the door, throwing herself directly into Grayson's arms. She was shaking so hard it took him twice as long as it should have to check her for injuries, his eyes and hands both lingering over the bloody cut on her face.

There was so much she wanted to tell him, but it wasn't

the right time. She pushed it down, determined to wait until she could give him the words properly. Instead, she looked down at Jared and then back at Grayson's terrified face.

"He didn't come inside." She pulled his hands away from her face, kissing the knuckles as she tried to reassure him she was fine. "This is just from the window and no one else is hurt either. I sent them all upstairs."

Behind them, Henry was standing over what might be an unconscious Jared, his face impassive even as he shook out the hand he'd used to knock him out. Becka had the distinct impression Jared should consider himself lucky he went down with the first hit, because she doubted that Henry would have minded throwing a few more punches.

Grayson either, if she had to bet based just on the pure hostile energy radiating off of him in waves. That did surprise her, given the way he'd always lectured her about keeping her own temper and violence in check.

"What took you so long?" She leaned into Grayson's chest, trying to distract him as she wrapped her arms around him and held on tight. "I promised you I wouldn't fight him again, but you didn't make it easy."

"I made it up from the beach in record time." He kissed the top of her head, refusing to rise to the bait. "Did you call the sheriff?"

"Payton did." Becka shifted away as Jared groaned and started to move around. "He should be on his way but—"

"That's fine." Henry bent down and hauled Jared to his feet, supporting him as he wobbled. "We're gonna step around the corner and have ourselves a little chat while we wait. Isn't that right, buddy? Seems we have a difference of opinion about who exactly is gonna be raising that baby and we need to get some shit sorted."

Becka almost felt sorry for him, and even knowing he

deserved it and more, she didn't want to stick around to listen as Henry handed out his version of a conversation.

"Let's go inside." She grabbed Grayson and pulled him toward the door as Henry and Jared disappeared toward the back of the house. "Payton's probably worried sick."

Payton, as it turned out, was not worried sick. It seemed that as soon as Becka had left, Edith and Elliot had gone to work reminding her exactly who was downstairs and why her pathetic ex-boyfriend didn't stand a chance against the combined might of the protective trio made up of Becka, Grayson, and Henry.

"Took you long enough." She had Ruffles in her lap, a sound asleep Finley in her bassinet, and a phone pressed to her ear. "I'm calling the damn sheriff back again. Someone should have been here by now."

"Well, by the time he shows up, Henry will have the situation handled." Grayson was still holding onto Becka's hand so hard it hurt, but he sounded fully confident in his friend's ass kicking abilities. "Mostly we just need Sheriff Levine to take the damn report. I don't think we'll need a restraining order after all this, but I still think we should try to get one, just in case."

Becka nodded and tried to gently pry her hand out of Grayson's stranglehold. "I agree. Not so much because I think the restraining order will actually keep him away, but because every paper trail we can make adds another layer of protection if he goes looking to take custody of Finley."

"He might." Payton rocked the bassinet with her free hand, her gaze never leaving the sleeping face of her child. "I know Henry's doing his best, but you all don't know Jared or what he's like. You can't change his mind about anything."

Edith sniffed as she got to her feet. "You think I have all this money for nothing? He can't afford the lawyers to get within a hundred feet of that baby without your permission."

Becka's jaw dropped, and Grayson chuckled. She'd known Edith had come to view them all as extensions of her family, but she hadn't known how far she was willing to go to keep them safe.

"Thank you."

Payton's eyes were misty with unshed tears, but Edith only patted her shoulder as she headed for the door. "I'm going to go down and wait for that no-good sheriff. Henry might need a few witnesses to back up whatever story he's planning on telling to explain the beating he's probably finishing up right about now."

They were all downstairs waiting for him when Sheriff Levine finally showed up thirty minutes later. Everyone was relieved to see him pull up the long driveway except Jared, who was sitting in a deck chair, shivering and muttering hateful comments under his breath. Grayson had taken his keys, so there was no chance of him running off, no matter how tempted he was.

Becka had been pleased to note that Henry had done a remarkably good job at not leaving visible bruises, so except for the initial punch that had rebroken his nose, Jared looked untouched. Not that anyone cared about his looks, she was just glad it would make it harder for him to play the victim.

"Afternoon." Sheriff Levine climbed out of his car and took in the scene. His eyes were unreadable behind a pair of sunglasses and his expression never changed as he ambled toward the front porch. "What's going on here?"

They'd already gone over it while they waited and decided to let Edith do most of the talking. He seemed to have the most goodwill toward her out of all the people present, and she was the least likely to lose her temper.

"Sheriff." Edith nodded from her seat and lifted a steaming cup of coffee to her lips. "Glad to see you. It seems we've run into a little bit of trouble here, again."

"This the same one you called about last time?" Sheriff Levine looked Jared over before turning back to Edith. "What happened to his nose?"

"He was trying to break in again, so I believe one of these gentlemen handled that for me." She looked sideways at Henry and Grayson, both of whom nodded to confirm. "You can see all the damage he did to my house."

"Bullshit." Now that the sheriff was there, Jared apparently forgot to be afraid of Henry. "They beat the hell out of me and then they refused to let me leave! This is kidnapping, damn it!"

Sheriff Levine lifted a brow as Henry shoved Jared back down in his chair, one hand on his shoulder to keep him in place. "That true?"

He seemed to be addressing the group as a whole, but it was Edith who answered, her voice cold. "Does he look like he's been beaten? Besides, the person Payton spoke to when she called 911 told her help should be here shortly. How were we supposed to know it would take so long?"

"What exactly are you trying to imply?"

"Imply?" Becka laughed, unable to hold her words back anymore even when Grayson shot her a warning look. "I think you're the expert on trying to implicate others. Wouldn't you agree?"

Sheriff Levine's face turned a mottled red and his eyebrows lifted, rising over the top of his sunglasses as a vein in his forehead throbbed. "Ms. Simmons, I don't know what you're talking about, but you need to let this man go before he presses charges."

"Gladly." Even from where she stood on the other side of the porch, Becka could tell the smile in Edith's voice didn't reach her eyes. "We just need you to take down the report for us. We want it on record that he tried to break into Barlow House, that he came here with the intention to harm Payton and her new baby, and that he's trespassing on my private property. I don't know about him, but I'd certainly like to press charges of my own."

"They invited me here," Jared lied desperately, struggling against Henry's restraining hand. He looked like he was about to start sobbing. The idea of going to jail must have been too much for him. "They told me I could come and visit the baby and then when I got here, they attacked me."

"Looks to me like it's his word against yours." Sheriff Levine shrugged and finally pulled the sunglasses off, his gaze immediately going to Grayson and Becka's joined hands. "Not much I can do in that case, you understand."

"Yes," Jared agreed, nodding wildly at everyone and no one. "I can just leave. I'll go and I will *never* come back. I swear. Please don't send me to jail. I don't think that's... I mean, I don't think I could ...."

Henry let him go and he stumbled down the steps toward his car before remembering he didn't have his keys. He turned back, a pleading look on his face, and Grayson threw them at the mud beneath his feet.

"Don't come back here again and leave Payton alone." Henry crossed his arms and made himself look as menacing as possible. "Next time, going to jail will be the least of your worries."

They all watched in silence as he clambered into his car and drove away, his pride in tatters and his belief that he could control Payton or her child even more broken. This time Becka was fully convinced he wasn't coming back.

Once he was out of sight, they turned their attention back to the sheriff. He looked entirely too pleased with himself, and Becka didn't like that at all.

"I guess that's taken care of then, isn't it? I'll just head back to town and—"

"Like hell it is." Grayson jumped in before Becka could say a word. "You think you're going to drive out of here patting yourself on the back for a job well done? You didn't do a damn thing."

Sheriff Levine started to bluster, but Grayson wasn't having any of it.

"You haven't done anything to keep Payton safe, just like you didn't do anything for all those years to keep Edith safe, to keep me safe."

Sheriff Levine had opened his car door, but he closed it again with a furious flick of his wrist. "I don't think you've got any room to talk about keeping people safe at Barlow House. Not after what happened to George. You think I'm the only one who knows there was something off about that situation? I could have these two arrested like *that*."

He snapped his fingers and Becka had to use all her remaining self-control not to skip down the porch steps and snap the bones in his leg.

"If you could have, you would have." Grayson didn't flinch under the provocation and even though Payton and Elliot looked curiously at the rest of them, a little lost as to what was going on, they also kept their mouths blessedly shut so he could finish talking. "You think your reputation as the sheriff of this town is enough to take on Barlow House?"

Grayson smiled as Sheriff Levine sputtered in humiliated silence.

"It's been months of you running around town with your little badge and your big mouth, but no one believes you, do they? No, I didn't think so."

Henry, having apparently run out of patience waiting for his turn to speak, cut in over Sheriff Levine's response. "Here's what's going to happen and do try to pay attention so you can't say later that we didn't warn you. First, you're going to leave Edith and the rest of Barlow House alone. Second, we're going to do everything we can to make sure you lose the next election."

"You can't do that." The sheriff's face, ruddy with rage a moment before, paled. "Everyone in this town loves me."

Becka clucked her tongue in disagreement. "I don't think so."

"I don't think so, either." Edith tipped her head and looked at him the way she might have looked at a bug. "And you know how much weight the Barlow name carries in Widow's Point. I could have you out of that job all by myself, but the fact is that I won't have to. Henry's family has just as much influence and I don't think he's playing around these days."

Henry stood in silent judgment with one arm wrapped protectively around Payton's waist. They were a united front, unassailable and without hesitation.

"To hell with all of you." Sheriff Levine climbed back into his car after tossing out one more barb, but there was no way for him to hide how shaken he was by an encounter he'd expected to go entirely in his favor.

"He didn't take down a report." Becka frowned, her irritation undimmed as the squad car disappeared from sight. "We needed that."

"I don't think Jared's coming back." Henry cracked his knuckles and gave them all a satisfied smile. "He talks tough but he's a coward and I gave him a few good reasons to stay away."

"Let's hope you're right." Payton pressed a kiss to Henry's cheek—the first show of affection she'd given him in front of the others—and carried Finley back inside. Henry stayed where he was for a moment, fingers pressed to his cheek, and then followed after her.

Elliot, who had been watching the events unfold with characteristic silent watchfulness, suddenly laughed so loud it made Becka jump. "Guess I'm on my way to that next sibling, huh?"

"Looks like it." Grayson gave the kid an aggressive

celebratory fist bump, giving her a curious look when Becka shook her head. He waited for them to go inside, probably to raid the kitchen for more food, before asking, "What?"

"It just seems like everyone around here is obsessed with babies these days." She tried to sound upset, infusing her voice with what she hoped was a healthy dose of frustration. "Even you can't stop smiling whenever someone mentions Finley."

Edith stood up, coffee cup in hand, and shuffled by them. "I think I'll just, uh, go check on Ruffles." She gave Becka a conspiratorial wink as she passed and Becka had to press a hand to her mouth to hide a smile.

Grayson waited for her to close the front door behind her before he spoke. "Not everyone is obsessed with babies. I admit, I love Finley and I am over the moon that I get to be that kid's uncle. I feel the same way about Elliot. But that doesn't mean—"

She stopped him with a finger on his lips. "I know."

"What do you mean, *you know*?" He had the audacity to look upset, his brows creasing and his lips turning down at the edges. It was a good thing she liked it when he was grumpy. "First you blew me off last time we talked about this, then you were barely even listening to Edith this morning—"

"I knew you set me up." She laughed, the last of her burdens having fallen aside and leaving her with no fear. All that remained were the feelings she'd tried to tell herself she couldn't have.

At least he had the decency to look embarrassed when she called him out on it. "Well, you wouldn't listen to me, so what was I supposed to do? Just let you ruin everything between us over some imagined conflict that doesn't even exist? I don't think so. You might have a problem with it, but I don't and I'm not about to ..."

"I love you, Grayson, and if you could stop talking for a

few seconds, I would really like to tell you how much I can't live without you."

"... let you go." He finished his sentence, the meaning of her words only penetrating his brain after he had stopped speaking. "What?"

"You heard me, Barlow, but I'll say it again, because I think you deserve to hear it more than once." She pushed herself up on tiptoe, arms wrapped around his neck and kissed him as he stared down at her with a blank face. "I love you."

"You love me? Just like that? After everything we've been through, all the ways you fought me, you're going to stand here and tell me you love me, just like that?"

She smiled at him, so happy she could feel it bubbling just under her skin, ready to burst out with a warm glow. "Yup. Just like that."

"Thank god." He pulled her in close, burying his answering smile in her hair. "Do you know what kind of hell you put me through?"

"I do." She rubbed his back and tried to pretend she didn't notice the wet plop of tears falling onto her skin where his face was pressed against her. "I really hope you'll forgive me someday."

He laughed, a sound that managed somehow to be both bright and extremely moist. "You love me. There's nothing to forgive."

Chapter Thirty

Grayson

Four Months Later

The summer breeze teased the ends of Becka's hair as she stepped out of the bookshop, arms laden with new additions for the library at Barlow House. It had taken Grayson some time to convince her that they could leave Edith for a weekend to make that trip up the coast he'd been dreaming about, but now that she was here with him, he knew it had been worth every minute of persuasion.

"Ice cream next?" He took the bags from her, adding them to the others already weighing him down, and nodded in the direction of a cute shop up the street. "I promised earlier, and I haven't forgotten."

She beamed at him, sunglasses perched on the tip of her nose as she looked up with sparkling eyes. Summer suited her. There was a light dusting of freckles across her cheeks again and she was wearing a short red sundress with white tennis shoes. His feral little gremlin was always beautiful, but she was putting in extra effort during this mini vacation, which was keeping him distracted in ways it was probably best not to focus on in public.

She found them a table while he put in their orders and was watching people pass by through the spotless window when he finally made his way over holding two dripping cones. Hers was chocolate on a waffle cone, and though she took it with a smile, there was a wisp of something else on her face.

"What's wrong? Did you change your mind about the flavor you wanted?" There was a teasing lilt to his question instead of the edge of impatience he would have had a few months ago. She rarely hid the reasons for her changing moods from him anymore, so he had no reason to worry that her sudden turn toward melancholy might not bode well for him.

"I was just thinking ..." She twisted the cone in her fingers, and she still hadn't taken a bite. "Maybe we should call and check on Edith."

Grayson shook his head. "She made us promise we wouldn't do that. I know you're worried about her, especially while Payton is at work, but Elliot agreed to hang out with her all weekend and if anything goes wrong, they'll call Henry."

"But—"

"We promised." He knew Becka hated it when he put his foot down, but Edith had been determined that they enjoy their time away without worrying, and she had been stern in her warning that they not waste even a single minute of it thinking about home.

"Fine." Becka finally gave in and licked the dripping side of her ice cream. "But I want it noted that this is over my strenuous objections."

"Noted." He leaned across the table to give her a kiss, enjoying the heat of her lips and the sweet taste of chocolate on her tongue.

Distracting.

Very distracting.

"Keep it up, Barlow, and we're not going to get any more sightseeing done today." She lifted a brow at him suggestively and he was tempted to let it get that far, thinking over the idea of pulling her out of here and seeing how fast they could make it to the nearest motel room.

"Eat your ice cream." He let the idea go with reluctance and sat back in his chair. They had a whole bedroom of their own back at Barlow House and endless nights to put it to good use. He wanted her to enjoy the trip, and that meant not keeping her under him for the entire weekend.

Her answering laugh had several heads turning in their direction, but Grayson didn't mind. Being with Becka meant being the center of attention, and he'd gotten used to it. Let them stare. Hadn't he done the same the first time he'd seen her and as often as possible since?

"Talk to me about something else, then," she demanded. "To keep my mind off of ..." She gave him a solid once over, eyes lingering on his lips, and he could feel his body reacting, blood rushing to the most inconvenient of places.

"Not helpful," he complained.

"Wasn't trying to be." She winked at him and waved her ice cream in his direction. "If you want to stay here instead of leaving to ..."

He scrambled to think of a topic, his mind running wild looking for the most mundane or unattractive topic possible. "I heard from Henry yesterday that Sheriff Levine was seen having a meltdown in the diner over the new signs they put up endorsing his opponent in the next election."

"Good." The teasing look on her face vanished, replaced with a vicious satisfaction. "I'm sure seeing him act like the big baby he is in such a public place will do even more to tarnish his reputation."

"Seems like it." Grayson took a lick of his own ice cream, letting the coffee flavor he'd chosen melt across his tongue. "Henry hears quite a bit of gossip in The Bakery and Edith picks up even more at all those meetings and events she goes to."

"Do you think he'll get voted out? Honestly?"

Grayson grinned, pleased and proud of the role he'd played in the man's downfall. "Absolutely. Once we started talking, it broke the dam on years of slowly building resentment. Lots of people started feeling safer telling their own stories and none of them looked very good for him. Without George to protect him, it was only a matter of time, but I think we sped things up a bit."

"It's not quite as satisfying as taking a baseball bat to his kneecaps, but I can see the appeal." She chuckled at her own joke when Grayson rolled his eyes, but he could tell she was genuinely happy to see the town would be better off because of something they'd done, and when she continued, her tone was completely serious. "I know we've been busy these last few months, helping out with the baby, moving our stuff into the same room, dealing with Sheriff Levine, but maybe now that we're more settled ..."

"Go on," he gave her an encouraging smile. It didn't really matter what she wanted, if it was within his power he was going to give it to her.

"I think we should spend some more time helping Edith." Becka took a deep breath, like this was something she'd been thinking about for a while and now she needed to get it all out in a rush. "She's getting older and it's time for her to start stepping back from some of those committees and boards that she's on. Maybe even attending fewer of the events she normally goes to. I think we should step up and start participating in those things."

"Oh." He wasn't sure what he thought she was going to

ask for, but it wasn't that. Most of his adult life had been spent running away from Widow's Point. He'd never considered getting involved in the politics of the place.

"I know what you're thinking." She held up her hand to hold him off. "You've never been interested in all of that and I'm not even a Barlow so what business do I have thinking about her legacy and family responsibilities, but—"

"What?"

"I said, I'm not really a Barlow—"

He reached into his pocket before he could think too much about it. It had been the primary reason he'd tried so hard to get her to come on this trip, and he'd thought he'd manage to pull it off in a more romantic way, but he'd be damned if she thought she wasn't "a real Barlow" for even one more minute.

He slid the ring box across the table and watched as her jaw dropped. "That's easily fixed. Now you're a real Barlow." She blinked at him, silent, and he tacked on an awkward, "Assuming you want to be, of course."

She continued to look at him, ice cream dripping down her hand unnoticed for several long seconds before blurting out an overly loud, "What the hell?" that had everyone turning to look at them again.

"Do you not want it?" He tried to take it back, but her reflexes were faster than he anticipated and he narrowly missed getting stabbed with a fork he hadn't even noticed sitting on the table beside her hand.

"Don't you dare!" She snatched the box up with her free hand and pushed it open with her thumb. A range of emotion played out across her face and nerves had butterflies dancing violently in his stomach.

He'd struggled with this choice for weeks, unsure of what kind of ring would be best, before settling on a simple, old-fashioned white diamond. Not too big, not too flashy.

Nothing that was going to get in her way or draw too much attention.

"Is this an antique?"

"Yeah?" He didn't know why he'd answered her question with a question. He knew it was an antique because he was the one that had bought the damn thing. "Yeah, it is."

"You know that's how you get ghosts, right?"

He snorted and looked at her pointedly as he took another bite of his ice cream. "I thought you didn't believe in ghosts."

"I don't." She was eyeing him and the ring with a critical expression that made his heart ache.

No reason to panic.

Okay, so she hadn't exactly done the whole dramatic weeping thing in response to his proposal, but he hadn't exactly done the whole getting down on one knee thing either. Maybe he should have done that. It didn't really feel right for them, but what if she was disappointed? What if she had, for just this one thing, wanted something more traditional?

He knew she liked old and interesting things, but what if she was offended that the ring wasn't new? He could still take it back. There was still time to return it and buy a newer, better ring. Yeah, he was just going to do that, he decided, reaching for the ring box...

"I love it." She pushed the box back toward him and held out her hand. "Put it on for me? I don't want to get it covered in ice cream." She waggled her messy hand at him, the cone still dripping chocolate down her fingers.

He could finally breathe again as he pulled the ring out and slid it onto her hand. It looked good on her and he couldn't wait to show the rest of the family when they made it back home.

"So, as I was saying," Becka continued, "a Barlow should step up to take Edith's place as she retires. We have a responsibility to the town and the people in it ..."

"I can't believe I let you talk me into this." She panted each word from beneath him as he fucked slowly into her, one hand on her breast and his teeth in her shoulder. Her left hand, the shiny ring in its new home on her finger, was buried in his hair.

"You love me," he reminded her. "That's why I get away with so much."

She didn't answer him, choosing instead to wrap her legs tighter around his waist, because they both knew it was true. Why else would she be naked beneath him in the back of her VW bug, crammed onto the too short bench seat while parked in a little secluded camping site in the Oregon forest instead of tucked into a luxurious bed at any of the nearby hotels?

He'd been dreaming of doing just this since that night she'd nearly let him do it in front of the diner, and while it was less comfortable than he'd hoped, it was satisfying some kind of primal itch he wasn't going to think too much about.

"You're just making up for all those lost teenage years," Becka said confidently, almost as though she could read his mind.

Some days he wasn't so sure she couldn't.

"I guess I didn't sow enough wild oats when I was young and now look at us." He punctuated it with a particularly hard thrust to make sure she knew he wasn't regretting his choices.

"Aren't you supposed to do this with some high school girlfriend and not your fiancée?"

Grayson froze for several seconds, and they both realized at the same time that neither of them had used that word, *fiancée*, before.

"Oh." She was looking up at him, gorgeous in the moonlight spilling in through the bus's windows, her mouth parted slightly in surprise. "I kind of like the sound of that."

"Yeah?" If the impossible, aching stiffness of his dick was any indication, he did, too. "You like being my fiancée, huh? Imagine what it's going to be like in a few months when you're my *wife*."

Her pupils contracted and he felt like he'd stumbled unexpectedly on some long-buried treasure. Watching her go limp for him over just a few whispered words might be the best experience of his life.

He grinned at her, wicked and full of ill intent, and kept talking as he went back to fucking her. "You'll be my wife and I'll be your husband and we'll be together forever..."

"Barlow, you need to stop that."

He could feel her quivering and nipped mischievously at her lower lip. "I don't think so. I like watching you come apart, and knowing it's because of me? Because you love me and you want the world to know it? I'm never going to shut up about it."

She groaned, frustration and desire spilling out from her well kissed lips, but she was wet and writhing beneath him and she didn't protest again when he went back to whispering nonsense in her ear. When she finally tipped over the edge into her release, it was the most intense he'd ever felt it, her whole body quaking and trembling even after he'd followed her into oblivion and tucked her against his side.

"You okay?" He was pretty sure she was, but it didn't hurt to check. "Becka?"

"Hmm?" She pushed the hair out of her face and pressed herself closer against him. "I'm okay. Happy and perfectly satisfied."

"Good." He relaxed once he knew she was feeling all right and had nearly slipped off into a light sleep when her voice, quiet and hesitant, roused him.

"Grayson?"

"Yeah?"

"How soon do you think we can get married?"

His heart skipped a full beat and then ran mad, thumping so hard he was sure she could hear it. "As soon as you're ready and we get the paperwork done, if you don't want a big ceremony."

Her answer didn't surprise him. "I don't want anything fancy. Just you and me and the family we've made. Let's do it as soon as possible. We'll do it before the end of summer, on the beach at Barlow House."

He remembered standing on that beach when he'd first come back, thinking that if there was a place in the world that would be haunted by George's spirit, it would be that one. Not a day had gone by since then that he hadn't looked at the pebbled shore and the water beyond and thought about his past, with all of its painful memories.

Now, she was giving him a chance to leave that behind, to stand on that same beach and look instead to his future. He would be a fool not to take it.

"That sounds perfect."

COMING 2026!

Prologue

Henry

Henry Schmidt would be the first to admit he was known as a man of few words, but it was rare for him to be truly speechless.

"Welcome to The ..."

Bakery.

That's what he'd meant to say when the bell above the door jingled and three people walked out of the rain and into the business his family had run in Widow's Point for generations. He'd recognized his friend Becka's ancient yellow VW bus when she'd pulled into the parking lot, and he was already reaching for the same donut she asked for every time she came in, but the minute he saw the woman next to her, the order and his greeting were forgotten.

He was so overwhelmed by the riot of unusual feelings she set off inside him that he was amazed he had the capacity to notice anything else, even the sudden and unexpected return of his childhood best friend, who made up the last man in their three person entourage.

Henry hadn't seen or spoken to Grayson Barlow in over a decade, but truth be told, he was grateful for the distraction the anger in his gut provided him. He was damn sure he would have made a fool of himself if seeing Grayson again, looking sheepish and guilty as all hell, hadn't provided him a reason to turn his attention elsewhere.

It would have taken him far too long to stop staring at Payton otherwise, and the second thing he noticed about her, after the fact that she was quite likely the most beautiful woman he'd ever seen, was that she was skittish.

Not the kind that made it seem like she wouldn't be the to type to enjoy a strange man lingering a little too long over a greeting, either. No, this was the kind of skittish that told him she might just up and run right out the door if he did anything more than mumble a quick hello. More than just timid, the woman was flat out scared, and it did something to him to imagine what could put that kind of haunted look in a person's eye.

She'd been through something, and since it wasn't his business yet to dig into what had made her so jumpy, he made a mental note to give her some space, to let her settle in before he got too close.

Watching her from the corner of his eye as he dealt with Grayson—he'd mostly forgiven the man long ago for taking off like that, but he wasn't going to admit to that just yet—he wondered about the circumstances that had brought her through his door. She was Becka's older sister, apparently, though Becka had never mentioned a sister before. Bad blood between them seemed like the most logical explanation for that, but Becka didn't act like there was any animosity there.

If anything she seemed even more protective over Payton than she was over Grayson's grandmother, Edith, and Henry knew for a fact that Becka had taken to the old woman the minute she'd started working as her caretaker at Barlow House, guarding her like a dog with a bone. To see her react even more strongly to Payton told him there was more to the story than a falling out between sisters.

Whatever it was, he'd get to the bottom of it eventually, and when he did, he'd offer whatever help he could. Not just because he was a good man, though he liked to think of himself that way, but because regardless of what had brought Payton to Widow's Point, he intended to make sure she never wanted to leave.

Acknowledgments

It amazes me that I'm already writing the acknowledgements for my third published book! Some days I honestly didn't think I would get this far, and I am grateful for every single person that has helped me or supported me on this journey. There are so many of you–from the friends and family that have cheered me on, to the publishing professional that have helped polish this book into the gem that it is, to the readers who have read and reviewed by previous books and given me reason to keep writing–and I am sure I will miss someone, so please know that if you have been there for me as I worked to make my dreams come true, you will always have a special place in my heart!

I want to begin by specially thanking my team at Creative James Media. They have taken a chance on my writing and have agreed to publish four of my books, which is such a miracle to me. Thank you, as always, to Jean Lowd for giving me my start and for guiding me through each step of the process. Also, a huge shout out to my editors, Staci Petroski and Rachel Burchett, for helping bring me from first draft to final finished project. I simply would not know where a comma goes without a good editor looking over my shoulder. I want to thank Matt Gabrielson for being my social media coordinator and helping me get my books in front of new readers. And last but certainly not least, I would not have seen the success I have with these books without Diana from Triumph Covers, because while we all know that as much as you may tell people not judge a book by its cover, they absolutely do!

I have many friends in publishing that have helped and guided me through the whole publishing process. Liana De la Rosa, Tristen Crone, Nichol Goldstein, and so many others in various groups and online communities, have all been vital in helping me get to where I am today. They have connected me with resources, critiqued my work, and dried my tears. I appreciate every single one of you. To Maria and Emily, who are my cheerleaders when I need someone to tell me a book isn't awful, and who are currently helping me get the sequel to this book ready for publication, you have become such a valuable part of the writing process for me and I am grateful for your wisdom.

No list of people who have helped with my author career would be complete without mentioning my friends and family. They have no idea how publishing works, but they love and support me without condition anyway, and that's something I will always cherish. My eternal gratitude goes to Sassy, my best friend of over twenty years, who always asks about my writing like she expects me to be famous any day now. Of course, I also need to thank my parents, for making me and for passing along all the traits that make me good at this, as well as for being so supportive of all the dreams I've shared with them over the years. I would like to thank my Grandma Charlotte for letting me read her Nora Roberts books as a kid, (I think my love of romantic suspense started in her upstairs guest bedroom) and my Granny who will be nearly ninety-eight by the time this book comes out and still read my first book just to show her love to me.

Nobody has shown me more support than my husband and my children. I am beyond blessed to be married to a man who has done the hard work of propping me up financially while I work on chasing my full time author dreams and has done it without a single word of question or complaint. He believes in me, and cheers for me, and wants the best for me every day, and I know how lucky I am to be able to say those words and mean them. My kids are the ones who have been the most patient with me, giving me quiet time to write and hiding out in their rooms to let me have privacy when I need to record an interview or am a guest on a podcast. They have sat with me at a book signing when I was nervous and hugged me on bad days. I would not be the woman I am without them, and every milestone I achieve on the road to success is theirs as much as mine.

To all of you- Thank you!

About the Author

Ashley Hawthorne is a contemporary romantic suspense author, an avid reader of many genres, and a strong believer in a better future for all. She writes love stories because she wants to help spread hope in a world that feels increasingly hopeless. No matter how dark the tale, there will always be a happily ever after. When she's not writing or reading romance, she chooses to spend time with her family, work with a local political activism group, or relax in nature, especially at the beach! She lives in Texas with her husband, her two teenagers, and a house full of rescue pets.

www.ingramcontent.com/pod-product-compliance
Lightning Source LLC
Chambersburg PA
CBHW020653010826
48969CB00013B/1362